Rafael Sabatini

THE SEA-HAWK

W. W. Norton & Company

New York / London

Introduction copyright © 2002 by Bernard Cornwell

The text of this book is composed in New Caledonia with the display set in
Bulmer and Miracolo
Composition by Adrian Kitzinger
Manufacturing by Quebecor World, Fairfield
Book design by Brooke Koven
Production manager: Amanda Morrison

Library of Congress Cataloging-in-Publication Data

Sabatini, Rafael, 1875–1950.
The Sea-hawk / Rafael Sabatini.
p. cm.
ISBN 0-393-32331-5 (pbk.)
1. Pirates—Fiction. 2. Muslims—Fiction. 3. Africa, North—Fiction.
4. British—Africa, North—Fiction. 5. Cornwall (England : County)—Fiction.
I. Title.

PR6037.A2 S357 2002
823'.912—dc21   2002069200

W. W. Norton & Company, Inc., 500 Fifth Avenue, New York, N.Y. 10110
www.wwnorton.com

W. W. Norton & Company Ltd., Castle House, 75/76 Wells Street,
London W1T 3QT

1 2 3 4 5 6 7 8 9 0

CONTENTS

INTRODUCTION

BERNARD CORNWELL

The Sea-Hawk begins with Sir Oliver Tresillian taking his ease in the comfort of his home, but anyone familiar with Rafael Sabatini's novels knows that trouble cannot be far away. Sabatini's most famous novel, *Captain Blood*, begins in much the same mood, with the hero smoking a pipe and watering his geraniums, and again we anticipate that this domestic contentment is about to be turned into ghastly ill-fortune and that the hero will need all his wit, guile, strength, and determination to endure. And not just endure, but undergo the most extraordinary adventures on his way to gaining revenge, winning the woman, and restoring the comfort that is the starting point of so many of Sabatini's books.

"How it came to happen that Sakr-el-Bahr, the Hawk of the Sea, the Muslim rover, the scourge of the Mediterranean, the terror of the Christians would be one and the same as Sir Oliver Tresillian, the Cornish gentleman of Penarrow is . . ." well, it is, in truth, a question that only Rafael Sabatini would dare ask, or indeed answer, for he was the master of such tales. In *The Sea-Hawk*, as in *Captain Blood*, a gentleman is plunged to the depths of society, robbed of everything and guilty of nothing, yet never succumbing to self pity.

This refusal to pity themselves is one of the most attractive characteristics of Sabatini's heroes; it seems likely that the trait came from Sabatini himself. There is, curiously, no full-length biography of him, but Jesse F. Knight, the foremost scholar of Sabatini's work, has published a biography on the Internet° and he suggests, convincingly, that Sabatini was born illegitimate. "Do you account birth of no importance?" the hero of *Scaramouche* is asked, to which he replies, and it seems like Sabatini speaking, "of none, madame—or else my own might trouble me."

Sabatini's birth was in 1875. His mother was Anna Trafford, an English singer who met Sabatini's Italian father, Vincenzo Sabatini, in the Phillippines, where both were appearing in opera. Rafael Sabatini was born at the home of Vincenzo's parents on Italy's Adriatic coast, but he was quickly sent to be raised in England by Anna's parents. He stayed in Cheshire till he was seven, then moved to Oporto, the port-wine city of Portugal, where his parents, by now married, had started a music school. From Oporto they moved back to Italy, to Milan, and the young Rafael Sabatini was sent to a Swiss boarding school. At the age of seventeen he was dispatched back to England in the belief that Liverpool, the greatest of all Britain's Atlantic ports and close to where his maternal grandparents lived, would provide him with employment. So, when a child, Sabatini was bounced between four countries and belonged to none of them. Any trace of self-pity in his character might well have been fatal; instead he showed the same resilience that makes his heroes so attractive. "You have never regretted your lack of parents' care?" André-Louis is asked in *Scaramouche*, and again we surely hear Sabatini's voice in the answer, "I tremble to think what they might have made of me, and I am grateful to have had the fashioning of myself."

° I have drawn heavily on Mr. Knight's work for these biographical notes. His own biography of Sabatini can be found at http://sabatini.virtualave.net.

That fashioning of himself had left him speaking English, Italian, Portuguese, German, and French, so when he arrived in Liverpool he had little trouble in finding employment as an interpreter for the Brazilian trade. That was his daytime job, but his dreams were anywhere but in Liverpool or Brazil.

Sabatini had always been a reader. As a child, whether in England, Milan, Portugal, or Switzerland, he had found his true home in books, especially books of heroic fiction. Alexandre Dumas, Jules Verne, Sir Walter Scott; all Europe's imagination was the young Rafael Sabatini's adventure playground, and he did not restrict himself to fiction, but traveled with the great historians to the alleys of revolutionary Paris or into the hard, sunlit waters of the pirate-haunted Caribbean. Sabatini's dreams were his escape and a young man who finds himself in rain-swept Liverpool, choking on coal smoke and translating dreary transactions about coffee and cassava, needs to dream. Sometime in the late 1890s, he began to write his dreams down.

He wrote what he wanted to read, stories of adventure, and by 1899 he was supplementing his translator's income by publishing short stories in London magazines. They were successful enough to encourage him to write his first novel, *The Suitors of Yvonne*, which was published in 1902. Three years later he married Ruth Dixon, the daughter of an affluent Liverpool merchant, and he felt confident enough in his abilities to abandon his interpreter's job and take up writing full time. Over the next forty-five years he was to write thirty-five novels, innumerable short stories, half a dozen nonfiction books, and a play, but his fame was gained by the novels which are quintessential swashbuckling adventures. This is red-blooded, heroic history.

Sabatini's success did not come quickly; indeed he had to wait until the 1920s before he became one of the world's most famous authors. *The Sea-Hawk* was published in 1915. It lacks the fluency of the later, more famous books, yet it has many of the author's virtues, especially his insight into character. Character drives motive and motive drives plot and plot is what keeps us reading, and Sabatini, in his depiction of the hero's brother, Lionel Tresillian, presents us with a villain as subtle as Iago. Lionel's self-justifications ring fatally true: "And then came the reflection that if he were guilty of emotional outbursts that could so outrageously play the traitor to his real desires, were not all men subject to the same?" That is sophisticated motivation, and we watch, appalled, as a weak man persuades himself into terrible treachery and a good man is sold into slavery. It is a splendid tale, and it made a good silent movie in 1924 (the second film, made with Errol Flynn in 1940, used only the novel's title and bears no resemblance to the book).

The other glowing virtue of *The Sea-Hawk*, shared with all Sabatini's work, is the fidelity to history. "To produce historical romance of any value," Sabatini once wrote, "it is necessary first to engage in researches so exhaustive as to qualify one to write a history of the epoch in which the romance is set." Some might think that the setting of *The Sea-Hawk* is so exotic that it cannot be true, but it is. The Muslim pirates of the Barbary coast were among the plagues of Christendom, and their depredations continued for almost four hundred years, until they were defeated by the U.S. Navy in 1815 (the great Stephen Decatur is one of the heroes of that episode). Sabatini's book takes us back to the sixteenth century, when the pirates of Algiers were at their most successful, and no western navy was capable of crushing them. The corsairs captured Christian ships not just for the value of ship and cargo, but also to take Christian prisoners. The wealthier of those prisoners could then be ransomed for a huge profit while the rest were condemned to be galley slaves (the most famous such prisoner was Miguel Cervantes, the author of *Don Quixote*). It is this brutal world, strange and cruel, that Sabatini uses to such effect in *The Sea-Hawk*.

Rafael Sabatini died in 1950. His second wife had the opening words of *Scaramouche* carved on his tombstone: "He was born with a gift of laughter and a sense that the world was mad." Here, then, is a tale of a man who knows how to meet disaster with laughter, who can suffer terrible privations and dreadful fate, yet win through to victory. A man not unlike his creator, the incomparable Rafael Sabatini.

NOTE

Lord Henry Goade, who had, as we shall see, some personal acquaintance with Sir Oliver Tressilian, tells us quite bluntly that he was ill-favored. But then his lordship is addicted to harsh judgments and his perceptions are not always normal. He says, for instance, of Anne of Cleves, that she was the "ugliest woman that ever I saw." As far as we can glean from his own voluminous writings it would seem to be extremely doubtful whether he ever saw Anne of Cleves at all, and we suspect him here of being no more than a slavish echo of the common voice, which attributed Cromwell's downfall to the ugliness of this bride he procured for his Bluebeard master. To the common voice I prefer the document from the brush of Holbein, which permits us to form our own opinions and shows us a lady who is certainly very far from deserving his lordship's harsh stricture. Similarly, I like to believe that Lord Henry was wrong in his pronouncement upon Sir Oliver, and I am encouraged in this belief by the pen-portrait which he himself appends to it. "He was," he says, "a tall, powerful fellow of a good shape, if we except that his arms were too long and that his feet and hands were of an uncomely bigness. In face he was swarthy, with black hair and a black forked beard; his nose was big and very high in the bridge, and his eyes sunk deep under beetling eyebrows were very pale-colored and very cruel and sinister. He had—and this I have ever remarked to be the sign of great virility in a man—a big, deep, rough voice, better suited to, and no doubt oftener employed in, quarter-deck oaths and foulnesses than the worship of his Maker."

Thus my Lord Henry Goade, and you observe how he permits his lingering disapproval of the man to intrude upon his description of him. The truth is that—as there is ample testimony in his prolific writings—his lordship was something of a misanthropist. It was, in fact, his misanthropy which drove him, as it has driven many another, to authorship. He takes up the pen, not so much that he may carry out his professed object of writing a chronicle of his own time, but to the end that he may vent the bitterness engendered in him by his fall from favor. As a consequence he has little that is good to say of anyone, and rarely mentions one of his contempo raries but to tap the sources of a picturesque invective. After all, it is possible to make excuses for him. He was at once a man of thought and a man of action—a combination as rare as it is usually deplorable. The man of action in him might have gone far had he not been ruined at the outset by the man of thought. A magnificent seaman, he might have become Lord High Admiral of England but for a certain proneness to intrigue. Fortunately for him—since otherwise he could hardly have kept his head where nature had placed it—he came betimes under a cloud of suspicion. His career suffered a check; but it was necessary to afford him some compensation since, after all, the suspicions could not be substantiated. Consequently he was removed from his command and appointed by the Queen's Grace her Lieutenant of Cornwall, a position in which it was judged that he could do little mischief. There, soured by this blighting of his ambitions, and living a life of comparative seclusion, he turned, as so many other men similarly placed have turned, to seek consolation in his pen. He wrote his singularly crabbed, narrow, and superficial *History of Lord Henry Goade: his own Times*—which is a miracle of injuvenations, distortions, misrepresentations, and eccentric spelling. In the eighteen enormous folio volumes, which he filled with his minute and gothic characters, he gives his own version of the story of what he terms his downfall, and, having, notwithstanding his prolixity, exhausted this subject in the first five of the eighteen tomes, he proceeds to deal with so much of the history of his own day as came immediately under his notice in his Cornish retirement.

For the purposes of English history his chronicles are entirely negligible, which is the reason why they have been allowed to remain unpublished and in oblivion. But to the student who attempts to follow the history of that extraordinary man, Sir Oliver Tressilian, they are entirely invaluable. And, since I have made this history my present task, it is fitting that I should here at the outset acknowledge my extreme indebtedness to those chronicles. Without them, indeed, it were impossible to reconstruct the life of that Cornish gentleman who became a renegade and a Barbary Corsair and might have become Basha of Algiers—or Argire, as his lordship terms it—but for certain matters which are to be set forth.

Lord Henry wrote with knowledge and authority, and the tale he has to tell is very complete and full of precious detail. He was, himself, an eyewitness of much that happened; he pursued a personal acquaintance with many of those who were connected with Sir Oliver's affairs that he might amplify his chronicles, and he considered no scrap of gossip that was to be gleaned along the countryside too trivial to be recorded. I suspect him also of having received no little assistance from Jasper Leigh in the matter of those events that happened out of England, which seem to me to constitute by far the most interesting portion of his narrative.

R.S.

PART ONE

SIR OLIVER TRESSILIAN

CHAPTER I

THE HUCKSTER

S IR OLIVER TRESSILIAN sat at his ease in the lofty dining room of the handsome house of Penarrow, which he owed to the enterprise of his father of lamented and lamentable memory and to the skill and invention of an Italian engineer named Bagnolo who had come to England half a century ago as one of the assistants of the famous Torrigiani.

This house of such a startlingly singular and Italianate grace for so remote a corner of Cornwall deserves, together with the story of its construction, a word in passing.

The Italian Bagnolo who combined with his salient artistic talents a quarrelsome, volcanic humor had the mischance to kill a man in a brawl in a Southwark tavern. As a result he fled the town, nor paused in his headlong flight from the consequences of that murderous deed until he had all but reached the very ends of England. Under what circumstances he became acquainted with Tressilian the elder I do not know. But certain it is that the meeting was a very timely one for both of them. To the fugitive, Ralph Tressilian—who appears to have been inveterately partial to the company of rascals of all denominations—afforded shelter; and Bagnolo repaid the service by offering to rebuild the decaying half-timbered house of Penarrow. Having taken the task in hand he went about it with all the enthusiasm of your true artist, and achieved for his protector a residence that was a marvel of grace in that crude age and outlandish district. There arose under the supervision of the gifted engineer, worthy associate of Messer Torrigiani, a noble two-storied mansion of mellow red brick, flooded with light and sunshine by the enormously tall mullioned windows that rose almost from base to summit of each pilastered façade. The main doorway was set in a projecting wing and was overhung by a massive balcony, the whole surmounted by a pillared pediment of extraordinary grace, now partly clad in a green mantle of creepers. Above the burnt red tiles of the roof soared massive twisted chimneys in lofty majesty.

But the glory of Penarrow—that is, of the new Penarrow begotten of the fertile brain of Bagnolo—was the garden fashioned out of the tangled wilderness about the old house that had crowned the heights above Penarrow point. To the labors of Bagnolo, Time and Nature had added their own. Bagnolo had cut those handsome esplanades, had built those noble balustrades bordering the three terraces with their fine connecting flights of steps: himself he had planned the fountain, and with his own hands had carved the granite faun presiding over it and the dozen other statues of nymphs and sylvan gods in a marble that gleamed in white brilliance amid the dusky green. But Time and Nature had smoothed the lawns to a velvet surface, had thickened the handsome boxwood hedges, and thrust up those black spear-like poplars that completed the very Italianate appearance of that Cornish demesne.

Sir Oliver took his ease in his dining-room considering all this as it was displayed before him in the mellowing September sunshine, and found it all very good to see, and life very good to live. Now no man has ever been known so to find life without some immediate cause, other than that of his environment, for his optimism. Sir

Oliver had several causes. The first of these—although it was one which he may have been far from suspecting—was his equipment of youth, wealth, and good digestion; the second was that he had achieved honor and renown both upon the Spanish Main and in the late harrying of the Invincible Armada—or, more aptly perhaps might it be said, in the harrying of the late Invincible Armada—and that he had received in that the twenty-fifth year of his life the honor of knighthood from the Virgin Queen; the third and last contributor to his pleasant mood—and I have reserved it for the end as I account this to be the proper place for the most important factor—was Dan Cupid who for once seemed compounded entirely of benignity and who had so contrived matters that Sir Oliver's wooing of Mistress Rosamund Godolphin ran an entirely smooth and happy course.

So, then, Sir Oliver sat at his ease in his tall, carved chair, his doublet untrussed, his long legs stretched before him, a pensive smile about the firm lips that as yet were darkened by no more than a small black line of moustachios. (Lord Henry's portrait of him was drawn at a much later period.) It was noon, and our gentleman had just dined, as the platters, the broken meats and the half-empty flagon on the board beside him testified. He pulled thoughtfully at a long pipe—for he had acquired this newly imported habit of tobacco-drinking—and dreamed of his mistress, and was properly and gallantly grateful that fortune had used him so handsomely as to enable him to toss a title and some measure of renown into his Rosamund's lap.

By nature Sir Oliver was a shrewd fellow ("cunning as twenty devils," is my Lord Henry's phrase) and he was also a man of some not inconsiderable learning. Yet neither his natural wit nor his acquired endowments appear to have taught him that of all the gods that rule the destinies of mankind there is none more ironic and malicious than that same Dan Cupid in whose honor, as it were, he was now burning the incense of that pipe of his. The ancients knew that innocent-seeming boy for a cruel, impish knave, and they mistrusted him. Sir Oliver either did not know or did not heed that sound piece of ancient wisdom. It was to be borne in upon him by grim experience, and even as his light pensive eyes smiled upon the sunshine that flooded the terrace beyond the long mullioned window, a shadow fell athwart it which he little dreamed to be symbolic of the shadow that was even then falling across the sunshine of his life.

After that shadow came the substance—tall and gay of raiment under a broad black Spanish hat decked with blood-red plumes. Swinging a long beribboned cane the figure passed the windows, stalking deliberately as Fate.

The smile perished on Sir Oliver's lips. His swarthy face grew thoughtful, his black brows contracted until no more than a single deep furrow stood between them. Then slowly the smile came forth again, but no longer that erstwhile gentle pensive smile. It was transformed into a smile of resolve and determination, a smile that tightened his lips even as his brows relaxed, and invested his brooding eyes with a gleam that was mocking, crafty, and almost wicked.

Came Nicholas his servant to announce Master Peter Godolphin, and close upon the lackey's heels came Master Godolphin himself, leaning upon his beribboned cane and carrying his broad Spanish hat. He was a tall, slender gentleman, with a shaven, handsome countenance, stamped with an air of haughtiness; like Sir Oliver, he had a highbridged, intrepid nose, and in age he was the younger by some two or three years. He wore his auburn hair rather longer than was the mode just then, but in his apparel there was no more foppishness than is tolerable in a gentleman of his years.

Sir Oliver rose and bowed from his great height in welcome. But a wave of tobacco-smoke took his graceful visitor in the throat and set him coughing and grimacing.

"I see,". he choked, "that ye have acquired that filthy habit."

"I have known filthier," said Sir Oliver composedly.

"I nothing doubt it," rejoined Master Godolphin, thus early giving indications of his humor and the object of his visit.

Sir Oliver checked an answer that must have helped his visitor to his ends, which was no part of the knight's intent.

"Therefore," said he ironically, "I hope you will be patient with my shortcomings. Nick, a chair for Master Godolphin and another cup. I bid you welcome to Penarrow."

A sneer flickered over the younger man's white face. "You pay me a compliment, sir, which I fear me 't is not mine to return to you."

"Time enough for that when I come to seek it," said Sir Oliver, with easy, if assumed, good humor.

"When you come to seek it?"

"The hospitality of your house," Sir Oliver explained.

"It is on that very matter I am come to talk with you."

"Will you sit?" Sir Oliver invited him, and spread a hand towards the chair which Nicholas had set. In the same gesture he waved the servant away.

Master Godolphin ignored the invitation. "You were," he said, "at Godolphin Court but yesterday, I hear." He paused, and as Sir Oliver offered no denial, he added stiffly: "I am come, sir, to inform you that the honor of your visits is one we shall be happy to forgo."

In the effort he made to preserve his self-control before so direct an affront Sir Oliver paled a little under his tan.

"You will understand, Peter," he replied slowly, "that you have said too much unless you add something more." He paused, considering his visitor a moment. "I do not know whether Rosamund has told you that yesterday she did me the honor to consent to become my wife. . . ."

"She is a child that does not know her mind," broke in the other.

"Do you know of any good reason why she should come to change it?" asked Sir Oliver, with a slight air of challenge.

Master Godolphin sat down, crossed his legs, and placed his hat on his knee.

"I know a dozen," he answered. "But I need not urge them. Sufficient should it be to remind you that Rosamund is but seventeen and that she is under my guardianship and that of Sir John Killigrew. Neither Sir John nor I can sanction this betrothal."

"Good lack!" broke out Sir Oliver. "Who asks your sanction or Sir John's? By God's grace your sister will grow to be a woman soon and mistress of herself. I am in no desperate haste to get me wed, and by nature—as you may be observing—I am a wondrous patient man. I'll even wait." And he pulled at his pipe.

"Waiting cannot avail you in this, Sir Oliver. 'T is best you should understand. We are resolved, Sir John and I."

"Are you so? God's light. Send Sir John to me to tell me of his resolves and I'll tell him something of mine. Tell him from me, Master Godolphin, that if he will trouble to come as far as Penarrow I'll do by him what the hangman should have done long since. I'll crop his pimpish ears for him, by this hand!"

"Meanwhile," said Master Godolphin whettingly, "will you not essay your rover's prowess upon me?"

"You?" quoth Sir Oliver, and looked him over with good-humored contempt. "I'm no butcher of fledgelings, my lad. Besides, you are your sister's brother, and 't is no aim of mine to increase the obstacles already in my path." Then his tone changed. He leaned across the table. "Come, now, Peter. What is at the root of all this matter? Can we not compose such differences as you conceive exist? Out with them. 'T is no matter for Sir John. He's a curmudgeon who signifies not a finger's snap. But you, 't is different. You are her brother. Out with your plaints, then. Let us be frank and friendly."

"Friendly?" The other sneered again. "Our fathers set us an example in that."

"Does it matter what our fathers did? More shame to them if, being neighbors, they could not be friends. Shall we follow so deplorable an example?"

"You'll not impute that the fault lay with *my* father," cried the other, with a show of ready anger.

"I impute nothing, lad. I cry shame upon them both."

"'Swounds!" swore Master Peter. "Do you malign the dead?"

"If I do, I malign them both. But I do not. I no more than condemn a fault that both must acknowledge could they return to life."

"Then, sir, confine your condemnings to your own father with whom no man of honor could have lived at peace. . . ."

"Softly, softly, good sir. . . ."

"There's no call to go softly. Ralph Tressilian was a dishonor, a scandal to the countryside. Not a hamlet between here and Truro, or between here and Helston, but swarms with big Tressilian noses like your own, in memory of your debauched parent."

Sir Oliver's eyes grew narrower: he smiled. "I wonder how you came by your own nose?" he wondered.

Master Godolphin got to his feet in a passion, and his chair crashed over behind him. "Sir," he blazed, "you insult my mother's memory!"

Sir Oliver laughed. "I make a little free with it, perhaps, in return for your pleasantries on the score of my father."

Master Godolphin pondered him in speechless anger, then swayed by his passion he leaned across the board, raised his long cane and struck Sir Oliver sharply on the shoulder.

That done, he strode off magnificently towards the door. Half-way thither he paused.

"I shall expect your friends and the length of your sword," said he.

Sir Oliver laughed again. "I don't think I shall trouble to send them," said he.

Master Godolphin wheeled, fully to face him again. "How? You will take a blow?"

Sir Oliver shrugged. "None saw it given," said he.

"But I shall publish it abroad that I have caned you."

"You'll publish yourself a liar if you do; for none will believe you." Then he changed his tone yet again. "Come, Peter, we are behaving unworthily. As for the blow, I confess that I deserved it. A man's mother is more sacred than his father. So we may cry quits on that score. Can we not cry quits on all else? What can it profit us to perpetuate a foolish quarrel that sprang up between our fathers?"

"There is more than that between us," answered Master Godolphin. "I'll not have my sister wed a pirate."

"A pirate? God's light! I am glad there's none to hear you, for since her grace has knighted me for my doings upon the seas, your words go very near to treason. Surely, lad, what the Queen approves, Master Peter Godolphin may approve and even your mentor Sir John Killigrew. You've been listening to him. 'T was he sent you hither."

"I am no man's lackey," answered the other hotly, resenting the imputation—and resenting it the more because of the truth in it.

"To call me a pirate is to say a foolish thing. Hawkins with whom I sailed has also received the accolade, and who dubs us pirates insults the Queen herself. Apart from that, which, as you see, is a very empty charge, what else have you against me? I am, I hope, as good as any other here in Cornwall; Rosamund honors me with her affection and I am rich and shall be richer still ere the wedding bells are heard."

"Rich with the fruit of thieving upon the seas, rich with the treasures of scuttled ships and the price of slaves captured in Africa and sold to the plantations, rich as the vampire is glutted—with the blood of dead men."

"Does Sir John say that?" asked Sir Oliver, in a soft deadly voice.

"I say it."

"I heard you; but I am asking where you learnt that pretty lesson. Is Sir John your preceptor? He is, he is. No need to tell me. I'll deal with him. Meanwhile let me disclose to you the pure and disinterested source of Sir John's rancor. You shall see what an upright and honest gentleman is Sir John, who was your father's friend and has been your guardian."

"I'll not listen to what you say of him."

"Nay, but you shall, in return for having made me listen to what he says of me. Sir John desires to obtain a licence to build at the mouth of the Fal. He hopes to see a town spring up above the haven there under the shadow of his own manor of Arwenack. He represents himself as nobly disinterested and all concerned for the prosperity of the country, and he neglects to mention that the land is his own and that it is his own prosperity and that of his family which he is concerned to foster. We met in London by a fortunate chance whilst Sir John was about this business at the Court. Now it happens that I, too, have interests in Truro and Penryn; but, unlike Sir John, I am honest in the matter, and proclaim it. If any growth should take place about Smithick it follows from its more advantageous situation that Truro and Penryn must suffer, and that suits me as little as the other matter would suit Sir John. I told him so, for I can be blunt, and I told the Queen in the form of a counter-petition to Sir John's." He shrugged. "The moment was propitious to me. I was one of the seamen who had helped to conquer the unconquerable Armada of King Philip. I was therefore not to be denied, and Sir John was sent home as empty-handed as he went to Court. D' ye marvel that he hates me? Knowing him for what he is, d' ye marvel that he dubs me pirate and worse? 'T is natural enough so to misrepresent my doings upon the sea, since it is those doings have afforded me the power to hurt his profit. He has chosen the weapons of calumny for this combat, but those weapons are not mine, as I shall show him this very day. If you do not credit what I say, come with me and be present at the little talk I hope to have with that curmudgeon."

"You forget," said Master Godolphin, "that I, too, have interests in the neighborhood of Smithick, and that you are hurting those."

"Soho!" crowed Sir Oliver. "Now at last the sun of truth peeps forth from all this cloud of righteous indignation at my bad Tressilian blood and pirate's ways! You, too, are but a trafficker. Now see what a fool am I to have believed you sincere, and to have stood here in talk with you as with an honest man." His voice swelled and his lip curled in a contempt that struck the other like a blow. "I swear I had not wasted breath with you had I known you for so mean and pitiful a fellow."

"These words . . ." began Master Godolphin, drawing himself up very stiffly.

"Are a deal less than your deserts," cut in the other, and he raised his voice to call—"Nick."

"You shall answer to them," snapped his visitor.

"I am answering now," was the stern answer. "To come here and prate to me of my dead father's dissoluteness and of an ancient quarrel between him and yours, to bleat of my trumped-up course of piracy and my own ways of life as a just cause why I may not wed your sister, whilst the real consideration in your mind, the real spur to your hostility is no more than the matter of some few paltry pounds a year that I hinder you from pocketing. A God's name get you gone."

Nick entered at that moment.

"You shall hear from me again, Sir Oliver," said the other, white with anger. "You shall account to me for these words."

"I do not fight with . . . with hucksters," flashed Sir Oliver.

"D' ye dare call me that?"

"Indeed, 't is to discredit an honorable class, I confess it. Nick, the door for Master Godolphin."

CHAPTER II

ROSAMUND

ANON, AFTER his visitor had departed, Sir Oliver grew calm again. Then being able in his calm to consider his position, he became angry anew at the very thought of the rage in which he had been, a rage which had so mastered him that he had erected additional obstacles to the already considerable ones that stood between Rosamund and himself. In full blast, his anger swung round and took Sir John Killigrew for its objective. He would settle with him at once. He would so, by Heaven's light!

He bellowed for Nick and his boots.

"Where is Master Lionel?" he asked when the boots had been fetched.

"He be just ridden in, Sir Oliver."

"Bid him hither."

Promptly, in answer to that summons, came Sir Oliver's half-brother—a slender lad favoring his mother, the dissolute Ralph Tressilian's second wife. He was as unlike Sir Oliver in body as in soul. He was comely in a very gentle, almost womanish way: his complexion was fair and delicate, his hair golden, and his eyes of a deep blue. He had a very charming stripling grace—for he was but in his twenty-first year—and he dressed with all the care of a Court-gallant.

"Has that whelp Godolphin been to visit you?" he asked as he entered.

"Aye," growled Sir Oliver. "He came to tell me some things and to hear some others in return."

"Ha, I passed him just beyond the gates, and he was deaf to my greeting. 'T is a most cursed insufferable pup."

"Art a judge of men, Lal." Sir Oliver stood up booted. "I am for Arwenack to exchange a compliment or two with Sir John."

His tight-pressed lips and resolute air supplemented his words so well that Lionel clutched his arm. "You're not . . . you're not . . .?"

"I am." And affectionately, as if to soothe the lad's obvious alarm, he patted his brother's shoulder. "Sir John," he explained, "talks too much. 'T is a fault that wants correcting. I go to teach him the virtue of silence."

"There will be trouble, Oliver."

"So there will—for him. If a man must be saying of me that I am a pirate, a slave-dealer, a murderer, and Heaven alone knows what else, he must be ready for the consequences. But you are late, Lal. Where have you been?"

"I rode as far as Malpas."

"As far as Malpas?" Sir Oliver's eyes narrowed, as was the trick with him. "I hear it whispered what magnet draws you thither," he said. "Be wary, boy. You go too much to Malpas."

"How?" quoth Lionel a trifle coldly.

"I mean that you are your father's son. Remember it, and strive not to follow in his ways lest they bring you to his own end. I have just been reminded of these predilections of his by good Master Peter. Go not over often to Malpas, I say. No more." But the arm which he flung about his younger brother's shoulders and the warmth of his embrace made resentment of his warning quite impossible.

When he was gone, Lionel sat him down to dine, with Nick to wait on him. He ate but little, and never addressed the old servant in the course of that brief repast. He was very pensive. In thought he followed his brother on that avenging visit of his to Arwenack. Killigrew was no babe, but a man of his hands, a soldier and a seaman. If any harm should come to Oliver. . . . He trembled at the thought; and then almost despite him his mind ran on to calculate the consequences to himself. His fortune would be in a very different case, he reflected. In a sort of horror, he sought to put so detestable a reflection from his mind; but it returned insistently. It would not be denied. It forced him to a consideration of his own circumstances.

All that he had he owed to his brother's bounty. That dissolute father of theirs had died as such men commonly die, leaving behind him heavily encumbered estates and many debts; the very house of Penarrow was mortgaged, and the moneys raised on it had been drunk, or gambled, or spent on one or another of Ralph Tressilian's many lights o' love. Then Oliver had sold some little property near Helston, inherited from his mother; he had sunk the money into a venture upon the Spanish Main. He had fitted out and manned a ship, and had sailed with Hawkins upon one of those ventures, which Sir John Killigrew was perfectly entitled to account pirate raids. He had returned with enough plunder in specie and gems to disencumber the Tressilian patrimony. He had sailed again and returned still wealthier. And meanwhile, Lionel had remained at home taking his ease. He loved his ease. His nature was inherently indolent, and he had the wasteful extravagant tastes that usually go with indolence. He was not born to toil and struggle, and none had sought to correct the shortcomings of his character in that respect. Sometimes he wondered what the future might hold for him should Oliver come to marry. He feared his life might not be as easy as it was at present. But he did not seriously fear. It was not in his nature—it never is in the natures of such men—to give any excess of consideration to the future. When his thoughts did turn to it in momentary uneasiness, he would abruptly dismiss them with the reflection that when all was said Oliver loved him, and Oliver would never fail to provide adequately for all his wants.

In this undoubtedly he was fully justified. Oliver was more parent than brother to him. When their father had been brought home to die for the wound dealt him by an outraged husband—and a shocking spectacle that sinner's death had been with its hasty terrified repentance—he had entrusted Lionel to his elder brother's care. At the time Oliver was seventeen and Lionel twelve. But Oliver had seemed by so many years older than his age that the twice-widowed Ralph Tressilian had come to depend upon this steady, resolute, and masterful child of his first marriage. It was into his ear that the dying man had poured the wretched tale of his repentance for the life he had lived and the state in which he was leaving his affairs with such scant provision for his sons. For Oliver he had no fear. It was as if with the prescience that comes to men in his pass he had perceived that Oliver was of those who must prevail, a man born to make the world his oyster. His anxieties were all for Lionel, whom he also judged with that same penetrating insight vouchsafed a man in his last hours. Hence his piteous recommendation of him to Oliver, and Oliver's ready promise to be father, mother, and brother to the youngster.

All this was in Lionel's mind as he sat musing there, and again he struggled with that hideous insistent thought that if things should go ill with his brother at Arwenack, there would be great profit to himself; that these things he now enjoyed upon another's bounty he would then enjoy in his own right. A devil seemed to mock him with the whispered sneer that were Oliver to die his own grief would not be long-lived. Then in revolt against that voice of an egoism so loathsome that in his better moments it inspired even himself with horror, he bethought him of Oliver's unvarying, unwavering affection; he pondered all the loving care and kindness that through these years past Oliver had ever showered upon him; and he cursed the rottenness of a mind that could even admit such thoughts as those which he had been entertaining. So wrought upon was he by the welter of his emotions, by that fierce strife between his conscience and his egotism, that he came abruptly to his feet, a cry upon his lips.

"Vade retro, Sathanas!"

Old Nicholas, looking up abruptly, saw the lad's face, waxen, his brow bedewed with sweat.

"Master Lionel! Master Lionel!" he cried, his small bright eyes concernedly scanning his young master's face.

"What be amiss?"

Lionel mopped his brow. "Sir Oliver has gone to Arwenack upon a punitive business," said he.

"An' what be that, zur?" quoth Nicholas.

"He has gone to punish Sir John for having maligned him."

A grin spread upon the weather-beaten countenance of Nicholas.

"Be that so? Marry, 't were time. Sir John he be over long i' th' tongue."

Lionel stood amazed at the man's easy confidence and supreme assurance of how his master must acquit himself.

"You . . . you have no fear, Nicholas. . . ." He did not add of what. But the servant understood, and his grin grew broader still.

"Fear? Lackaday! I bain't afeeard for Sir Oliver, and doan't ee be afeeard. Sir Oliver'll be home to sup with a sharp-set appetite—'t is the only difference fighting ever made to he."

The servant was justified of his confidence by the events, though through a slight error of judgment Sir Oliver did not quite accomplish all that he promised and intended. In anger, and when he deemed that he had been affronted, he was—as his chronicler never wearies of insisting, and as you shall judge before the end of this tale is reached—of a tigerish ruthlessness. He rode to Arwenack fully resolved to kill his calumniator. Nothing less would satisfy him. Arrived at that fine embattled castle of the Killigrews which commanded the entrance to the estuary of the Fal, and from whose crenels the country might be surveyed as far as the Lizard, fifteen miles away, he found Peter Godolphin there before him; and because of Peter's presence Sir Oliver was more deliberate and formal in his accusation of Sir John than he had intended. He desired, in accusing Sir John, also to clear himself in the eyes of Rosamund's brother, to make the latter realize how entirely odious were the calumnies which Sir John had permitted himself, and how basely prompted.

Sir John however, came halfway to meet the quarrel. His rancor against the Pirate of Penarrow—as he had come to dub Sir Oliver—rendered him almost as eager to engage as was his visitor.

They found a secluded corner of the deer-park for their business, and there Sir John—a slim, sallow gentleman of some thirty years of age—made an onslaught with sword and dagger upon Sir Oliver, full worthy of the onslaught he had made earlier with his tongue. But his impetuosity availed him less than nothing. Sir Oliver was come there with a certain purpose, and it was his way that he never failed to carry through a thing to which he set his hand.

In three minutes it was all over and Sir Oliver was carefully wiping his blade, whilst Sir John lay coughing upon the turf tended by white-faced Peter Godolphin and a scared groom who had been bidden thither to make up the necessary tale of witnesses.

Sir Oliver sheathed his weapons and resumed his coat, then came to stand over his fallen foe, considering him critically.

"I think I have silenced him for a little time only," he said. "And I confess that I intended to do better. I hope, however, that the lesson will suffice and that he will lie no more—at least concerning me."

"Do you mock a fallen man?" was Master Godolphin's angry protest.

"God forbid!" said Sir Oliver soberly. "There is no mockery in my heart. There is, believe me, nothing but regret—regret that I should not have done the thing more thoroughly. I will send assistance from the house as I go. Give you good day, Master Peter."

From Arwenack he rode round by Penryn on his homeward way. But he did not go straight home. He paused at the Gates of Godolphin Court, which stood above Trefusis Point commanding the view of Carrick Roads. He turned in under the old gateway and drew up in the courtyard. Leaping to the kidney-stones that paved it, he announced himself a visitor to Mistress Rosamund.

He found her in her bower—a light, turreted chamber on the mansion's eastern side, with windows that looked out upon that lovely sheet of water and the wooded slopes beyond. She was sitting with a book in her lap in the deep of that tall window when he entered, preceded and announced by Sally Pentreath, who, now her tire-woman, had once been her nurse.

She rose with a little exclamation of gladness when he appeared under the lintel—scarce high enough to admit him without stooping—and stood regarding him across the room with brightened eyes and flushing cheeks.

What need is there to describe her? In the blaze of notoriety into which she was anon to be thrust by Sir Oliver Tressilian there was scarce a poet in England who did not sing the grace and loveliness of Rosamund Godolphin, and in all conscience enough of those fragments have survived. Like her brother she was tawny headed and she was divinely tall, though as yet her figure in its girlishness was almost too slender for her height.

"I had not looked for you so early . . ." she was beginning, when she observed that his countenance was oddly stern. "Why . . . what has happened?" she cried, her intuitions clamoring loudly of some mischance.

"Naught to alarm you, sweet; yet something that may vex you." He set an arm about that lissom waist of hers above the swelling farthingale, and gently led her back to her chair, then flung himself upon the window-seat beside her. "You hold Sir John Killigrew in some affection?" he said between statement and inquiry.

"Why, yes. He was our guardian until my brother came of full age."

Sir Oliver made a wry face. "Aye, there's the rub. Well, I've all but killed him."

She drew back into her chair, recoiling before him, and he saw horror leap to her eyes and blanch her face. He made haste to explain the causes that had led to this; he told her briefly of the calumnies concerning him that Sir John had put about to vent his spite at having been thwarted in the matter of his coveted licence to build at Smithick.

"That mattered little," he concluded. "I knew these tales concerning me were abroad, and I held them in the same contempt as I hold their utterer. But he went further, Rose: he poisoned your brother's mind against me, and he stirred up in him the slumbering rancor that in my father's time was wont to lie between our houses. To-day Peter came to me with the clear intent to make a quarrel. He affronted me as no man has ever dared."

She cried out at that, her already great alarm redoubled. He smiled.

"Do not suppose that I could harm him. He is your brother, and, so, sacred to me. He came to tell me that no betrothal was possible between us, forbade me ever again to visit Godolphin Court, dubbed me pirate and vampire to my face and reviled my father's memory. I tracked the evil of all this to its source in Killigrew, and rode straight to Arwenack to dam that source of falsehood for all time. I did not accomplish quite so much as I intended. You see, I am frank, my Rose. It may be that Sir John will live; if so I hope that he may profit by this lesson. I have come straight to you," he concluded, "that you may hear the tale from me before another comes to malign me with false stories of this happening."

"You . . . you mean Peter?" she cried.

"Alas!" he sighed.

She sat very still and white, looking straight before her and not at all at Sir Oliver. At length she spoke.

"I am not skilled in reading men," she said in a sad, small voice. "How should I be, that am but a maid who has led a cloistered life? I was told of you that you were violent and passionate, a man of bitter enmities, easily stirred to hatreds, cruel and ruthless in the persecution of them."

"You, too, have been listening to Sir John," he muttered, and laughed shortly.

"All this was I told," she pursued as if he had not spoken, "and all did I refuse to believe because my heart was given to you. Yet . . . yet of what have you made proof to-day?"

"Of forbearance," said he shortly.

"Forbearance?" she echoed, and her lips writhed in a smile of weary irony. "Surely you mock me!"

He set himself to explain.

"I have told you what Sir John had done. I have told you that the greater part of it—and matter all that touched my honor—I know Sir John to have done long since. Yet I suffered it in silence and contempt. Was that to show myself easily stirred to ruthlessness? What was it but forbearance? When, however, he carries his petty huckster's rancor so far as to seek to choke for me my source of happiness in life and sends your brother to affront me, I am still so forbearing that I recognize your brother to be no more than a tool and go straight to the hand that wielded him. Because I know of your affection for Sir John I gave him such latitude as no man of honor in England would have given him."

Then seeing that she still avoided his regard, still sat in that frozen attitude of horror at learning that the man she loved had imbrued his hands with the blood of another whom she also loved, his pleading quickened to a warmer note. He flung himself upon his knees beside her chair, and took in his great sinewy hands the slender fingers which she listlessly surrendered. "Rose," he cried, and his deep voice quivered with intercession, "dismiss all that you have heard from out your mind. Consider only this thing that has befallen. Suppose that Lionel my brother came to you, and that, having some measure of power and authority to support him, he swore to you that you should never wed me, swore to prevent this marriage because he deemed you such a woman as could not bear my name with honor to myself; and suppose that to all this he added insult to the memory of your dead father, what answer would you return him? Speak, Rose! Be honest with thyself and me. Deem yourself in my place, and say in honesty if you can still condemn me for what I have done. Say if it differs much from what you would wish to do in such a case as I have named."

Her eyes scanned now his upturned face, every line of which was pleading to her and calling for impartial judgment. Her face grew troubled, and then almost fierce. She set her hands upon his shoulders, and looked deep into his eyes.

"You swear to me, Noll, that all is as you have told it me—you have added naught, you have altered naught to make the tale more favorable to yourself?"

"You need such oaths from me?" he asked, and she saw sorrow spread upon his countenance.

"If I did I should not love thee, Noll. But in such an hour I need your own assurance. Will you not be generous and bear with me, strengthen me to withstand anything that may be said hereafter?"

"As God's my witness, I have told you true in all," he answered solemnly.

She sank her head to his shoulder. She was weeping softly, overwrought by this climax to all that in silence and in secret she had suffered since he had come a-wooing her.

"Then," she said, "I believe you acted rightly. I believe with you that no man of honor could have acted otherwise. I must believe you, Noll, for did I not, then I could believe in naught and hope for naught. You are as a fire that has seized upon the better part of me and consumed it all to ashes that you may hold it in your heart. I am content so you be true."

"True I shall ever be, sweetheart," he whispered fervently. "Could I be less since you are sent to make me so?"

She looked at him again, and now she was smiling wistfully through her tears.

"And you will bear with Peter?" she implored him.

"He shall have no power to anger me," he answered, "I swear that too. Do you know that but to-day he struck me?"

"Struck you? You did not tell me that!"

"My quarrel was not with him but with the rogue that sent him. I laughed at the blow. Was he not sacred to me?"

"He is good at heart, Noll," she pursued. "In time he will come to love you as you deserve, and you will come to know that he, too, deserves your love."

"He deserves it now, for the love he bears to you."

"And you will think ever thus during the little while of waiting that perforce must lie before us?"

"I shall never think otherwise, sweet. Meanwhile I shall avoid him, and that no harm may come should he forbid me Godolphin Court I'll even stay away. In less than a year you will be of full age, and none may hinder you to come and go. What is a year, with such hope as mine to still impatience?"

She stroked his face. "Art very gentle with me ever, Noll," she murmured fondly. "I cannot credit you are ever harsh to any, as they say."

"Heed them not," he answered her. "I may have been something of all that, but you have purified me, Rose. What man that loved you could be aught but gentle." He kissed her, and stood up. "I had best be going now," he said. "I shall walk along the shore towards Trefusis Point to-morrow morning. If you should chance to be similarly disposed . . ."

She laughed, and rose in her turn. "I shall be there, dear Noll."

"'T were best so hereafter," he assured her, smiling, and so took his leave.

She followed him to the stair-head, and watched him as he descended with eyes that took pride in the fine upright carriage of that stalwart, masterful lover.

CHAPTER III

THE FORGE

S IR OLIVER'S WISDOM in being the first to bear Rosamund the story of that day's happenings was established anon when Master Godolphin returned home. He went straight in quest of his sister; and in a frame of mind oppressed by fear and sorrow for Sir John, by his general sense of discomfiture at the hands of Sir Oliver and by the anger begotten of all this he was harsh in manner and disposed to hector.

"Madam," he announced abruptly, "Sir John is like to die."

The astounding answer she returned him—that is, astounding to him—did not tend to soothe his sorely ruffled spirit.

"I know," she said. "And I believe him to deserve no less. Who deals in calumny should be prepared for the wages of it."

He stared at her in a long, furious silence, then exploded into oaths, and finally inveighed against her unnaturalness and pronounced her bewitched by that foul dog Tressilian.

"It is fortunate for me," she answered him composedly, "that he was here before you to give me the truth of this affair." Then her assumed calm and the anger with which she had met his own all fell away from her. "Oh, Peter, Peter," she cried in anguish, "I hope that Sir John will recover. I am distraught by this event. But be just, I implore you. Sir Oliver has told me how hard-driven he has been."

"He shall be driven harder yet, as God's my life! If you think this deed shall go unpunished. . . ."

She flung herself upon his breast and implored him to carry this quarrel no further. She spoke of her love for Sir Oliver, and announced her firm resolve to marry him in despite of all opposition that could be made, all of which did not tend to soften her brother's humor. Yet because of the love that ever had held these two in closest bonds he went so far in the end as to say that should Sir John recover he would not himself pursue the matter further. But if Sir John should die—as was very likely—honor compelled him to seek vengeance of a deed to which he had himself so very largely contributed.

"I read that man as if he were an open book," the boy announced, with callow boastfulness. "He has the subtlety of Satan, yet he does not delude me. It was at me he struck through Killigrew. Because he desires you, Rosamund, he could not—as he bluntly told me—deal with me however I provoked him, not even though I went the length of striking him. He might have killed me for 't; but he knew that to do so would place a barrier 'twixt him and you. Oh! he is calculating as all the fiends of Hell. So, to wipe out the dishonor which I did him, he shifts the blame of it upon Killigrew and goes out to kill him, which he further thinks may act as a warning to me. But if Killigrew dies . . ." And thus he rambled on, filling her gentle heart with anguish to see this feud increasing between the two men she loved best in all the world. If the outcome of it should be that either were to kill the other, she knew that she could never again look upon the survivor.

She took heart at last in the memory of Sir Oliver's sworn promise that her brother's life should be inviolate to him, betide what might. She trusted him; she depended upon his word and that rare strength of his which rendered possible to him a course that no weaker man would dare pursue. And in this reflection her pride in him increased, and she thanked God for a lover who in all things was a giant among men.

But Sir John Killigrew did not die. He hovered between this world and a better one for some seven days, at the end of which he began to recover. By October he was abroad again, gaunt and pale, reduced to half the bulk that had been his before, a mere shadow of a man.

One of his first visits was to Godolphin Court. He went to remonstrate with Rosamund upon her betrothal, and he did so at the request of her brother. But his remonstrances were strangely lacking in the force that she had looked for.

The odd fact is that in his near approach to death, and with his earthly interest dwindling, Sir John had looked matters frankly in the face, and had been driven to the conclusion—a conclusion impossible to him in normal health—that he had got no more than he deserved. He realized that he had acted unworthily, if unconscious at the time of the unworthiness of what he did; that the weapons with which he had fought Sir Oliver were not the weapons that become a gentleman or in which there is credit to be won. He perceived that he had permitted his old enmity for the house of Tressilian, swollen by a sense of injury lately suffered in the matter of the licence to build at Smithick, to warp his judgment and to persuade him that Sir Oliver was all he had dubbed him. He realized that jealousy, too, had taken a hand in the matter. Sir Oliver's exploits upon the seas had brought him wealth, and with this wealth he was building up once more the Tressilian sway in those parts, which Ralph Tressilian had so outrageously diminished, so that he threatened to eclipse the importance of the Killigrews of Arwenack.

Nevertheless, in the hour of reaction he did not go so far as to admit that Sir Oliver Tressilian was a fit mate for Rosamund

Godolphin. She and her brother had been placed in his care by their late father, and he had nobly discharged his tutelage until such time as Peter had come to full age. His affection for Rosamund was tender as that of a lover, but tempered by a feeling entirely paternal. He went very near to worshiping her, and when all was said, when he had cleared his mind of all dishonest bias, he still found overmuch to dislike in Oliver Tressilian, and the notion of his becoming Rosamund's husband was repellent.

First of all there was that bad Tressilian blood—-notoriously bad, and never more fragrantly displayed than in the case of the late Ralph Tressilian. It was impossible that Oliver should have escaped the taint of it; nor could Sir John perceive any signs that he had done so. He displayed the traditional Tressilian turbulence. He was passionate and brutal, and the pirate's trade to which he had now set his hand was of all trades the one for which he was by nature best equipped. He was harsh and overbearing, impatient of correction, and prone to trample other men's feelings underfoot. Was this, he asked himself in all honesty, a mate for Rosamund? Could he entrust her happiness to the care of such a man? Assuredly he could not.

Therefore, being whole again, he went to remonstrate with her as he accounted it his duty and as Master Peter had besought him. Yet knowing the bias that had been his, he was careful to understate rather than to overstate his reasons.

"But, Sir John," she protested, "if every man is to be condemned for the sins of his forbears, but few could escape condemnation, and wherever shall you find me a husband deserving your approval?"

"His father . . ." began Sir John.

"Tell me not of his father, but of himself," she interrupted.

He frowned impatiently—they were sitting in that bower of hers above the river.

"I was coming to 't," he answered, a thought testily, for these interruptions which made him keep to the point robbed him of his best arguments. "However, suffice it that many of his father's vicious qualities he has inherited, as we see in his ways of life; that he has not inherited others only the future can assure us."

"In other words," she mocked him, yet very seriously, "I am to wait until he dies of old age to make quite sure that he has no such sins as must render him an unfitting husband?"

"No, no," he cried. "Good lack! what a perverseness in thine!"

"The perverseness is your own, Sir John. I am but the mirror of it."

He shifted in his chair and grunted. "Be it so, then," he snapped. "We will deal with the qualities that already he displays." And Sir John enumerated them.

"But this is no more than your judgment of him—no more than what you think him."

"'T is what all the world thinks him."

"But I shall not marry a man for what others think of him, but for what I think of him myself. And in my view you cruelly malign him. I discover no such qualities in Sir Oliver."

"'T is that you should be spared such a discovery that I am beseeching you not to wed him."

"Yet unless I wed him I shall never make such a discovery; and until I make it I shall ever continue to love him and to desire to wed him. Is all my life to be spent so?" She laughed outright, and came to stand beside him. She put an arm about his neck as she might have put it about the neck of her father, as she had been in the habit of doing any day in these past ten years—and thereby made him feel himself to have reached an unconscionable age. With her hand she rubbed his brow.

"Why, here are wicked wrinkles of ill-humor," she cried to him. "You are all undone, and by a woman's wit, and you do not like it."

"I am undone by a woman's wilfulness, by a woman's headstrong resolve not to see."

"You have naught to show me, Sir John."

"Naught? Is all that I have said naught?"

"Words are not things; judgments are not facts. You say that he is so, and so and so. But when I ask you upon what facts you judge him, your only answer is that you think him to be what you say he is. Your thoughts may be honest, Sir John, but your logic is contemptible." And she laughed again at his gaping discomfiture. "Come, now, deal like an honest upright judge, and tell me one act of his—one thing that he has ever done and of which you have sure knowledge—that will bear him out to be what you say he is. Now, Sir John!"

He looked up at her impatiently. Then, at last he smiled.

"Rogue!" he cried—and upon a distant day he was to bethink him of those words. "If ever he be brought to judgment I can desire him no better advocate than thou."

Thereupon following up her advantage swiftly, she kissed him. "Nor could I desire him a more honest judge than you."

What was the poor man to do thereafter? What he did. Live up to her pronouncement, and go forthwith to visit Sir Oliver and compose their quarrel.

The acknowledgment of his fault was handsomely made, and Sir Oliver received it in a spirit no less handsome. But when Sir John came to the matter of Mistress Rosamund he was, out of his sense of duty to her, less generous. He announced that since he could not bring himself to look upon Sir Oliver as a suitable husband for her, nothing that he had now said must mislead Sir Oliver into supposing him a consenting party to any such union.

"But that," he added, "is not to say that I oppose it. I disapprove, but I stand aside. Until she is of full age her brother will refuse his sanction. After that, the matter will concern neither him nor myself."

"I hope," said Sir Oliver, "he will take as wise a view. But whatever view he takes will be no matter. For the rest, Sir John, I thank you for your frankness, and I rejoice to know that if I may not count you for my friend, at least I need not reckon you among my enemies."

But if Sir John was thus won round to a neutral attitude, Master Peter's rancor abated nothing; rather it increased each day, and presently there came another matter to feed it, a matter of which Sir Oliver had no suspicion.

He knew that his brother Lionel rode almost daily to Malpas, and he knew the object of those daily rides. He knew of the lady who kept a sort of court there for the rustic bucks of Truro, Penryn, and Helston, and he knew something of the ill-repute that had attached to her in town—a repute, in fact, which had been the cause of her withdrawal into the country. He told his brother some frank and ugly truths concerning her, by way of warning him, and therein, for the first time, the twain went very near to quarreling.

After that he mentioned her no more. He knew that in his indolent way Lionel could be headstrong, and he knew human nature well enough to be convinced that interference here would but set up a breach between himself and his brother without in the least achieving its real object. So Oliver shrugged resignedly, and held his peace.

There he left the affair, nor ever spoke again of Malpas and the siren who presided there. And meanwhile the autumn faded into winter, and with the coming of stormy weather Sir Oliver and Rosamund had fewer opportunities of meeting. To Godolphin Court he would not go since she did not desire it; and himself he deemed it best to remain away since otherwise he must risk a quarrel with its master, who had forbidden him the place. In those days he saw Peter Godolphin but little, and on the rare occasions when they did meet they passed each other with a very meager salute.

Sir Oliver was entirely happy, and men noticed how gentler were his accents, how sunnier had become a countenance that they had known for haughty and forbidding. He waited for his coming happiness with the confidence of an immortal in the future. Patience was all the service Fate asked of him, and he gave that service blithely, depending upon the reward that soon now would be his own. Indeed, the year drew near its close; and ere another winter should come round Penarrow House would own a mistress. That to him seemed as inevitable as the season itself. And yet for all his supreme confidence, for all his patience and the happiness he culled from it, there were moments when he seemed oppressed by some elusive sense of overhanging doom, by some subconsciousness of an evil in the womb of Destiny. Did he challenge his oppression, did he seek to translate it into terms of reason, he found nothing upon which his wits could fasten, and he came ever to conclude that it was his very happiness by its excessiveness that was oppressing him, giving him at times that sense of premonitory weight about the heart as if to check its joyous soarings.

One day, a week from Christmas, he had occasion to ride to Helston on some trifling affair. For half a week a blizzard had whirled about the coast, and he had been kept chafing indoors what time layer upon layer of snow was spread upon the countryside. On the fourth day, the storm being spent, the sun came forth, the skies were swept clear of clouds and all the countryside lay robed in a sun-drenched, dazzling whiteness. Sir Oliver called for his horse and rode forth alone through the crisp snow. He turned homeward very early in the afternoon, but when a couple of miles from Helston he found that his horse had cast a shoe. He dismounted, and bridle over arm tramped on through the sunlit vale between the heights of Pendennis and Arwenack, singing as he went. He came thus to Smithick and the door of the forge. About it stood a group of fishermen and rustics, for, in the absence of any inn just there, this forge was ever a point of congregation. In addition to the rustics and an itinerant merchant with his pack-horses, there were present Sir Andrew Flack, the parson from Penryn, and Master Gregory Baine, one of the Justices from the neighborhood of

Truro. Both were well known to Sir Oliver, and he stood in friendly gossip with them what time he waited for his horse.

It was all very unfortunate, from the casting of that shoe to the meeting with those gentlemen; for as Sir Oliver stood there, down the gentle slope from Arwenack rode Master Peter Godolphin.

It was said afterwards by Sir Andrew and Master Baine that Master Peter appeared to have been carousing, so flushed was his face, so unnatural the brightness of his eye, so thick his speech and so extravagant and foolish what he said. There can be little doubt that it was so. He was addicted to Canary, and so indeed was Sir John Killigrew, and he had been dining with Sir John. He was of those who turn quarrelsome in wine—which is but another way of saying that when the wine was in and the restraint out, his natural humor came uppermost untrammeled. The sight of Sir Oliver standing there gave the lad precisely what he needed to indulge that evil humor of his, and he may have been quickened in his purpose by the presence of those other gentlemen. In his half fuddled state of mind he may have recalled that once he had struck Sir Oliver and Sir Oliver had laughed and told him that none would believe it.

He drew rein suddenly as he came abreast of the group, so suddenly that he pulled his horse until it almost sat down like a cat; yet he retained his saddle. Then he came through the snow that was all squelched and mudded just about the forge, and leered at Sir Oliver.

"I am from Arwenack," he announced unnecessarily. "We have been talking of you."

"You could have had no better subject of discourse," said Sir Oliver, smiling, for all that his eyes were hard and something scared—though his fears did not concern himself.

"Marry, you are right; you make an engrossing topic—you and your debauched father."

"Sir," replied Sir Oliver, "once already have I deplored your mother's utter want of discretion."

The words were out of him in a flash under the spur of the gross insult flung at him, uttered in the momentary blind rage aroused by that inflamed and taunting face above him. No sooner were they sped than he repented them, the more bitterly because they were greeted by a guffaw from the rustics. He would have given half his fortune in that moment to have recalled them.

Master Godolphin's face had changed as utterly as if he had removed a mask. From flushed that it had been it was livid now and the eyes were blazing, the mouth twitching. Thus a moment he glowered upon his enemy. Then standing in his stirrups he swung aloft his whip.

"You dog!" he cried, in a snarling sob. "You dog!" And his lash came down and cut a long red wheal across Sir Oliver's dark face.

With cries of dismay and anger the others, the parson, the Justice and the rustics got between the pair, for Sir Oliver was looking very wicked, and all the world knew him for a man to be feared.

"Master Godolphin, I cry shame upon you," exclaimed the parson. "If evil comes of this I shall testify to the grossness of your aggression. Get you gone from here!"

"Go to the devil, sir," said Master Godolphin thickly. "Is my mother's name to be upon the lips of that bastard? By God, man, the matter rests not here. He shall send his friends to me, or I will horsewhip him every time we meet. You hear, Sir Oliver?"

Sir Oliver made him no reply.

"You hear?" he roared. "There is no Sir John Killigrew this time upon whom you can shift the quarrel. Come you to me and get the punishment of which that whiplash is but an earnest." Then with a thick laugh he drove spurs into his horse's flanks, so furiously that he all but sent the parson and another sprawling.

"Stay but a little while for me," roared Sir Oliver after him. "You'll ride no more, my drunken fool!"

And in a rage he bellowed for his horse, flinging off the parson and Master Baine, who endeavored to detain and calm him. He vaulted to the saddle when the nag was brought him, and whirled away in furious pursuit.

The parson looked at the Justice and the Justice shrugged, his lips tight-pressed.

"The young fool is drunk," said Sir Andrew, shaking his white head. "He's in no case to meet his Maker."

"Yet he seems very eager," quoth Master Justice Baine. "I doubt I shall hear more of the matter." He turned and looked into the forge where the bellows now stood idle, the smith himself grimy and aproned in leather in the doorway, listening to the rustics' account of the happening. Master Baine it seems had a taste for analogies. "Faith," he said, "the place was excellently well chosen. They have forged here to-day a sword which it will need blood to temper."

CHAPTER IV

THE INTERVENER

THE PARSON HAD notions of riding after Sir Oliver, and begged Master Baine to join him. But the Justice looked down his long nose and opined that no good purpose was to be served: that Tressilians were ever wild and bloody men; and that an angry Tressilian was a thing to be avoided. Sir Andrew, who was far from valorous, thought there might be wisdom in the Justice's words, and remembered that he had troubles enough of his own with a froward wife without taking up the burdens of others. Master Godolphin and Sir Oliver between them, quoth the Justice, had got up this storm of theirs. A God's name let them settle it, and if in the settling they should cut each other's throats haply the countryside would be well rid of a brace of turbulent fellows. The pedlar deemed them a couple of madmen, whose ways were beyond the understanding of a sober citizen. The others—the fishermen and the rustics—had not the means to follow even had they had the will.

They dispersed to put abroad the news of that short furious quarrel and to prophesy that blood would be let in the adjusting of it. This prognostication they based entirely upon their knowledge of the short Tressilian way. But it was a matter in which they were entirely wrong. It is true that Sir Oliver went galloping along that road that follows the Penryn river and that he pounded over the bridge in the town of Penryn in Master Godolphin's wake with murder in his heart. Men who saw him riding wildly thus with the red wheal across his white furious face said that he looked a very devil.

He crossed the bridge at Penryn a half-hour after sunset, as dusk was closing into night, and it may be that the sharp, frosty air had a hand in the cooling of his blood. For as he reached the river's eastern bank he slackened his breakneck pace, even as he slackened the angry galloping of his thoughts. The memory of that oath he had sworn three months ago to Rosamund smote him like a physical blow. It checked his purpose, and, reflecting this, his pace fell to an amble. He shivered to think how near he had gone to wrecking all the happiness that lay ahead of him. What was a boy's whip lash, that his resentment of it should set all his future life in jeopardy? Even though men should call him a coward for submitting to it and leaving the insult unavenged, what should that matter? Moreover, upon the body of him who did so proclaim him he could brand the lie of a charge so foolish. Sir Oliver raised his eyes to the deep sapphire dome of heaven where an odd star was glittering frostily, and thanked God from a swelling heart that he had not overtaken Peter Godolphin whilst his madness was upon him.

A mile or so below Penryn, he turned up the road that ran down to the ferry there, and took his way home over the shoulder of the hill with a slack rein. It was not his usual way. He was wont ever to go round by Trefusis Point that he might take a glimpse at the walls of the house that harbored Rosamund and a glance at the window of her bower. But to-night he thought the shorter road over the hill would be the safer way. If he went by Godolphin Court he might chance to meet Peter again, and his past anger warned him against courting such a meeting, warned him to avoid it lest evil should betide. Indeed, so imperious was the warning, and such were his fears of himself after what had just passed, that he resolved to leave Penarrow on the next day. Whither he would go he did not then determine. He might repair to London, and he might even go upon another cruise—an idea which he had lately dismissed under Rosamund's earnest intercession. But it was imperative that he should quit the neighborhood, and place a distance between Peter Godolphin and himself until such time as he might take Rosamund to wife. Eight months or so of exile; but what matter? Better so than that he should be driven into some deed that would compel him to spend his whole lifetime apart from her. He would write, and she would understand and approve when he told her what had passed that day.

The resolve was firmly implanted in him by the time he reached Penarrow, and he felt himself uplifted by it and by the promise it afforded him that thus his future happiness would be assured.

Himself he stabled his horse; for of the two grooms he kept, one had by his leave set out yesterday to spend Christmas in Devon with his parents, the other had taken a chill and had been ordered to bed that very day by Sir Oliver, who was considerate with those that served him.

In the dining-room he found supper spread, and a great log fire blazed in the enormous cowled fireplace, diffusing a pleasant warmth through the vast room and flickering ruddily upon the trophies of weapons that adorned the walls, upon the tapestries and the portraits of dead Tressilians. Hearing his step, old Nicholas entered bearing a great candle-branch which he set upon the table.

"You 'm late, Sir Oliver," said the servant, "and Master Lionel bain't home yet neither."

Sir Oliver grunted and scowled as he crunched a log and set it sizzling under his wet heel. He thought of Malpas and cursed Lionel's folly, as, without a word, he loosed his cloak and flung it on an oaken coffer by the wall where already he had cast his hat. Then he sat down, and Nicholas came forward to draw off his boots.

When that was done and the old servant stood up again, Sir Oliver shortly bade him to serve supper.

"Master Lionel cannot be long now," said he. "And give me to drink, Nick. 'T is what I most require."

"I've brewed ee a posset o' canary sack," announced Nicholas; "there 'm no better supping o' a frosty winter's night, Sir Oliver."

He departed to return presently with a black jack that was steaming fragrantly. He found his master still in the same attitude, staring at the fire, and frowning darkly. Sir Oliver's thoughts were still of his brother and Malpas, and so insistent were they that his own concerns were for the moment quite neglected; he was considering whether it was not his duty, after all, to attempt a word of remonstrance. At length he rose with a sigh and got to table. There he bethought him of his sick groom, and asked Nicholas for news of him. Nicholas reported the fellow to be much as he had been, whereupon Sir Oliver took up a cup and brimmed it with the steaming posset.

"Take him that," he said. "There's no better medicine for such an ailment."

Outside fell a clatter of hooves.

"Here be Master Lionel at last," said the servant.

"No doubt," agreed Sir Oliver. "No need to stay for him. Here is all he needs. Carry that to Tom ere it cools."

It was his object to procure the servant's absence when Lionel should arrive, resolved as he was to greet him with a sound rating for his folly. Reflection had brought him the assurance that this was become his duty in view of his projected absence from Penarrow; and in his brother's interest he was determined not to spare him.

He took a deep draught of the posset, and as he set it down he heard Lionel's step without. Then the door was flung open, and his brother stood on the threshold a moment at gaze.

Sir Oliver looked round with a scowl, the well-considered reproof already on his lips.

"So . . ." he began, and got no further. The sight that met his eyes drove the ready words from his lips and mind; instead it was with a sharp gasp of dismay that he came immediately to his feet. "Lionel!"

Lionel lurched in, closed the door, and shot home one of its bolts. Then he leaned against it, facing his brother again. He was deathly pale, with great dark stains under his eyes; his ungloved right hand was pressed to his side, and the fingers of it were all smeared with blood that was still oozing and dripping from between them. Over his yellow doublet on the right side there was a spreading dark stain whose nature did not intrigue Sir Oliver a moment.

"My God!" he cried, and ran to his brother. "What's happened, Lal? Who has done this?"

"Peter Godolphin," came the answer from lips that writhed in a curious smile.

Never a word said Sir Oliver, but he set his teeth and clenched his hands until the nails cut into his palms. Then he put an arm about this lad he loved above all save one in the whole world, and with anguish in his mind he supported him forward to the fire. There Lionel dropped to the chair that Sir Oliver had lately occupied.

"What is your hurt, lad? Has it gone deep?" he asked, in terror almost.

"'T is naught—a flesh wound; but I have lost a mort of blood. I thought I should have been drained or ever I got me home."

With fearful speed Sir Oliver drew his dagger and ripped away doublet, vest, and shirt, laying bare the lad's white flesh. A moment's examination, and he breathed more freely.

"Art a very babe, Lal," he cried in his relief. "To ride without thought to stanch so simple a wound, and so lose all this blood—bad Tressilian blood though it be." He laughed in the immensity of his reaction from that momentary terror. "Stay thou there whilst I call Nick to help us dress this scratch."

"No, no!" There was note of sudden fear in the lad's voice, and his hand clutched at his brother's sleeve. "Nick must not know. None must know, or I am undone else."

Sir Oliver stared, bewildered. Lionel smiled again that curious twisted, rather frightened smile.

"I gave better than I took, Noll," said he. "Master Godolphin is as cold by now as the snow on which I left him."

His brother's sudden start and the fixed stare from out of his slowly paling face scared Lionel a little. He observed, almost sub-consciously, the dull red wheal that came into prominence as the color faded out of Sir Oliver's face, yet never thought to ask how it came there. His own affairs possessed him too completely.

"What's this?" quoth Oliver at last, hoarsely.

Lionel dropped his eyes, unable longer to meet a glance that was becoming terrible.

"He would have it," he growled almost sullenly, answering the reproach that was written in every line of his brother's taut body. "I had warned him not to cross my path. But to-night I think some madness had seized upon him. He affronted me, Noll; he said things which it was beyond human power to endure, and . . ." He shrugged to complete his sentence.

"Well, well," said Oliver in a small voice. "First let us tend this wound of yours."

"Do not call Nick," was the other's swift admonition. "Don't you see, Noll?" he explained in answer to the inquiry of his brother's stare, "don't you see that we fought there almost in the dark and without witnesses. It . . ." he swallowed. "it will be called murder, fair fight though it was; and should it be discovered that it was I . . ." He shivered and his glance grew wild; his lips twitched.

"I see," said Oliver, who understood at last, and he added bit-terly: "You fool!"

"I had no choice," protested Lionel. "He came at me with his drawn sword. Indeed, I think he was half-drunk. I warned him of what must happen to the other did either of us fall, but he bade me not concern myself with the fear of any such consequences to himself. He was full of foul words of me and you and all whoever bore our name. He struck me with the flat of his blade and threatened to run me through as I stood unless I drew to defend myself. What choice had I? I did not mean to kill him—as God's my witness, I did not, Noll."

Without a word Oliver turned to a side-table, where stood a metal basin and ewer. He poured water, then came in the same silence to treat his brother's wound. The tale that Lionel told made blame impossible, at least from Oliver. He had but to recall the mood in which he himself had ridden after Peter Godolphin; he had but to remember, that only the consideration of Rosamund—only, indeed, the consideration of his future—had set a curb upon his own bloodthirsty humor.

When he had washed the wound he fetched some table linen from a press and ripped it into strips with his dagger; he threaded out one of these and made a preliminary crisscross of the threads across the lips of the wound—for the blade had gone right through the muscles of the breast, grazing the ribs; these threads would help the formation of a clot. Then with the infinite skill and cunning acquired in the course of his rovings he proceeded to the bandaging.

That done, he opened the window and flung out the blood-tinted water. The cloths with which he had mopped the wound and all other similar evidence of the treatment he cast upon the fire. He must remove all traces even from the eyes of Nicholas. He had the most implicit trust in the old servant's fidelity. But the matter was too grave to permit of the slightest risk. He realized fully the justice of Lionel's fears that however fair the fight might have been, a thing done thus in secret must be accounted murder by the law.

Bidding Lionel wrap himself in his cloak, Sir Oliver unbarred the door, and went upstairs in quest of a fresh shirt and doublet for his brother. On the landing he met Nicholas descending. He held him a moment in talk of the sick man above, and outwardly at least he was now entirely composed. He dispatched him upstairs again upon a trumped-up errand that must keep him absent for some little time, whilst himself he went to get the things he needed.

He returned below with them, and when he had assisted his brother into fresh garments with as little movement as possible so as not to disturb his dressing of the wound or set it bleeding afresh, he took the blood-stained doublet, vest, and shirt which he had ripped and flung them, too, into the great fire.

When some moments later Nicholas entered the vast room he found the brothers sitting composedly at table. Had he faced Lionel he would have observed little amiss with him beyond the deep pallor of his face. But he did not even do so much. Lionel sat with his back to the door, and the servant's advance into the room was checked by Sir Oliver with the assurance that they did not require him. Nicholas withdrew again, and the brothers were once more alone.

Lionel ate very sparingly. He thirsted and would have emptied the measure of posset, but that Sir Oliver restrained him, and refused him anything but water lest he should contract a fever. Such a sparing meal as they made—for neither had much appetite—was made in silence. At last Sir Oliver rose, and with slow, heavy steps, suggestive of his humor, he crossed the fireplace. He threw fresh logs on the blaze, and took from the tall mantelshelf his pipe and a leaden jar of tobacco. He filled the pipe pensively, then with the short iron tongs seized a fragment of glowing wood and applied it to the herb.

He returned to the table, and standing over his brother, he broke at last the silence that had now endured some time.

"What," he asked gruffly, "was the cause of your quarrel?"

Lionel started and shrank a little; between finger and thumb he kneaded a fragment of bread, his eyes upon it. "I scarce know," he replied.

"Lal, that is not the truth."

"How?"

"'T is not the truth. I am not to be put off with such an answer. Yourself you said that you had warned him not to cross your path. What path was in your mind?"

Lionel leaned his elbows on the table and took his head in his hands. Weak from loss of blood, overwrought mentally as well, in a state of revulsion and reaction also from the pursuit which had been the cause of to-night's tragic affair, he had not strength to withhold the confidence his brother asked. On the contrary, it seemed to him that in making such a confidence, he would find a haven and refuge in Sir Oliver.

"'T was that wanton at Malpas was the cause of all," he complained. And Sir Oliver's eye flashed at the words. "I deemed her quite other; I was a fool, a fool! I"—he choked, and a sob shook him—"I thought she loved me. I would have married her, I would so, by God."

Sir Oliver swore softly under his breath.

"I believed her pure and good, and . . ." He checked. "After all, who am I to say even now that she was not? 'T was no fault of hers. 'T was he, that foul dog Godolphin, who perverted her. Until he came all was well between us. And then . . ."

"I see," said Sir Oliver quietly. "I think you have something for which to thank him, if he revealed to you the truth of that strumpet's nature. I would have warned thee, lad. But . . . Perhaps I have been weak in that."

"It was not so; it was not she . . ."

"I say it was, and if I say so I am to be believed, Lionel. I'd smirch no woman's reputation without just cause. Be very sure of that."

Lionel stared up at him. "O God!" he cried presently, "I know not what to believe. I am a shuttlecock flung this way and that way."

"Believe me," said Sir Oliver grimly. "And set all doubts to rest." Then he smiled. "So that was the virtuous Master Peter's secret pastime, eh? The hypocrisy of man! There is no plumbing the endless depths of it!"

He laughed outright, remembering all the things that Master Peter had said of Ralph Tressilian—delivering himself as though he were some chaste and self-denying anchorite. Then on that laugh he caught his breath quite suddenly. "Would she know?" he asked fearfully. "Would that harlot know, would she suspect that 't was your hand did this?"

"Aye—would she," replied the other. "I told her to-night, when she flouted me and spoke of him, that I went straight to find him and pay the score between us. I was on my way to Godolphin Court when I came upon him in the park."

"Then you lied to me again, Lionel. For you said 't was he attacked you."

"And so he did," Lionel countered instantly. "He never gave me time to speak, but flung down from his horse and came at me snarling like a cross-grained mongrel. Oh, he was as ready for the fight as I—as eager."

"But the woman at Malpas knows," said Sir Oliver gloomingly. "And if she tells . . ."

"She'll not," cried Lionel. "She dare not for her reputation's sake."

"Indeed, I think you are right," agreed his brother with relief. "She dare not for other reasons, when I come to think of it. Her reputation is already such, and so well detested is she that were it known she had been the cause, however indirect, of this, the countryside would satisfy certain longings that it entertains concerning her. You are sure none saw you either going or returning?"

"None."

Sir Oliver strode the length of the room and back, pulling at his pipe. "All should be well, then, I think," said he at last. "You were best abed. I'll carry you thither."

He took up his stripling brother in his powerful arms and bore him upstairs as though he were a babe. When he had seen him safely disposed for slumber, he returned below, shut the door in the hall, drew up the great oaken chair to the fire, and sat there far into the night smoking and thinking.

He had said to Lionel that all should be well. All should be well for Lionel. But what of himself with the burden of this secret on his soul? Were the victim another than Rosamund's brother the matter would have plagued him but little. The fact that Godolphin was slain, it must be confessed, was not in itself the source of his oppression. Godolphin had more than deserved his end, and he would have come by it months ago at Sir Oliver's own hand but for the fact that he was Rosamund's brother, as we know. There was the rub, the bitter, cruel rub. Her own brother had fallen by the hand of his. She loved her brother more than any living being next to himself, just as he loved Lionel above any other but herself. The pain that must be hers he knew; he experienced some of it in anticipation, participating it because it was hers and because all things that were hers he must account in some measure his own.

He rose up at last, cursing that wanton at Malpas who had come to fling this fresh and terrible difficulty where already he had to face so many. He stood leaning upon the overmantel, his foot upon one of the dogs of the fender, and considered what to do. He must bear his burden in silence, that was all. He must keep this secret even from Rosamund. It split his heart to think that he must practice this deceit with her. But naught else was possible short of relinquishing her, and that was far beyond his strength.

The resolve adopted, he took up a taper and went off to bed.

CHAPTER V

THE BUCKLER

IT WAS OLD Nicholas who brought the news next morning to the brothers as they were breaking their fast.

Lionel should have kept his bed that day, but dared not, lest the fact should arouse suspicion. He had a little fever, the natural result both of his wound and of his loss of blood; he was inclined to welcome rather than deplore it, since it set a flush on cheeks that otherwise must have looked too pale.

So leaning upon his brother's arm he came down to a breakfast of herrings and small ale before the tardy sun of that December morning was well risen.

Nicholas burst in upon them with a white face and shaking limbs. He gasped out his tale of the event in a voice of terror, and both brothers affected to be shocked, dismayed, and incredulous. But the worst part of that old man's news, the true cause of his terrible agitation, was yet to be announced.

"And they do zay," he cried with anger quivering through his fear, "they do zay that it were you that killed he, Sir Oliver."

"I?" quoth Sir Oliver, staring, and suddenly like a flood there burst upon his mind a hundred reasons, overlooked until this moment, that inevitably must urge the countryside to this conclusion, and to this conclusion only. "Where heard you that foul lie?"

In the tumult of his mind he never heeded what answer was returned by Nicholas. What could it matter where the fellow had heard the thing; by now it would be the accusation on the lips of every man. There was one course to take and he must take it instantly—as he had taken it once before in like case. He must straight to Rosamund to forestall the tale that others would carry to her. God send he did not come too late already.

He stayed for no more than to get his boots and hat, then to the stables for a horse, and he was away over the short mile that divided Penarrow from Godolphin Court, going by bridle and track meadow straight to his goal. He met none until he fetched up in the courtyard at Godolphin Court. Thence a babble of excited voices had reached him as he approached. But at sight of him there fell a general silence, ominous and staring. A dozen men or more were assembled there, and their eyes considered him first with amazement and curiosity, then with sullen anger.

He leapt down from his saddle, and stood a moment waiting for one of the three Godolphin grooms he had perceived in that assembly to take his reins. Seeing that none stirred—

"How now?" he cried. "Does no one wait here? Hither, sirrah, and hold my horse."

The groom addressed hesitated a moment, then, under the stare of Sir Oliver's hard, commanding eye, he shuffled sullenly forward to do as he was bid. A murmur ran through the group. Sir Oliver flashed a glance upon it, and every tongue trembled into silence.

In that silence he strode up the steps, and entered the rush-strewn hall. As he vanished he heard the hubbub behind him break out anew, fiercer than it had been before. But he nothing heeded it.

He found himself face to face with a servant, who shrank before him, staring as those in the courtyard had stared. His heart sank. It was plain that he came a little late already; that the tale had got there ahead of him.

"Where is your mistress?" said he.

"I . . . I will tell her you are here, Sir Oliver," the man replied in a voice that faltered; and he passed through a doorway on the right.

Sir Oliver stood a moment tapping his boots with his whip, his face pale, a deep line between his brows. Then the man reappeared, closing the door after him.

"Mistress Rosamund bids you depart, sir. She will not see you."

A moment Sir Oliver scanned the servant's face—or appeared to scan it, for it is doubtful if he saw the fellow at all. Then for only answer he strode forward towards the door from which the man had issued. The servant set his back to it, his face resolute.

"Sir Oliver, my mistress will not see you."

"Out of my way!" he muttered in his angry, contemptuous fashion, and as the man persistent in his duty stood his ground, Sir Oliver took him by the breast of his jacket, heaved him aside and went in.

She was standing in mid-apartment, dressed by an odd irony all in bridal white, that yet was not as white as was her face. Her eyes looked like two black stains, solemn and haunting as they fastened upon this intruder who would not be refused. Her lips parted, but she had no word for him. She just stared in a horror that routed all his audacity and checked the masterfulness of his advance. At last he spoke.

"I see that you have heard," said he, "the lie that runs the countryside. That is evil enough. But I see that you have lent an ear to it; and that is worse."

She continued to regard him with a cold look of loathing, this child that but two days ago had lain against his heart gazing up at him in trust and adoration.

"Rosamund!" he cried, and approached her by another step. "Rosamund! I am here to tell you that it is a lie."

"You had best go," she said, and her voice had in it a quality that made him tremble.

"Go?" he echoed stupidly. "You bid me go? You will not hear me?"

"I consented to hear you more than once; refused to hear others who knew better than I, and was heedless of their warnings. There is no more to be said between us. I pray God that they may take and hang you."

He was white to the lips, and for the first time in his life he knew fear and felt his great limbs trembling under him.

"They may hang me and welcome since you believe this thing. They could not hurt me more than you are doing, nor by hanging me could they deprive me of aught I value, since your faith in me is a thing to be blown upon by the first rumor of the countryside."

He saw the pale lips twist themselves into a dreadful smile. "There is more than rumor, I think," said she. "There is more than all your lies will ever serve to cloak."

"My lies?" he cried. "Rosamund, I swear to you by my honor that I have had no hand in the slaying of Peter. May God rot me where I stand if this be not true!"

"It seems," said a harsh voice behind him, "that you fear God as little as aught else."

He wheeled sharply to confront Sir John Killigrew, who had entered after him.

"So," he said slowly, and his eyes grew hard and bright as agates, "this is your work." And he waved a hand towards Rosamund. It was plain to what he alluded.

"My work?" quoth Sir John. He closed the door, and advanced into the room. "Sir, it seems your audacity, your shamelessness, transcends all bounds. Your . . ."

"Have done with that," Sir Oliver interrupted him, and smote his great fist upon the table. He was suddenly swept by a gust of passion. "Leave words to fools, Sir John, and criticisms to those that can defend them better."

"Aye, you talk like a man of blood. You come hectoring it here in the very house of the dead—in the very house upon which you have cast this blight of sorrow and murder. . ."

"Have done, I say, or murder there will be!"

His voice was a roar, his mien terrific. And bold man though Sir John was, he recoiled. Instantly Sir Oliver had conquered himself again. He swung to Rosamund. "Ah, forgive me!" he pleaded. "I am mad—stark mad with anguish at the thing imputed. I have not loved your brother, it is true. But as I swore to you, so have I done. I have taken blows from him, and smiled; but yesterday in a public place he affronted me, lashed me across the face with his riding-whip, as I still bear the mark. The man who says I were not justified in having killed him for it is a liar and a hypocrite. Yet the thought of you, Rosamund, the thought that he was your brother sufficed to quench the rage in which he left me. And now that by some grim mischance he has met his death, my recompense for all my patience, for all my thought for you is that I am charged with slaying him, and that you believe this charge."

"She has no choice," rasped Killigrew.

"Sir John," he cried, "I pray you do not meddle with her choice. That you believe it, marks you for a fool, and a fool's counsel is a rotten staff to lean upon at any time. Why God o' mercy! assume that I desired to take satisfaction for the affront he had put upon me; do you know so little of men, and of me of all men, that you suppose I should go about my vengeance in this hole-and-corner fashion to set a hangman's noose about my neck? A fine vengeance that, as God lives. Was it so I dealt with you, Sir John, when you permitted your tongue to wag too freely, as you have yourself confessed? Heaven's light, man; take a proper view; consider was this matter likely. I take it you are a more fearsome antagonist than was ever poor Peter Godolphin, yet when I sought satisfaction of you I sought it boldly and openly, as is my way. When we measured swords in your park at Arwenack we did so before witnesses in proper form, that the survivor might not be troubled with the Justices. You know me well, and what manner of man I am with my weapons. Should I not have done the like by Peter if I had sought his life? Should I not have sought it in the same open fashion, and so killed him at my pleasure and leisure, and without risk or reproach from any?"

Sir John was stricken thoughtful. Here was logic hard and clear as ice; and the knight of Arwenack was no fool. But whilst he stood frowning and perplexed at the end of that long tirade, it was Rosamund who gave Sir Oliver his answer.

"You ran no risk of reproach from any, do you say?"

He turned, and was abashed. He knew the thought that was running in her mind.

"You mean," he said slowly, gently, his accents charged with reproachful incredulity, "that I am so base and false that I could in this fashion do what I dared not for your sake do openly? 'T is what you mean. Rosamund! I burn with shame for you that you can think such thoughts of one whom . . . whom you professed to love."

Her coldness fell from her. Under the lash of his bitter, half-scornful accents, her anger mounted, whelming for a moment even her anguish in her brother's death.

"You false deceiver!" she cried. "There are those who heard you vow his death. Your very words have been reported to me. And from where he lay they found a trail of blood upon the snow that ran to your own door. Will you still lie?"

They saw the color leave his face. They saw his arms drop limply to his sides, and his eyes dilate with obvious sudden fear.

"A . . . a trail of blood?" he faltered stupidly.

"Aye, answer that!" cut in Sir John, fetched suddenly from out his doubts by that reminder.

Sir Oliver turned upon Killigrew again. The knight's words restored to him the courage of which Rosamund's had bereft him. With a man he could fight; with a man there was no need to mince his words.

"I cannot answer it," he said, but very firmly, in a tone that brushed aside all implications. "If you say it was so, so it must have been. Yet when all is said, what does it prove? Does it set it beyond doubt that it was I who killed him? Does it justify the woman who loved me to believe me a murderer and something worse?" He paused, and looked at her again, a world of reproach in his glance. She had sunk to a chair, and rocked there, her fingers locking and interlocking, her face a mask of pain unutterable.

"Can you suggest what else it proves, sir?" quoth Sir John, and there was doubt in his voice.

Sir Oliver caught the note of it, and a sob broke from him.

"O God of pity!" he cried out. "There is doubt in your voice, and there is none in hers. You were my enemy once, and have since been in a mistrustful truce with me, yet you can doubt that I did this thing. But she . . . she who loved me has no room for any doubt!"

"Sir Oliver," she answered him, "the thing you have done has broken quite my heart. Yet knowing all the taunts by which you were brought to such a deed I could have forgiven it, I think, even though I could no longer be your wife; I could have forgiven it, I say, but for the baseness of your present denial."

He looked at her, white-faced an instant, then turned on his heel and made for the door. There he paused.

"Your meaning is quite plain," said he. "It is your wish that I shall take my trial for this deed." He laughed. "Who will accuse me to the Justices? Will you, Sir John?"

"If Mistress Rosamund so desires me," replied the knight.

"Ha! Be it so. But do not think I am the man to suffer myself to be sent to the gallows upon such paltry evidence as satisfies that lady. If any accuser comes to bleat of a trail of blood reaching to my door, and of certain words I spoke yesterday in anger, I will take my trial—but it shall be trial by battle upon the body of my accuser. That is my right, and I will have every ounce of it. Do you doubt how God will pronounce? I call upon him solemnly to pronounce between me and such a one. If I am guilty of this thing may He wither my arm when I enter the lists."

"Myself I will accuse you," came Rosamund's dull voice. "And if you will, you may claim your rights against me, and butcher me as you butchered him."

"God forgive you, Rosamund!" said Sir Oliver, and went out.

He returned home with hell in his heart. He knew not what the future might hold in store for him; but such was his resentment against Rosamund that there was no room in his bosom for despair. They should not hang him. He would fight them tooth and claw, and yet Lionel should not suffer. He would take care of that. And then the thought of Lionel changed his mood a little. How easily could he have shattered their accusation, how easily have brought her to her proud knees imploring pardon of him! By a word he could have done it, yet he feared lest that word must jeopardize his brother.

In the calm, still watches of that night, as he lay sleepless upon his bed and saw things without heat, there crept a change into his mental attitude. He reviewed all the evidence that had led her to her conclusions, and he was forced to confess that she was in some measure justified of them. If she had wronged him, he had wronged her yet more. For years she had listened to all the poisonous things that were said of him by his enemies—and his arrogance had made him not a few. She had disregarded all because she loved him; her relations with her brother had become strained on that account, yet now, all this returned to crush her; repentance played its part in her cruel belief that it was by his hand Peter Godolphin had fallen. It must almost seem to her that in a sense she had been a party to his murder by the headstrong course to which she had kept in loving the man her brother hated.

He saw it now, and was more merciful in judging her. She had been more than human if she had not felt as he now saw that she must feel, and since reactions are to be measured by the mental exaltations from which they spring, so was it but natural that now she must hate him fiercely whom she had loved wellnigh as fiercely.

It was a heavy cross to bear. Yet for Lionel's sake he must bear it with what fortitude he could. Lionel must not be sacrificed to his egoism for a deed that in Lionel he could not account other than justified. He were base indeed did he so much as contemplate such a way of escape as that.

But if he did not contemplate it, Lionel did, and went in terror during those days, a terror that kept him from sleep and so fostered the fever in him that on the second day after that grim affair he had the look of a ghost, hollow-eyed and gaunt. Sir Oliver remonstrated with him, and in such terms as to put heart into him anew. Moreover, there was other news that day to allay his terrors: the Justices at Truro had been informed of the event and the accusation that was made; but they had refused point-blank to take action in the matter. The reason of it was that one of them was that same Master Anthony Baine who had witnessed the affront offered Sir Oliver. He declared that whatever had happened to Master Godolphin as a consequence was no more than he deserved, no more than he had brought upon himself, and he gave it as his decision that his conscience as a man of honor would not permit him to issue any warrant to the constable.

Sir Oliver received this news from that other witness, the parson, who himself had suffered such rudeness at Godolphin's hands, and who, man of the Gospel and of peace though he was, entirely supported the Justice's decision—or so he declared.

Sir Oliver thanked him, protesting that it was kind in him and in Master Baine to take such a view, but for the rest avowing that he had had no hand in the affair, however much appearances might point to him.

When, however, it came to his knowledge two days later that the whole countryside was in a ferment against Master Baine as a consequence of the attitude he had taken up, Sir Oliver summoned the parson and straightway rode with him to the Justice's house at Truro, there to afford certain evidence which he had withheld from Rosamund and Sir John Killigrew.

"Master Baine," he said, when the three of them were closeted in that gentleman's library, "I have heard of the just and gallant pronouncement you have made, and I am come to thank you and to express my admiration of your courage."

Master Baine bowed gravely. He was a man whom Nature had made grave.

"But since I would not that any evil consequences might attend your action, I am come to lay proof before you that you have acted more rightly even than you think, and that I am not the slayer."

"You are not?" ejaculated Master Baine in amazement.

"Oh, I assure you I use no subterfuge with you, as you shall judge. I have proof to show you, as I say; and I am come to do so now before time might render it impossible. I do not desire it to be made public just yet, Master Baine; but I wish you to draw up some such document as would satisfy the courts at any future time should this matter be taken further, as well it may."

It was a shrewd plea. The proof that was not upon himself was upon Lionel; but time would efface it, and if anon publication were made of what he was now about to show, it would then be too late to look elsewhere.

"I assure you, Sir Oliver, that had you killed him after what happened I could not hold you guilty of having done more than punish a boorish and arrogant offender."

"I know, sir. But it was not so. One of the pieces of evidence against me—indeed the chief item—is that from Godolphin's body to my door there was a trail of blood."

The other two grew tensely interested. The parson watched him with unblinking eyes.

"Now it follows logically, I think, inevitably indeed, that the murderer must have been wounded in the encounter. The blood could not possibly have been the victim's, therefore it must have been the slayer's. That the slayer was wounded indeed we know, since there was blood upon Godolphin's sword. Now, Master Baine, and you, Sir Andrew, shall be witnesses that there is upon my body not so much as a scratch of recent date. I will strip me here as naked as when first I had the mischance to stray into this world, and you shall satisfy yourselves of that. Thereafter I shall beg you, Master Baine, to indite the document I have mentioned." And he removed his doublet as he spoke. "But since I will not give these louts who accuse me so much satisfaction, lest I seem to go in fear of them, I must beg, sirs, that you will keep this matter entirely private until such time as its publication may be rendered necessary by events."

They saw the reasonableness of his proposal, and they consented, still entirely sceptical. But when they had made their examination they were utterly dumbfoundered to find all their notions entirely overset. Master Baine, of course, drew up the required document, and signed and sealed it, whilst Sir Andrew added his own signature and seal as witness thereunto.

With this parchment that should be his buckler against any future need, Sir Oliver rode home, uplifted. For once it were safe to do so, that parchment should be spread before the eyes of Sir John Killigrew and Rosamund, and all might yet be well.

CHAPTER VI

JASPER LEIGH

I F THAT CHRISTMAS was one of sorrow at Godolphin Court, it
was nothing less at Penarrow.

Sir Oliver was moody and silent in those days, given to sit for
long hours staring into the heart of the fire and repeating to himself
again and again every word of his interview with Rosamund, now in
a mood of bitter resentment against her for having so readily
believed his guilt, now in a gentler sorrowing humor which made
full allowance for the strength of the appearances against him.

His half-brother moved softly about the house now in a sort of
self-effacement, never daring to intrude upon Sir Oliver's abstractions. He was well acquainted with their cause. He knew what had
happened at Godolphin Court, knew that Rosamund had dismissed
Sir Oliver for all time, and his heart smote him to think that he
should leave his brother to bear this burden that rightly belonged
to his own shoulders.

The thing preyed so much upon his mind that in an expansive
moment one evening he gave it tongue.

"Noll," he said, standing beside his brother's chair in the firelit gloom, and resting a hand upon his brother's shoulder. "were it not best to tell the truth?"

Sir Oliver looked up quickly, frowning. "Art mad?" quoth he. "The truth would hang thee, Lal."

"It might not. And in any case you are suffering something worse than hanging. Oh, I have watched you every hour this past week, and I know the pain that abides in you. It is not just." And he insisted—"We had best tell the truth."

Sir Oliver smiled wistfully. He put out a hand and took his brother's.

"'T is noble in you to propose it, Lal."

"Not half so noble as it is in you to bear all the suffering for a deed that was my own."

"Bah!" Sir Oliver shrugged impatiently; his glance fell away from Lionel's face and returned to the consideration of the fire. "After all, I can throw off the burden when I will. Such knowledge as that will enhearten a man through any trial."

He had spoken in a harsh, cynical tone, and Lionel had turned cold at his words. He stood a long while in silence there, turning them over in his mind and considering the riddle which they presented him. He thought of asking his brother bluntly for the key to it, for the precise meaning of his disconcerting statement; but courage failed him. He feared lest Sir Oliver should confirm his own dread interpretation of it.

He drew away after a time, and soon after went to bed. For days thereafter the phrase rankled in his mind—"I can throw off the burden when I will." Conviction grew upon him that Sir Oliver meant that he was enheartened by the knowledge that by speaking if he chose he could clear himself. That Sir Oliver would so speak he could not think. Indeed, he was entirely assured that Sir Oliver was very far from intending to throw off his burden. Yet he might come to change his mind. The burden might grow too heavy, his longings for Rosamund too clamorous, his grief at being in her eyes her brother's murderer too overwhelming.

Lionel's soul shuddered to contemplate the consequences to himself. His fears were self-revelatory. He realized how far from sincere had been his proposal that they should tell the truth; he perceived that it had been no more than the emotional outburst of the moment, a proposal which if accepted he must most bitterly have repented. And then came the reflection that if he were guilty of emotional outbursts that could so outrageously play the traitor to his real desires, were not all men subject to the same? Might not his brother, too, come to fall a prey to one of those moments of mental storm when in a climax of despair he would find his burden altogether too overwhelming and in rebellion cast it from him?

Lionel sought to assure himself that his brother was a man of stern fibers, a man who never lost control of himself. But against this he would argue that what had happened in the past was no guarantee of what might happen in the future; that a limit was set to the endurance of every man be he never so strong, and that it was far from impossible that the limit of Sir Oliver's endurance might be reached in this affair. If that happened, in what case should he find himself? The answer to this was a picture beyond his fortitude to contemplate. The danger of his being sent to trial and made to suffer the extreme penalty of the law would be far greater now than if he had spoken at once. The tale he could then have told must have compelled some attention, for he was accounted a man of unsmirched honor and his word must carry some weight. But now none would believe him. They would argue from his silence and from his having suffered his brother to be unjustly accused that he was craven-hearted and dishonorable, and that if he had acted thus it was because he had no good defence to offer for his deed. Not only would he be irrevocably doomed, but he would be doomed with ignominy, he would be scorned by all upright men and become a thing of contempt over whose end not a tear would be shed.

Thus he came to the dread conclusion that in his endeavors to screen himself he had but enmeshed himself the more inextricably. If Oliver but spoke he was lost. And back he came to the question: What assurance had he that Oliver would not speak?

The fear of this from occurring to him occasionally began to haunt him day and night, and for all that the fever had left him and his wound was entirely healed, he remained pale and thin and hollow-eyed. Indeed the secret terror that was in his soul glared out of his eyes at every moment. He grew nervous and would start up at the least sound, and he went now in a perpetual mistrust of Oliver, which became manifest in a curious petulance of which there were outbursts at odd times.

Coming one afternoon into the dining-room, which was ever Sir Oliver's favorite haunt in the mansion of Penarrow, Lionel found his half-brother in that brooding attitude, elbow on knee and chin on palm, staring into the fire. This was so habitual now in Sir Oliver that it had begun to irritate Lionel's tense nerves; it had come to seem to him that in this listlessness was a studied tacit reproach aimed at himself.

"Why do you sit ever thus over the fire like some old crone?" he growled, voicing at last the irritability that so long had been growing in him.

Sir Oliver looked round with mild surprise in his glance. Then from Lionel his eyes traveled to the long windows.

"It rains," he said.

"It was not your wont to be driven to the fireside by rain. But rain or shine 't is ever the same. You never go abroad."

"To what end?" quoth Sir Oliver, with the same mildness, but a wrinkle of bewilderment coming gradually between his dark brows. "Do you suppose I love to meet lowering glances, to see heads approach one another so that confidential curses of me may be muttered?"

"Ha!" cried Lionel, short and sharp, his sunken eyes blazing suddenly. "It has come to this, then, that having voluntarily done this thing to shield me, you now reproach me with it."

"I?" cried Sir Oliver, aghast.

"Your very words are a reproach. D' ye think I do not read the meaning that lies under them?"

Sir Oliver rose slowly, staring at his brother. He shook his head and smiled.

"Lal, Lal!" he said. "Your wound has left you disordered, boy. With what have I reproached you? What was this hidden meaning of my words? If you will read aright you will see it to be that to go abroad is to involve myself in fresh quarrels, for my mood is become short, and I will not brook sour looks and mutterings. That is all."

He advanced and set his hands upon his brother's shoulders. Holding him so at arm's length he considered him, what time Lionel drooped his head and a slow flush overspread his cheeks. "Dear fool!" he said, and shook him. "What ails you? You are pale and gaunt, and not yourself at all. I have a notion. I'll furnish me a ship and you shall sail with me to my old hunting-grounds. There is life out yonder—life that will restore your vigor and your zest, and perhaps mine as well. How say you, now?"

Lionel looked up, his eye brightening. Then a thought occurred to him; a thought so mean that again the color flooded into his cheeks, for he was shamed by it. Yet it clung. If he sailed with Oliver, men would say that he was a partner in the guilt attributed to his brother.

He knew—from more than one remark addressed him here or there, and left by him uncontradicted—that the belief was abroad on the countryside that a certain hostility was springing up between himself and Sir Oliver on the score of that happening in Godolphin Park. His pale looks and hollow eyes had contributed to the opinion that his brother's sin was weighing heavily upon him. He had ever been known for a gentle, kindly lad, in all things the very opposite of the turbulent Sir Oliver, and it was assumed that Sir Oliver in his present increasing harshness used his brother ill because the lad would not condone his crime. A deal of sympathy was consequently arising for Lionel and was being testified to him on every hand. Were he to accede to such a proposal as Oliver now made him, assuredly he must jeopardize all that.

He realized to the full the contemptible quality of his thought and hated himself for conceiving it. But he could not shake off its dominion. It was stronger than his will.

His brother observing this hesitation, and misreading it, drew him to the fireside and made him sit.

"Listen," he said, as he dropped into the chair opposite, "There is a fine ship standing in the roads below, off Smithick. You'll have seen her. Her master is a desperate adventurer named Jasper Leigh, who is to be found any afternoon in the alehouse at Penycumwick. I know him of old, and he and his ship are to be acquired. He is ripe for any venture, from scuttling Spaniards to trading in slaves, and so that the price be high enough we may buy him body and soul. His is a stomach that refuses nothing, so there be money in the venture. So here is ship and master ready found; the rest I will provide—the crew, the munitions, the armament, and by the end of March we shall see the Lizard dropping astern. What do you say, Lal? 'T is surely better than to sit moping here in this place of gloom."

"I'll . . . I'll think of it," said Lionel, but so listlessly that all Sir Oliver's quickening enthusiasm perished again at once and no more was said of the venture.

But Lionel did not altogether reject the notion. If on the one hand he was repelled by it, on the other he was attracted almost despite himself. He went so far as to acquire the habit of riding daily over to Penycumwick, and there he made the acquaintance of that hardy and scarred adventurer of whom Sir Oliver had spoken, and listened to the marvels the fellow had to tell—many of them too marvelous to be true—of hazards upon distant seas.

But one day in early March Master Jasper Leigh had a tale of another kind for him, news that dispelled from Lionel's mind all interest in the captain's ventures on the Spanish Main. The seaman had followed the departing Lionel to the door of the little inn and stood by his stirrup after he had got to horse.

"A word in your ear, good Master Tressilian," said he. "D' ye know what is being concerted here against your brother?"

"Against my brother?"

"Ay—in the matter of the killing of Master Peter Godolphin last Christmas. Seeing that the Justices would not move of theirselves, some folk ha' petitioned the Lieutenant of Cornwall to command them to grant a warrant for Sir Oliver's arrest on a charge o' murder. But the Justices ha' refused to be driven by his lordship, answering that they hold their office direct from the Queen and that in such a matter they are answerable to none but her grace. And now I hear that a petition be gone to London to the Queen herself, begging her to command her Justices to perform their duty or quit their office."

Lionel drew a sharp breath, and with dilating eyes regarded the mariner, but made him no answer.

Jasper laid a long finger against his nose and his eyes grew cunning.

"I thought I'd warn you, sir, so as you may bid Sir Oliver look to hisself. 'T is a fine seaman and fine seamen be none so plentiful."

Lionel drew his purse from his pocket and without so much as looking into its contents dropped it into the seaman's ready hand, with a muttered word of thanks.

He rode home in terror almost. It was come. The blow was about to fall, and his brother would at last be forced to speak. At Penarrow a fresh shock awaited him. He learnt from old Nicholas that Sir Oliver was from home, that he had ridden over to Godolphin Court.

The instant conclusion prompted by Lionel's terror was that

already the news had reached Sir Oliver and that he had instantly taken action; for he could not conceive that his brother should go to Godolphin Court upon any other business.

But his fears on that score were very idle. Sir Oliver, unable longer to endure the present state of things, had ridden over to lay before Rosamund that proof with which he had taken care to furnish himself. He could do so at last without any fear of hurting Lionel. His journey, however, had been entirely fruitless. She had refused point-blank to receive him, and for all that with a humility entirely foreign to him he had induced a servant to return to her with a most urgent message, yet had he been denied. He returned stricken to Penarrow, there to find his brother awaiting him in a passion of impatience.

"Well?" Lionel greeted him. "What will you do now?"

Sir Oliver looked at him from under brows that scowled darkly in reflection of his thoughts.

"Do now? Of what do you talk?" quoth he.

"Have you not heard?" And Lionel told him the news.

Sir Oliver stared long at him when he had done, then his lips tightened and he smote his brow.

"So!" he cried. "Would that be why she refused to see me? Did she conceive that I went perhaps to plead? Could she think that? Could she?"

He crossed to the fireplace and stirred the logs with his boot angrily. "Oh! 'T were too unworthy. Yet of a certainty 't is her doing, this."

"What shall you do?" insisted Lionel, unable to repress the question that was uppermost in his mind; and his voice shook.

"Do?" Sir Oliver looked at him over his shoulder. "Prick this bubble, by heaven! Make an end of it for them, confound them and cover them with shame."

He said it roughly, angrily, and Lionel recoiled, deeming that roughness and anger aimed at himself. He sank into a chair, his knees loosened by his sudden fear. So it seemed that he had had more than cause for his apprehensions. This brother of his who boasted such affection for him was not equal to bearing this matter through. And yet the thing was so unlike Oliver that a doubt still lingered with him.

"You . . . you will tell them the truth?" he said, in small, quavering voice.

Sir Oliver turned and considered him more attentively.

"A God's name, Lal, what's in thy mind now?" he asked, almost roughly. "Tell them the truth? Why, of course—but only as it concerns myself. You're not supposing that I shall tell them it was you? You'll not be accounting me capable of that?"

"What other way is there?"

Sir Oliver explained the matter. The explanation brought Lionel relief. But this relief was ephemeral. Further reflection presented a new fear to him. It came to him that if Sir Oliver cleared himself, of necessity his own implication must follow. His terrors very swiftly magnified a risk that in itself was so slender as to be entirely negligible. In his eyes it ceased to be a risk; it became a certain and inevitable danger. If Sir Oliver put forward this proof that the trail of blood had not proceeded from himself, it must, thought Lionel, inevitably be concluded that it was his own. As well might Sir Oliver tell them the whole truth, for surely they could not fail to infer it. Thus he reasoned in his terror, accounting himself lost irrevocably.

Had he but gone with those fears of his to his brother, or had he but been able to abate them sufficiently to allow reason to prevail, he must have been brought to understand how much further they carried him than was at all justified by probability. Oliver would have shown him this, would have told him that with the collapsing of the charge against himself no fresh charge could be leveled against any there, that no scrap of suspicion had ever attached to Lionel, or ever could. But Lionel dared not seek his brother in this matter. In his heart he was ashamed of his fears; in his heart he knew himself for a craven. He realized to the full the hideousness of his selfishness, and yet, as before, he was not strong enough to conquer it. In short his love of himself was greater than his love of his brother, or of twenty brothers.

The morrow—a blustering day of late March—found him again at that ale-house at Penycumwick in the company of Jasper Leigh. A course had occurred to him, as the only course now possible. Last night his brother had muttered something of going to Killigrew with his proofs since Rosamund refused to receive him. Through Killigrew he would reach her, he had said; and he would yet see her on her knees craving his pardon for the wrong she had done him, for the cruelty she had shown him.

Lionel knew that Killigrew was absent from home just then; but he was expected to return by Easter, and to Easter there was but a week. Therefore he had little time in which to act, little time in which to execute the project that had come into his mind. He cursed himself for conceiving it, but held to it with all the strength of a weak nature.

Yet when he came to sit face to face with Jasper Leigh in that little inn-parlor with the scrubbed table of plain deal between them, he lacked the courage to set his proposal forth. They drank sherry sack stiffly laced with brandy by Lionel's suggestion, instead of the more customary mulled ale. Yet not until he had consumed the best part of a pint of it did Lionel feel himself heartened to broaching his loathsome business. Through his head hummed the words his brother had said some time ago when first the name of Jasper Leigh had passed between them—"a desperate adventurer ripe for anything. So the price be high enough you may buy him body and soul." Money enough to buy Jasper Leigh was ready to Lionel's hand; but it was Sir Oliver's money—the money that was placed at Lionel's disposal by his half-brother's open-handed bounty. And this money he was to employ for Oliver's utter ruin!

He cursed himself for a filthy, contemptible hound; he cursed the foul fiend that whispered such suggestions into his mind; he knew himself, despised himself, and reviled himself until he came to swear to be strong and to go through with whatever might await him sooner than be guilty of such a baseness; the next moment that same resolve would set him shuddering again as he viewed the inevitable consequences that must attend it.

Suddenly the captain set him a question, very softly, that fired the train and blew all his lingering self-resistance into shreds.

"You'll ha' borne my warning to Sir Oliver?" he asked, lowering his voice so as not to be overheard by the vintner who was stirring beyond the thin wooden partition.

Master Lionel nodded, nervously fingering the jewel in his ear, his eyes shifting from their consideration of the seaman's coarse, weather-tanned and hairy countenance.

"I did," he said. "But Sir Oliver is headstrong. He will not stir."

"Will he not?" The captain stroked his bushy red beard and cursed profusely and horribly after the fashion of the sea. "Od's wounds! He's very like to swing if he bides him here."

"Ay," said Lionel, "if he bides." He felt his mouth turn dry as he spoke; his heart thudded, but its thuds were softened by a slight insensibility which the liquor had produced in him.

He uttered the words in so curious a tone that the sailor's dark eyes peered at him from under his heavy sandy eyebrows. There was alert inquiry in that glance. Master Lionel got up suddenly.

"Let us take a turn outside, captain," said he.

The captain's eyes narrowed. He scented business. There was something plaguily odd about this young gentleman's manner. He tossed off the remains of his sack, slapped down the pot and rose.

"Your servant, Master Tressilian," said he.

Outside our gentleman untethered his horse from the iron ring to which he had attached the bridle; leading his horse he turned seaward and strode down the road that wound along the estuary towards Smithick.

A sharp breeze from the north was whipping the water into white peaks of foam; the sky was of a hard brightness and the sun shone brilliantly. The tide was running out, and the rock in the very neck of the haven was thrusting its black crest above the water. A cable's length this side of it rode the black hull and naked spars of the *Swallow*—Captain Leigh's ship.

Lionel stepped along in silence, very gloomy and pensive, hesitating even now. And the crafty mariner reading this hesitation, and anxious to conquer it for the sake of such profit as he conceived might lie in the proposal which he scented, paved the way for him at last.

"I think that ye'll have some matter to propose to me," said he slyly. "Out with it, sir, for there never was a man more ready to serve you."

"The fact is," said Lionel, watching the other's face with a side-long glance, "I am in a difficult position, Master Leigh."

"I've been in a many," laughed the captain, "but never yet in one through which I could not win. Strip forth your own, and haply I can do as much for you as I am wont to do for myself."

"Why, it is this wise," said the other. "My brother will assuredly hang as you have said if he bides him here. He is lost if they bring him to trial. And in that case, faith, I am lost too. It dishonors a man's family to have a member of it hanged. 'T is a horrible thing to have happen."

"Indeed, indeed!" the sailor agreed encouragingly.

"I would abstract him from this," pursued Lionel, and at the same time cursed the foul fiend that prompted him such specious words to cloak his villainy. "I would abstract him from it, and yet 't is against my conscience that he should go unpunished; for I swear to you, Master Leigh, that I abhor the deed—a cowardly, murderous deed!"

"Ah!" said the captain. And lest that grim ejaculation should check his gentleman he made haste to add—"To be sure! To be sure!"

Master Lionel stopped and faced the other squarely, his shoulders to his horse. They were quite alone in as lonely a spot as any conspirator could desire. Behind him stretched the empty beach, ahead of him the ruddy cliffs that rise gently to the wooded heights of Arwenack.

"I'll be quite plain and open with you, Master Leigh. Peter Godolphin was my friend. Sir Oliver is no more than my half-brother. I would give a deal to the man who would abstract Sir Oliver secretly from the doom that hangs over him, and yet do the thing in such a way that Sir Oliver should not thereby escape the punishment he deserves."

It was strange, he thought, even as he said it, that he could bring his lips so glibly to utter words that his heart detested.

The captain looked grim. He laid a finger upon Master Lionel's velvet doublet in line with that false heart of his.

"I am your man," said he. "But the risk is great. Yet ye say that ye'ld give a deal . . ."

"Yourself shall name the price," said Lionel quickly, his eyes burning feverishly, his cheeks white.

"Oh, I can contrive it, never fear," said the captain. "I know to a nicety what you require. How say you now: if I was to carry him overseas to the plantations where they lack toilers of just such thews as his?" He lowered his voice and spoke with some slight hesitation, fearing that he proposed perhaps more than his prospective employer might desire.

"He might return," was the answer that dispelled all doubts on that score.

"Ah!" said the skipper. "What o' the Barbary rovers, then! They lack slaves and are ever ready to trade, though they be niggardly payers. I never heard of none that returned once they had him safe aboard their galleys. I ha' done some trading with them, bartering human freights for spices and eastern carpets and the like."

Master Lionel breathed hard. "'T is a horrible fate, is 't not?"

The captain stroked his beard. "Yet 't is the only really safe bestowal, and when all is said 't is not so horrible as hanging, and certainly less dishonoring to a man's kin. Ye'ld be serving Sir Oliver and yourself."

"'T is so, 't is so," cried Master Lionel almost fiercely. "And the price?"

The seaman shifted on his short, sturdy legs, and his face grew pensive. "A hundred pound?" he suggested tentatively.

"Done with you for a hundred pounds," was the prompt answer—so prompt that Captain Leigh realized he had driven a fool's bargain which it was incumbent upon him to amend.

"That is, a hundred pound for myself," he corrected slowly. "Then there be the crew to reckon for—to keep their counsel and lend a hand; 't will mean another hundred at the least."

Master Lionel considered a moment. "It is more than I can lay my hands on at short notice. But, look you, you shall have a hundred and fifty pounds in coin and the balance in jewels. You shall not be the loser in that, I promise you. And when you come again, and bring me word that all is done as you now undertake there shall be the like again."

Upon that the bargain was settled. And when Lionel came to talk of ways and means he found that he had allied himself to a man who understood his business thoroughly. All the assistance that the skipper asked was that Master Lionel should lure his gentleman to some concerted spot conveniently near the waterside. There Leigh would have a boat and his men in readiness, and the rest might very safely be left to him.

In a flash Lionel bethought him of the proper place for this. He swung round, and pointed across the water to Trefusis Point and the grey pile of Godolphin Court all bathed in sunshine now.

"Yonder, at Trefusis Point in the shadow of Godolphin Court at eight to-morrow night, when there will be no moon. I'll see that he is there. But on your life do not miss him."

"Trust me," said Master Leigh. "And the money?"

"When you have him safely aboard come to me at Penarrow," he replied, which showed that after all he did not trust Master Leigh any further than he was compelled.

The captain was quite satisfied. For should his gentleman fail to disburse he could always return Sir Oliver to shore.

On that they parted. Lionel mounted and rode away, whilst Master Leigh made a trumpet of his hands and hallooed to the ship.

As he stood waiting for the boat that came off to fetch him, a smile slowly overspread the adventurer's rugged face. Had Master Lionel seen it he might have asked himself how far it was safe to drive such bargains with a rogue who kept faith only insofar as it was profitable. And in this matter Master Leigh saw a way to break faith with profit. He had no conscience, but he loved as all rogues love to turn the tables upon a superior rogue. He would play Master Lionel most finely, most poetically false; and he found a deal to chuckle over in the contemplation of it.

CHAPTER VII

TREPANNED

MASTER LIONEL was absent most of the following day from Penarrow, upon a pretext of making certain purchases in Truro. It would be half-past seven when he returned; and as he entered he met Sir Oliver in the hall.

"I have a message for you from Godolphin Court," he announced, and saw his brother stiffen and his face change color. "A boy met me at the gates and bade me tell you that Mistress Rosamund desires a word with you forthwith."

Sir Oliver's heart almost stopped, then went off at a gallop. She asked for him! She had softened perhaps from her yesterday's relentlessness. She would consent at last to see him!

"Be thou blessed for these good tidings!" he answered on a note of high excitement. "I go at once." And on the instant he departed. Such was his eagerness, indeed, that under the hot spur of it he did not even stay to fetch that parchment which was to be his unanswerable advocate. The omission was momentous.

Master Lionel said no word as his brother swept out. He shrank back a little into the shadows. He was white to the lips and felt as if he would stifle. As the door closed he moved suddenly. He sprang to follow Sir Oliver. Conscience cried out to him that he could not do this thing. But Fear was swift to answer that outcry. Unless he permitted what was planned to take its course, his life might pay the penalty.

He turned, and lurched into the dining-room upon legs that trembled.

He found the table set for supper as on that other night when he had staggered in with a wound in his side to be cared for and sheltered by Sir Oliver. He did not approach the table; he crossed to the fire, and sat down there holding out his hands to the blaze. He was very cold and could not still his trembling. His very teeth chattered.

Nicholas came in to know if he would sup. He answered unsteadily that despite the lateness of the hour he would await Sir Oliver's return.

"Is Sir Oliver abroad?" quoth the servant in surprise.

"He went out a moment since, I know not whither," replied Lionel. "But since he has not supped he is not like to be long absent."

Upon that he dismissed the servant, and sat huddled there, a prey to mental tortures which were not to be repressed. His mind would turn upon naught but the steadfast, unwavering affection of which Sir Oliver ever had been prodigal towards him. In this very matter of Peter Godolphin's death, what sacrifices had not Sir Oliver made to shield him? From so much love and self-sacrifice in the past he inclined to argue now that not even in extreme peril would his brother betray him. And then that bad streak of fear which made a villain of him reminded him that to argue thus was to argue upon supposition, that it would be perilous to trust such an assumption; that if, after all, Sir Oliver should fail him in the crucial test, then was he lost indeed.

When all is said, a man's final judgment of his fellows must be based upon his knowledge of himself; and Lionel, knowing himself

incapable of any such sacrifice for Sir Oliver, could not believe Sir
Oliver capable of persisting in such a sacrifice as future events
might impose. He reverted to those words Sir Oliver had uttered in
that very room two nights ago, and more firmly than ever he concluded that they could have but one meaning.

Then came doubt, and, finally, assurance of another sort, assurance that this was not so and that he knew it; assurance that he lied
to himself, seeking to condone the thing he did. He took his head in
his hands and groaned aloud. He was a villain, a black hearted,
soulless villain! He reviled himself again. There came a moment
when he rose shuddering, resolved even in this eleventh hour to go
after his brother and save him from the doom that awaited him out
yonder in the night.

But again that resolve was withered by the breath of selfish fear.
Limply he resumed his seat, and his thoughts took a fresh turn.
They considered now those matters which had engaged them on
that day when Sir Oliver had ridden to Arwenack to claim satisfaction of Sir John Killigrew. He realized again that Oliver being
removed, what he now enjoyed by his brother's bounty he would
enjoy henceforth in his own unquestioned right. The reflection
brought him a certain consolation. If he must suffer for his villainy,
at least there would be compensations.

The clock over the stables chimed the hour of eight. Master
Lionel shrank back in his chair at the sound. The thing would be
doing even now. In his mind he saw it all—saw his brother come
running in his eagerness to the gates of Godolphin Court, and then
dark forms resolve themselves from the surrounding darkness and
fall silently upon him. He saw him struggling a moment on the
ground, then, bound hand and foot, a gag thrust into his mouth, he
beheld him in fancy borne swiftly down the slope to the beach and
so to the waiting boat.

Another half-hour sat he there. The thing was done by now, and
this assurance seemed to quiet him a little.

Then came Nicholas again to babble of some possible mischance having overtaken his master.

"What mischance should have overtaken him?" growled Lionel, as if in scorn of the idea.

"I pray none indeed," replied the servant. "But Sir Oliver lacks not for enemies nowadays, and 't is scarce zafe for he to be abroad after dark."

Master Lionel dismissed the notion contemptuously. For pretence's sake he announced that he would wait no longer, whereupon Nicholas brought in his supper, and left him again to go and linger about the door, looking out into the night and listening for his master's return. He had paid a visit to the stables, and knew that Sir Oliver had gone forth afoot.

Meanwhile Master Lionel must make pretence of eating, though actual eating must have choked him. He smeared his platter, broke food, and avidly drank a bumper of claret. Then he, too, feigned a growing anxiety and went to join Nicholas. Thus they spent the weary night, watching for the return of one who Master Lionel knew would return no more.

At dawn they roused the servants and sent them to scour the countryside and put the news of Sir Oliver's disappearance abroad. Lionel himself rode out to Arwenack to ask Sir John Killigrew bluntly if he knew aught of this matter.

Sir John showed a startled face, but swore readily enough that he had not so much as seen Sir Oliver for days. He was gentle with Lionel, whom he liked, as everybody liked him. The lad was so mild and kindly in his ways, so vastly different from his arrogant overbearing brother, that his virtues shone the more brightly by that contrast.

"I confess it is natural you should come to me," said Sir John. "But, my word on it, I have no knowledge of him. It is not my way to beset my enemies in the dark."

"Indeed, indeed, Sir John, I had not supposed it in my heart," replied the afflicted Lionel. "Forgive me that I should have come to ask a question so unworthy. Set it down to my distracted state. I have not been the same man these months, I think, since that happening in Godolphin Park. The thing has preyed upon my mind. It is a fearsome burden to know your own brother—though I thank God he is no more than my half-brother—guilty of so foul a deed."

"How?" cried Killigrew, amazed. "You say that? You believed it yourself?"

Master Lionel looked confused, a look which Sir John entirely misunderstood and interpreted entirely in the young man's favor. And it was thus and in that moment that was sown the generous seed of the friendship that was to spring up between these two men, its roots fertilized by Sir John's pity that one so gentle-natured, so honest, and so upright should be cursed with so villainous a brother.

"I see, I see," he said. And he sighed. "You know that we are daily expecting an order from the Queen to her Justices to take the action which hitherto they have refused against your . . . against Sir Oliver." He frowned thoughtfully. "D' ye think Sir Oliver had news of this?"

At once Master Lionel saw the drift of what was in the other's mind.

"I know it," he replied. "Myself I bore it him. But why do you ask?"

"Does it not help us perhaps to understand and explain Sir Oliver's disappearance? God lack! Surely, knowing that, he were a fool to have tarried here, for he would hang beyond all doubt did he stay for the coming of her grace's messenger."

"My God!" said Lionel, staring. "You . . . you think he is fled, then?"

Sir John shrugged. "What else is to be thought?"

Lionel hung his head. "What else, indeed?" said he, and took his leave like a man overwrought, as indeed he was. He had never considered that so obvious a conclusion must follow upon his work so fully to explain the happening and to set at rest any doubt concerning it.

He returned to Penarrow, and bluntly told Nicholas what Sir John suspected and what he feared himself must be the true reason of Sir Oliver's disappearance. The servant, however, was none so easy to convince.

"But do ee believe that he done it?" cried Nicholas. "Do ee believe it, Master Lionel?" There was reproach amounting to horror in the servant's voice.

"God help me, what else can I believe now that he is fled."

Nicholas sidled up to him with tightened lips. He set two gnarled fingers on the young man's arm.

"He 'm not fled, Master Lionel," he announced with grim impressiveness. "He 'm never a turntail. Sir Oliver he don't fear neither man nor devil, and if so be him had killed Master Godolphin, he'd never ha' denied it. Don't ee believe Sir John Killigrew. Sir John ever hated he."

But in all that countryside the servant was the only one to hold this view. If a doubt had lingered anywhere of Sir Oliver's guilt, that doubt was now dispelled by this flight of his before the approach of the expected orders from the Queen.

Later that day came Captain Leigh to Penarrow inquiring for Sir Oliver.

Nicholas brought word of his presence and his inquiry to Master Lionel, who bade him be admitted.

The thick-set little seaman rolled in on his bowed legs, and leered at his employer when they were alone.

"He's snug and safe aboard," he announced. "The thing were done as clean as peeling an apple, and as quiet."

"Why did you ask for him?" quoth Master Lionel.

"Why?" Jasper leered again. "My business was with him. There was some talk between us of him going a voyage with me. I've heard the gossip over at Smithick. This will fit in with it." He laid that finger of his to his nose. "Trust me to help a sound tale along. 'T were a clumsy business to come here asking for you, sir. Ye'll know now how to account for my visit."

Lionel paid him the price agreed and dismissed him upon receiving the assurance that the *Swallow* would put to sea upon the next tide.

When it became known that Sir Oliver had been in treaty with Master Leigh for a passage overseas, and that it was but on that account that Master Leigh had tarried in that haven, even Nicholas began to doubt.

Gradually Lionel recovered his tranquillity as the days flowed on. What was done was done, and, in any case, being now beyond recall, there was no profit in repining. He never knew how fortune aided him, as fortune will sometimes aid a villain. The royal poursuivants arrived some six days later, and Master Baine was the recipient of a curt summons to render himself to London, there to account for his breach of trust in having refused to perform his sworn duty. Had Sir Andrew Flack but survived the chill that had carried him off a month ago, Master Justice Baine would have made short work of the accusation lodged against him. As it was, when he urged the positive knowledge he possessed, and told them how he had made the examination to which Sir Oliver had voluntarily submitted, his single word carried no slightest conviction. Not for a moment was it supposed that this was aught but the subterfuge of one who had been lax in his duty and who sought to save himself from the consequences of that laxity. And the fact that he cited as his fellow-witness a gentleman now deceased but served to confirm his judges in this opinion. He was deposed from his office and subjected to a heavy fine, and there the matter ended, for the hue and cry that was afoot entirely failed to discover any trace of the missing Sir Oliver.

For Master Lionel a new existence set in from that day. Looked

upon as one in danger of suffering for his brother's sins, the countryside determined to help him as far as possible to bear his burden. Great stress was laid upon the fact that after all he was no
more than Sir Oliver's half-brother; some there were who would
have carried their kindness to the lengths of suggesting that perhaps he was not even that, and that it was but natural that Ralph
Tressilian's second wife should have repaid her husband in kind for
his outrageous infidelities. This movement of sympathy was led by
Sir John Killigrew, and it spread in so rapid and marked a manner
that very soon Master Lionel was almost persuaded that it was no
more than he deserved, and he began to sun himself in the favor of
a countryside that hitherto had shown little but hostility for men of
the Tressilian blood.

CHAPTER VIII

THE SPANIARD

THE *Swallow,* having passed through a gale in the Bay of Biscay—a gale which she weathered like the surprisingly steady old tub she was—rounded Cape Finisterre and so emerged from tempest into peace, from leaden skies and mountainous seas into a sunny azure calm. It was like a sudden transition from winter into spring, and she ran along now, close hauled to the soft easterly breeze, with a gentle list to port.

It had never been Master Leigh's intent to have got so far as this without coming to an understanding with his prisoner. But the wind had been stronger than his intentions, and he had been compelled to run before it and to head to southward until its fury should abate. Thus it fell out—and all marvelously to Master Lionel's advantage, as you shall see—that the skipper was forced to wait until they stood along the coast of Portugal—but well out to sea, for the coast of Portugal was none too healthy just then to English seamen—before commanding Sir Oliver to be haled into his presence.

In the cramped quarters of the cabin in the poop of the little vessel sat her captain at a greasy table, over which a lamp was swinging faintly to the gentle heave of the ship. He was smoking a foul pipe, whose fumes hung heavily upon the air of that little chamber, and there was a bottle of Nantes at his elbow.

To him, sitting thus in state, was Sir Oliver introduced—his wrists still pinioned behind him. He was haggard and hollow-eyed, and he carried a week's growth of beard on his chin. Also his garments were still in disorder from the struggle he had made when taken, and from the fact that he had been compelled to lie in them ever since.

Since his height was such that it was impossible for him to stand upright in that low-ceilinged cabin, a stool was thrust forward for him by one of the ruffians of Leigh's crew who had haled him from his confinement beneath the hatchway.

He sat down quite listlessly, and stared vacantly at the skipper. Master Leigh was somewhat discomposed by this odd calm when he had looked for angry outbursts. He dismissed the two seamen who had fetched Sir Oliver, and when they had departed and closed the cabin door he addressed his captive.

"Sir Oliver," said he, stroking his red beard, "ye've been most foully abused."

The sunshine filtered through one of the horn windows and beat full upon Sir Oliver's expressionless face.

"It was not necessary, you knave, to bring me hither to tell me so much," he answered.

"Quite so," said Master Leigh. "But I have something more to add. Ye'll be thinking that I ha' done you a disservice. There ye wrong me. Through me you are brought to know true friends from secret enemies; henceforward ye'll know which to trust and which to mistrust."

Sir Oliver seemed to rouse himself a little from his passivity, stimulated despite himself by the impudence of this rogue. He stretched a leg and smiled sourly.

"You'll end by telling me that I am in your debt," said he.

"You'll end by saying so yourself," the captain assured him. "D' ye know what I was bidden do with you?"

"Faith, I neither know nor care," was the surprising answer, wearily delivered. "If it is for my entertainment that you propose to tell me, I beg you'll spare yourself the trouble."

It was not an answer that helped the captain. He pulled at his pipe a moment.

"I was bidden," said he presently, "to carry you to Barbary and sell you there into the service of the Moors. That I might serve you, I made believe to accept this task."

"God's death!" swore Sir Oliver. "You carry make-believe to an odd length."

"The weather has been against me. It were no intention o' mine to ha' come so far south with you. But we've been driven by the gale. That is overpast, and so that ye'll promise to bear no plaint against me, and to make good some of the loss I'll make by going out of my course, and missing a cargo that I wot of, I'll put about and fetch you home again within a week."

Sir Oliver looked at him and smiled grimly. "Now what a rogue are you that can keep faith with none!" he cried. "First you take money to carry me off; and then you bid me pay you to carry me back again."

"Ye wrong me, sir, I vow ye do! I can keep faith when honest men employ me, and ye should know it, Sir Oliver. But who keeps faith with rogues is a fool—and that I am not, as ye should also know. I ha' done this thing that a rogue might be revealed to you and thwarted, as well as that I might make some little profit out of this ship o' mine. I am frank with ye, Sir Oliver. I ha' had some two hundred pounds in money and trinkets from your brother. Give me the like and . . ."

But now of a sudden Sir Oliver's listlessness was all dispelled. It fell from him like a cloak, and he sat forward, wide awake and with some show of anger even.

"How do you say?" he cried, on a sharp, high note.

The captain stared at him, his pipe neglected. "I say that if so be as ye'll pay me the same sum which your brother paid me to carry you off . . ."

"My brother?" roared the knight. "Do you say my brother?"

"I said your brother."

"Master Lionel?" the other demanded still.

"What other brothers have you?" quoth Master Leigh.

There fell a pause and Sir Oliver looked straight before him, his head sunken a little between his shoulders. "Let me understand," he said at length. "Do you say that my brother Lionel paid you money to carry me off—in short, that my presence aboard this foul hulk of yours is due to him?"

"Whom else had ye suspected? Or did ye think that I did it for my own personal diversion?"

"Answer me," bellowed Sir Oliver, writhing in his bonds.

"I ha' answered you more than once already. Still, I tell you once again, since ye are slow to understand it, that I was paid a matter of two hundred pound by your brother, Master Lionel Tressilian, to carry you off to Barbary and there sell you for a slave. Is that plain to you?"

"As plain as it is false. You lie, you dog!"

"Softly, softly!" quoth Master Leigh good-humoredly.

"I say you lie!"

Master Leigh considered him a moment. "Sets the wind so!" said he at length, and without another word he rose and went to a sea-chest ranged against the wooden wall of the cabin. He opened it and took thence a leather bag. From this he produced a handful of jewels. He thrust them under Sir Oliver's nose. "Haply," said he, "ye'll be acquainted with some of them. They was given me to make up the sum since your brother had not the whole two hundred pound in coin. Take a look at them."

Sir Oliver recognized a ring and a long pear-shaped pearl earring that had been his brother's; he recognized a medallion that he himself had given Lionel two years ago; and so, one by one, he recognized every trinket placed before him.

His head drooped to his breast, and he sat thus awhile like a man stunned. "My God!" he groaned miserably, at last. "Who, then, is left to me! Lionel too! Lionel!" A sob shook the great frame. Two tears slowly trickled down that haggard face and were lost in the stubble of beard upon his chin. "I am accursed!" he said.

Never without such evidence could he have believed this thing. From the moment that he was beset outside the gates of Codolphin Court he had conceived it to be the work of Rosamund, and his listlessness was begotten of the thought that she could have suffered conviction of his guilt and her hatred of him to urge her to such lengths as these. Never for an instant had he doubted the message delivered him by Lionel that it was Mistress Rosamund who summoned him. And just as he believed himself to be going to Godolphin Court in answer to her summons, so did he conclude that the happening there was the real matter to which she had bidden him, a thing done by her contriving, her answer to his attempt on the previous day to gain speech with her, her manner of ensuring that such an impertinence should never be repeated.

This conviction had been gall and wormwood to him; it had drugged his very senses, reducing him to a listless indifference to any fate that might be reserved him. Yet it had not been so bitter a draught as this present revelation. After all, in her case there were some grounds for the hatred that had come to take the place of her erstwhile love. But in Lionel's what grounds were possible? What motives could exist for such an action as this, other than a monstrous, a loathly egoism which desired perhaps to ensure that the blame for the death of Peter Godolphin should not be shifted from the shoulders that were unjustly bearing it, and the accursed desire to profit by the removal of the man who had been brother, father, and all else to him? He shuddered in sheer horror. It was incredible, and yet beyond a doubt it was true. For all the love which he had showered upon Lionel, for all the sacrifices of self which he had made to shield him, this was Lionel's return. Were all the world against him he still must have believed Lionel true to him, and in that belief must have been enheartened a little. And now . . . His sense of loneliness, of utter destitution overwhelmed him. Then slowly of his sorrow resentment was begotten, and being begotten it grew rapidly until it filled his mind and whelmed in its turn all else. He threw back his great head, and his bloodshot, gleaming eyes fastened upon Captain Leigh, who seated now upon the sea-chest was quietly observing him and waiting patiently until he should recover the wits which this revelation had scattered.

"Master Leigh," said he, "what is your price to carry me home again to England?"

"Why, Sir Oliver," said he, "I think the price I was paid to carry you off would be a fair one. The one would wipe out t' other as it were."

"You shall have twice the sum when you land me on Trefusis Point again," was the instant answer.

The captain's little eyes blinked and his shaggy red eyebrows came together in a frown. Here was too speedy an acquiescence. There must be guile behind it, or he knew nought of the ways of men.

"What mischief are ye brooding?" he sneered.

"Mischief, man? To you?" Sir Oliver laughed hoarsely. "God's light, knave, d' ye think I consider you in this matter, or d' ye think I've room in my mind for such petty resentments together with that other?"

It was the truth. So absolute was the bitter sway of his anger against Lionel that he could give no thought to this rascally seaman's share in the adventure.

"Will ye give me your word for that?"

"My word? Pshaw, man! I have given it already. I swear that you shall be paid the sum I've named the moment you set me ashore

again in England. Is that enough for you? Then cut me these
bonds, and let us make an end of my present condition."

"Faith, I am glad to deal with so sensible a man! Ye take it in the
proper spirit. Ye see that what I ha' done I ha' but done in the way
of my calling, that I am but a tool, and that what blame there be
belongs to them which hired me to this deed."

"Aye, ye're but a tool—a dirty tool, whetted with gold; no more.
'T is admitted. Cut me these bonds, a God's name! I'm weary o'
being trussed like a capon."

The captain drew his knife, crossed to Sir Oliver's side and
slashed his bonds away without further word. Sir Oliver stood up so
suddenly that he smote his head against the low ceiling of the
cabin, and so sat down again at once. And in that moment from
without and above there came a cry which sent the skipper to the
cabin door. He flung it open, and so let out the smoke and let in the
sunshine. He passed out on to the poop-deck, and Sir Oliver—conceiving himself at liberty to do so—followed him.

In the waist below a little knot of shaggy seamen were crowding
to the larboard bulwarks, looking out to sea; on the forecastle there
was another similar assembly, all staring intently ahead and towards
the land. They were off Cape Roca at the time, and when Captain
Leigh saw by how much they had lessened their distance from
shore since last he had conned the ship, he swore ferociously at his
mate who had charge of the wheel. Ahead of them away on their
larboard bow and in line with the mouth of the Tagus from which
she had issued—and where not a doubt but she had been lying in
wait for such stray craft as this—came a great tall-masted ship,
equipped with topgallants, running wellnigh before the wind with
every foot of canvas spread.

Close-hauled as was the *Swallow* and with her topsails and
mizzen reefed she was not making more than one knot to the
Spaniard's five—for that she was a Spaniard was beyond all doubt
judging by the haven whence she issued.

"Luff alee!" bawled the skipper, and he sprang to the wheel, thrusting the mate aside with a blow of his elbow that almost sent him sprawling.

"'T was yourself set the course," the fellow protested.

"Thou lubberly fool," roared the skipper. "I bade thee keep the same distance from shore. If the land comes jutting out to meet us, are we to keep straight on until we pile her up?" He spun the wheel round in his hands, and turned her down the wind. Then he relinquished the helm to the mate again. "Hold her thus," he commanded, and bellowing orders as he went, he heaved himself down the companion to see them executed. Men sprang to the ratlines to obey him, and went swarming aloft to let out the reefs of the topsails; others ran astern to do the like by the mizzen, and soon they had her leaping and plunging through the green water with every sheet unfurled, racing straight out to sea.

From the poop Sir Oliver watched the Spaniard. He saw her veer a point or so to starboard, heading straight to intercept them, and he observed that although this maneuver brought her fully a point nearer to the wind than the *Swallow*, yet, equipped as she was with half as much canvas again as Captain Leigh's piratical craft, she was gaining steadily upon them none the less.

The skipper came back to the poop, and stood there moodily watching that other ship's approach, cursing himself for having sailed into such a trap, and cursing his mate more fervently still.

Sir Oliver meanwhile took stock of so much of the *Swallow*'s armament as was visible and wondered what like were those on the main-deck below. He dropped a question on that score to the captain, dispassionately, as though he were no more than an indifferently interested spectator, and with never a thought to his position aboard.

"Should I be racing her afore the wind if I was properly equipped?" growled Leigh. "Am I the man to run before a Spaniard? As it is I do no more than lure her well away from land."

Sir Oliver understood, and was silent thereafter. He observed a bo'sun and his mates staggering in the waist under loads of cutlasses and small arms which they stacked in a rack about the mainmast. Then the gunner, a swarthy, massive fellow, stark to the waist with a faded scarf tied turban-wise about his head, leapt up the companion to the brass carronade on the larboard quarter, followed by a couple of his men.

Master Leigh called up the bo'sun, bade him take the wheel, and dispatched the mate forward to the forecastle, where another gun was being prepared for action.

Thereafter followed a spell of racing, the Spaniard ever lessening the distance between them, and the land dropping astern until it was no more than a hazy line above the shimmering sea. Suddenly from the Spaniard appeared a little cloud of white smoke, and the boom of a gun followed, and after it came a splash a cable's length ahead of the *Swallow*'s bows.

Linstock in hand the brawny gunner on the poop stood ready to answer them when the word should be given. From below came the gunner's mate to report himself ready for action on the main-deck and to receive his orders.

Came another shot from the Spaniard, again across the bows of the *Swallow*.

"'T is a clear invitation to heave to," said Sir Oliver.

The skipper snarled in his fiery beard. "She has a longer range than most Spaniards," said he. "But I'll not waste powder yet for all that. We've none to spare."

Scarcely had he spoken when a third shot boomed. There was a splintering crash overhead followed by a sough and a thud as the maintopmast came hurtling to the deck and in its fall stretched a couple of men in death. Battle was joined, it seemed. Yet Captain Leigh did nothing in a hurry.

"Hold there!" he roared to the gunner who swung his linstock at that moment in preparation.

She was losing way as a result of that curtailment of her main-mast, and the Spaniard came on swiftly now. At last the skipper accounted her near enough, and gave the word with an oath. The *Swallow* fired her first and last shot in that encounter. After the deafening thunder of it and through the cloud of suffocating smoke, Sir Oliver saw the high forecastle of the Spaniard rent open.

Master Leigh was cursing his gunner for having aimed too high. Then he signaled to the mate to fire the culverin of which he had charge. That second shot was to be the signal for the whole broad-side from the main-deck below. But the Spaniard anticipated them. Even as the skipper of the *Swallow* signaled the whole side of the Spaniard burst into flame and smoke.

The *Swallow* staggered under the blow, recovered an instant, then listed ominously to larboard.

"Hell!" roared Leigh. "She's bilging!" and Sir Oliver saw the Spaniard standing off again, as if satisfied with what she had done. The mate's gun was never fired, nor was the broadside from below. Indeed that sudden list had set the muzzles pointing to the sea; within three minutes of it they were on a level with the water. The *Swallow* had received her death-blow, and she was settling down.

Satisfied that she could do no further harm, the Spaniard luffed and hove to, awaiting the obvious result and intent upon picking up what slaves she could to man the galleys of his Catholic Majesty on the Mediterranean.

Thus the fate intended Sir Oliver by Lionel was to be fulfilled; and it was to be shared by Master Leigh himself, which had not been at all in that venal fellow's reckoning.

PART TWO

ŞAKR-EL-BAHR

CHAPTER I

THE CAPTIVE

Sakr-el-Bahr, the hawk of the sea, the scourge of the Mediterranean and the terror of Christian Spain, lay prone on the heights of Cape Spartel.

Above him on the crest of the cliff ran the dark green line of the orange groves of Araish—the reputed Garden of the Hesperides of the ancients, where the golden apples grew. A mile or so to eastward were dotted the huts and tents of a Bedouin encampment on the fertile emerald pasture-land that spread away, as far as eye could range, towards Ceuta. Nearer, astride of a gray rock an almost naked goatherd, a lithe brown stripling with a cord of camel-hair about his shaven head, intermittently made melancholy and unmelodious sounds upon a reed pipe. From somewhere in the blue vault of heaven overhead came the joyous trilling of a lark, from below the silken rustling of the tideless sea.

Sakr-el-Bahr lay prone upon a cloak of woven camel-hair amid luxuriating fern and samphire, on the very edge of the shelf of cliff to which he had climbed. On either side of him squatted a negro from the Sus, both naked of all save white loin-cloths, their muscular bodies glistening like ebony in the dazzling sunshine of mid-May. They wielded crude fans fashioned from the yellowing leaves of date palms, and their duty was to wave these gently to and fro above their lord's head, to give him air and to drive off the flies.

Sakr-el-Bahr was in the very prime of life, a man of a great length of body, with a deep Herculean torso and limbs that advertised a giant strength. His hawk-nosed face ending in a black forked beard was of a swarthiness accentuated to exaggeration by the snowy white turban wound about his brow. His eyes, by contrast, were singularly light. He wore over his white shirt a long green tunic of very light silk, woven along its edges with arabesques in gold; a pair of loose calico breeches reached to his knees; his brown muscular calves were naked, and his feet were shod in a pair of Moorish shoes of crimson leather, with up-curling and very pointed toes. He had no weapons other than the heavy-bladed knife with a jewelled hilt that was thrust into his girdle of plaited leather.

A yard or two away on his left lay another supine figure, elbows on the ground, and hands arched above his brow to shade his eyes, gazing out to sea. He, too, was a tall and powerful man, and when he moved there was a glint of armor from the chain mail in which his body was cased, and from the steel casque about which he had swathed his green turban. Beside him lay an enormous curved scimitar in a sheath of brown leather that was heavy with steel ornaments. His face was handsome, and bearded, but swarthier far than his companion's, and the backs of his long fine hands were almost black.

Sakr-el-Bahr paid little heed to him. Lying there he looked down the slope, clad with stunted cork-trees and evergreen oaks; here and there was the golden gleam of broom; yonder over a spur of whitish rock sprawled the green and living scarlet of a cactus. Below him about the caves of Hercules was a space of sea whose clear depths shifted with its slow movement from the deep green of emerald to all the colors of the opal. A little farther off behind a projecting screen of rock that formed a little haven two enormous masted galleys, each of fifty oars, and a smaller galliot of thirty rode gently on the slight heave of the water, the vast yellow oars standing out almost horizontally from the sides of each vessel like the pinions of some gigantic bird. That they lurked there either in concealment or in ambush was very plain. Above them circled a flock of seagulls noisy and insolent.

Sakr-el-Bahr looked out to sea, across the straits towards Tarifa and the faint distant European coast line just visible through the limpid summer air. But his glance was not concerned with that hazy horizon; it went no further than a fine white-sailed ship that, close-hauled, was beating up the straits some four miles off. A gentle breeze was blowing from the east, and with every foot of canvas spread to catch it she stood as close to it as was possible. Nearer she came on her larboard tack, and not a doubt but her master would be scanning the hostile African littoral for a sight of those desperate rovers who haunted it and who took toll of every Christian ship that ventured over-near. Sakr-el-Bahr smiled to think how little the presence of his galleys could be suspected, how innocent must look the sun-bathed shore of Africa to the Christian skipper's diligently searching spyglass. And there from his height, like the hawk they had dubbed him, poised in the cobalt heavens to plumb down upon his prey, he watched the great white ship and waited until she should come within striking distance.

A promontory to eastward made something of a lee that reached out almost a mile from shore. From the watcher's eyrie the line of demarcation was sharply drawn; they could see the point at which the white crests of the wind-whipped wavelets ceased and the water became smoother. Did she but venture as far southward on her present tack, she would be slow to go about again, and that should be their opportunity. And all unconscious of the lurking peril she held steadily to her course, until not half a mile remained between her and that inauspicious lee.

Excitement stirred the mail-clad corsair; he kicked his heels in the air, then swung round to the impassive and watchful Sakr-el-Bahr.

"She will come! She will come!" he cried in the Frankish jargon—the lingua franca of the African littoral.

"Insh' Allah!" was the laconic answer—"If God will."

A tense silence fell between them again as the ship drew nearer so that now with each forward heave of her they caught a glint of the white belly under her black hull. Sakr-el-Bahr shaded his eyes, and concentrated his vision upon the square ensign flying from her mainmast. He could make out not only the red and yellow quarterings, but the devices of the castle and the lion.

"A Spanish ship, Biskaine," he growled to his companion. "It is very well. The praise to the One!"

"Will she venture in?" wondered the other.

"Be sure she will venture," was the confident answer. "She suspects no danger, and it is not often that our galleys are to be found so far westward. Aye, there she comes in all her Spanish pride."

Even as he spoke she reached that line of demarcation. She crossed it, for there was still a moderate breeze on the leeward side of it, intent no doubt upon making the utmost of that southward run.

"Now!" cried Biskaine—Biskaine-el-Borak was he called from the lightning-like impetuousness in which he was wont to strike. He quivered with impatience, like a leashed hound.

"Not yet," was the calm, restraining answer. "Every inch nearer shore she creeps the more certain is her doom. Time enough to sound the charge when she goes about. Give me to drink, Abiad," he said to one of his negroes, whom in irony he had dubbed "the White."

The slave turned aside, swept away a litter of ferns and produced an amphora of porous red clay; he removed the palm-leaves from the mouth of it and poured water into a cup. Sakr-el-Bahr drank slowly, his eyes never leaving the vessel, whose every ratline was clearly defined by now in the pellucid air. They could see men moving on her decks, and the watchman stationed in the foremast fighting-top. She was not more than half a mile away when suddenly came the maneuver to go about.

Sakr-el-Bahr leapt instantly to his great height and waved a long green scarf. From one of the galleys behind the screen of rocks a trumpet rang out in immediate answer to that signal; it was followed by the shrill whistles of the bo'suns, and that again by the splash and creak of oars, as the two larger galleys swept out from their ambush. The long armored poops were a-swarm with turbaned corsairs, their weapons gleaming in the sunshine; a dozen at least were astride of the cross-tree of each mainmast, all armed with bows and arrows, and the ratlines on each side of the galleys were black with men who swarmed there like locusts ready to envelop and smother their prey.

The suddenness of the attack flung the Spaniard into confusion. There was a frantic stir aboard her, trumpet blasts and shoutings and wild scurryings of men hither and thither to the posts to which they were ordered by their too reckless captain. In that confusion her maneuver to go about went all awry, and precious moments were lost during which she stood floundering, with idly flapping sails. In his desperate haste the captain headed her straight to leeward, thinking that by running thus before the wind he stood the best chance of avoiding the trap. But there was not wind enough in that sheltered spot to make the attempt successful. The galleys sped straight on at an angle to the direction in which the Spaniard was moving, their yellow dripping oars flashing furiously, as the bo'suns plied their whips to urge every ounce of sinew in the slaves.

Of all this Sakr-el-Bahr gathered an impression, as, followed by Biskaine and the negroes, he swiftly made his way down from that eyrie that had served him so well. He sprang from red oak to cork-tree and from cork-tree to red oak; he leapt from rock to rock, or lowered himself from ledge to ledge, gripping a handful of heath or a projecting stone, but all with the speed and nimbleness of an ape. He dropped at last to the beach, then sped across it at a run, and went bounding along a black reef until he stood alongside of the galliot which had been left behind by the other corsair vessels. She awaited him in deep water, the length of her oars from the rock, and as he came alongside, these oars were brought to the horizontal, and held there firmly. He leapt down upon them, his companions following him, and using them as a gangway, reached the bulwarks. He threw a leg over the side, and alighted on a decked space between two oars and the two rows of six slaves that were manning each of them.

Biskaine followed him and the negroes came last. They were still astride of the bulwarks when Sakr-el-Bahr gave the word. Up the middle gangway ran a bo'sun and two of his mates cracking their long whips of bullock-hide. Down went the oars, there was a heave, and they shot out in the wake of the other two to join the fight.

Sakr-el-Bahr, scimitar in hand, stood on the prow, a little in advance of the mob of eager babbling corsairs who surrounded him, quivering in their impatience to be let loose upon the Christian foe. Above, along the yardarm and up the ratlines swarmed his bowmen. From the mast-head floated out his standard, of crimson charged with a green crescent.

The naked Christian slaves groaned, strained, and sweated under the Moslem lash that drove them to the destruction of their Christian brethren.

Ahead the battle was already joined. The Spaniard had fired one single hasty shot which had gone wide, and now one of the corsairs' grappling-irons had seized her on the larboard quarter, a withering hail of arrows was pouring down upon her decks from the Muslim crosstrees; up her sides crowded the eager Moors, ever most eager when it was a question of tackling the Spanish dogs who had driven them from their Andalusian Caliphate. Under her quarter sped the other galley to take her on the starboard side, and even as she went her archers and slingers hurled death aboard the galleon.

It was a short, sharp fight. The Spaniards in confusion from the beginning, having been taken utterly by surprise, had never been able to order themselves in a proper manner to receive the onslaught. Still, what could be done they did. They made a gallant stand against this pitiless assailant. But the corsairs charged home as gallantly, utterly reckless of life, eager to slay in the name of Allah and His Prophet and scarcely less eager to die if it should please the All-pitiful that their destinies should be here fulfilled. Up they went, and back fell the Castilians, outnumbered by at least ten to one.

When Sakr-el-Bahr's galliot came alongside, that brief encounter was at an end, and one of his corsairs was aloft, hacking from the mainmast the standard of Spain and the wooden crucifix that was nailed below it. A moment later and to a thundering roar of "Alhamdollilah!" the green crescent floated out upon the breeze.

Sakr-el-Bahr thrust his way through the press in the galleon's waist; his corsairs fell back before him, making way, and as he advanced they roared his name deliriously and waved their scimitars to acclaim him this hawk of the sea, as he was named, this most valiant of all the servants of Islam. True he had taken no actual part in the engagement. It had been too brief and he had arrived too late for that. But his had been the daring to conceive an ambush at so remote a western point, and his the brain that had guided them to this swift sweet victory in the name of Allah the One.

The decks were slippery with blood, and strewn with wounded and dying men, whom already the Muslimeen were heaving overboard—dead and wounded alike when they were Christians, for to what end should they be troubled with maimed slaves?

About the mainmast were huddled the surviving Spaniards,

weaponless and broken in courage, a herd of timid, bewildered sheep.

Sakr-el-Bahr stood forward, his light eyes considering them grimly. They must number close upon a hundred, adventurers in the main who had set out from Cadiz in high hope of finding fortune in the Indies. Their voyage had been a very brief one; their fate they knew—to toil at the oars of the Muslim galleys, or, at best, to be taken to Algiers or Tunis and sold there into the slavery of some wealthy Moor.

Sakr-el-Bahr's glance scanned them appraisingly, and rested finally on the captain, who stood slightly in advance, his face livid with rage and grief. He was richly dressed in the Castilian black, and his velvet thimble-shaped hat was heavily plumed and decked by a gold cross.

Sakr-el-Bahr salaamed ceremoniously to him. "Fortuna de guerra, señor capitan," said he in fluent Spanish. "What is your name?"

"I am Don Paulo de Guzman," the man answered, drawing himself erect, and speaking with conscious pride in himself and manifest contempt of his interlocutor.

"So! A gentleman of family! And well-nourished and sturdy, I should judge. In the sôk at Algiers you might fetch two hundred philips. You shall ransom yourself for five hundred."

"Por las Entrañas de Dios!" swore Don Paulo, who, like all pious Spanish Catholics, favored the oath anatomical. What else he would have added in his fury is not known, for Sakr-el-Bahr waved him contemptuously away.

"For your profanity and want of courtesy we will make the ransom a thousand philips, then," said he. And to his followers—"Away with him! Let him have courteous entertainment against the coming of his ransom."

He was borne away cursing.

Of the others Sakr-el-Bahr made short work. He offered the

privilege of ransoming himself to any who might claim it, and the
privilege was claimed by three. The rest he consigned to the care of
Biskaine, who acted as his Kayia, or lieutenant. But before doing so
he bade the ship's bo'sun stand forward, and demanded to know
what slaves there might be on board. There were, he learnt, but a
dozen, employed upon menial duties on the ship—three Jews,
seven Muslimeen, and two heretics—and they had been driven
under the hatches when the peril threatened.

By Sakr-el-Bahr's orders these were dragged forth from the
blackness into which they had been flung. The Muslimeen upon
discovering that they had fallen into the hands of their own people
and that their slavery was at an end, broke into cries of delight, and
fervent praise of Allah than whom they swore there was no other
God. The three Jews, lithe, stalwart young men in black tunics that
fell to their knees and black skull-caps upon their curly black locks,
smiled ingratiatingly, hoping for the best since they were fallen into
the hands of people who were nearer akin to them than Christians
and allied to them, at least, by the bond of common enmity to
Spain and common suffering at the hands of Spaniards. The two
heretics stood in stolid apathy, realizing that with them it was but a
case of passing from Charybdis to Scylla, and that they had as little
to hope for from heathen as from Christian. One of these was a
sturdy bowlegged fellow, whose garments were little better than
rags; his weather-beaten face was of the color of mahogany and his
eyes of a dark blue under tufted eyebrows that once had been
red—like his hair and beard—but were now thickly intermingled
with gray. He was spotted like a leopard on the hands by enormous
dark brown freckles.

Of the entire dozen he was the only one that drew the attention
of Sakr-el-Bahr. He stood despondently before the corsair, with
bowed head and his eyes upon the deck, a weary, dejected, spirit-
less slave who would as soon die as live. Thus some few moments
during which the stalwart Muslim stood regarding him; then as if

drawn by that persistent scrutiny he raised his dull, weary eyes. At once they quickened, the dullness passed out of them; they were bright and keen as of old. He thrust his head forward, staring in his turn; then, in a bewildered way he looked about him at the ocean of swarthy faces under turbans of all colors, and back again at Sakr-el-Bahr.

"God's light!" he said at last, in English, to vent his infinite amazement. Then reverting to the cynical manner that he had ever affected, and effacing all surprise—

"Good day to you, Sir Oliver," said he. "I suppose ye'll give yourself the pleasure of hanging me."

"Allah is great!" said Sakr-el-Bahr impassively.

CHAPTER II

THE RENEGADE

How it came to happen that Sakr-el-Bahr, the Hawk of the Sea, the Muslim rover, the scourge of the Mediterranean, the terror of Christians, and the beloved of Asad ed Din, Basha of Algiers, would be one and the same as Sir Oliver Tressilian, the Cornish gentleman of Penarrow, is at long length set forth in the chronicles of Lord Henry Goade. His lordship conveys to us some notion of how utterly overwhelming he found that fact by the tedious minuteness with which he follows step by step this extraordinary metamorphosis. He devotes to it two entire volumes of those eighteen which he has left us. The whole, however, may with advantage be summarized into one short chapter.

Sir Oliver was one of a score of men who were rescued from the sea by the crew of the Spanish vessel that had sunk the *Swallow*; another was Jasper Leigh, the skipper. All of them were carried to Lisbon, and there handed over to the Court of the Holy Office. Since they were heretics all—or nearly all—it was fit and proper that the Brethren of St. Dominic should undertake their conversion in the first place. Sir Oliver came of a family that never had been famed for rigidity in religious matters, and he was certainly not going to burn alive if the adoption of other men's opinions upon an extremely hypothetical future state would suffice to save him from the stake. He accepted Catholic baptism with an almost contemptuous indifference. As for Jasper Leigh, it will be conceived that the elasticity of the skipper's conscience was no less than Sir Oliver's, and he was certainly not the man to be roasted for a trifle of faith.

No doubt there would be great rejoicings in the Holy House over the rescue of these two unfortunate souls from the certain perdition that had awaited them. It followed that as converts to the Faith they were warmly cherished, and tears of thanksgiving were profusely shed over them by the Hounds of God. So much for their heresy. They were completely purged of it, having done penance in proper form at an Auto held on the Rocio at Lisbon, candle in hand and sanbenito on their shoulders. The Church dismissed them with her blessing and an injunction to persevere in the ways of salvation to which with such meek kindness she had inducted them.

Now this dismissal amounted to a rejection. They were, as a consequence, thrown back upon the secular authorities, and the secular authorities had yet to punish them for their offence upon the seas. No offence could be proved, it is true. But the courts were satisfied that this lack of offence was but the natural result of a lack of opportunity. Conversely, they reasoned, it was not to be doubted that with the opportunity the offence would have been forthcoming. Their assurance of this was based upon the fact that when the Spaniard fired across the bows of the *Swallow* as an invitation to heave to, she had kept upon her course. Thus, with unanswerable Castilian logic was the evil conscience of her skipper proven.

Captain Leigh protested on the other hand that his action had been dictated by his lack of faith in Spaniards and his firm belief that all Spaniards were pirates to be avoided by every honest seaman who was conscious of inferior strength of armaments. It was a plea that won him no favor with his narrow-minded judges.

Sir Oliver fervently urged that he was no member of the crew of the *Swallow*, that he was a gentleman who found himself aboard her very much against his will, being the victim of a villainous piece of trepanning executed by her venal captain. The court heard his plea with respect, and asked to know his name and rank. He was so very indiscreet as to answer truthfully. The result was extremely educative to Sir Oliver; it showed him how systematically conducted was the keeping of the Spanish archives. The court produced documents enabling his judges to recite to him most of that portion of his life that had been spent upon the seas, and many an awkward little circumstance which had slipped his memory long since, which he now recalled, and which certainly was not calculated to make his sentence lighter.

Had he not been in the Barbados in such a year, and had he not there captured the galleon *Maria de las Dolores*? What was that but an act of villainous piracy? Had he not scuttled a Spanish carack four years ago in the bay of Funchal? Had he not been with that pirate Hawkins in the affair at San Juan de Ulloa? And so on. Questions poured upon him and engulfed him.

He almost regretted that he had given himself the trouble to accept conversion and all that it entailed at the hands of the Brethren of St. Dominic. It began to appear to him that he had but wasted time and escaped the clerical fire to be dangled on a secular rope as an offering to the vengeful gods of outraged Spain.

So much, however, was not done. The galleys in the Mediterranean were in urgent need of men at the time, and to this circumstance Sir Oliver, Captain Leigh, and some others of the luckless crew of the *Swallow* owed their lives, though it is to be doubted whether any of them found the matter one for congratulation. Chained each man to a fellow, ankle to ankle, with but a short length of links between, they formed part of a considerable herd of unfortunates who were driven across Portugal into Spain and then southward to Cadiz. The last that Sir Oliver saw of Captain Leigh was on the morning on which they set out from the reeking Lisbon jail. Thereafter throughout that weary march each knew the other to be somewhere in that wretched regiment of galley-slaves; but they never came face to face again.

In Cadiz Sir Oliver spent a month in a vast enclosed space that was open to the sky, but nevertheless of an indescribable foulness, a place of filth, disease, and suffering beyond human conception, the details of which the curious may seek for himself in my Lord Henry's chronicles. They are too revolting by far to be retailed here.

At the end of that month he was one of those picked out by an officer who was manning a galley that was to convey the Infanta to Naples. He owed this to his vigorous constitution which had successfully withstood the infections of that mephitic place of torments, and to the fine thews which the officer pummelled and felt as though he were acquiring a beast of burden—which, indeed, is precisely what he was doing.

The galley to which our gentleman was dispatched was a vessel of fifty oars, each manned by seven men. They were seated upon a sort of staircase that followed the slope of the oar, running from the gangway in the vessel's middle down to the shallow bulwarks.

The place allotted to Sir Oliver was that next the gangway. Here, stark naked as when he was born, he was chained to the bench, and in those chains, let us say at once, he remained, without a single moment's intermission, for six whole months.

Between himself and the hard timbers of his seat there was naught but a flimsy and dirty sheepskin. From end to end the bench was not more than ten feet in length, whilst the distance separating it from the next one was a bare four feet. In that cramped space of ten feet by four, Sir Oliver and his six oar-mates had their miserable existence, waking and sleeping—for they slept in their chains at the oar without sufficient room in which to lie at stretch.

Anon Sir Oliver became hardened and inured to that unspeakable existence, that living death of the galley-slave. But that first

long voyage to Naples was ever to remain the most terrible experience of his life. For spells of six or eight endless hours at a time,
and on one occasion for no less than ten hours, did he pull at his oar
without a single moment's pause. With one foot on the stretcher,
the other on the bench in front of him, grasping his part of that
appallingly heavy fifteen-foot oar, he would bend his back to thrust
forward—and upwards so to clear the shoulders of the groaning,
sweating slaves in front of him—then he would lift the end so as to
bring the blade down to the water, and having gripped he would
rise from his seat to throw his full weight into the pull, and so fall
back with clank of chain upon the groaning bench to swing forward
once more, and so on until his senses reeled, his sight became
blurred, his mouth parched and his whole body a living, straining
ache. Then would come the sharp fierce cut of the boatswain's whip
to revive energies that flagged however little, and sometimes to
leave a bleeding stripe upon his naked back.

Thus day in day out, now broiled and blistered by the pitiless
southern sun, now chilled by the night dews whilst he took his
cramped and unrefreshing rest, indescribably filthy and dishev-
elled, his hair and beard matted with endless sweat, unwashed
save by the rains which in that season were all too rare, choked
almost by the stench of his miserable comrades and infested by
filthy crawling things begotten of decaying sheepskins and
Heaven alone knows what other foulnesses of that floating hell.
He was sparingly fed upon weeviled biscuit and vile messes of tal-
lowy rice, and to drink he was given luke-warm water that was
often stale, saving that sometimes when the spell of rowing was
more than usually protracted the boatswains would thrust lumps
of bread sodden in wine into the mouths of the toiling slaves to
sustain them.

The scurvy broke out on that voyage, and there were other dis-
eases among the rowers, to say nothing of the festering sores begotten of the friction of the bench which were common to all, and

which each must endure as best he could. With the slave whose disease conquered him or who, reaching the limit of his endurance, permitted himself to swoon, the boatswains had a short way. The diseased were flung overboard; the swooning were dragged out upon the gangway or bridge and flogged there to revive them; if they did not revive they were flogged on until they were a horrid bleeding pulp, which was then heaved into the sea.

Once or twice when they stood to windward the smell of the slaves being wafted abaft and reaching the fine gilded poop where the Infanta and her attendants traveled, the helmsmen were ordered to put about, and for long weary hours the slaves would hold the galley in position, backing her up gently against the wind so as not to lose way.

The number that died in the first week of that voyage amounted to close upon a quarter of the total. But there were reserves in the prow, and these were drawn upon to fill the empty places. None but the fittest could survive this terrible ordeal.

Of these was Sir Oliver, and of these too was his immediate neighbor at the oar, a stalwart, powerful, impassive, uncomplaining young Moor, who accepted his fate with a stoicism that aroused Sir Oliver's admiration. For days they exchanged no single word together, their religions marking them out, they thought, for enemies despite the fact that they were fellows in misfortune. But one evening when an aged Jew who had collapsed in merciful unconsciousness was dragged out and flogged in the usual manner, Sir Oliver, chancing to behold the scarlet prelate who accompanied the Infanta looking on from the poop-rail with hard unmerciful eyes, was filled with such a passion at all this inhumanity and at the cold pitilessness of that professed servant of the Gentle and Pitiful Savior, that aloud he cursed all Christians in general and that scarlet Prince of the Church in particular.

He turned to the Moor beside him, and addressing him in Spanish—

"Hell," he said, "was surely made for Christians, which may be why they seek to make earth like it."

Fortunately for him the creak and dip of the oars, the clank of chains, and the lashes beating sharply upon that wretched Jew were sufficient to muffle his voice. But the Moor heard him, and his dark eyes gleamed.

"There is a furnace seven times heated awaiting them, O my brother," he replied, with a confidence which seemed to be the source of his present stoicism. "But art thou, then, not a Christian?"

He spoke in that queer language of the North African seaboard, that lingua franca, which sounded like some French dialect interspersed with Arabic words. But Sir Oliver made out his meaning almost by intuition. He answered him in Spanish again, since although the Moor did not appear to speak it yet it was plain he understood it.

"I renounce from this hour," he answered in his passion. "I will acknowledge no religion in whose name such things are done. Look me at that scarlet fruit of hell up yonder. See how daintily he sniffs at his pomander lest his saintly nostrils be offended by the exhalations of our misery. Yet are we God's creatures, made in God's image like himself. What does he know of God? Religion he knows as he knows good wine, rich food, and soft women. He preaches self-denial as the way to heaven, and by his own tenets is he damned." He growled an obscene oath as he heaved the great oar forward. "A Christian I?" he cried, and laughed for the first time since he had been chained to that bench of agony. "I am done with Christians and Christianity!"

"Verily we are God's, and to Him shall we return," said the Moor.

That was the beginning of a friendship between Sir Oliver and this man, whose name was Yusuf-ben-Moktar. The Muslim conceived that in Sir Oliver he saw one upon whom the grace of Allah had descended, one who was ripe to receive the Prophet's message.

Yusuf was devout, and he applied himself to the conversion of his fellow-slave. Sir Oliver listened to him, however, with indifference. Having discarded one creed he would need a deal of satisfying on the score of another before he adopted it, and it seemed to him that all the glorious things urged by Yusuf in praise of Islam he had heard before in praise of Christianity. But he kept his counsel on that score, and meanwhile his intercourse with the Muslim had the effect of teaching him the lingua franca, so that at the end of six months he found himself speaking it like a Mauretanian with all the Muslim's imagery and with more than the ordinary seasoning of Arabic.

It was towards the end of that six months that the event took place which was to restore Sir Oliver to liberty. In the meanwhile those limbs of his which had ever been vigorous beyond the common wont had acquired an elephantine strength. It was ever thus at the oar. Either you died under the strain, or your thews and sinews grew to be equal to their relentless task. Sir Oliver in those six months was become a man of steel and iron, impervious to fatigue, superhuman almost in his endurance.

They were returning home from a trip to Genoa when one evening as they were standing off Minorca in the Balearic Isles they were surprised by a fleet of four Muslim galleys which came skimming round a promontory to surround and engage them.

Aboard the Spanish vessel there broke a terrible cry of "Asad-ed-Din"—the name of the most redoubtable Muslim corsair since the Italian renegade Ochiali—the Ali Pasha who had been killed at Lepanto. Trumpets blared and drums beat on the poop, and the Spaniards in morion and corselet, armed with calivers and pikes, stood to defend their lives and liberty. The gunners sprang to the culverins. But fire had to be kindled and linstocks ignited, and in the confusion much time was lost—so much that not a single cannon shot was fired before the grappling irons of the first galley clanked upon and gripped the Spaniard's bulwarks. The shock of

the impact was terrific. The armored prow of the Muslim galley—Asad-ed-Din's own—smote the Spaniard a slanting blow
amidships that smashed fifteen of the oars as if they had been so
many withered twigs.

There was a shriek from the slaves, followed by such piteous
groans as the damned in hell may emit. Fully two score of them
had been struck by the shafts of their oars as these were hurled
back against them. Some had been killed outright, others lay limp
and crushed, some with broken backs, others with shattered limbs
and ribs.

Sir Oliver would assuredly have been of these but for the warning, advice, and example of Yusuf, who was well versed in
galley-fighting and who foresaw clearly what must happen. He
thrust the oar upward and forward as far as it would go, compelling
the others at his bench to accompany his movement. Then he
slipped down upon his knees, released his hold of the timber, and
crouched down until his shoulders were on a level with the bench.
He had shouted to Sir Oliver to follow his example, and Sir Oliver,
without even knowing what the maneuver should portend, but
gathering its importance from the other's urgency of tone,
promptly obeyed. The oar was struck an instant later, and ere it
snapped off it was flung back, braining one of the slaves at the bench
and mortally injuring the others, but passing clean over the heads of
Sir Oliver and Yusuf. A moment later the bodies of the oarsmen of
the bench immediately in front were flung back atop of them with
yells and curses.

When Sir Oliver staggered to his feet he found the battle
joined. The Spaniards had fired a volley from their calivers and a
dense cloud of smoke hung above the bulwarks; through this
surged now the corsairs, led by a tall, lean, elderly man with a flowing white beard and a swarthy eagle face. A crescent of emeralds
flashed from his snowy turban; above it rose the peak of a steel cap,
and his body was cased in chain mail. He swung a great scimitar,

before which Spaniards went down like wheat to the reaper's sickle. He fought like ten men, and to support him poured a never-ending stream of Muslimeen to the cry of "Din! Din! Allah, Y'Allah!" Back and yet back went the Spaniards before that irresistible onslaught.

Sir Oliver found Yusuf struggling in vain to rid himself of his chain, and went to his assistance. He stooped, seized it in both hands, set his feet against the bench, exerted all his strength, and tore the staple from the wood. Yusuf was free, save, of course, that a length of heavy chain was dangling from his steel anklet. In his turn he did the like service by Sir Oliver, though not quite as speedily, for strong man though he was, either his strength was not equal to the Cornishman's or else the latter's staple had been driven into sounder timber. In the end, however, it yielded, and Sir Oliver too was free. Then he set the foot that was hampered by the chain upon the bench, and with the staple that still hung from the end of it he prised open the link that attached it to his anklet.

That done he took his revenge. Crying "Din!" as loudly as any of the Muslimeen boarders, he flung himself upon the rear of the Spaniards brandishing his chain. In his hands it became a terrific weapon. He used it as a scourge, lashing it to right and left of him, splitting here a head and crushing there a face, until he had hacked a way clean through the Spanish press, which bewildered by this sudden rear attack made but little attempt to retaliate upon the escaped galley-slave. After him, whirling the remaining ten feet of the broken oar, came Yusuf.

Sir Oliver confessed afterwards to knowing very little of what happened in those moments. He came to a full possession of his senses to find the fight at an end, a cloud of turbaned corsairs standing guard over a huddle of Spaniards, others breaking open the cabin and dragging thence the chests that it contained, others again armed with chisels and mallets passing along the benches liberating the surviving slaves, of whom the great majority were children of Islam.

Sir Oliver found himself face to face with the white-bearded leader of the corsairs, who was leaning upon his scimitar and regarding him with eyes at once amused and amazed. Our gentleman's naked body was splashed from head to foot with blood, and in his right hand he still clutched that yard of iron links with which he had wrought such ghastly execution. Yusuf was standing at the corsair leader's elbow speaking rapidly.

"By Allah, was ever such a lusty fighter seen!" cried the latter. "The strength of the Prophet is within him thus to smite the unbelieving pigs."

Sir Oliver grinned savagely.

"I was returning them some of their whip-lashes—with interest," said he.

And those were the circumstances under which he came to meet the formidable Asad-ed-Din, Basha of Algiers, those the first words that passed between them.

Anon, when aboard Asad's own galley he was being carried to Barbary, he was washed and his head was shaved all but the forelock, by which the Prophet should lift him up to heaven when his earthly destiny should come to be fulfilled. He made no protest. They washed and fed him and gave him ease; and so that they did these things to him they might do what else they pleased. At last arrayed in flowing garments that were strange to him, and with a turban wound about his head, he was conducted to the poop, where Asad sat with Yusuf under an awning, and he came to understand that it was in compliance with the orders of Yusuf that he had been treated as if he were a True-Believer.

Yusuf-ben-Moktar was discovered as a person of great consequence, the nephew of Asad-ed-Din, and a favorite with that Exalted of Allah the Sublime Portal himself, a man whose capture by Christians had been a thing profoundly deplored. Accordingly his delivery from that thraldom was matter for rejoicing. Being delivered, he bethought him of his oar-mate, concerning whom indeed Asad-ed-Din manifested the greatest curiosity, for in all this world there was nothing the old corsair loved so much as a fighter, and in all his days, he vowed, never had he seen the equal of that stalwart galley-slave, never the like of his performance with that murderous chain. Yusuf had informed him that the man was a fruit ripe for the Prophet's plucking, that the grace of Allah was upon him, and in spirit already he must be accounted a good Muslim.

When Sir Oliver, washed, perfumed, and arrayed in white caftan and turban, which gave him the air of being even taller than he was, came into the presence of Asad-ed-Din, it was conveyed to him that if he would enter the ranks of the Faithful of the Prophet's House and devote the strength and courage with which Allah the One had endowed him to the upholding of the True Faith and to the chastening of the enemies of Islam, great honor, wealth, and dignity were in store for him.

Of all that proposal, made at prodigious length and with great wealth of Eastern circumlocution, the only phrase that took root in his rather bewildered mind was that which concerned the chastening of the enemies of Islam. The enemies of Islam he conceived, were his own enemies; and he further conceived that they stood in great need of chastening, and that to take a hand in that chastening would be a singularly grateful task. So he considered the proposals made him. He considered, too, that the alternative—in the event of his refusing to make the protestations of Faith required of him—was that he must return to the oar of a galley, of a Muslim galley now. Now that was an occupation of which he had had more than his fill, and since he had been washed and restored to the normal sensations of a clean human being he found that whatever might be within the scope of his courage he could not envisage returning to the oar. We have seen the ease with which he had abandoned the religion in which he was reared for the Roman faith, and how utterly deluded he had found himself. With the same degree of ease did he now go over to Islam, and with much greater profit. Moreover, he embraced the Religion of Mahomet with a measure of fierce conviction that had been entirely lacking from his earlier apostasy.

He had arrived at the conclusion whilst aboard the galley of Spain, as we have seen, that Christianity as practiced in his day was a grim mockery of which the world were better rid. It is not to be supposed that his convictions that Christianity was at fault went the length of making him suppose that Islam was right, or that his conversion to the Faith of Mahomet was anything more than superficial. But forced as he was to choose between the rower's bench and the poop-deck, the oar and the scimitar, he boldly and resolutely made the only choice that in his case could lead to liberty and life.

Thus he was received into the ranks of the Faithful whose pavilions wait them in Paradise, set in an orchard of never-failing fruit, among rivers of milk, of wine, and of clarified honey. He became the Kayia or lieutenant to Yusuf on the galley of that corsair's command, and seconded him in half a score of engagements with an ability and a conspicuity that made him swiftly famous throughout the ranks of the Mediterranean rovers. Some six months later in a fight off the coast of Sicily with one of the galleys of the Religion—as the vessels of the Knights of Malta were called—Yusuf was mortally wounded in the very moment of the victory. He died an hour later in the arms of Sir Oliver, naming the latter his successor in the command of the galley, and enjoining upon all implicit obedience to him until they should be returned to Algiers and the Basha should make known his further will in the matter.

The Basha's will was to confirm his nephew's dying appointment of a successor, and Sir Oliver found himself in full command of a galley. From that hour he became Oliver-Reis, but very soon his valor and fury earned him the by-name of Sakr-el-Bahr, the Hawk of the Sea. His fame grew rapidly, and it spread across the tideless sea to the very shores of Christendom. Soon he became Asad's lieutenant, the second in command of all the Algerine galleys, which meant in fact that he was the commander-in-chief, for Asad was growing old and took the sea more and more rarely now. Sakr-el-Bahr sallied forth in his name and his stead, and such was his courage, his address, and his good fortune that never did he go forth to return empty-handed.

It was clear to all that the favor of Allah was upon him, that he had been singled out by Allah to be the very glory of Islam. Asad, who had ever esteemed him, grew to love him. An intensely devout man, could he have done less in the case of one for whom the Pitying the Pitiful showed so marked a predilection? It was freely accepted that when the destiny of Asad-ed-Din should come to be fulfilled, Sakr-el-Bahr must succeed him in the Bashalik of Algiers, and that thus Oliver-Reis would follow in the footsteps of Barbarossa, Ochiali, and other Christian renegades who had become corsair-princes of Islam.

In spite of certain hostilities which his rapid advancement begot, and of which we shall hear more presently, once only did his power stand in danger of suffering a check. Coming one morning into the reeking bagnio at Algiers, some six months after he had been raised to his captaincy, he found there a score of countrymen of his own, and he gave orders that their fetters should instantly be struck off and their liberty restored them.

Called to account by the Basha for this action he took a high-handed way, since no other was possible. He swore by the beard of the Prophet that if he were to draw the sword of Mahomet and to serve Islam upon the seas, he would serve it in his own way, and one of his ways was that his own countrymen were to have immunity from the edge of that same sword. Islam, he swore, should not be the loser, since for every Englishman he restored to liberty he would bring two Spaniards, Frenchmen, Greeks, or Italians into bondage.

He prevailed, but only upon condition that since captured slaves were the property of the state, if he desired to abstract them from the state he must first purchase them for himself. Since they would then be his own property he could dispose of them at his good pleasure. Thus did the wise and just Asad resolve the difficulty which had arisen, and Oliver-Reis bowed wisely to that decision.

Thereafter what English slaves were brought to Algiers he purchased, manumitted, and found means to send home again. True, it cost him a fine price yearly, but he was fast amassing such wealth as could easily support this tax.

As you read Lord Henry Goade's chronicles you might come to the conclusion that in the whorl of that new life of his Sir Oliver had entirely forgotten the happenings in his Cornish home and the woman he had loved, who so readily had believed him guilty of the slaying of her brother. You might believe this until you come upon the relation of how he found one day among some English seamen brought captive to Algiers by Biskaine-el-Borak—who was become his own second in command—a young Cornish lad from Helston named Pitt, whose father he had known.

He took this lad home with him to the fine palace which he inhabited near the Bab-el-Oueb, treated him as an honored guest, and sat through a whole summer night in talk with him, questioning him upon this person and that person, and thus gradually drawing from him all the little history of his native place during the two years that were sped since he had left it. In this we gather an impression of the wistful longings, the fierce nostalgia that must have overcome the renegade and his endeavors to allay it by his endless questions. The Cornish lad had brought him up sharply and agonizingly with that past of his upon which he had closed the door when he became a Muslim and a corsair. The only possible inference is that in those hours of that summer's night repentance stirred in him, and a wild longing to return. Rosamund should reopen for him that door which, hard-driven by misfortune, he had slammed. That she would do so when once she knew the truth he had no faintest doubt. And there was now no reason why he should conceal the truth, why he should continue to shield that dastardly half-brother of his, whom he had come to hate as fiercely as he had erstwhile loved him.

In secret he composed a long letter giving the history of all that had happened to him since his kidnapping, and setting forth the entire truth of that and of the deed that had led to it. His chronicler opines that it was a letter that must have moved a stone to tears. And, moreover, it was not a mere matter of passionate protestations of innocence, or of unsupported accusation of his brother. It told her of the existence of proofs that must dispel all doubt. It told her of that parchment indited by Master Baine and witnessed by the parson, which document was to be delivered to her together with the letter. Further, it bade her seek confirmation of that document's genuineness, did she doubt it, at the hands of Master Baine himself. That done, it besought her to lay the whole matter before the Queen, and thus secure him faculty to return to England and immunity from any consequences of his subsequent renegade act to which his sufferings had driven him. He loaded the young Cornishman with gifts, gave him that letter to deliver in person, and added instructions that should enable him to find the document he was to deliver with it. That precious parchment had been left between the leaves of an old book on falconry in the library at Penarrow, where it would probably be found still undisturbed since his brother would not suspect its presence and was himself no scholar. Pitt was to seek out Nicholas at Penarrow and enlist his aid to obtain possession of that document, if it still existed.

Then Sakr-el-Bahr found means to conduct Pitt to Genoa, and there put him aboard an English vessel.

Three months later he received an answer—a letter from Pitt, which reached him by way of Genoa—which was at peace with the Algerines, and served then as a channel of communication with Christianity. In this letter Pitt informed him that he had done all that Sir Oliver had desired him; that he had found the document by the help of Nicholas, and that in person he had waited upon Mis-

tress Rosamund Godolphin, who dwelt now with Sir John Killigrew
at Arwenack, delivering to her the letter and the parchment; but
that upon learning on whose behalf he came she had in his presence flung both unopened upon the fire and dismissed him with his
tale untold.

Sakr-el-Bahr spent the night under the skies in his fragrant
orchard, and his slaves reported in terror that they had heard sobs
and weeping. If indeed his heart wept, it was for the last time;
thereafter he was more inscrutable, more ruthless, cruel and mocking than men had ever known him, nor from that day did he ever
again concern himself to manumit a single English slave. His heart
was become a stone.

Thus five years passed, counting from that spring night when he
was trepanned by Jasper Leigh, and his fame spread, his name
became a terror upon the seas, and fleets put forth from Malta,
from Naples, and from Venice to make an end of him and his ruthless piracy. But Allah kept watch over him, and Sakr-el-Bahr never
delivered battle but he wrested victory to the scimitars of Islam.

Then in the spring of that fifth year there came to him another
letter from the Cornish Pitt, a letter which showed him that gratitude was not as dead in the world as he supposed it, for it was purely
out of gratitude that the lad whom he had delivered from thraldom
wrote to inform him of certain matters that concerned him. This letter reopened that old wound; it did more; it dealt him a fresh one.
He learnt from it that the writer had been constrained by Sir John
Killigrew to give such evidence of Sir Oliver's conversion to Islam as
had enabled the courts to pronounce Sir Oliver as one to be pre-
sumed dead at law, granting the succession to his half-brother, Master Lionel Tressilian. Pitt professed himself deeply mortified at
having been forced unwittingly to make Sir Oliver so evil a return
for the benefits received from him, and added that sooner would he
have suffered them to hang him than have spoken could he have
foreseen the consequences of his testimony.

So far Sir Oliver read unmoved by any feeling other than cold contempt. But there was more to follow. The letter went on to tell him that Mistress Rosamund was newly returned from a two years' sojourn in France to become betrothed to his half-brother Lionel, and that they were to be wed in June. He was further informed that the marriage had been contrived by Sir John Killigrew in his desire to see Rosamund settled and under the protection of a husband, since he himself was proposing to take the seas and was fitting out a fine ship for a voyage to the Indies. The writer added that the marriage was widely approved, and was deemed to be an excellent measure for both houses, since it would weld into one the two contiguous estates of Penarrow and Godolphin Court.

Oliver-Reis laughed when he had read thus far. The marriage was approved not for itself, it would seem, but because by means of it two stretches of earth were united into one. It was a marriage of two parks, of two estates, of two tracts of arable and forest, and that two human beings were concerned in it was apparently no more than an incidental circumstance.

Then the irony of it all entered his soul and spread it with bitterness. After dismissing him for the supposed murder of her brother, she was to take the actual murderer to her arms. And he—that cur, that false villain!—out of what depths of hell did he derive the courage to go through with this mummery?—had he no heart, no conscience, no sense of decency, no fear of God?

He tore the letter into fragments and set about effacing the matter from his thoughts. Pitt had meant kindly by him, but had dealt cruelly. In his efforts to seek distraction from the torturing images ever in his mind he took to the sea with three galleys, and thus some two weeks later came face to face with Master Jasper Leigh aboard the Spanish carack which he captured under Cape Spartel.

CHAPTER III

HOMEWARD BOUND

I N THE cabin of the captured Spaniard, Jasper Leigh found himself that evening face to face with Sakr-el-Bahr, haled thither by the corsair's gigantic Nubians.

Sakr-el-Bahr had not yet pronounced his intentions concerning the piratical little skipper, and Master Leigh, full conscious that he was a villain, feared the worst, and had spent some miserable hours in the forecastle awaiting a doom which he accounted foregone.

"Our positions have changed, Master Leigh, since last we talked in a ship's cabin," was the renegade's inscrutable greeting.

"Indeed," Master Leigh agreed. "But I hope ye'll remember that on that occasion I was your friend."

"At a price," Sakr-el-Bahr reminded him. "And at a price you may find me your friend to-day."

The rascally skipper's heart leapt with hope. "Name it, Sir Oliver," he answered eagerly. "And so that it lies within my wretched power I swear I'll never boggle at it. I've had enough of slavery," he ran on in a plaintive whine. "Five years of it, and four of them spent aboard the galleys of Spain, and no day in all of them but that I prayed for death. Did you but know what I ha' suffered."

"Never was suffering more merited, never punishment more fitting, never justice more poetic," said Sakr-el-Bahr in a voice that made the skipper's blood run cold. "You would have sold me, a man who did you no hurt, indeed a man who once befriended you—you would have sold me into slavery for a matter of two hundred pounds. . . ."

"Nay, nay," cried the other fearfully, "as God's my witness, 't was never part of my intent. Ye'll never ha' forgot the words I spoke to you, the offer that I made to carry you back home again."

"Ay, at a price, 't is true," Sakr-el-Bahr repeated. "And it is fortunate for you that you are to-day in a position to pay a price that should postpone your dirty neck's acquaintance with a rope. I need a navigator," he added in explanation, "and what five years ago you would have done for two hundred pounds, you shall do to-day for your life. How say you: will you navigate this ship for me?"

"Sir," cried Jasper Leigh, who could scarce believe that this was all that was required of him, "I'll sail it to hell at your bidding."

"I am not for Spain this voyage," answered Sakr-el-Bahr. "You shall sail me precisely as you would have done five years ago, back to the mouth of the Fal, and set me ashore there. Is that agreed?"

"Ay, and gladly," replied Master Leigh without a second's pause.

"The conditions are that you shall have your life and your liberty," Sakr-el-Bahr explained. "But do not suppose that arrived in England you are to be permitted to depart. You must sail us back again, though once you have done that I shall find a way to send you home if you so desire it, and perhaps there will be some measure of reward for you if you serve me faithfully throughout. Follow the habits of a lifetime by playing me false and there's an end to you. You shall have for constant bodyguard these two lilies of the desert," and he pointed to the colossal Nubians who stood there invisible almost in the shadow but for the flash of teeth and eyeballs. "They shall watch over you, and see that no harm befalls you so long as you are honest with me, and they shall strangle you at the first sign of treachery. You may go. You have the freedom of the ship, but you are not to leave it here or elsewhere save at my express command."

Jasper Leigh stumbled out counting himself fortunate beyond his expectations or deserts, and the Nubians followed him and hung behind him ever after like some vast twin shadow.

To Sakr-el-Bahr entered now Biskaine with a report of the prize captured. Beyond the prisoners, however, and the actual vessel, which had suffered nothing in the fight, the cargo was of no account. Outward bound as she was it was not to be expected that any treasures would be discovered in her hold. They found great store of armaments and powder and a little money; but naught else that was worthy of the corsairs' attention.

Sakr-el-Bahr briefly issued his surprising orders.

"Thou'lt set the captives aboard one of the galleys, Biskaine, and thyself convey them to Algiers, there to be sold. All else thou'lt leave aboard here, and two hundred picked corsairs to go a voyage with me overseas, men that will act as mariners and fighters."

"Art thou, then, not returning to Algiers, O Sakr-el-Bahr?"

"Not yet. I am for a longer voyage. Convey my service to Asad-ed-Din, whom Allah guard and cherish, and tell him to look for me in some six weeks' time."

This sudden resolve of Oliver-Reis created no little excitement aboard the galleys. The corsairs knew nothing of navigation upon the open seas, none of them had ever been beyond the Mediterranean, few of them indeed had ever voyaged as far west as Cape Spartel, and it is doubtful if they would have followed any other leader into the perils of the open Atlantic. But Sakr-el-Bahr, the child of Fortune, the protected of Allah, had never yet led them to aught but victory, and he had but to call them to heel and they would troop after him whithersoever he should think well to go. So now there was little trouble in finding the two hundred Muslimeen he desired for his fighting crew. Rather was the difficulty to keep the number of those eager for the adventure within the bounds he had indicated.

You are not to suppose that in all this Sir Oliver was acting upon any preconcerted plan. Whilst he had lain on the heights watching that fine ship beating up against the wind it had come to him that with such a vessel under him it were a fond adventure to sail to England, to descend upon that Cornish coast abruptly as a thunderbolt, and present the reckoning to his craven dastard of a brother. He had toyed with the fancy, dreamily almost as men build their castles in Spain. Then in the heat of conflict it had entirely escaped his mind, to return in the shape of a resolve when he came to find himself face to face with Jasper Leigh.

The skipper and the ship conjointly provided him with all the means to realize that dream he had dreamt. There was none to oppose his will, no reason not to indulge his cruel fancy. Perhaps, too, he might see Rosamund again, might compel her to hear the truth from him. And there was Sir John Killigrew. He had never been able to determine whether Sir John had been his friend or his foe in the past; but since it was Sir John who had been instrumental in setting up Lionel in Sir Oliver's place—by inducing the courts to presume Sir Oliver's death on the score that being a renegade he must be accounted dead at law—and since it was Sir John who was contriving this wedding between Lionel and Rosamund, why, Sir John, too, should be paid a visit and should be informed of the precise nature of the thing he did.

With the forces at his disposal in those days of his absolute lordship of life and death along the African littoral, to conceive was with Oliver-Reis no more than the prelude to execution. The habit of swift realization of his every wish had grown with him, and that habit guided now his course.

He made his preparations quickly, and on the morrow the Spanish carack—lately labeled *Nuestra Señora de las Llagas,* but with

that label carefully effaced from her quarter—trimmed her sails
and stood out for the open Atlantic, navigated by Captain Jasper
Leigh. The three galleys under the command of Biskaine-el-Borak
crept slowly eastward and homeward to Algiers, hugging the coast,
as was the corsair habit.

The wind favored Oliver so well that within ten days of round-
ing Cape St. Vincent he had his first glimpse of the Lizard.

CHAPTER IV

THE RAID

I N THE estuary of the River Fal a splendid ship, on the building of which the most cunning engineers had been employed and no money spared, rode proudly at anchor just off Smithick under the very shadow of the heights crowned by the fine house of Arwenack. She was fitting out for a distant voyage, and for days the work of bringing stores and munitions aboard had been in progress, so that there was an unwonted bustle about the little forge and the huddle of cottages that went to make up the fishing village, as if in earnest of the great traffic that in future days was to be seen about that spot. For Sir John Killigrew seemed at last to be on the eve of prevailing and of laying there the foundations of the fine port of his dreams.

To this state of things his friendship with Master Lionel Tressilian had contributed not a little. The opposition made to his project by Sir Oliver—and supported, largely at Sir Oliver's suggestion, by Truro and Helston—had been entirely withdrawn by Lionel; more, indeed Lionel had actually gone so far in the opposite direction as to support Sir John in his representations to Parliament and the

Queen. It followed naturally enough that just as Sir Oliver's opposition of that cherished project had been the seed of the hostility between Arwenack and Penarrow, so Lionel's support of it became the root of the staunch friendship that sprang up between himself and Sir John.

What Lionel lacked of his brother's keen intelligence he made up for in cunning. He realized that although at some future time it was possible that Helston and Truro and the Tressilian property there might come to suffer as a consequence of the development of a port so much more advantageously situated, yet that could not be in his own lifetime; and meanwhile he must earn in return Sir John's support for his suit of Rosamund Godolphin and thus find the Godolphin estates merged with his own. This certain immediate gain was to Master Lionel well worth the other future possible loss.

It must not, however, be supposed that Lionel's courtship had thenceforward run a smooth and easy course. The mistress of Godolphin Court showed him no favor, and it was mainly that she might abstract herself from the importunities of his suit that she had sought and obtained Sir John Killigrew's permission to accompany the latter's sister to France when she went there with her husband, who was appointed English ambassador to the Louvre. Sir John's authority as her guardian had come into force with the decease of her brother.

Master Lionel moped awhile in her absence; but cheered by Sir John's assurance that in the end he should prevail, he quitted Cornwall in his turn and went forth to see the world. He spent some time in London about the Court, where, however, he seems to have prospered little, and then he crossed to France to pay his devoirs to the lady of his longings.

His constancy, the humility with which he made his suit, the obvious intensity of his devotion, began at last to wear away that gentlewoman's opposition, as dripping water wears away a stone. Yet she could not bring herself to forget that he was Sir Oliver's brother—the brother of the man she had loved, and the brother of the man who had killed her own brother. Between them stood, then, two things; the ghost of that old love of hers and the blood of Peter Godolphin.

Of this she reminded Sir John on her return to Cornwall after an absence of some two years, urging these matters as reasons why an alliance between herself and Lionel Tressilian must be impossible.

Sir John did not at all agree with her.

"My dear," he said, "there is your future to be thought of. You are now of full age and mistress of your own actions. Yet it is not well for a woman and a gentlewoman to dwell alone. As long as I live, or as long as I remain in England, all will be well. You may continue indefinitely your residence here at Arwenack, and you have been wise, I think, in quitting the loneliness of Godolphin Court. Yet consider that that loneliness may be yours again when I am not here."

"I should prefer that loneliness to the company you would thrust upon me," she answered him.

"Ungracious speech!" he protested. "Is this your gratitude for that lad's burning devotion, for his patience, his gentleness, and all the rest!"

"He is Oliver Tressilian's brother," she replied.

"And has he not suffered enough for that already? Is there to be no end to the price that he must pay for his brother's sins? Besides, consider that when all is said they are not even brothers. They are but half-brothers."

"Yet too closely kin," she said. "If you must have me wed I beg you'll find me another husband."

To this he would answer that expediently considered no husband could be better than the one he had chosen her. He pointed out the contiguity of their two estates, and how fine and advantageous a thing it would be to merge these two into one.

He was persistent, and his persistence was increased when he came to conceive his notion to take the seas again. His conscience would not permit him to heave anchor until he had bestowed her safely in wedlock. Lionel too was persistent, in a quiet, almost self-effacing way that never set a strain upon her patience, and was therefore the more difficult to combat.

In the end she gave way under the pressure of these men's wills, and did so with the best grace she could summon, resolved to drive from her heart and mind the one real obstacle of which, for very shame, she had made no mention to Sir John. The fact is that in spite of all, her love for Sir Oliver was not dead. It was stricken down, it is true, until she herself failed to recognize it for what it really was. But she caught herself thinking of him frequently and wistfully; she found herself comparing him with his brother; and for all that she had bidden Sir John find her some other husband than Lionel, she knew full well that any suitor brought before her must be submitted to that same comparison to his inevitable undoing. All this she accounted evil in herself. It was in vain that she lashed her mind with the reminder that Sir Oliver was Peter's murderer. As time went on she found herself actually making excuses for her sometime lover; she would admit that Peter had driven him to the step, that for her sake Sir Oliver had suffered insult upon insult from Peter, until, being but human, the cup of his endurance had overflowed in the end, and weary of submitting to the other's blows he had risen up in his anger and smitten in his turn.

She would scorn herself for such thoughts as these, yet she could not dismiss them. In act she could be strong—as witness how she had dealt with that letter which Oliver sent her out of Barbary by the hand of Pitt—but her thoughts she could not govern, and her thoughts were full often traitors to her will. There were longings in her heart for Oliver which she could not stifle, and there was ever the hope that he would one day return, although she realized that from such a return she might look for nothing.

When Sir John finally slew the hope of that return he did a

wiser thing than he conceived. Never since Oliver's disappearance had they heard any news of him until Pitt came to Arwenack with that letter and his story. They had heard, as had all the world, of the corsair Sakr-el-Bahr, but they had been far indeed from connecting him with Oliver Tressilian. Now that his identity was established by Pitt's testimony, it was an easy matter to induce the courts to account him dead and to give Lionel the coveted inheritance.

This to Rosamund was a small matter. But a great one was that Sir Oliver was dead at law, and must be so in fact, should he ever again set foot in England. It extinguished finally that curiously hopeless and almost subconscious hope of hers that one day he would return. Thus it helped her perhaps to face and accept the future which Sir John was resolved to thrust upon her.

Her betrothal was made public, and she proved if not an ardently loving, at least a docile and gentle mistress to Lionel. He was content. He could ask no more in reason at the moment, and he was buoyed up by every lover's confidence that given opportunity and time he could find the way to awaken a response. And it must be confessed that already during their betrothal he gave some proof of his reason for his confidence. She had been lonely, and he dispelled her loneliness by his complete surrender of himself to her; his restraint and his cautious, almost insidious creeping along a path which a more clumsy fellow would have taken at a dash made companionship possible between them and very sweet to her. Upon this foundation her affection began gradually to rise, and seeing them together and such excellent friends, Sir John congratulated himself upon his wisdom and went about the fitting out of that fine ship of his—the *Silver Heron*—for the coming voyage.

Thus they came within a week of the wedding, and Sir John all impatience now. The marriage bells were to be his signal for departure; as they fell silent the *Silver Heron* should spread her wings.

It was the evening of the first of June; the peal of the curfew had faded on the air and lights were being set in the great dining-room at Arwenack where the company was to sup. It was a small party. Just Sir John and Rosamund with Lionel, who had lingered on that day, and Lord Henry Goade—our chronicler—the Queen's Lieutenant of Cornwall, together with his lady. They were visiting Sir John and they were to remain yet a week his guests at Arwenack that they might grace the coming nuptials.

Above in the house there was great stir of preparation for the departure of Sir John and his ward, the latter into wedlock, the former into unknown seas. In the turret chamber a dozen seamstresses were at work upon the bridal outfit under the directions of that Sally Pentreath who had been no less assiduous in the preparation of swaddling clothes and the like on the eve of Rosamund's appearance in this world.

At the very hour at which Sir John was leading his company to table Sir Oliver Tressilian was setting foot ashore not a mile away.

He had deemed it wiser not to round Pendennis Point. So in the bay above Swanpool on the western side of that promontory he had dropped anchor as the evening shadows were deepening. He had launched the ship's two boats, and in these he had conveyed some thirty of his men ashore. Twice had the boats returned, until a hundred of his corsairs stood ranged along that foreign beach. The other hundred he left on guard aboard. He took so great a force upon an expedition for which a quarter of the men would have sufficed so as to ensure by overwhelming numbers the avoidance of all unnecessary violence.

Absolutely unobserved he led them up the slope towards Arwenack through the darkness that had now closed in. To tread his native soil once more went near to drawing tears from him. How familiar was the path he followed with such confidence in the night; how well known each bush and stone by which he went with his silent multitude hard upon his heels. Who could have foretold him such a return as this? Who could have dreamt when he roamed amain in his youth here with dogs and fowling-piece, that he would creep one night over these dunes a renegade Muslim leading a horde of infidels to storm the house of Sir John Killigrew of Arwenack?

Such thoughts begot a weakness in him; but he made a quick recovery when his mind swung to all that he had so unjustly suffered, when he considered all that he came thus to avenge.

First to Arwenack to Sir John and Rosamund to compel them to hear the truth at least, and then away to Penarrow for Master Lionel and the reckoning. Such was the project that warmed him, conquered his weakness and spurred him, relentless, onward and upward to the heights and the fortified house that dominated them.

He found the massive iron-studded gates locked, as was to have been expected at that hour. He knocked, and presently the postern gaped, and a lantern was advanced. Instantly that lantern was dashed aside and Sir Oliver had leapt over the sill into the courtyard. With a hand gripping the porter's throat to choke all utterance, Sir Oliver heaved him out to his men, who swiftly gagged him.

That done they poured silently through that black gap of the postern into the spacious gateway. On he led them, at a run almost, towards the tall mullioned windows whence a flood of golden light seemed invitingly to beckon them.

With the servants who met them in the hall they dealt in the same swift silent fashion as they had dealt with the gatekeeper, and such was the speed and caution of their movements that Sir John and his company had no suspicion of their presence until the door of the dining-room crashed open before their eyes.

The sight which they beheld was one that for some moments left them mazed and bewildered. Lord Henry tells us how at first he imagined that here was some mummery, some surprise prepared for the bridal couple by Sir John's tenants or the folk of Smithick and Penycumwick, and he adds that he was encouraged in this belief by the circumstance that not a single weapon gleamed in all that horde of outlandish intruders. Although they came full armed against any eventualities, yet by their leader's orders not a blade was bared. What was to do was to be done with their naked hands alone and without bloodshed. Such were the orders of Sakr-el-Bahr, and Sakr-el-Bahr's were not orders to be disregarded.

Himself he stood forward at the head of that legion of brown-skinned men arrayed in all the colors of the rainbow, their heads swathed in turbans of every hue. He considered the company in grim silence, and the company in amazement considered this turbaned giant with the masterful face that was tanned to the color of mahogany, the black forked beard, and those singularly light eyes glittering like steel under his black brows.

Thus a little while in silence, then with a sudden gasp Lionel Tressilian sank back in his tall chair as if bereft of strength.

The agate eyes flashed upon him smiling, cruelly.

"I see that you, at least, recognize me," said Sakr-el-Bahr in his deep voice. "I was assured I could depend upon the eyes of brotherly love to pierce the change that time and stress have wrought in me."

Sir John was on his feet, his lean swarthy face flushing darkly, an oath on his lips. Rosamund sat on as if frozen with horror, considering Sir Oliver with dilating eyes, whilst her hands clawed the table before her. They too recognized him now, and realized that here was no mummery. That something sinister was intended Sir John could not for a moment doubt. But of what that something might be he could form no notion. It was the first time that Barbary rovers were seen in England. That famous raid of theirs upon Baltimore in Ireland did not take place until some thirty years after this date.

"Sir Oliver Tressilian!" Killigrew gasped, and "Sir Oliver Tressilian!" echoed Lord Henry Goade, to add—"By God!"

"Not Sir Oliver Tressilian," came the answer, "but Sakr-el-Bahr, the scourge of the sea, the terror of Christendom, the desperate corsair your lies, cupidity, and false-heartedness have fashioned out of a sometime Cornish gentleman." He embraced them all in his denunciatory gesture. "Behold me here with my sea-hawks to present a reckoning long overdue."

Writing now of what his own eyes beheld, Lord Henry tells us how Sir John leapt to snatch a weapon from the armored walls; how Sakr-el-Bahr barked out a single word in Arabic, and how at that word a half-dozen of his supple blackamoors sprang upon the knight like greyhounds upon a hare and bore him writhing to the ground.

Lady Henry screamed; her husband does not appear to have done anything, or else modesty keeps him silent on the score of it. Rosamund, white to the lips, continued to look on, whilst Lionel, overcome, covered his face with his hands in sheer horror. One and all of them expected to see some ghastly deed of blood performed there, coldly and callously as the wringing of a capon's neck. But no such thing took place. The corsairs merely turned Sir John upon his face, dragged his wrists behind him to make them fast, and having performed that duty with a speedy, silent dexterity they abandoned him.

Sakr-el-Bahr watched their performance with those grimly smiling eyes of his. When it was done he spoke again and pointed to Lionel, who leapt up in sudden terror, with a cry that was entirely inarticulate. Lithe brown arms encircled him like a legion of snakes. Powerless, he was lifted in the air and borne swiftly away. For an instant he found himself held face to face with his turbaned brother. Into that pallid, terror-stricken human mask the renegade's eyes stabbed like two daggers. Then deliberately and after the fashion of the Muslim he was become he spat upon it.

"Away!" he growled, and through the press of corsairs that thronged the hall behind him a lane was swiftly opened and Lionel was swallowed up, lost to the view of those within the room.

"What murderous deed do you intend?" cried Sir John indomitably. He had risen and stood grimly dignified in his bonds.

"Will you murder your own brother as you murdered mine?"

demanded Rosamund, speaking now for the first time, and rising as she spoke, a faint flush coming to overspread her pallor. She saw him wince; she saw the mocking lustful anger perish in his face, leaving it vacant for a moment. Then it became grim again with a fresh resolve. Her words had altered all the current of his intentions. They fixed in him a dull, fierce rage. They silenced the explanations which he was come to offer, and which he scorned to offer here after that taunt.

"It seems you love that—whelp, that thing that was my brother," he said, sneering. "I wonder will you love him still when you come to be better acquainted with him? Though, faith, naught would surprise me in a woman and her love. Yet I am curious to see—curious to see." He laughed. "I have a mind to gratify myself. I will not separate you—not just yet."

He advanced upon her. "Come thou with me, lady," he commanded, and held out his hand.

And now Lord Henry seems to have been stirred to futile action.

"At that," he writes, "I thrust myself between to shield her. 'Thou dog,' I cried, 'thou shalt be made to suffer!'

"'Suffer?' quoth he, and mocked me with his deep laugh 'I have suffered already. 'T is for that reason I am here.'

"'And thou shalt suffer again, thou pirate out of hell!' I warned him. 'Thou shalt suffer for this outrage as God's my life!'

"'Shall I so?' quoth he, very calm and sinister. 'And at whose hands, I pray you?'

"'At mine, sir,' I roared, being by now stirred to a great fury.

"'At thine?' he sneered. 'Thou'lt hunt the hawk of the sea? Thou? Thou plump partridge! Away! Hinder me not!'"

And he adds that again Sir Oliver spoke that short Arabic command, whereupon a dozen blackamoors whirled the Queen's Lieutenant aside and bound him to a chair.

Face to face stood now Sir Oliver with Rosamund—face to face after five long years, and he realized that in every moment of that time the certainty had never departed from him of some such future meeting.

"Come, lady," he bade her sternly.

A moment she looked at him with hate and loathing in the clear depths of her deep blue eyes. Then swiftly as lightning she snatched a knife from the board and drove it at his heart. But his hand moved as swiftly to seize her wrist, and the knife clattered to the ground, its errand unfulfilled.

A shuddering sob escaped her then to express at once her horror of her own attempt and of the man who held her. That horror mounting until it overpowered her, she sank suddenly against him in a swoon.

Instinctively his arms went round her, and a moment he held her thus, recalling the last occasion on which she had lain against his breast, on an evening five years and more ago under the gray wall of Godolphin Court above the river. What prophet could have told him that when next he so held her the conditions would be these? It was all grotesque and incredible, like the fantastic dream of some sick mind. But it was all true, and she was in his arms again.

He shifted his grip to her waist, heaved her to his mighty shoulder, as though she were a sack of grain, and swung about, his business at Arwenack accomplished—indeed, more of it accomplished than had been his intent, and also something less.

"Away, away!" he cried to his rovers, and away they sped as fleetly and silently as they had come, no man raising now so much as a voice to hinder them.

Through the hall and across the courtyard flowed that human tide; out into the open and along the crest of the hill it surged, then away down the slope towards the beach where their boats awaited them. Sakr-el-Bahr ran as lightly as though the swooning woman he bore were no more than a cloak he had flung across his shoulder. Ahead of him went a half-dozen of his fellows carrying his gagged and pinioned brother.

Once only before they dipped from the heights of Arwenack did

Oliver check. He paused to look across the dark shimmering water to the woods that screened the house of Penarrow from his view. It had been part of his purpose to visit it, as we know. But the necessity had now been removed, and he was conscious of a pang of disappointment, of a hunger to look again upon his home. But to shift the current of his thoughts just then came two of his officers—Othmani and Ali, who had been muttering one with the other. As they overtook him, Othmani set now a hand upon his arm, and pointed down towards the twinkling lights of Smithick and Penycumwick.

"My lord," he cried, "there will be lads and maidens there should fetch fat prices in the Sôk-el-Abeed."

"No doubt," said Sakr-el-Bahr, scarce heeding him, heeding indeed little in this world but his longings to look upon Penarrow.

"Why, then, my lord, shall I take fifty True-Believers and make a raid upon them? It were an easy task, all unsuspicious as they must be of our presence."

Sakr-el-Bahr came out of his musings. "Othmani," said he, "art a fool, the very father of fools, else wouldst thou have come to know by now that those who once were of my own race, those of the land from which I am sprung, are sacred to me. Here we take no slave but these we have. On, then, in the name of Allah!"

But Othmani was not yet silenced. "And is our perilous voyage across these unknown seas into this far heathen land to be rewarded by no more than just these two captives? Is that a raid worthy of Sakr-el-Bahr?"

"Leave Sakr-el-Bahr to judge," was the curt answer.

"But reflect, my lord: there is another who will judge. How shall our Basha, the glorious Asad-ed-Din, welcome thy return with such poor spoils as these? What questions will he set thee, and what account shalt thou render him for having imperiled the lives of all these True-Believers upon the seas for so little profit?"

"He shall ask me what he pleases, and I shall answer what I please and as Allah prompts me. On, I say!"

And on they went, Sakr-el-Bahr conscious now of little but the

warmth of that body upon his shoulder, and knowing not, so tumul-
tuous were his emotions, whether it fired him to love or hate.

They gained the beach; they reached the ship whose very presence had continued unsuspected. The breeze was fresh and they
stood away at once. By sunrise there was no more sign of them than
there had been at sunset, there was no more clue to the way they
had taken than to the way they had come. It was as if they had
dropped from the skies in the night upon that Cornish coast, and
but for the mark of their swift, silent passage, but for the absence of
Rosamund and Lionel Tressilian, the thing must have been
accounted no more than a dream of those few who had witnessed it.

Aboard the carack, Sakr-el-Bahr bestowed Rosamund in the
cabin over the quarter, taking the precaution to lock the door that
led to the stern-gallery. Lionel he ordered to be dropped into a
dark hole under the hatchway, there to lie and meditate upon the
retribution that had overtaken him until such time as his brother
should have determined upon his fate—for this was a matter upon
which the renegade was still undecided.

Himself he lay under the stars that night and thought of many
things. One of these things, which plays some part in the story,
though it is probable that it played but a slight one in his thoughts,
was begotten of the words Othmani had used. What, indeed, would
be Asad's welcome of him on his return if he sailed into Algiers with
nothing more to show for that long voyage and the imperiling of the
lives of two hundred True-Believers than just those two captives
whom he intended, moreover, to retain for himself? What capital
would not be made out of that circumstance by his enemies in
Algiers and by Asad's Sicilian wife who hated him with all the bitterness of a hatred that had its roots in the fertile soil of jealousy?

This may have spurred him in the cool dawn to a very daring
and desperate enterprise which Destiny sent his way in the shape
of a tall-masted Dutchman homeward bound. He gave chase, for
all that he was full conscious that the battle he invited was one of

which his corsairs had no experience, and one upon which they must have hesitated to venture with another leader than himself. But the star of Sakr-el-Bahr was a star that never led to aught but victory, and their belief in him, the very Javelin of Allah, overcame any doubts that may have been begotten of finding themselves upon an unfamiliar craft and on a rolling, unfamiliar sea.

This fight is given in great detail by my Lord Henry from the particulars afforded him by Jasper Leigh. But it differs in no great particular from other sea-fights, and it is none of my purpose to surfeit you with such recitals. Enough to say that it was stern and fierce, entailing great loss to both combatants; that cannon played little part in it, for knowing the quality of his men Sakr-el-Bahr made haste to run in and grapple. He prevailed of course as he must ever prevail by the very force of his personality and the might of his example. He was the first to leap aboard the Dutchman, clad in mail and whirling his great scimitar, and his men poured after him shouting his name and that of Allah in a breath.

Such was ever his fury in an engagement that it infected and inspired his followers. It did so now, and the shrewd Dutchmen came to perceive that this heathen horde was as a body to which he supplied the brain and soul. They attacked him fiercely in groups, intent at all costs upon cutting him down, convinced almost by instinct that were he felled the victory would easily be theirs. And in the end they succeeded. A Dutch pike broke some links of his mail and dealt him a flesh wound which went unheeded by him in his fury; a Dutch rapier found the breach thus made in his defences, and went through it to stretch him bleeding upon the deck. Yet he staggered up, knowing as fully as did they that if he succumbed then all was lost. Armed now with a short axe which he had found under his hand when he went down, he hacked a way to the bulwarks, set his back against the timbers, and hoarse of voice, ghastly of face, spattered with the blood of his wound he urged on his men until the victory was theirs—and this was fortunately soon.

And then, as if he had been sustained by no more than the very force of his will, he sank down in a heap among the dead and wounded huddled against the vessel's bulwarks.

Grief-stricken his corsairs bore him back aboard the carack. Were he to die then was their victory a barren one indeed. They laid him on a couch prepared for him amidships on the main deck, where the vessel's pitching was least discomfiting. A Moorish surgeon came to tend him, and pronounced his hurt a grievous one, but not so grievous as to close the gates of hope.

This pronouncement gave the corsairs all the assurance they required. It could not be that the Gardener would already pluck so fragrant a fruit from Allah's garden. The Pitiful must spare Sakr-el-Bahr to continue the glory of Islam.

Yet they were come to the straits of Gibraltar before his fever abated and he recovered complete consciousness, to learn of the final issue of that hazardous fight into which he had led those children of the Prophet.

The Dutchman, Othmani informed him, was following in their wake, with Ali and some others aboard her, steering ever in the wake of the carack which continued to be navigated by the Nasrani dog, Jasper Leigh. When Sakr-el-Bahr learnt the value of the capture, when he was informed that in addition to a hundred able-bodied men under the hatches, to be sold as slaves in the Sôk-el-Abeed, there was a cargo of gold and silver, pearls, amber, spices, and ivory, and such lesser matters as gorgeous silken fabrics, rich beyond anything that had ever been seen upon the seas at any one time, he felt that the blood he had shed had not been wasted.

Let him sail safely into Algiers with these two ships both captured in the name of Allah and his Prophet, one of them an argosy so richly fraught, a floating treasure-house, and he need have little fear of what his enemies and the crafty evil Sicilian woman might have wrought against him in his absence.

Then he made inquiry touching his two English captives, to be informed that Othmani had taken charge of them, and that he had continued the treatment meted out to them by Sakr-el-Bahr himself when first they were brought aboard.

He was satisfied, and fell into a gentle healing sleep, whilst, on the decks above, his followers rendered thanks to Allah the Pitying the Pitiful, the Master of the Day of Judgment, who Alone is All Wise, All-Knowing.

CHAPTER V

THE LION OF
THE FAITH

ASAD-ED-DIN, the Lion of the Faith, Basha of Algiers,
walked in the evening cool in the orchard of the Kasbah
upon the heights above the city, and at his side, stepping
daintily, came Fenzileh, his wife, the first lady of his hareem, whom
eighteen years ago he had carried off in his mighty arms from that
little whitewashed village above the Straits of Messina which his
followers had raided.

She had been a lissom maid of sixteen in those far-off days, the
child of humble peasant-folk, and she had gone uncomplaining to
the arms of her swarthy ravisher. To-day, at thirty-six, she was still
beautiful, more beautiful indeed than when first she had fired the
passion of Asad-Reis—as he then was, one of the captains of the
famous Ali-Basha. There were streaks of red in her heavy black
tresses, her skin was of a soft pearliness that seemed translucent,
her eyes were large, of a golden-brown, agleam with somber fires,
her lips were full and sensuous. She was tall and of a shape that in
Europe would have been accounted perfect, which is to say that
she was a thought too slender for Oriental taste; she moved along
beside her lord with a sinuous, languorous grace, gently stirring her

fan of ostrich plumes. She was unveiled; indeed it was her immod-
est habit to go naked of face more often than was seemly, which is
but the least of the many undesirable infidel ways which had survived her induction into the Faith of Islam—a necessary step
before Asad, who was devout to the point of bigotry, would consent
to make her his wife. He had found her such a wife as it is certain
he could never have procured at home; a woman who, not content
to be his toy, the plaything of his idle hour, insinuated herself into
affairs, demanded and obtained his confidences, and exerted over
him much the same influence as the wife of a European prince
might exert over her consort. In the years during which he had
lain under the spell of her ripening beauty he had accepted the
situation willingly enough; later, when he would have curtailed
her interferences, it was too late; she had taken a firm grip of the
reins, and Asad was in no better case than many a European husband—an anomalous and outrageous condition this for a Basha of
the Prophet's House. It was also a dangerous one for Fenzileh; for
should the burden of her at any time become too heavy for her lord
there was a short and easy way by which he could be rid of it. Do
not suppose her so foolish as not to have realized this—she realized
it fully; but her Sicilian spirit was daring to the point of recklessness; her very dauntlessness which had enabled her to seize a control so unprecedented in a Muslim wife urged her to maintain it in
the face of all risks.

Dauntless was she now, as she paced there in the cool of the
orchard, under the pink and white petals of the apricots, the flaming scarlet of pomegranate blossoms, and through orange-groves
where the golden fruit glowed amid foliage of somber green. She
was at her eternal work of poisoning the mind of her lord against
Sakr-el-Bahr, and in her maternal jealousy she braved the dangers
of such an undertaking, fully aware of how dear to the heart of
Asad-ed-Din was that absent renegade corsair. It was this very
affection of the Basha's for his lieutenant that was the fomenter of
her own hate of Sakr-el-Bahr, for it was an affection that tran-

scended Asad's love for his own son and hers, and it led to the common rumor that for Sakr-el-Bahr was reserved the high destiny of succeeding Asad in the Bashalik.

"I tell thee thou'rt abused by him, O source of my life."

"I hear thee," answered Asad sourly. "And were thine own hearing less infirm, woman, thou wouldst have heard me answer thee that thy words weigh for naught with me against his deeds. Words may be but a mask upon our thoughts; deeds are ever the expression of them. Bear thou that in mind, O Fenzileh."

"Do I not bear in mind thine every word, O fount of wisdom?" she protested, and left him, as she often did, in doubt whether she fawned or sneered. "And it is his deeds I would have speak for him, not indeed my poor words and still less his own."

"Then, by the head of Allah, let those same deeds speak, and be thou silent."

The harsh tone of his reproof and the scowl upon his haughty face, gave her pause for a moment. He turned about.

"Come!" he said. "Soon it will be the hour of prayer." And he paced back towards the yellow huddle of walls of the Kasbah that overtopped the green of that fragrant place.

He was a tall, gaunt man, stooping slightly at the shoulders under the burden of his years; but his eagle face was masterful, and some lingering embers of his youth still glowed in his dark eyes. Thoughtfully, with a jeweled hand, he stroked his long white beard; with the other he leaned upon her soft plump arm, more from habit than for support, for he was full vigorous still.

High in the blue overhead a lark burst suddenly into song, and from the depths of the orchard came a gentle murmur of doves as if returning thanks for the lessening of the great heat now that the sun was sinking rapidly towards the world's edge and the shadows were lengthening.

Came Fenzileh's voice again, more musical than either, yet laden with words of evil, poison wrapped in honey.

"O my dear lord, thou'rt angered with me now. Woe me! that never may I counsel thee for thine own glory as my heart prompts me, but I must earn thy coldness."

"Abuse not him I love," said the Basha shortly. "I have told thee so full oft already."

She nestled closer to him, and her voice grew softer, more akin to the amorous cooing of the doves. "And do I not love thee, O master of my soul? Is there in all the world a heart more faithful to thee than mine? Is not thy life my life? Have not my days been all devoted to the perfecting of thine happiness? And wilt thou then frown upon me if I fear for thee at the hands of an intruder of yesterday?"

"Fear for me?" he echoed, and laughed jeeringly. "What shouldst thou fear for me from Sakr-el-Bahr?"

"What all believers must ever fear from one who is no true Muslim, from one who makes a mock and travesty of the True Faith that he may gain advancement."

The Basha checked in his stride, and turned upon her angrily.

"May thy tongue rot, thou mother of lies!"

"I am as the dust beneath thy feet, O my sweet lord, yet am I not what thine heedless anger calls me."

"Heedless?" quoth he. "Not heedless but righteous to hear one whom the Prophet guards, who is the very Javelin of Islam against the breast of the unbeliever, who carries the scourge of Allah against the infidel Frankish pigs, so maligned by thee! No more, I say! Lest I bid thee make good thy words, and pay the liar's price if thou shouldst fail."

"And should I fear the test?" she countered, nothing daunted. "I tell thee, O father of Marzak, that I should hail it gladly. Why, hear me now. Thou settest store by deeds, not words. Tell me, then, is it the deed of a True-Believer to waste substance upon infidel slaves, to purchase them that he may set them free?"

Asad moved on in silence. That erstwhile habit of Sakr-el-Bahr's was one not easy to condone. It had occasioned him his moments of uneasiness, and more than once had he taxed his lieutenant with the practice ever to receive the same answer, the answer which he now made to Fenzileh. "For every slave that he so manumitted, he brought a dozen into bondage."

"Perforce, else would he be called to account. 'T was so much dust he flung into the face of true Muslimeen. Those manumissions prove a lingering fondness for the infidel country whence he springs. Is there room for that in the heart of a true member of the Prophet's immortal House? Hast ever known me languish for the Sicilian shore from which in thy might thou wrested me, or have I ever besought of thee the life of a single Sicilian infidel in all these years that I have lived to serve thee? Such longings are betrayed, I say, by such a practice, and such longings could have no place in one who had uprooted infidelity from his heart. And now this voyage of his beyond the seas—risking a vessel that he captured from the arch-enemy of Islam, which is not his to risk but thine in whose name he captured it; and together with it he imperils the lives of two hundred True-Believers. To what end? To bear him overseas, perchance that he may look again upon the unhallowed land that gave him birth. So Biskaine reported. And what if he should founder on the way?"

"Thou at least wouldst be content, thou fount of malice," growled Asad.

"Call me harsh names, O sun that warms me! Am I not thine to use and abuse at thy sweet pleasure? Pour salt upon the heart thou woundest; since it is thy hand I'll never murmur a complaint. But heed me—heed my words; or since words are of no account with thee, then heed his deeds which I am drawing to thy tardy notice. Heed them, I say, as my love bids me even though thou shouldst give me to be whipped or slain for my temerity."

"Woman, thy tongue is like the clapper of a bell with the devil swinging from the rope. What else dost thou impute?"

"Naught else, since thou dost but mock me, withdrawing thy love from thy fond slave."

"The praise to Allah, then," said he. "Come, it is the hour of prayer!"

But he praised Allah too soon. Woman-like, though she protested she had done, she had scarce begun as yet.

"There is thy son, O father of Marzak."

"There is, O mother of Marzak."

"And a man's son should be the partner of his soul. Yet is Marzak passed over for this foreign upstart; yet does this Nasrani of yesterday hold the place in thy heart and at thy side that should be Marzak's."

"Could Marzak fill that place?" he asked. "Could that beardless boy lead men as Sakr-el-Bahr leads them, or wield the scimitar against the foes of Islam and increase as Sakr-el-Bahr increases the glory of the Prophet's Holy Law upon the earth?"

"If Sakr-el-Bahr does this, he does it by thy favor, O my lord. And so might Marzak, young though he be. Sakr-el-Bahr is but what thou hast made him—no more, no less."

"There art thou wrong, indeed, O mother of error. Sakr-el-Bahr is what Allah hath made him. He is what Allah wills. He shall become what Allah wills. Hast yet to learn that Allah has bound the fate of each man about his neck?"

And then a golden glory suffused the deep sapphire of the sky heralding the setting of the sun and made an end of that altercation, conducted by her with a daring as singular as the patience that had endured it. He quickened his steps in the direction of the courtyard. That golden glow paled as swiftly as it had spread, and night fell as suddenly as if a curtain had been dropped.

In the purple gloom that followed the white cloisters of the courtyard glowed with a faintly luminous pearliness. Dark forms of slaves stirred as Asad entered from the garden followed by Fenzileh, her head now veiled in a thin blue silken gauze. She flashed across the quadrangle and vanished through one of the archways, even as the distant voice of a Mueddin broke plaintively upon the brooding stillness reciting the Shehad—

"La illaha, illa Allah! Wa Muhammad er Rasool Allah!"

A slave spread a carpet, a second held a great silver bowl, into which a third poured water. The Basha, having washed, turned his face towards Mecca, and testified to the unity of Allah, the Compassionate, the Merciful, King of the Day of Judgment, whilst the cry of the Meuddin went echoing over the city from minaret to minaret.

As he rose from his devotions, there came a quick sound of steps without, and a sharp summons. Turkish janissaries of the Basha's guard, invisible almost in their flowing black garments, moved to answer that summons and challenge those who came.

From the dark vaulted entrance of the courtyard leapt a gleam of lanterns containing tiny clay lamps in which burned a wick that was nourished by mutton fat. Asad, waiting to learn who came, halted at the foot of the white glistening steps, whilst from doors and lattices of the palace flooded light to suffuse the courtyard and set the marbles shimmering.

A dozen Nubian javelin-men advanced, then ranged themselves aside whilst into the light stepped the imposing, gorgeously robed figure of Asad's wazeer, Tsamanni. After him came another figure in mail that clanked faintly and glimmered as he moved.

"Peace and the Prophet's blessings upon thee, O mighty Asad!" was the wazeer's greeting.

"And peace upon thee, Tsamanni," was the answer. "Art the bearer of news?"

"Of great and glorious tidings, O exalted one! Sakr-el-Bahr is returned."

"The praise to Him!" exclaimed the Basha, with uplifted hands; and there was no mistaking the thrill of his voice.

There fell a soft step behind him and a shadow from the doorway. He turned. A graceful stripling in turban and caftan of cloth of gold salaamed to him from the topmost step. And as he came upright and the light of the lanterns fell full upon his face the astonishingly white fairness of it was revealed—a woman's face it might have been, so softly rounded was it in its beardlessness.

Asad smiled wrily in his white beard, guessing that the boy had been sent by his ever-watchful mother to learn who came and what the tidings that they bore.

"Thou hast heard, Marzak?" he said. "Sakr-el-Bahr is returned."

"Victoriously, I hope," the lad lied glibly.

"Victorious beyond aught that was ever known," replied Tsamanni. "He sailed at sunset into the harbor, his company aboard two mighty Frankish ships, which are but the lesser part of the great spoil he brings."

"Allah is great," was the Basha's glad welcome of this answer to those insidious promptings of his Sicilian wife. "Why does he not come in person with his news?"

"His duty keeps him yet awhile aboard, my lord," replied the wazeer. "But he hath sent his kayia Othmani here to tell the tale of it."

"Thrice welcome be thou, Othmani." He beat his hands together, whereat slaves placed cushions for him upon the ground. He sat, and beckoned Marzak to his side. "And now thy tale!"

And Othmani standing forth related how they had voyaged to distant England in the ship that Sakr-el-Bahr had captured, through seas that no corsair yet had ever crossed, and how on their return they had engaged a Dutchman that was their superior in strength and numbers; how none the less Sakr-el-Bahr had wrested victory by the help of Allah, his protector, how he had been dealt a wound that must have slain any but one miraculously preserved for the greater glory of Islam, and of the surpassing wealth of the booty which at dawn to-morrow should be laid at Asad's feet for his division of it.

CHAPTER VI

THE CONVERT

THAT TALE of Othmani's being borne anon to Fenzileh by her son was gall and wormwood to her jealous soul. Evil enough to know that Sakr-el-Bahr was returned in spite of the fervent prayers for his foundering which she had addressed both to the God of her forefathers and to the God of her adoption. But that he should have returned in triumph bringing with him heavy spoils that must exalt him further in the affection of Asad and the esteem of the people was bitterness indeed. It left her mute and stricken, bereft even of the power to curse him.

Anon, when her mind recovered from the shock she turned it to the consideration of what at first had seemed a trivial detail in Othmani's tale as reported by Marzak.

"It is most singularly odd that he should have undertaken that long voyage to England to wrest thence just those two captives; that being there he should not have raided in true corsair fashion and packed his ship with slaves. Most singularly odd!"

They were alone behind the green lattices through which filtered the perfumes of the garden and the throbbing of a nightingale's voice laden with the tale of its love for the rose. Fenzileh reclined upon a divan that was spread with silken Turkey carpets, and one of her gold-embroidered slippers had dropped from her henna-stained toes. Her lovely arms were raised to support her head, and she stared up at the lamp of many colors that hung from the fretted ceiling.

Marzak paced the length of the chamber back and forth, and there was silence save for the soft swish of his slippers along the floor.

"Well?" she asked him impatiently at last. "Does it not seem odd to thee?"

"Odd, indeed, O my mother," the youth replied, coming to a halt before her.

"And canst think of naught that was the cause of it?"

"The cause of it?" quoth he, his lovely young face, so closely modeled upon her own, looking blank and vacant.

"Ay, the cause of it," she cried impatiently. "Canst do naught but stare? Am I the mother of a fool? Wilt thou simper and gape and trifle away thy days whilst that dog-descended Frank tramples thee underfoot, using thee but as a stepping-stone to the power that should be thine own? And that be so, Marzak, I would thou hadst been strangled in my womb."

He recoiled before the Italian fury of her, was dully resentful even, suspecting that in such words from a woman, were she twenty times his mother, there was something dishonoring to his manhood.

"What can I do?" he cried.

"Dost ask me? Art thou not a man to think and act? I tell thee that misbegotten son of a Christian and a Jew will trample thee in the dust. He is greedy as the locust, wily as the serpent, and ferocious as the panther. By Allah! I would I had never borne a son. Rather might men point at me the finger of scorn and call me mother of the wind than that I should have brought forth a man who knows not how to be a man."

"Show me the way," he cried. "Set me a task; tell me what to do and thou shalt not find me lacking, O my mother. Until then spare me these insults, or I come no more to thee."

At this threat that strange woman heaved herself up from her soft couch. She ran to him and flung her arms about his neck, set her cheek against his own. Not eighteen years in the Basha's hareem had stifled the European mother in her, the passionate Sicilian woman, fierce as a tiger in her maternal love.

"O my child, my lovely boy," she almost sobbed. "It is my fear for thee that makes me harsh. If I am angry it is but my love that speaks, my rage for thee to see another come usurping the place beside thy father that should be thine. Ah! but we will prevail, sweet son of mine. I shall find a way to return that foreign offal to the dung-heap whence it sprang. Trust me, O Marzak! Sh! Thy father comes. Away! Leave me alone with him."

She was wise in that, for she knew that alone Asad was more easily controlled by her, since the pride was absent which must compel him to turn and rend her did she speak so before others. Marzak vanished behind the screen of fretted sandalwood that masked one doorway even as Asad loomed in the other.

He came forward smiling, his slender brown fingers combing his long beard, his white djellaba trailing behind him along the ground.

"Thou hast heard, not a doubt, O Fenzileh," said he. "Art thou answered enough?"

She sank down again upon her cushions and idly considered herself in a steel mirror set in silver.

"Answered?" she echoed lazily, with infinite scorn and a hint of rippling contemptuous laughter running through the word. "Answered indeed. Sakr-el-Bahr risks the lives of two hundred children of Islam and a ship that being taken was become the property of the State upon a voyage to England that has no object but the capturing of two slaves—two slaves, when, had his purpose been sincere, it might have been two hundred."

"Ha! And is that all that thou hast heard?" he asked her, mocking in his turn.

"All that signifies," she replied, still mirroring herself. "I heard as a matter of lesser import that on his return, meeting fortuitously a Frankish ship that chanced to be richly laden, he seized it in thy name."

"Fortuitously, sayest thou?"

"What else?" She lowered the mirror, and her bold, insolent eyes met his own quite fearlessly. "Thou'lt not tell me that it was any part of his design when he went forth?"

He frowned; his head sank slowly in thought. Observing the advantage gained she thrust it home.

"It was a lucky wind that blew that Dutchman into his path, and luckier still her being so richly fraught that he may dazzle thine eyes with the sight of gold and gems, and so blind thee to the real purpose of his voyage."

"Its real purpose?" he asked dully. "What was its real purpose?"

She smiled a smile of infinite knowledge to hide her utter ignorance, her inability to supply even a reason that should wear an air of truth.

"Dost ask me, O perspicuous Asad? Are not thine eyes as sharp, thy wits as keen at least as mine, that what is clear to me should be hidden from thee? Or hath this Sakr-el-Bahr bewitched thee with enchantments of Babyl?"

He strode to her and caught her wrist in a cruelly rough grip of his sinewy old hand.

"His purpose, thou jade! Pour out the foulness of thy mind. Speak!"

She sat up, flushed and defiant.

"I will not speak," said she.

"Thou wilt not? Now, by the Head of Allah! dost dare to stand before my face and defy me, thy Lord? I'll have thee whipped, Fenzileh. I have been too tender of thee these many years—so tender that thou hast forgot the rods that await the disobedient wife. Speak then ere thy flesh is bruised or speak thereafter, at thy pleasure."

"I will not," she repeated. "Though I be flung to the hooks, not another word will I say of Sakr-el-Bahr. Shall I unveil the truth to be spurned and scorned and dubbed a liar and the mother of lies?" Then abruptly changing she fell to weeping. "O source of my life!" she cried to him, "how cruelly unjust to me thou art!" She was groveling now, a thing of supplest grace, her lovely arms entwining his knees. "When my love for thee drives me to utter what I see, I earn but thy anger, which is more than I can endure. I swoon beneath the weight of it."

He flung her off impatiently. "What a weariness is a woman's tongue!" he cried, and stalked out again, convinced from past experiences that did he linger he would be whelmed in a torrent of words.

But her poison was shrewdly administered, and slowly did its work. It abode in his mind to torture him with the doubts that were its very essence. No reason, however well founded, that she might have urged for Sakr-el-Bahr's strange conduct could have been half so insidious as her suggestion that there was a reason. It gave him something vague and intangible to consider. Something that he could not repel since it had no substance he could grapple with. Impatiently he awaited the morning and the coming of Sakr-el-Bahr himself, but he no longer awaited it with the ardent whole-hearted eagerness as of a father awaiting the coming of a beloved son.

Sakr-el-Bahr himself paced the poop deck of the carack and watched the lights perish one by one in the little town that straggled up the hillside before him. The moon came up and bathed it in a white hard light, throwing sharp inky shadows of rustling date palm and spearlike minaret, and flinging shafts of silver athwart the peaceful bay.

His wound was healed and he was fully himself once more. Two days ago he had come on deck for the first time since the fight with the Dutchman, and he had spent there the greater portion of the time since then. Once only had he visited his captives. He had risen from his couch to repair straight to the cabin in the poop where Rosamund was confined. He had found her pale and very wistful, but with her courage entirely unbroken. The Godolphins were a stiff-necked race, and Rosamund bore in her frail body the spirit of a man. She looked up when he entered, started a little in surprise to see him at last, for it was the first time he stood before her since he had carried her off from Arwenack some four weeks ago. Then she had averted her eyes, and sat there, elbows on the table, as if carved of wood, as if blind to his presence and deaf to his words.

To the expressions of regret—and they were sincere, for already he repented him his unpremeditated act so far as she was concerned—she returned no slightest answer, gave no sign indeed that she heard a word of it. Baffled, he stood gnawing his lip a moment, and gradually, unreasonably perhaps, anger welled up from his heart. He turned and went out again. Next he had visited his brother, to consider in silence a moment the haggard, wild-eyed, unshorn wretch who shrank and cowered before him in the consciousness of guilt. At last he returned to the deck, and there, as I have said, he spent the greater portion of the last three days of that strange voyage, reclining for the most part in the sun and gathering strength from its ardor.

To-night as he paced under the moon a stealthy shadow crept up the companion to call him gently by his English name—

"Sir Oliver!"

He started as if a ghost had suddenly leapt up to greet him. It was Jasper Leigh who hailed him thus.

"Come up," he said. And when the fellow stood before him on the poop—"I have told you already that here is no Sir Oliver. I am Oliver-Reis or Sakr-el-Bahr, as you please, one of the Faithful of the Prophet's House. And now what is your will?"

"Have I not served you faithfully and well?" quoth Captain Leigh.

"Who has denied it?"

"None. But neither has any acknowledged it. When you lay wounded below it had been an easy thing for me to ha' played the traitor. I might ha' sailed these ships into the mouth of Tagus. I might so, by God!"

"You'ld have been carved in pieces on the spot," said Sakr-el-Bahr.

"I might have hugged the land and run the risk of capture and then claimed my liberation from captivity."

"And found yourself back on the galleys of his Catholic Majesty. But there! I grant that you have dealt loyally by me. You have kept your part of the bond. I shall keep mine, never doubt it."

"I do not. But your part of the bond was to send me home again."

"Well?"

"The hell of it is that I know not where to find a home, I know not where home may be after all these years. If ye send me forth, I shall become a wanderer of no account."

"What else am I to do with you?"

"Faith now, I am as full weary of Christians and Christendom as you was yourself when the Muslims took the galley on which you toiled. I am a man of parts, Sir Ol— Sakr-el-Bahr. No better navigator ever sailed a ship from an English port, and I ha' seen a mort o' fighting and know the art of it upon the sea. Can ye make naught of me here?"

"You would become a renegade like me?" His tone was bitter.

"I ha' been thinking that 'renegade' is a word that depends upon which side you're on. I'ld prefer to say that I've a wish to be converted to the faith of Mahound."

"Converted to the faith of piracy and plunder and robbery upon the seas is what you mean," said Sakr-el-Bahr.

"Nay, now. To that I should need no converting, for all that I were afore," Captain Leigh admitted frankly. "I ask but to sail under another flag than the Jolly Roger."

"You'll need to abjure strong drink," said Sakr-el-Bahr.

"There be compensations," said Master Leigh.

Sakr-el-Bahr considered. The rogue's appeal smote a responsive chord in his heart. It would be good to have a man of his own race beside him, even though it were but such a rascal as this.

"Be it as you will," he said at last. "You deserve to be hanged in spite of what promises I made you. But no matter for that. So that you become a Muslim I will take you to serve beside me, one of my own lieutenants to begin with, and so long as you are loyal to me, Jasper, all will be well. But at the first sign of faithlessness, a rope and the yard-arm, my friend, and an airy dance into hell for you."

The rascally skipper stooped in his emotion, caught up Sakr-el-Bahr's hand and bore it to his lips.

"It is agreed," he said. "Ye have shown me mercy who have little deserved it from you. Never fear for my loyalty. My life belongs to you, and worthless thing though it may be, ye may do with it as ye please."

Despite himself Sakr-el-Bahr tightened his grip upon the rogue's hand, and Jasper shuffled off and down the companion again, touched to the heart for once in his rough villainous life by a clemency that he knew to be undeserved, but which he swore should be deserved ere all was done.

CHAPTER VII

MARZAK-BEN-ASAD

IT TOOK no less than forty camels to convey the cargo of that
Dutch argosy from the mole to the Kasbah, and the procession—carefully marshaled by Sakr-el-Bahr, who knew the
value of such pageants to impress the mob—was such as never yet
had been seen in the narrow streets of Algiers upon the return of
any corsair. It was full worthy of the greatest Muslim conqueror
that sailed the seas, of one who, not content to keep to the tideless
Mediterranean as had hitherto been the rule of his kind, had ventured forth upon the wider ocean.

Ahead marched a hundred of his rovers in their short caftans of
every conceivable color, their waists swathed in gaudy scarves,
some of which supported a very arsenal of assorted cutlery; many
wore body armor of mail and the gleaming spike of a casque thrust
up above their turbans. After them, dejected and in chains, came
the five score prisoners taken aboard the Dutchman, urged along
by the whips of the corsairs who flanked them. Then marched
another regiment of corsairs, and after these the long line of
stately, sneering camels, shuffling cumbrously along and led by

shouting Saharowis. After them followed yet more corsairs, and then mounted, on a white Arab jennet, his head swathed in a turban of cloth of gold, came Sakr-el-Bahr. In the narrower streets, with their white and yellow washed houses, which presented blank windowless walls broken here and there by no more than a slit to admit light and air, the spectators huddled themselves fearfully into doorways to avoid being crushed to death by the camels, whose burdens bulging on either side entirely filled those narrow ways. But the more open spaces, such as the strand on either side of the mole, the square before the sôk, and the approaches of Asad's fortress, were thronged with a motley roaring crowd. There were stately Moors in flowing robes cheek by jowl with half-naked blacks from the Sus and the Draa; lean, enduring Arabs in their spotless white djellabas rubbed shoulders with Berbers from the highlands in black camel-hair cloaks; there were Levantine Turks, and Jewish refugees from Spain ostentatiously dressed in European garments, tolerated there because bound to the Moor by ties of common suffering and common exile from that land that once had been their own.

Under the glaring African sun this amazing crowd stood assembled to welcome Sakr-el-Bahr; and welcome him it did, with such vocal thunder that an echo of it from the mole reached the very Kasbah on the hill-top to herald his approach.

By the time, however, that he reached the fortress his procession had dwindled by more than half. At the sôk his forces had divided, and his corsairs, headed by Othmani, had marched the captives away to the bagnio—or banyard, as my Lord Henry calls it—whilst the camels had continued up the hill. Under the great gateway of the Kasbah they padded into the vast courtyard to be ranged along two sides of it by their Saharowi drivers, and there brought clumsily to their knees. After them followed but some two score corsairs as a guard of honor to their leader. They took their stand upon either side of the gateway after profoundly salaaming to Asad-ed-Din. The Basha sat in the shade of an awning enthroned upon a divan, attended by his wazeer Tsamanni and by Marzak, and guarded by a half-dozen janissaries, whose sable garments made an effective background to the green and gold of his jeweled robes. In his white turban glowed an emerald crescent.

The Basha's countenance was dark and brooding as he watched the advent of that line of burdened camels. His thoughts were still laboring with the doubt of Sakr-el-Bahr which Fenzileh's crafty speech and craftier reticence had planted in them. But at sight of the corsair leader himself his countenance cleared suddenly, his eyes sparkled, and he rose to his feet to welcome him as a father might welcome a son who had been through perils in a service dear to both.

Sakr-el-Bahr entered the courtyard on foot, having dismounted at the gate. Tall and imposing, with his head high and his forked beard thrusting forward, he stalked with great dignity to the foot of the divan, followed by Ali and a mahogany-faced fellow, turbaned and red-bearded, in whom it needed more than a glance to recognize the rascally Jasper Leigh, now in all the panoply of your complete renegado.

Sakr-el-Bahr went down upon his knees and prostrated himself solemnly before his prince.

"The blessing of Allah and His peace upon thee, my lord," was his greeting.

And Asad, stooping to lift that splendid figure in his arms, gave him a welcome that caused the spying Fenzileh to clench her teeth behind the fretted lattice that concealed her.

"The praise to Allah and to our Lord Mahomet that thou art returned and in health, my son. Already hath my old heart been gladdened by the news of thy victories in the service of the Faith."

Then followed the display of all those riches wrested from the Dutch, and greatly though Asad's expectations had been fed already by Othmani, the sight now spread before his eyes by far exceeded all those expectations.

In the end all was dismissed to the treasury, and Tsamanni was bidden to go cast up the account of it and mark the share that fell to the portion of those concerned—for in these ventures all were partners, from the Basha himself, who represented the State, down to the meanest corsair who had manned the victorious vessels of the Faith, and each had his share of the booty, greater or less according to his rank, one twentieth of the total falling to Sakr-el-Bahr himself.

In the courtyard were left none but Asad, Marzak, and the janissaries, and Sakr-el-Bahr with Ali and Jasper. It was then that Sakr-el-Bahr presented his new officer to the Basha, as one upon whom the grace of Allah had descended, a great fighter and a skilled seaman, who had offered up his talents and his life to the service of Islam, who had been accepted by Sakr-el-Bahr, and stood now before Asad to be confirmed in his office.

Marzak interposed petulantly, to exclaim that already were there too many erstwhile Nasrani dogs in the ranks of the soldiers of the Faith, and that it was unwise to increase their number and presumptuous in Sakr-el-Bahr to take so much upon himself.

Sakr-el-Bahr measured him with an eye in which scorn and surprise were nicely blended.

"Dost say that it is presumptuous to win a convert to the banner of Our Lord Mahomet?" quoth he. "Go read the Most Perspicuous Book and see what is there enjoined as a duty upon every True-Believer. And bethink thee, O son of Asad, that when thou dost in thy little wisdom cast scorn upon those whom Allah has blessed and led from the night wherein they dwelt into the bright noontide of Faith, thou dost cast scorn upon me and upon thine own mother, which is but a little matter, and thou dost blaspheme the Blessed name of Allah, which is to tread the ways that lead unto the Pit."

Angry but defeated and silenced, Marzak fell back a step and stood biting his lip and glowering upon the corsair, what time Asad nodded his head and smiled approval.

"Verily art thou full learned in the True Belief, Sakr-el-Bahr," he said. "Thou art the very father of wisdom as of valor." And thereupon he gave welcome to Master Leigh, whom he hailed to the ranks of the Faithful under the designation of Jasper-Reis.

That done, the renegade and Ali were both dismissed, as were also the janissaries, who, quitting their position behind Asad, went to take their stand on guard at the gateway. Then the Basha beat his hands together, and to the slaves who came in answer to his summons he gave orders to set food, and he bade Sakr-el-Bahr to come sit beside him on the divan.

Water was brought that they might wash. That done, the slaves placed before them a savory stew of meat and eggs with olives, limes, and spices.

Asad broke bread with a reverently pronounced "Bismillah!" and dipped his fingers into the earthenware bowl, leading the way for Sakr-el-Bahr and Marzak, and as they ate he invited the corsair himself to recite the tale of his adventure.

When he had done so, and again Asad had praised him in high and loving terms, Marzak set him a question.

"Was it to obtain just these two English slaves that thou didst undertake this perilous voyage to that distant land?"

"That was but a part of my design," was the calm reply. "I went to rove the seas in the Prophet's service, as the result of my voyage gives proof."

"Thou didst not know that this Dutch argosy would cross thy path," said Marzak, in the very words his mother had prompted him.

"Did I not?" quoth Sakr-el-Bahr, and he smiled confidently, so confidently that Asad scarce needed to hear the words that so cunningly gave the lie to the innuendo. "Had I no trust in Allah, the All-wise, the All-knowing?"

"Well answered, by the Koran!" Asad approved him heartily, the more heartily since it rebutted insinuations which he desired above all to hear rebutted.

But Marzak did not yet own himself defeated. He had been soundly schooled by his guileful Sicilian mother.

"Yet there is something in all this I do not understand," he murmured, with false gentleness.

"All things are possible to Allah!" said Sakr-el-Bahr, in tones of incredulity, as if he suggested—not without a suspicion of irony—that it was incredible there should be anything in all the world that could elude the penetration of Marzak.

The youth bowed to him in acknowledgment. "Tell me, O mighty Sakr-el-Bahr," he begged, "how it came to pass that having reached those distant shores thou wert content to take thence but two poor slaves, since with thy followers and the favor of the All-seeing thou might easily have taken fifty times that number." And he looked ingenuously into the corsair's swarthy, rugged face, whilst Asad frowned thoughtfully, for the thought was one that had occurred to him already.

It became necessary that Sakr-el-Bahr should lie to clear himself. Here no high-sounding phrase of Faith would answer. An explanation was unavoidable, and he was conscious that he could not afford one that did not go a little lame.

"Why, as to that," said he, "these prisoners were wrested from the first house upon which we came, and their capture occasioned some alarm. Moreover, it was night-time when we landed, and I dared not adventure the lives of my followers by taking them farther from the ship and attacking a village which might have risen to cut off our good retreat."

The frown remained stamped upon the brow of Asad, as Marzak slyly observed.

"Yet Othmani," said he, "urged thee to fall upon a slumbering village all unconscious of thy presence, and thou didst refuse."

Asad looked up sharply at that, and Sakr-el-Bahr realized with a tightening about the heart something of the undercurrents at work

against him and all the pains that had been taken to glean information that might be used to his undoing.

"Is it so?" demanded Asad, looking from his son to his lieutenant with that lowering look that rendered his face evil and cruel.

Sakr-el-Bahr took a high tone. He met Asad's glance with an eye
of challenge.

"And if it were so, my lord?" he demanded.

"I asked thee is it so?"

"Ay, but knowing thy wisdom I disbelieved my ears," said
Sakr-el-Bahr. "Shall it signify what Othmani may have said? Do I
take my orders or am I to be guided by Othmani? If so, best set
Othmani in my place, give him the command and the responsibility
for the lives of the Faithful who fight beside him." He ended with
an indignant snort.

"Thou art over-quick to anger," Asad reproved him, scowling still.

"And by the Head of Allah, who will deny my right to it? Am I
to conduct such an enterprise as this from which I am returned
laden with spoils that might well be the fruits of a year's raiding, to
be questioned by a beardless stripling as to why I was not guided by
Othmani?"

He heaved himself up and stood towering there in the intensity
of a passion that was entirely simulated. He must bluster here,
and crush down suspicion with whorling periods and broad, fierce
gesture.

"To what should Othmani have guided me?" he demanded
scornfully. "Could he have guided me to more than I have this day
laid at thy feet? What I have done speaks eloquently with its own
voice. What he would have had me do might well have ended in
disaster. Had it so ended, would the blame of it have fallen upon
Othmani? Nay, by Allah! but upon me. And upon me rests then the
credit, and let none dare question it without better cause."

Now these were daring words to address to the tyrant Asad, and
still more daring was the tone, the light hard eyes aflash and the
sweeping gestures of contempt with which they were delivered.

But of his ascendancy over the Basha there was no doubt. And here now was proof of it.

Asad almost cowered before his fury. The scowl faded from his face to be replaced by an expression of dismay.

"Nay, nay, Sakr-el-Bahr, this tone!" he cried.

Sakr-el-Bahr, having slammed the door of conciliation in the face of the Basha, now opened it again. He became instantly submissive.

"Forgive it," he said. "Blame the devotion of thy servant to thee and to the Faith he serves with little reck to life. In this very expedition was I wounded nigh unto death. The livid scar of it is a dumb witness to my zeal. Where are thy scars, Marzak?"

Marzak quailed before the sudden blaze of that question, and Sakr-el-Bahr laughed softly in contempt.

"Sit," Asad bade him. "I have been less than just."

"Thou art the very fount and spring of justice, O my lord, as this thine admission proves," protested the corsair. He sat down again, folding his legs under him. "I will confess to you that being come so near to England in that cruise of mine I determined to land and seize one who some years ago did injure me, and between whom and me there was a score to settle. I exceeded my intentions in that I carried off two prisoners instead of one. These prisoners," he ran on, judging that the moment of reaction in Asad's mind was entirely favorable to the preferment of the request he had to make, "are not in the bagnio with the others. They are still confined aboard the carack I seized."

"And why is this?" quoth Asad, but without suspicion now.

"Because, my lord, I have a boon to ask in some reward for the service I have rendered."

"Ask it, my son."

"Give me leave to keep these captives for myself."

Asad considered him, frowning again slightly. Despite himself, despite his affection for Sakr-el-Bahr, and his desire to soothe him now that rankling poison of Fenzileh's infusing was at work again in his mind.

"My leave thou hast," said he. "But not the law's, and the law runs that no corsair shall subtract so much as the value of an asper from his booty until the division has been made and his own share allotted him," was the grave answer.

"The law?" quoth Sakr-el-Bahr. "But thou art the law, exalted lord."

"Not so, my son. The law is above the Basha, who must himself conform to it so that he be just and worthy of his high office. And the law I have recited thee applies even should the corsair raider be the Basha himself. These slaves of thine must forthwith be sent to the bagnio to join the others that to-morrow all may be sold in the sôk. See it done, Sakr-el-Bahr."

The corsair would have renewed his pleadings, but that his eye caught the eager white face of Marzak and the gleaming expectant eyes, looking so hopefully for his ruin. He checked, and bowed his head with an assumption of indifference.

"Name thou their price then, and forthwith will I pay it into thy treasury."

But Asad shook his head. "It is not for me to name their price, but for the buyers," he replied. "I might set the price too high, and that were unjust to thee, or too low, and that were unjust to others who would acquire them. Deliver them over to the bagnio."

"It shall be done," said Sakr-el-Bahr, daring to insist no further and dissembling his chagrin.

Very soon thereafter he departed upon that errand, giving orders, however, that Rosamund and Lionel should be kept apart from the other prisoners until the hour of the sale on the morrow, when perforce they must take their place with the rest.

Marzak lingered with his father after Oliver had taken his leave, and presently they were joined there in the courtyard by Fenzileh—this woman who had brought, said many, the Frankish ways of Shaltan into Algiers.

CHAPTER VIII

MOTHER AND SON

EARLY ON the morrow—so early that scarce had the Shehad been recited—came Biskaine-el-Borak to the Basha. He had just landed from a galley which had come upon a Spanish fishing boat, aboard of which there was a young Morisco who was being conducted over seas to Algiers. The news of which the fellow was the bearer was of such urgency that for twenty hours without intermission the slaves had toiled at the oars of Biskaine's vessel—the capitana of his fleet—to bring her swiftly home.

The Morisco had a cousin—a New-Christian like himself, and like himself, it would appear, still a Muslim at heart—who was employed in the Spanish treasury at Malaga. This man had knowledge that a galley was fitting out for sea to convey to Naples the gold destined for the pay of the Spanish troops in garrison there. Through parsimony this treasure-galley was to be afforded no escort, but was under orders to hug the coast of Europe, where she should be safe from all piratical surprise. It was judged that she would be ready to put to sea in a week, and the Morisco had set out at once to bring word of it to his Algerine brethren that they might intercept and capture her.

Asad thanked the young Morisco for his news, bade him be housed and cared for, and promised him a handsome share of the plunder should the treasure-galley be captured. That done he sent for Sakr-el-Bahr, whilst Marzak, who had been present at the interview, went with the tale of it to his mother, and beheld her fling into a passion when he added that it was Sakr-el-Bahr had been summoned that he might be entrusted with this fresh expedition, thus proving that all her crafty innuendoes and insistent warnings had been so much wasted labor.

With Marzak following at her heels, she swept like a fury into the darkened room where Asad took his ease.

"What is this I hear, O my lord?" she cried, in tone and manner more the European shrew than the submissive Eastern slave. "Is Sakr-el-Bahr to go upon this expedition against the treasure-galley of Spain?"

Reclining on his divan he looked her up and down with a languid eye.

"Dost know of any better fitted to succeed?" quoth he.

"I know of one whom it is my lord's duty to prefer to that foreign adventurer. One who is entirely faithful and entirely to be trusted. One who does not attempt to retain for himself a portion of the booty garnered in the name of Islam."

"Bah!" said Asad. "Wilt thou talk forever of those two slaves? And who may be this paragon of thine?"

"Marzak," she answered fiercely, flinging out an arm to drag forward her son. "Is he to waste his youth here in softness and idleness? But yesternight that ribald mocked him with his lack of scars. Shall he take scars in the orchard of the Kasbah here? Is he to be content with those that come from the scratch of a bramble, or is he to learn to be a fighter and leader of the Children of the Faith that himself he may follow in the path his father trod?"

"Whether he so follows," said Asad, "is as the Sultan of Istambul, the Sublime Portal, shall decree. We are but his vicegerents here."

"But shall the Grand Sultan appoint him to succeed thee if thou hast not equipped him so to do? I cry shame on thee, O father of Marzak, for that thou art lacking in due pride in thine own son."

"May Allah give me patience with thee! Have I not said that he is still over young."

"At his age thyself thou wert upon the seas, serving with the great Ochiali."

"At his age I was, by the favor of Allah, taller and stronger than is he. I cherish him too dearly to let him go forth and perchance be lost to me before his strength is full grown."

"Look at him," she commanded. "He is a man, Asad, and such a son as another might take pride in. Is it not time he girt a scimitar about his waist and trod the poop of one of thy galleys?"

"Indeed, indeed, O my father!" begged Marzak himself.

"What?" barked the old Moor. "And is it so? And wouldst thou go forth then against the Spaniard? What knowledge hast thou that shall equip thee for such a task?"

"What can his knowledge be since his father has never been concerned to school him?" returned Fenzileh. "Dost thou sneer at shortcomings that are the natural fruits of thine own omissions?"

"I will be patient with thee," said Asad, showing every sign of losing patience. "I will ask thee only if in thy judgment he is in case to win a victory for Islam? Answer me straightly now."

"Straightly I answer thee that he is not. And, as straightly, I tell thee that it is full time he were. Thy duty is to let him go upon this expedition that he may learn the trade that lies before him."

Asad considered a moment. Then: "Be it so," he answered slowly. "Shalt set forth, then, with Sakr-el-Bahr, my son."

"With Sakr-el-Bahr?" cried Fenzileh aghast.

"I could find him no better preceptor."

"Shall thy son go forth as the servant of another?"

"As the pupil," Asad amended. "What else?"

"Were I a man, O fountain of my soul," said she, "and had I a son, none but myself should be his preceptor. I should so mold and fashion him that he should be another me. That, O my dear lord, is thy duty to Marzak. Entrust not his training to another, and to one whom despite thy love for him I cannot trust. Go forth thyself upon this expedition with Marzak here for thy kayia."

Asad frowned. "I grow too old," he said. "I have not been upon the seas these two years past. Who can say that I may not have lost the art of victory. No, no." He shook his head, and his face grew overcast and softened by wistfulness. "Sakr-el-Bahr commands this time, and if Marzak goes, he goes with him."

"My lord . . ." she began, then checked. A Nubian had entered to announce that Sakr-el-Bahr was come and was awaiting the orders of his lord in the courtyard. Asad rose instantly and for all that Fenzileh, greatly daring as ever, would still have detained him, he shook her off impatiently, and went out.

She watched his departure with anger in those dark lovely eyes of hers, an anger that went near to filming them in tears, and after he had passed out into the glaring sunshine beyond the door, a silence dwelt in the cool darkened chamber—a silence disturbed only by distant trills of silvery laughter from the lesser women of the Basha's house. The sound jarred her taut nerves. She moved with an oath and beat her hands together. To answer her came a negress, lithe and muscular as a wrestler and naked to the waist; the slave ring in her ear was of massive gold.

"Bid them make an end of that screeching," she snapped to vent some of her fierce petulance. "Tell them I will have the rods to them if they again disturb me."

The negress went out, and silence followed, for those other lesser ladies of the Basha's hareem were more obedient to the commands of Fenzileh than to those of the Basha himself.

Then she drew her son to the fretted lattice commanding the courtyard, a screen from behind which they could see and hear all that passed out yonder. Asad was speaking, informing Sakr-el-Bahr of what he had learnt, and what there was to do.

"How soon canst thou put to sea again?" he ended.

"As soon as the service of Allah and thyself require," was the prompt answer.

"It is well, my son." Asad laid a hand affectionately upon the corsair's shoulder, entirely conquered by this readiness. "Best set out at sunrise to-morrow. Thou'lt need so long to make thee ready for the sea."

"Then by thy leave I go forthwith to give orders to prepare," replied Sakr-el-Bahr, for all that he was a little troubled in his mind by this need to depart again so soon.

"What galleys shalt thou take?"

"To capture one galley of Spain? My own galeasse, no more; she will be full equal to such an enterprise, and I shall be the better able, then, to lurk and take cover—a thing which might well prove impossible with a fleet."

"Ay—thou art wise in thy daring," Asad approved him. "May Allah prosper thee upon the voyage."

"Have I thy leave to go?"

"A moment yet. There is my son Marzak. He is approaching manhood, and it is time he entered the service of Allah and the State. It is my desire that he sail as thy lieutenant on this voyage, and that thou be his preceptor even as I was thine of old."

Now here was something that pleased Sakr-el-Bahr as little as it pleased Marzak. Knowing the bitter enmity borne him by the son of Fenzileh he had every cause to fear trouble if this project of Asad's were realized.

"As I was thine of old!" he answered with crafty wistfulness. "Wilt thou not put to sea with us to-morrow, O Asad? There is none like thee in all Islam, and what a joy were it not to stand beside thee on the prow as of old when we grapple with the Spaniard."

Asad considered him. "Dost thou, too, urge this?" quoth he.

"Have others urged it?" The man's sharp wits, rendered still sharper by his sufferings, were cutting deeply and swiftly into this matter. "They did well, but none could have urged it more fervently than I, for none knows so well as I the joy of battle against the infidel under thy command and the glory of prevailing in thy sight. Come, then, my lord, upon this enterprise, and be thyself thine own son's preceptor, since 't is the highest honor thou canst bestow upon him."

Thoughtfully Asad stroked his long white beard, his eagle eyes growing narrow. "Thou temptest me, by Allah!"

"Let me do more . . ."

"Nay, more thou canst not. I am old and worn, and I am needed here. Shall an old lion hunt a young gazelle? Peace, peace! The sun has set upon my fighting day. Let the brood of fighters I have raised up keep that which my arm conquered and maintain my name and the glory of the Faith upon the seas." He leaned upon Sakr-el-Bahr's shoulder and sighed, his eyes wistfully dreamy. "It were a fond adventure in good truth. But no . . . I am resolved. Go thou and take Marzak with thee, and bring him safely home again."

"I should not return myself else," was the answer. "But my trust is in the All-knowing."

Upon that he departed, dissembling his profound vexation both at the voyage and the company, and went to bid Othmani make ready his great galeasse, equipping it with carronades, three hundred slaves to row it, and three hundred fighting men.

Asad-el-Din returned to that darkened room in the Kasbah overlooking the courtyard, where Fenzileh and Marzak still lingered. He went to tell them that in compliance with the desires of both Marzak should go forth to prove himself upon this expedition.

But where he had left impatience he found thinly veiled wrath.

"O sun that warms me," Fenzileh greeted him, and from long experience he knew that the more endearing were her epithets the more vicious was her mood, "do then my counsels weigh as naught with thee, are they but as the dust upon thy shoes?"

"Less," said Asad, provoked out of his habitual indulgence of her licences of speech.

"That is the truth, indeed!" she cried, bowing her head whilst behind her the handsome face of her son was overcast.

"It is," Asad agreed. "At dawn, Marzak, thou settest forth upon the galeasse of Sakr-el-Bahr to take the seas under his tutelage and to emulate the skill and valor that have rendered him the stoutest bulwark of Islam, the very Javelin of Allah."

But Marzak felt that in this matter his mother was to be supported, whilst his detestation of this adventurer who threatened to usurp the place that should rightly be his own spurred him to mad lengths of daring.

"When I take the seas with that dog-descended Nasrani," he answered hoarsely, "he shall be where rightly he belongs—at the rowers' bench."

"How?" It was a bellow of rage. Upon the word Asad swung to confront his son, and his face, suddenly inflamed, was so cruel and evil in its expression that it terrified that intriguing pair. "By the beard of the Prophet! what words are these to me?" He advanced upon Marzak until Fenzileh in sudden terror stepped between and faced him, like a lioness springing to defend her cub. But the Basha, enraged now by this want of submission in his son, enraged both against that son and the mother who he knew had prompted him, caught her in his sinewy old hands, and flung her furiously aside, so that she stumbled and fell in a panting heap amid the cushions of her divan.

"The curse of Allah upon thee!" he screamed, and Marzak recoiled before him. "Has this presumptuous hellcat who bore thee taught thee to stand before my face, to tell me what thou wilt and wilt not do? By the Koran! too long have I endured her evil foreign ways, and now it seems she has taught thee how to tread them after her and how to beard thy very father! To-morrow thou'lt take the sea with Sakr-el-Bahr. I have said it. Another word and thou'lt go aboard his galeasse even as thou saidst should be the case with him—at the rower's bench, to learn submission under the slave-master's whip."

Terrified, Marzak stood numb and silent, scarcely daring to draw breath. Never in all his life had he seen his father in a rage so royal. Yet it seemed to inspire no fear in Fenzileh, that congenital shrew whose tongue not even the threat of rods or hooks could silence.

"I shall pray Allah to restore sight to thy soul, O father of Marzak," she panted, "to teach thee to discriminate between those that love thee and the self-seekers that abuse thy trust."

"How?" he roared at her. "Art not yet done?"

"Nor ever shall be until I am lain dumb in death for having counseled thee out of my great love, O light of these poor eyes of mine."

"Maintain this tone," he said, with concentrated anger, "and that will soon befall."

"I care not so that the sleek mask be plucked from the face of that dog-descended Sakr-el-Bahr. May Allah break his bones! What of those slaves of his—those two from England, O Asad? I am told that one is a woman, tall and of that white beauty which is the gift of Eblis to these Northerners. What is his purpose with her—that he would not show her in the sôk as the law prescribes, but comes slinking here to beg thee set aside the law for him? Ha! I talk in vain. I have shown thee graver things to prove his vile disloyalty, and yet thou'lt fawn upon him whilst thy fangs are bared to thine own son."

He advanced upon her, stooped, caught her by the wrist, and heaved her up.

His face showed gray under its deep tan. His aspect terrified her at last, and made an end of her reckless forward courage.

He raised his voice to call.

"Ya anta! Ayoub!"

She gasped, livid in her turn with sudden terror. "My lord, my lord!" she whimpered. "Stream of my life, be not angry! What wilt thou do?"

He smiled evilly. "Do?" he growled. "What I should have done ten years ago and more. We'll have the rods to thee." And again he called, more insistently—"Ayoub!"

"My lord, my lord!" she gasped in shuddering horror now that at last she found him set upon the thing to which so often she had dared him. "Pity! Pity!" She groveled and embraced his knees. "In the name of the Pitying the Pitiful be merciful upon the excesses to which my love for thee may have driven this poor tongue of mine. O my sweet lord! O father of Marzak!"

Her distress, her beauty, and perhaps, more than either, her unusual humility and submission may have moved him. For even as at that moment Ayoub—the sleek and portly eunuch, who was her wazeer and chamberlain—loomed in the inner doorway, salaaming, he vanished again upon the instant, dismissed by a peremptory wave of the Basha's hand.

Asad looked down upon her, sneering. "That attitude becomes thee best," he said. "Continue it in future." Contemptuously he shook himself free of her grasp, turned and stalked majestically out, wearing his anger like a royal mantle, and leaving behind him two terror-shaken beings, who felt as if they had looked over the very edge of death.

There was a long silence between them. Then at long length Fenzileh rose and crossed to the meshrabiyah—the latticed window-box. She opened it and took from one of its shelves an earthenware jar, placed there so as to receive the slightest breeze. From it she poured water into a little cup and drank greedily. That she could perform this menial service for herself when a mere clapping of hands would have brought slaves to minister to her need betrayed something of her disordered state of mind.

She slammed the inner lattice and turned to Marzak.

"And now?" quoth she.

"Now?" said the lad.

"Ay, what now? What are we to do? Are we to lie crushed under his rage until we are ruined indeed? He is bewitched. That jackal has enchanted him, so that he must deem well done all that is done by him. Allah guide us here, Marzak, or thou'lt be trampled into dust by Sakr-el-Bahr."

Marzak hung his head; slowly he moved to the divan and flung himself down upon its pillows; there he lay prone, his hands cupping his chin, his heels in the air.

"What can I do?" he asked at last.

"That is what I most desire to know. Something must be done, and soon. May his bones rot! If he lives thou art destroyed."

"Ay," said Marzak, with sudden vigor and significance. "If he lives!" And he sat up. "Whilst we plan and plot, and our plans and plots come to naught save to provoke the anger of my father, we might be better employed in taking the shorter way."

She stood in the middle of the chamber, pondering him with gloomy eyes.

"I too have thought of that," said she. "I could hire me men to do the thing for a handful of gold. But the risk of it. . . ."

"Where would be the risk once he is dead?"

"He might pull us down with him, and then what would our profit be in his death? Thy father would avenge him terribly."

"If it were craftily done we should not be discovered."

"Not be discovered?" she echoed, and laughed without mirth. "How young and blind thou art, O Marzak! We should be the first to be suspected. I have made no secret of my hate of him, and the people do not love me. They would urge thy father to do justice even were he himself averse to it, which I will not credit would be the case. This Sakr-el-Bahr—may Allah wither him!—is a god in their eyes. Bethink thee of the welcome given him! What Basha returning in triumph was ever greeted by the like? These victories that fortune has vouchsafed him have made them account him divinely favored and protected. I tell thee Marzak, that did thy father die to-morrow Sakr-el-Bahr would be proclaimed Basha of

Algiers in his stead, and woe betide us then. And Asad-el-Din grows old. True, he does not go forth to fight. He clings to life and may last long. But if he should not, and if Sakr-el-Bahr should still walk the earth when thy father's destiny is fulfilled, I dare not think what then will be thy fate and mine."

"May his grave be defiled!" growled Marzak.

"His grave?" said she. "The difficulty is to dig it for him without hurt to ourselves. Shaitan protects the dog."

"May he make his bed in hell!" said Marzak.

"To curse him will not help us. Up, Marzak, and consider how the thing is to be done."

Marzak came to his feet, nimble and supple as a greyhound.

"Listen now," he said. "Since I must go this voyage with him, perchance upon the seas on some dark night opportunity may serve me."

"Wait! Let me consider it. Allah guide me to find some way!" She beat her hands together and bade the slave girl who answered her to summon her wazeer Ayoub, and bid a litter be prepared for her. "We'll to the sôk, O Marzak, and see these slaves of his. Who knows but that something may be done by means of them! Guile will serve us better than mere strength against that misbegotten son of shame."

"May his house be destroyed!" said Marzak.

CHAPTER IX

COMPETITORS

THE OPEN space before the gates of the Sôk-el-Abeed was thronged with a motley, jostling, noisy crowd that at every moment was being swelled by the human streams pouring to mingle in it from the debouching labyrinth of narrow, unpaved streets.

There were brown-skinned Berbers in black goat-hair cloaks that were made in one piece with a cowl and decorated by a lozenge of red or orange color on the back, their shaven heads encased in skull-caps or simply bound in a cord of plaited camel-hair; there were black Saharowi who went almost naked, and stately Arabs who seemed over-muffled in their flowing robes of white with the cowls overshadowing their swarthy, finely featured faces; there were dignified and prosperous-looking Moors in brightly colored selhams astride of sleek mules that were richly caparisoned; and there were Tagareenes, the banished Moors of Andalusia, most of whom followed the trade of slave-dealers; there were native Jews in somber black djellabas, and Christian-Jews —so-called because bred in Christian countries, whose garments they still wore; there were Levantine Turks, splendid of dress and arrogant of demeanor, and there were humble Cololies, Kabyles and Biscaries. Here a water-seller, laden with his goatskin vessel, tinkled his little bell; there an orange-hawker, balancing a basket of the golden fruit upon his ragged turban, bawled his wares. There were men on foot and men on mules, men on donkeys and men on slim Arab horses, an ever-shifting medley of colors, all jostling, laughing, cursing in the ardent African sunshine under the blue sky where pigeons circled. In the shadow of the yellow tapia wall squatted a line of whining beggars and cripples soliciting alms; near the gates a little space had been cleared and an audience had gathered in a ring about a Meddah—a beggar-troubadour—who, to the accompaniment of gimbri and gaitah from two acolytes, chanted a doleful ballad in a thin, nasal voice.

Those of the crowd who were patrons of the market held steadily amain, and, leaving their mounts outside, passed through the gates through which there was no admittance for mere idlers and mean folk. Within the vast quadrangular space of bare, dry ground, enclosed by dust-colored walls, there was more space. The sale of slaves had not yet begun and was not due to begin for another hour, and meanwhile a little trading was being done by those merchants who had obtained the coveted right to set up their booths against the walls; they were vendors of wool, of fruit, of spices, and one or two traded in jewels and trinkets for the adornment of the Faithful.

A well was sunk in the middle of the ground, a considerable octagon with a low parapet in three steps. Upon the nethermost of these sat an aged, bearded Jew in a black djellaba, his head swathed in a colored kerchief. Upon his knees reposed a broad, shallow black box, divided into compartments, each filled with lesser gems and rare stones, which he was offering for sale; about him stood a little group of young Moors and one or two Turkish officers, with several of whom the old Israelite was haggling at once.

The whole of the northern wall was occupied by a long penthouse, its contents completely masked by curtains of camel-hair; from behind it proceeded a subdued murmur of human voices. These were the pens in which were confined the slaves to be offered for sale that day. Before the curtains, on guard, stood some dozen corsairs with attendant negro slaves.

Beyond and above the wall glistened the white dome of a zowla, flanked by a spear-like minaret and the tall heads of a few date palms whose long leaves hung motionless in the hot air.

Suddenly in the crowd beyond the gates there was a commotion. From one of the streets six colossal Nubians advanced with shouts of—

"Oâk! Oâk! Warda! Way! Make way!"

They were armed with great staves, grasped in their two hands, and with these they broke a path through that motley press, hurling men to right and left and earning a shower of curses in return.

"Balâk! Make way! Way for the Lord Asad-ed-Din, the exalted of Allah! Way!"

The crowd, pressing back, went down upon its knees and groveled as Asad-ed-Din on a milk-white mule rode forward, escorted by Tsamanni his wazeer and a cloud of black-robed janissaries with flashing scimitars.

The curses that had greeted the violence of his negroes were suddenly silenced; instead, blessings as fervent filled the air.

"May Allah increase thy might! May Allah lengthen thy days! The blessings of our Lord Mahomet upon thee! Allah send thee more victories!" were the benedictions that showered upon him on every hand. He returned them as became a man who was supremely pious and devout.

"The peace of Allah upon the Faithful of the Prophet's House," he would murmur in response from time to time, until at last he had reached the gates. There he bade Tsamanni fling a purse to the crouching beggars—for is it not written in the Most Perspicuous

Book that of alms ye shall bestow what ye can spare, for such as are
saved from their own greed shall prosper, and whatever ye give in
alms, as seeking the face of Allah, shall be doubled unto you?

Submissive to the laws as the meanest of his subjects, Asad dismounted and passed on foot into the sôk. He came to a halt by the
well, and, facing the curtained penthouse, he blessed the kneeling
crowd and commanded all to rise.

He beckoned Sakr-el-Bahr's officer Ali—who was in charge of
the slaves of the corsair's latest raid—and announced his will to
inspect the captives. At a sign from Ali, the negroes flung aside the
camel-hair curtains and let the fierce sunlight beat in upon those
pent-up wretches; they were not only the captives taken by
Sakr-el-Bahr, but some others who were the result of one or two
lesser raids by Biskaine.

Asad beheld a huddle of men and women—though the propor-
tion of women was very small—of all ages, races, and conditions;
there were pale, fair haired men from France or the North,
olive-skinned Italians and swarthy Spaniards, negroes and
half-castes; there were old men, young men, and mere children,
some handsomely dressed, some almost naked, others hung with
rags. In the hopeless dejection of their countenances alone was
there any uniformity. But it was not a dejection that could awaken
pity in the pious heart of Asad. They were unbelievers who would
never look upon the face of God's Prophet, accursed and unworthy
of any tenderness from man. For a moment his glance was held by
a lovely black-haired Spanish girl, who sat with her locked hands
held fast between her knees, in an attitude of intense despair and
suffering—the glory of her eyes increased and magnified by the
dark brown stains of sleeplessness surrounding them. Leaning on
Tsamanni's arm, he stood considering her for a little while; then his
glance traveled on. Suddenly he tightened his grasp of Tsamanni's
arm, and a quick interest leapt into his sallow face.

On the uppermost tier of the pen that he was facing sat a very glory of womanhood, such a woman as he had heard tell existed but the like of which he had never yet beheld. She was tall and graceful as a cypress-tree; her skin was white as milk, her eyes two darkest sapphires, her head of a coppery golden that seemed to glow like metal as the sunlight caught it. She was dressed in a close gown of white, the bodice cut low and revealing the immaculate loveliness of her neck.

Asad-ed-Din turned to Ali. "What pearl is this that hath been cast upon this dung-heap?" he asked.

"She is the woman our lord Sakr-el-Bahr carried off from England."

Slowly the Basha's eyes returned to consider her, and insensible though she had deemed herself by now, he saw her cheeks slowly reddening under the cold insult of his steady, insistent glance. The glow heightened her beauty, effacing the weariness which the face had worn.

"Bring her forth," said the Basha shortly.

She was seized by two of the negroes, and to avoid being roughly handled by them she came at once, bracing herself to bear with dignity whatever might await her. A golden-haired young man beside her, his face haggard and stubbled with a beard of some growth, looked up in alarm as she was taken from his side. Then, with a groan, he made as if to clutch her, but a rod fell upon his raised arms and beat them down.

Asad was thoughtful. It was Fenzileh who had bidden him come look at the infidel maid whom Sakr-el-Bahr had risked so much to snatch from England, suggesting that in her he would behold some proof of the bad faith which she was forever urging against the corsair leader. He beheld the woman, but he discovered about her no such signs as Fenzileh had suggested he must find, nor indeed did he look for any. Out of curiosity had he obeyed her prompting. But that and all else were forgotten now in the contemplation of this noble ensample of Northern womanhood, statuesque almost in her terrible restraint.

He put forth a hand to touch her arm, and she drew it back as if his fingers were of fire.

He sighed. "How inscrutable are the ways of Allah, that He should suffer so luscious a fruit to hang from the foul tree of infidelity!"

Tsamanni watching him craftily, a master-sycophant profoundly learned in the art of playing upon his master's moods, made answer:

"Even so perchance that a Faithful of the Prophet's House may pluck it. Verily all things are possible to the One!"

"Yet is it not set down in the Book to be Read that the daughters of the infidel are not for True-Believers?" And again he sighed.

But Tsamanni, knowing full well how the Basha would like to be answered, trimmed his reply to that desire.

"Allah is great, and what hath befallen once may well befall again, my lord."

Asad's kindling eyes flashed a glance at his wazeer.

"Thou meanest Fenzileh. But then, by the mercy of Allah, I was rendered the instrument of her enlightenment."

"It may well be written that thou shalt be the same again, my lord," murmured the insidious Tsamanni. There was more stirring in his mind than the mere desire to play the courtier now. 'Twixt Fenzileh and himself there had long been a feud begotten of the jealousy which each inspired the other where Asad was concerned. Were Fenzileh removed the wazeer's influence must grow and spread to his own profit. It was a thing of which he had often dreamed, but a dream he feared that was never like to be realized, for Asad was aging, and the fires that had burned so fiercely in his earlier years seemed now to have consumed in him all thought of women. Yet here was one as by a miracle, of a beauty so amazing and so diverse from any that ever yet had feasted the Basha's sight, that plainly she had acted as a charm upon his senses.

"She is white as the snows upon the Atlas, luscious as the dates of Tafilalt," he murmured fondly, his gleaming eyes considering her what time she stood immovable before him. Suddenly he looked about him, and wheeled upon Tsamanni, his manner swiftly becoming charged with anger.

"Her face has been bared to a thousand eyes and more," he cried.

"Even that has been so before," replied Tsamanni.

And then quite suddenly at their elbow a voice that was naturally soft and musical of accent but now rendered harsh, cut in to ask:

"What woman may this be?"

Startled, both the Basha and his wazeer swung round. Fenzileh, becomingly veiled and hooded, stood before them, escorted by Marzak. A little behind them were the eunuchs and the litter in which, unperceived by Asad, she had been borne thither. Beside the litter stood her wazeer Ayoub-el-Samin.

Asad scowled down upon her, for he had not yet recovered from the resentment she and Marzak had provoked in him. Moreover, that in private she should be lacking in the respect which was his due was evil enough, though he had tolerated it. But that she should make so bold as to thrust in and question him in this peremptory fashion before all the world was more than his dignity could suffer. Never yet had she dared so much, nor would she have dared it now but that her sudden anxiety had effaced all caution from her mind. She had seen the look with which Asad had been considering that lovely slave, and not only jealousy but positive fear awoke in her. Her hold upon Asad was growing tenuous. To snap it utterly no more was necessary than that he who of late years had scarce bestowed a thought or glance upon a woman should be taken with the fancy to bring some new recruit to his hareem.

Hence her desperate, reckless courage to stand thus before him now, for although her face was veiled there was hardy arrogance in every line of her figure. Of his scowl she took no slightest heed.

"If this be the slave fetched by Sakr-el-Bahr from England, then rumor has lied to me," she said. "I vow it was scarce worth so long a voyage and the endangering so many valuable Muslim lives to fetch this yellow-faced, long-shanked daughter of perdition into Barbary."

Asad's surprise beat down his anger. He was not subtle.

"Yellow-faced? Long-shanked?" quoth he. Then reading Fenzileh at last, he displayed a slow, crooked smile. "Already have I observed thee to grow hard of hearing, and now thy sight is failing too, it seems. Assuredly thou art growing old." And he looked her over with such an eye of displeasure that she recoiled.

He stepped close up to her. "Too long already hast thou queened it in my hareem with thine infidel, Frankish ways," he muttered, so that none but those immediately about overheard his angry words. "Thou art become a very scandal in the eyes of the Faithful," he added very grimly. "It were well, perhaps, that we amended that."

Abruptly then he turned away, and by a gesture he ordered Ali to return the slave to her place among the others. Leaning on the arm of Tsamanni he took some steps towards the entrance, then halted, and turned again to Fenzileh:

"To thy litter," he bade her peremptorily, rebuking her thus before all, "and get thee to the house as becomes a seemly Muslim woman. Nor ever again let thyself be seen roving the public places afoot."

She obeyed him instantly, without a murmur; and he himself lingered at the gates with Tsamanni until her litter had passed out, escorted by Ayoub, and Marzak walking each on one side of it and neither daring to meet the angry eye of the Basha.

Asad looked sourly after that litter, a sneer on his heavy lips.

"As her beauty wanes so her presumption waxes," he growled. "She is growing old, Tsamanni—old and lean and shrewish, and no fit mate for a Member of the Prophet's House. It were perhaps a pleasing thing in the sight of Allah that we replaced her." And then, referring obviously to that other one, his eye turning towards the penthouse the curtains of which were drawn again, he changed his tone.

"Didst thou mark, O Tsamanni, with what a grace she moved?—lithely and nobly as a young gazelle. Verily, so much beauty was never created by the All-Wise to be cast into the Pit."

"May it not have been sent to comfort some True-Believer?" wondered the subtle wazeer. "To Allah all things are possible."

"Why else, indeed?" said Asad. "It was written; and even as none may obtain what is not written, so none may avoid what is. I am resolved. Stay thou here, Tsamanni. Remain for the outcry and purchase her. She shall be taught the True Faith. She shall be saved from the furnace."

The command had come, the thing that Tsamanni had so ardently desired.

He licked his lips. "And the price, my lord?" he asked, in a small voice.

"Price?" quoth Asad. "Have I not bid thee purchase her? Bring her to me, though her price be a thousand philips."

"A thousand philips!" echoed Tsamanni amazed. "Allah is great!"

But already Asad had left his side and passed out under the arched gateway, where the crowd was groveling anew at sight of him.

It was a fine thing for Asad to bid him remain for the sale. But the dalal would part with no slave until the money was forthcoming, and Tsamanni had no considerable sum upon his person. Therefore in the wake of his master he set out forthwith to the Kasbah. It wanted still an hour before the sale would be held and he had time and to spare in which to go and return.

It happened, however, that Tsamanni was malicious, and that the hatred of Fenzileh which so long he had consumed in silence and dissembled under fawning smiles and profound salaams included also her servants. There was none in all the world of whom he entertained a greater contempt than her sleek and greasy eunuch Ayoub-el-Samin of the majestic, rolling gait and fat, supercilious lips.

It was written, too, that in the courtyard of the Kasbah he should stumble upon Ayoub, who indeed had by his mistress's commands been set to watch for the wazeer. The fat fellow rolled forward, his hands supporting his paunch, his little eyes agleam.

"Allah increase thy health, Tsamanni," was his courteous greeting. "Thou bearest news?"

"News? What news?" quoth Tsamanni. "In truth none that will gladden thy mistress."

"Merciful Allah! What now? Doth it concern that Frankish slave girl?"

Tsamanni smiled, a thing that angered Ayoub, who felt that the ground he trod was becoming insecure; it followed that if his mistress fell from influence he fell with her, and became as the dust upon Tsamanni's slippers.

"By the Koran thou tremblest, Ayoub!" Tsamanni mocked him. "Thy soft fat is all a-quivering; and well it may, for thy days are numbered, O father of nothing."

"Dost deride me, dog?" came the other's voice, shrill now with anger.

"Callest me dog? Thou?" Deliberately Tsamanni spat upon his shadow. "Go tell thy mistress that I am bidden by my lord to buy the Frankish girl. Tell her that my lord will take her to wife, even as he took Fenzileh, that he may lead her into the True Belief and cheat Shaitan of so fair a jewel. Add that I am bidden to buy her though she cost my lord a thousand philips. Bear her that message, O father of wind, and may Allah increase thy paunch!" And he was gone, lithe, active, and mocking.

"May thy sons perish and thy daughters become harlots,"

roared the eunuch, maddened at once by this evil news and the insult with which it was accompanied.

But Tsamanni only laughed, as he answered him over his shoulder—

"May thy sons be sultans all, Ayoub!"

Quivering still with a rage that entirely obliterated his alarm at what he had learnt, Ayoub rolled into the presence of his mistress with that evil message.

She listened to him in a dumb white fury. Then she fell to reviling her lord and the slave-girl in a breath, and called upon Allah to break their bones and blacken their faces and rot their flesh with all the fervor of one born and bred in the True Faith. When she recovered from that burst of fury it was to sit brooding awhile. At length she sprang up and bade Ayoub see that none lurked to listen about the doorways.

"We must act, Ayoub, and act swiftly, or I am destroyed and with me will be destroyed Marzak, who alone could not stand against his father's face. Sakr-el-Bahr will trample us into the dust." She checked on a sudden thought. "By Allah it may have been a part of his design to have brought hither that white-faced wench. But we must thwart him and we must thwart Asad, or thou art ruined too, Ayoub."

"Thwart him?" quoth her wazeer, gaping at the swift energy of mind and body with which this woman was endowed, the like of which he had never seen in any woman yet. "Thwart him?" he repeated.

"First, Ayoub, to place this Frankish girl beyond his reach."

"That is well thought—but how?"

"How? Can thy wit suggest no way? Hast thou wits at all in that fat head of thine? Thou shalt outbid Tsamanni, or, better still, set someone else to do it for thee, and so buy the girl for me. Then we'll contrive that she shall vanish quietly and quickly before Asad can discover a trace of her."

His face blanched, and the wattles about his jaws were shaking. "And . . . and the cost? Hast thou counted the cost, O Fenzileh? What will happen when Asad gains knowledge of this thing?"

"He shall gain no knowledge of it," she answered him. "Or if he does, the girl being gone beyond recall, he shall submit him to what was written. Trust me to know how to bring him to it."

"Lady, lady!" he cried, and wrung his bunches of fat fingers. "I dare not engage in this!"

"Engage in what? If I bid thee go buy this girl, and give thee the money thou'lt require, what else concerns thee, dog? What else is to be done, a man shall do. Come now, thou shalt have the money, all I have, which is a matter of some fifteen hundred philips, and what is not laid out upon this purchase thou shalt retain for thyself."

He considered an instant, and conceived that she was right. None could blame him for executing the commands she gave him. And there would be profit in it, clearly—ay, and it would be sweet to outbid that dog Tsamanni and send him empty-handed home to face the wrath of his frustrated master.

He spread his hands and salaamed in token of complete acquiescence.

CHAPTER X

THE SLAVE-MARKET

A T THE Sôk-el-Abeed it was the hour of the outcry, announced by a blast of trumpets and the thudding of tom-toms. The traders that until then had been licensed to ply within the enclosure now put up the shutters of their little booths. The Hebrew pedlar of gems closed his box and effaced himself, leaving the steps about the well clear for the most prominent patrons of the market. These hastened to assemble there, surrounding it and facing outwards, whilst the rest of the crowd was ranged against the southern and western walls of the enclosure.

Came negro water-carriers in white turbans with aspersers made of palmetto leaves to sprinkle the ground and lay the dust against the tramp of slaves and buyers. The trumpets ceased for an instant, then wound a fresh imperious blast and fell permanently silent. The crowd about the gates fell back to right and left, and very slowly and stately three tall dalals, dressed from head to foot in white and with immaculate turbans wound about their heads, advanced into the open space. They came to a halt at the western end of the long wall, the chief dalal standing slightly in advance of the other two.

The chattering of voices sank upon their advent, it became a hissing whisper, then a faint drone like that of bees, and then utter silence. In the solemn and grave demeanor of the dalals there was something almost sacerdotal, so that when that silence fell upon the crowd the affair took on the aspect of a sacrament.

The chief dalal stood forward a moment as if in an abstraction, with downcast eyes; then with hands outstretched to catch a blessing he raised his voice and began to pray in a monotonous chant.

"In the name of Allah the Pitying the Pitiful Who created man from clots of blood! All that is in the Heavens and in the Earth praiseth Allah, Who is the Mighty, the Wise! His the kingdom of the Heavens and of the Earth. He maketh alive and killeth, and He hath power over all things. He is the first and the last, the seen and the unseen, and He knoweth all things."

"Ameen," intoned the crowd.

"The praise to Him who sent us Mahomet His Prophet to give the world the True Belief, and curses upon Shaitan the stoned who wages war upon Allah and His children."

"Ameen."

"The blessings of Allah and our Lord Mahomet upon this market and upon all who may buy and sell herein, and may Allah increase their wealth and grant them length of days in which to praise Him."

"Ameen," replied the crowd, as with a stir and rustle the close ranks relaxed from the tense attitude of prayer, and each man sought elbow-room.

The dalal beat his hands together, whereupon the curtains were drawn aside and the huddled slaves displayed—some three hundred in all, occupying three several pens.

In the front rank of the middle pen—the one containing Rosamund and Lionel—stood a couple of stalwart young Nubians, sleek and muscular, who looked on with completest indifference, no whit appalled by the fate which had haled them thither. They caught the eye of the dalal, and although the usual course was for a buyer to indicate a slave he was prepared to purchase, yet to the end that good beginning should be promptly made, the dalal himself pointed out that stalwart pair to the corsairs who stood on guard. In compliance the two negroes were brought forth.

"Here is a noble twain," the dalal announced, "strong of muscle and long of limb, as all may see, whom it were a shameful thing to separate. Who needs such a pair for strong labor let him say what he will give." He set out on a slow circuit of the well, the corsairs urging the two slaves to follow him that all buyers might see and inspect them.

In the foremost ranks of the crowd near the gate stood Ali, sent thither by Othmani to purchase a score of stout fellows required to make up the contingent of the galeasse of Sakr-el-Bahr. He had been strictly enjoined to buy naught but the stoutest stuff the market could afford—with one exception. Aboard that galeasse they wanted no weaklings who would trouble the boatswain with their swoonings. Ali announced his business forthwith.

"I need such tall fellows for the oars of Sakr-el-Bahr," said he with loud importance, thus drawing upon himself the eyes of the assembly, and sunning himself in the admiring looks bestowed upon one of the officers of Oliver-Reis, one of the rovers who were the pride of Islam and a sword-edge to the infidel.

"They were born to toil nobly at the oar, O Ali-Reis," replied the dalal in all solemnity. "What wilt thou give for them?"

"Two hundred philips for the twain."

The dalal paced solemnly on, the slaves following in his wake.

"Two hundred philips am I offered for a pair of the lustiest slaves that by the favor of Allah were ever brought into this market. Who will say fifty philips more?"

A portly Moor in a flowing blue selham rose from his seat on the step of the well as the dalal came abreast of him, and the slaves scenting here a buyer, and preferring any service to that of the galleys with which they were threatened, came each in turn to kiss his hands and fawn upon him, for all the world like dogs.

Calm and dignified he ran his hands over them feeling their muscles, and then forced back their lips and examined their teeth and mouths.

"Two hundred and twenty for the twain," he said, and the dalal passed on with his wares, announcing the increased price he had been offered.

Thus he completed the circuit and came to stand once more before Ali.

"Two hundred and twenty is now the price, O Ali! By the Koran, they are worth three hundred at the least. Wilt say three hundred?"

"Two hundred and thirty," was the answer.

Back to the Moor went the dalal. "Two hundred and thirty I am now offered, O Hamet. Thou wilt give another twenty?"

"Not I, by Allah!" said Hamet, and resumed his seat. "Let him have them."

"Another ten philips?" pleaded the dalal.

"Not another asper."

"They are thine, then, O Ali, for two hundred and thirty. Give thanks to Allah for so good a bargain."

The Nubians were surrendered to Ali's followers, whilst the dalal's two assistants advanced to settle accounts with the corsair.

"Wait, wait," said he, "is not the name of Sakr-el-Bahr good warranty?"

"The inviolable law is that the purchase money be paid ere a slave leaves the market, O valiant Ali."

"It shall be observed," was the impatient answer, "and I will so pay before they leave. But I want others yet, and we will make one account and it please thee. That fellow yonder now. I have orders to buy him for my captain." And he indicated Lionel, who stood at Rosamund's side, the very incarnation of woefulness and debility.

Contemptuous surprise flickered an instant in the eyes of the dalal. But this he made haste to dissemble.

"Bring forth that yellow-haired infidel," he commanded.

The corsairs laid hands on Lionel. He made a vain attempt to struggle, but it was observed that the woman leaned over to him and said something quickly, whereupon his struggles ceased and he suffered himself to be dragged limply forth into the full view of all the market.

"Dost want him for the oar, Ali?" cried Ayoub-el-Samin across the quadrangle, a jest this that evoked a general laugh.

"What else?" quoth Ali. "He should be cheap at least."

"Cheap?" quoth the dalal in an affectation of surprise. "Nay, now. 'T is a comely fellow and a young one. What wilt thou give, now? a hundred philips?"

"A hundred philips!" cried Ali derisively. "A hundred philips for that skinful of bones! Ma'sh'-Allah! Five philips is my price, O dalal."

Again laughter crackled through the mob. But the dalal stiffened with increasing dignity. Some of that laughter seemed to touch himself, and he was not a person to be made the butt of mirth.

"'T is a jest, my master," said he, with a forgiving yet contemptuous wave. "Behold how sound he is." He signed to one of the corsairs, and Lionel's doublet was slit from neck to girdle and wrenched away from his body, leaving him naked to the waist, and displaying better proportions than might have been expected. In a passion at that indignity Lionel writhed in the grip of his guards, until one of the corsairs struck him a light blow with a whip in earnest of what to expect if he continued to be troublesome. "Consider him now," said the dalal, pointing to that white torso. "And behold how sound he is. See how excellent are his teeth." He seized Lionel's head and forced the jaws apart.

"Ay," said Ali, "but consider me those lean shanks and that woman's arm."

"'T is a fault the oar will mend," the dalal insisted.

"You filthy blackamoors!" burst from Lionel in a sob of rage.

"He is muttering curses in his infidel tongue," said Ali. "His temper is none too good, you see. I have said five philips. I'll say no more."

With a shrug the dalal began his circuit of the well, the corsairs thrusting Lionel after him. Here one rose to handle him, there another, but none seemed disposed to purchase.

"Five philips is the foolish price offered me for this fine young Frank," cried the dalal. "Will no True-Believer pay ten for such a slave? Wilt not thou, O Ayoub? Thou, Hamet—ten philips?"

But one after another those to whom he was offered shook their heads. The haggardness of Lionel's face was too unprepossessing. They had seen slaves with that look before, and experience told them that no good was ever to be done with such fellows. Moreover, though shapely, his muscles were too slight, his flesh looked too soft and tender. Of what use a slave who must be hardened and nourished into strength, and who might very well die in the process? Even at five philips he would be dear. So the disgusted dalal came back to Ali.

"He is thine, then, for five philips—Allah pardon thy avarice."

Ali grinned, and his men seized upon Lionel and bore him off into the background to join the two negroes previously purchased.

And then, before Ali could bid for another of the slaves he desired to acquire, a tall, elderly Jew, dressed in black doublet and hose like a Castilian gentleman, with a ruffle at his neck, a plumed bonnet on his gray locks, and a serviceable dagger hanging from his girdle of hammered gold, had claimed the attention of the dalal.

In the pen that held the captives of the lesser raids conducted by Biskaine sat an Andalusian girl of perhaps some twenty years, of a beauty entirely Spanish. Her face was of the warm pallor of ivory, her massed hair of an ebony black, her eyebrows were finely penciled, and her eyes of deepest and softest brown. She was dressed in the becoming garb of the Castilian peasant, the folded kerchief of red and yellow above her bodice leaving bare the glories of her neck. She was very pale, and her eyes were wild in their look, but this detracted nothing from her beauty.

She had attracted the Jew's notice, and it is not impossible that there may have stirred in him a desire to avenge upon her some of the cruel wrongs, some of the rackings, burning, confiscations, and banishment suffered by the men of his race at the hands of the men of hers. He may have bethought him of invaded ghettos, of Jewish maidens ravished, and Jewish children butchered in the name of the God those Spanish Christians worshiped, for there was something almost of contemptuous fierceness in his dark eyes and in the hand he flung out to indicate her.

"Yonder is a Castilian wench for whom I will give fifty philips, O dalal," he announced. The dalal made a sign, whereupon the corsairs dragged her struggling forth.

"So much loveliness may not be bought for fifty philips, O Ibrahim," said he. "Yusuf here will pay sixty at least." And he stood expectantly before a resplendent Moor.

The Moor, however, shook his head.

"Allah knows I have three wives who would destroy her loveliness within the hour, and so leave me the loser."

The dalal moved on, the girl following him, but contesting every step of the way with those who impelled her forward, and reviling them too in hot Castilian. She drove her nails into the arms of one and spat fiercely into the face of another of her corsair guards. Rosamund's weary eyes quickened to horror as she watched her—a horror prompted as much by the fate awaiting that poor child as by the undignified fury of the futile battle she waged against it. But it happened that her behavior impressed a Levantine Turk quite differently. He rose, a short squat figure, from his seat on the steps of the well.

"Sixty philips will I pay for the joy of taming that wild cat," said he.

But Ibrahim was not to be outbidden. He offered seventy, the

Turk countered with a bid of eighty, and Ibrahim again raised the price to ninety, and there fell a pause.

The dalal spurred on the Turk. "Wilt thou be beaten then, and by an Israelite? Shall this lovely maid be given to a perverter of the Scriptures, to an inheritor of the fire, to one of a race that would not bestow on their fellow-men so much as the speck out of a date-stone? It were a shame upon a True-Believer."

Urged thus the Turk offered another five philips, but with obvious reluctance. The Jew, however, entirely unabashed by a tirade against him, the like of which he heard a score of times a day in the course of trading, pulled forth a heavy purse from his girdle.

"Here are one hundred philips," he announced. "'T is overmuch. But I offer it."

Ere the dalal's pious and seductive tongue could urge him further the Turk sat down again with a gesture of finality.

"I give him joy of her," said he.

"She is thine, then, O Ibrahim, for one hundred philips."

The Israelite relinquished the purse to the dalal's white-robed assistants and advanced to receive the girl. The corsairs thrust her forward against him, still vainly battling, and his arms closed about her for a moment.

"Thou has cost me dear, thou daughter of Spain," said he. "But I am content. Come." And he made shift to lead her away. Suddenly, however, fierce as a tiger-cat she writhed her arms upwards and clawed at his face. With a scream of pain he relaxed his hold of her, and in that moment, quick as lightning she plucked the dagger that hung from his girdle so temptingly within her reach.

"Valga me Dios!" she cried, and ere a hand could be raised to prevent her she had buried the blade in her lovely breast and sank in a laughing, coughing heap at his feet. A final convulsive heave and she lay there quite still, whilst Ibrahim glared down at her with eyes of dismay, and over all the market there hung a hush of sudden awe. Rosamund had risen in her place, and a faint color came to warm her pallor, a faint light kindled in her eyes. God had shown her the way through this poor Spanish girl, and assuredly God would give her the means to take it when her own turn came. She felt herself suddenly uplifted and enheartened. Death was a sharp, swift severing, an easy door of escape from the horror that threatened her, and God in His mercy, she knew, would justify self-murder under such circumstances as were her own and that poor dead Andalusian maid's.

At length Ibrahim roused himself from his momentary stupor. He stepped deliberately across the body, his face inflamed, and stood to beard the impassive dalal.

"She is dead!" he bleated. "I am defrauded. Give me back my gold!"

"Are we to give back the price of every slave that dies?" the dalal questioned him.

"But she was not yet delivered to me," raved the Jew. "My hands had not touched her. Give me back my gold."

"Thou liest, son of a dog," was the answer, dispassionately delivered. "She was thine already. I had so pronounced her. Bear her hence, since she belongs to thee."

The Jew, his face empurpling, seemed to fight for breath.

"How?" he choked. "Am I to lose a hundred philips?"

"What is written is written," replied the serene dalal.

Ibrahim was frothing at the lips, his eyes were blood-injected. "But it was never written that . . ."

"Peace," said the dalal. "Had it not been written it could not have come to pass. It is the will of Allah! Who dares rebel against it?"

The crowd began to murmur.

"I want my hundred philips," the Jew insisted, whereupon the murmur swelled into a sudden roar.

"Thou hearest?" said the dalal. "Allah pardon thee, thou art disturbing the peace of this market. Away, ere ill betide thee."

"Hence! hence!" roared the crowd, and some advanced threat-

eningly upon the luckless Ibrahim. "Away, thou perverter of Holy
Writ! thou filth! thou dog! Away!"

Such was the uproar, such the menace of angry countenances
and clenched fists shaken in his very face, that Ibrahim quailed and
forgot his loss in fear.

"I go, I go," he said, and turned hastily to depart.

But the dalal summoned him back. "Take hence thy property,"
said he, and pointed to the body. And so Ibrahim was forced to suffer the further mockery of summoning his slaves to bear away the
lifeless body for which he had paid in lively potent gold.

Yet by the gates he paused again. "I will appeal me to the
Basha," he threatened. "Asad-ed-Din is just, and he will have my
money restored to me."

"So he will," said the dalal, "when thou canst restore the dead to
life," and he turned to the portly Ayoub, who was plucking at his
sleeve. He bent his head to catch the muttered words of Fenzileh's
wazeer. Then, in obedience to them, he ordered Rosamund to be
brought forward.

She offered no least resistance, advancing in a singularly lifeless
way, like a sleep-walker or one who had been drugged. In the heat
and glare of the open market she stood by the dalal's side at the
head of the well, whilst he dilated upon her physical merits in that
lingua franca which he used since it was current coin among all the
assorted races represented there—a language which the knowledge of French that her residence in France had taught her she
was to her increasing horror and shame able to understand.

The first to make an offer for her was that same portly Moor
who had sought to purchase the two Nubians. He rose to scrutinize
her closely, and must have been satisfied, for the price he offered
was a good one, and he offered it with contemptuous assurance
that he would not be outbidden.

"One hundred philips for the milk-faced girl."

"'T is not enough. Consider me the moon-bright loveliness of

her face," said the dalal as he moved on. "Chigil yields us fair
women, but no woman of Chigi was ever half so fair."

"One hundred and fifty," said the Levantine Turk with a snap.

"Not yet enough. Behold the stately height which Allah hath
vouchsafed her. See the noble carriage of her head, the luster of
her eye! By Allah, she is worthy to grace the Sultan's own hareem."

He said no more than the buyers recognized to be true, and
excitement stirred faintly through their usually impassive ranks. A
Tagareen Moor named Yusuf offered at once two hundred.

But still the dalal continued to sing her praises. He held up one
of her arms for inspection, and she submitted with lowered eyes,
and no sign of resentment beyond the slow flush that spread across
her face and vanished again.

"Behold me these limbs, smooth as Arabian silks and whiter
than ivory. Look at those lips like pomegranate blossoms. The price
is now two hundred philips. What wilt thou give, O Hamet?"

Hamet showed himself angry that his original bid should so
speedily have been doubled. "By the Koran, I have purchased
three sturdy girls from the Sus for less."

"Wouldst thou compare a squat-faced girl from the Sus with
this narcissus-eyed glory of womanhood?" scoffed the dalal.

"Two hundred and ten, then," was Hamet's sulky grunt.

The watchful Tsamanni considered that the time had come to
buy her for his lord as he had been bidden.

"Three hundred," he said curtly, to make an end of matters,
and—

"Four hundred," instantly piped a shrill voice behind him.

He spun round in his amazement and met the leering face of
Ayoub. A murmur ran through the ranks of the buyers, the people
craned their necks to catch a glimpse of this openhanded purchaser.

Yusuf the Tagareen rose up in a passion. He announced angrily
that never again should the dust of the sôk of Algiers defile his slippers, that never again would he come there to purchase slaves.

"By the Well of Zem-Zem," he swore, "all men are bewitched in this market. Four hundred philips for a Frankish girl! May Allah increase your wealth, for verily you'll need it." And in his supreme disgust he stalked to the gates, and elbowed his way through the crowd, and so vanished from the sôk.

Yet ere he was out of earshot her price had risen further. Whilst Tsamanni was recovering from his surprise at the competitor that had suddenly appeared before him, the dalal had lured an increased offer from the Turk.

"'T is a madness," the latter deplored. "But she pleaseth me, and should it seem good to Allah the Merciful to lead her into the True Faith she may yet become the light of my hareem. Four hundred and twenty philips, then, O dalal, and Allah pardon me my prodigality."

Yet scarcely was his little speech concluded than Tsamanni with laconic eloquence rapped out: "Five hundred."

"Y' Allah!" cried the Turk, raising his hands to heaven, and "Y' Allah!" echoed the crowd.

"Five hundred and fifty," shrilled Ayoub's voice above the general din.

"Six hundred," replied Tsamanni, still unmoved.

And now such was the general hubbub provoked by these unprecedented prices that the dalal was forced to raise his voice and cry for silence.

When this was restored Ayoub at once raised the price to seven hundred.

"Eight hundred," snapped Tsamanni, showing at last a little heat.

"Nine hundred," replied Ayoub.

Tsamanni swung round upon him again, white now with fury. "Is this a jest, O father of wind?" he cried, and excited laughter by the taunt implicit in that appellation.

"And thou'rt the jester," replied Ayoub with forced calm, "thou'lt find the jest a costly one."

With a shrug Tsamanni turned again to the dalal. "A thousand philips," said he shortly.

"Silence there!" cried the dalal again. "Silence, and praise Allah who sends good prices."

"One thousand and one hundred," said Ayoub the irrepressible.

And now Tsamanni not only found himself outbidden, but he had reached the outrageous limit appointed by Asad. He lacked authority to go further, dared not do so without first consulting the Basha. Yet if he left the sôk for that purpose Ayoub would meanwhile secure the girl. He found himself between sword and wall. On the one hand did he permit himself to be outbidden his master might visit upon him his disappointment. On the other, did he continue beyond the limit so idly mentioned as being far beyond all possibility, it might fare no less ill with him.

He turned to the crowd, waving his arms in furious gesticulation. "By the beard of the Prophet, this bladder of wind and grease makes sport of us. He has no intent to buy. What man ever heard of the half of such a price for a slave girl?"

Ayoub's answer was eloquent; he produced a fat bag and flung it on the ground, where it fell with a mellow chink. "There is my sponsor," he made answer, grinning in the very best of humors, savoring to the full his enemy's rage and discomfiture, and savoring it at no cost to himself. "Shall I count out one thousand and one hundred philips, O dalal?"

"If the wazeer Tsamanni is content."

"Dost thou know for whom I buy?" roared Tsamanni. "For the Basha himself, Asad-ed-Din, the exalted of Allah." He advanced upon Ayoub with hands upheld. "What shalt thou say to him, O dog, when he calls thee to account for daring to outbid him?"

But Ayoub remained unruffled before all this fury. He spread his fat hands, his eyes twinkling, his great lips pursed. "How should I know, since Allah has not made me all-knowing? Thou shouldst have said so earlier. 'T is thus I shall answer the Basha should he question me, and the Basha is just."

"I would not be thee, Ayoub—not for the throne of Istambul."

"Nor I thee, Tsamanni; for thou are jaundiced with rage."

And so they stood glaring each at the other until the dalal called them back to the business that was to do.

"The price is now one thousand and one hundred philips. Wilt thou suffer defeat, O wazeer?"

"Since Allah wills. I have no authority to go further."

"Then at one thousand and one hundred philips, Ayoub, she is . . ."

But the sale was not yet to be completed. From the dense and eager throng about the gates rang a crisp voice—

"One thousand and two hundred philips for the Frankish girl."

The dalal, who had conceived that the limits of madness had been already reached, stood gaping now in fresh amazement. The mob crowed and cheered and roared between enthusiasm and derision, and even Tsamanni brightened to see another champion enter the lists who perhaps would avenge him upon Ayoub. The crowd parted quickly to right and left, and through it into the open strode Sakr-el-Bahr. They recognized him instantly, and his name was shouted in acclamation by that idolizing multitude.

That Barbary name of his conveyed no information to Rosamund, and her back being turned to the entrance she did not see him. But she had recognized his voice, and she had shuddered at the sound. She could make nothing of the bidding, nor what the purpose that surely underlay it to account for the extraordinary excitement of the traders. Vaguely had she been wondering what dastardly purpose Oliver might intend to serve, but now that she heard his voice that wonder ceased and understanding took its place. He had hung there somewhere in the crowd waiting until all competitors but one should have been outbidden, and now he stepped forth to buy her for his own—his slave! She closed her eyes a moment and prayed God that he might not prevail in his intent. Any fate but that; she would rob him even of the satisfaction of driving her to sheathe a poniard in her heart as that poor Andalusian girl had done. A wave almost of unconsciousness passed over her in the intensity of her horror. For a moment the ground seemed to rock and heave under her feet. Then the dizziness passed, and she was herself again. She heard the crowd thundering. "Ma'sh 'Allah!" and "Sakr-el-Bahr!" and the dalal clamoring sternly for silence. When this was at last restored she heard his exclamation—

"The glory to Allah who sends eager buyers! What sayest thou, O wazeer Ayoub?"

"Ay!" sneered Tsamanni, "what now?"

"One thousand and three hundred," said Ayoub with a quaver of uneasy defiance.

"Another hundred, O dalal," came from Sakr-el-Bahr in a quiet voice.

"One thousand and five hundred," screamed Ayoub, thus reaching not only the limit imposed by his mistress, but the very limit of the resources at her immediate disposal. Gone, too, with that bid was all hope of profit to himself.

But Sakr-el-Bahr, impassive as Fate, and without so much as deigning to bestow a look upon the quivering eunuch, said again—

"Another hundred, O dalal."

"One thousand and six hundred philips!" cried the dalal, more in amazement than to announce the figure reached. Then controlling his emotions he bowed his head in reverence and made confession of his faith. "All things are possible if Allah wills them. The praise to Him who sends wealthy buyers."

He turned to the crestfallen Ayoub, so crestfallen that in the contemplation of him Tsamanni was fast gathering consolation for his own discomfiture, vicariously tasting the sweets of vengeance. "What say you now, O perspicuous wazeer?"

"I say," choked Ayoub, "that since by the favor of Shaitan he hath so much wealth he must prevail."

But the insulting words were scarcely uttered than Sakr-el-Bahr's great hand had taken the wazeer by the nape of his fat neck, a growl of anger running through the assembly to approve him.

"By the favor of Shaitan, sayest thou, thou sexless dog?" he growled, and tightened his grip so that the wazeer squirmed and twisted in an agony of pain. Down was his head thrust, and still down, until his fat body gave way and he lay supine and writhing in the dust of the sôk. "Shall I strangle thee, thou father of filth, or shall I fling thy soft flesh to the hooks to teach thee what is a man's due from thee?" And as he spoke he rubbed the too daring fellow's face roughly on the ground.

"Mercy!" squealed the wazeer. "Mercy, O mighty Sakr-el-Bahr, as thou lookest for mercy!"

"Unsay thy words, thou offal. Pronounce thyself a liar and a dog."

"I do unsay them. I have foully lied. Thy wealth is the reward sent thee by Allah for thy glorious victories over the unbelieving."

"Put out thine offending tongue," said Sakr-el-Bahr, "and cleanse it in the dust. Put it forth, I say."

Ayoub obeyed him in fearful alacrity, whereupon Sakr-el-Bahr released his hold and allowed the unfortunate fellow to rise at last, half-choked with dirt, livid of face, and quaking like a jelly, an object of ridicule and cruel mockery to all assembled.

"Now get thee hence, ere my sea-hawks lay their talons on thee. Go!"

Ayoub departed in all haste to the increasing jeers of the multitude and the taunts of Tsamanni, whilst Sakr-el-Bahr turned him once more to the dalal.

"At one thousand and six hundred philips this slave is thine, O Sakr-el-Bahr, thou glory of Islam. May Allah increase thy victories!"

"Pay him, Ali," said the corsair shortly, and he advanced to receive his purchase.

Face to face stood he now with Rosamund, for the first time since that day before the encounter with the Dutch argosy when he had sought her in the cabin of the carack.

One swift glance she bestowed on him, then, her senses reeling with horror at her circumstance, she shrank back, her face of a deathly pallor. In his treatment of Ayoub she had just witnessed the lengths of brutality of which he was capable, and she was not to know that this brutality had been a deliberate piece of mummery calculated to strike terror into her.

Pondering her now he smiled a tight-lipped cruel smile that only served to increase her terror.

"Come," he said in English.

She cowered back against the dalal as if for protection. Sakr-el-Bahr reached forward, caught her by the wrists, and almost tossed her to his Nubians, Abiad and Zal-Zer, who were attending him.

"Cover her face," he bade them. "Bear her to my house. Away!"

CHAPTER XI

THE TRUTH

THE SUN was dipping swiftly to the world's rim when Sakr-el-Bahr with his Nubians and his little retinue of corsairs came to the gates of that white house of his on its little eminence outside the Bab-el-Oueb, and beyond the walls of the city.

When Rosamund and Lionel, brought in the wake of the corsair, found themselves in the spacious courtyard beyond the dark and narrow entrance, the blue of the sky contained but the paling embers of the dying day, and suddenly, sharply upon the evening stillness, came a mueddin's voice calling the faithful unto prayer.

Slaves fetched water from the fountain that played in the middle of the quadrangle and tossed aloft a slender silvery spear of water to break into a myriad gems and so shower down into the broad marble basin. Sakr-el-Bahr washed, as did his followers, and then he went down upon the praying-mat that had been set for him, whilst his corsairs detached their cloaks and spread them upon the ground to serve them in like stead.

The Nubians turned the two slaves about, lest their glances should defile the orisons of the faithful, and left them so, facing the wall and the green gate that led into the garden whence were wafted on the cooling air the perfumes of jessamine and lavender. Through the laths of the gate they might have caught a glimpse of the riot of color there, and they might have seen the slaves arrested by the Persian waterwheel at which they had been toiling and chanting until the call to prayer had come to strike them into statues.

Sakr-el-Bahr rose from his devotions, uttered a sharp word of command, and entered the house. The Nubians followed him, urging their captives before them up the narrow stairs, and so brought them out upon the terrace on the roof, that space which in Eastern houses is devoted to the women, but which no woman's foot had ever trodden since this house had been tenanted by Sakr-el-Bahr the wifeless.

This terrace, which was surrounded by a parapet some four feet high, commanded a view of the city straggling up the hillside to eastward from the harbor and of the island at the end of the mole which had been so laboriously built by the labor of Christian slaves from the stones of the ruined fortress—the Peñon, which Kheyr-ed-Din Barbarossa had wrested from the Spaniards. The deepening shroud of evening was now upon all, transmuting white and yellow walls alike to a pearly grayness. To westward stretched the fragrant gardens of the house, where the doves were murmuring fondly among the mulberries and lotus trees. Beyond it a valley wound its way between the shallow hills, and from a pool fringed with sedges and bullrushes above which a great stork was majestically sailing came the harsh croak of frogs.

An awning supported upon two gigantic spears hung out from the southern wall of the terrace which rose to twice the height of that forming the parapet on its other three sides. Under this was a divan and silken cushions, and near it a small Moorish table of ebony inlaid with mother of pearl and gold. Over the opposite parapet, where a lattice had been set, rioted a trailing rose-tree charged with blood-red blossoms, though now their colors were merged into the all-encompassing grayness.

Here Lionel and Rosamund looked at each other in the dim light, their faces gleaming ghostly each to each, whilst the Nubians stood like twin statues by the door that opened from the stair-head.

The man groaned, and clasped his hands before him. The doublet which had been torn from him in the sôk had since been restored and temporarily repaired by a strand of palmetto cord. But he was woefully bedraggled. Yet his thoughts, if his first words are to be taken as an indication of them, were for Rosamund's condition rather than his own.

"O God, that you should be subjected to this!" he cried. "That you should have suffered what you have suffered! The humiliation of it, the barbarous cruelty! Oh!" He covered his haggard face with his hands.

She touched him gently on the arm.

"What I have suffered is but a little thing," she said, and her voice was wonderfully steady and soothing. Have I not said that these Godolphins were brave folk? Even their women were held to have something of the male spirit in their breasts; and to this none can doubt that Rosamund now bore witness. "Do not pity me, Lionel, for my sufferings are at an end or very nearly." She smiled strangely, the smile of exaltation that you may see upon the martyr's face in the hour of doom.

"How?" quoth he, in faint surprise.

"How?" she echoed. "Is there not always a way to thrust aside life's burden when it grows too heavy—heavier than God would have us bear?"

His only answer was a groan. Indeed, he had done little but groan in all the hours they had spent together since they were brought ashore from the carack; and had the season permitted her so much reflection, she might have considered that she had found him singularly wanting during those hours of stress when a man of worth would have made some effort, however desperate, to enhearten her rather than repine upon his own plight.

Slaves entered bearing four enormous flaming torches, which they set in iron sconces protruding from the wall of the house. Thence they shed a lurid ruddy glow upon the terrace. The slaves departed again, and presently, in the black gap of the doorway between the Nubians, a third figure appeared unheralded. It was Sakr-el-Bahr.

He stood a moment at gaze, his attitude haughty, his face expressionless; then slowly he advanced. He was dressed in a short white caftan that descended to his knees, and was caught about his waist in a shimmering girdle of gold that quivered like fire in the glow of the torches as he moved. His arms from the elbow and his legs from the knee were bare, and his feet were shod with gold-embroidered red Turkish slippers. He wore a white turban decked by a plume of osprey attached by a jeweled clasp.

He signed to the Nubians and they vanished silently, leaving him alone with his captives.

He bowed to Rosamund. "This, mistress," he said, "is to be your domain henceforth, which is to treat you more as wife than slave. For it is to Muslim wives that the housetops in Barbary are allotted. I hope you like it."

Lionel staring at him out of a white face, his conscience bidding him fear the very worst, his imagination painting a thousand horrid fates for him and turning him sick with dread, shrank back before his half-brother, who scarce appeared to notice him just then.

But Rosamund confronted him, drawn to the full of her splendid height, and if her face was pale, yet it was as composed and calm as his own; if her bosom rose and fell to betray her agitation, yet her glance was contemptuous and defiant, her voice calm and steady, when she answered him with the question—

"What is your intent with me?"

"My intent?" said he, with a little twisted smile. Yet for all that he believed he hated her and sought to hurt, to humble and to crush her, he could not stifle his admiration of her spirit's gallantry in such an hour as this.

From behind the hills peeped the edge of the moon—a sickle of burnished copper.

"My intent is not for you to question," he replied. "There was a time, Rosamund, when in all the world you had no slave more utter than was I. Yourself in your heartlessness, and in your lack of faith, you broke the golden fetters of that servitude. You'll find it less easy to break the shackles I now impose upon you."

She smiled her scorn and quiet confidence. He stepped close to her.

"You are my slave, do you understand?—bought in the market-place as I might buy me a mule, a goat, or a camel—and belonging to me body and soul. You are my property, my thing, my chattel, to use or abuse, to cherish or break as suits my whim, without a will that is not my will, holding your very life at my good pleasure."

She recoiled a step before the dull hatred that throbbed in his words, before the evil mockery of his swarthy bearded face.

"You beast!" she gasped.

"So now you understand the bondage into which you are come in exchange for the bondage which in your own wantonness you dissolved."

"May God forgive you," she panted.

"I thank you for that prayer," said he. "May He forgive you no less."

And then from the background came an inarticulate sound, a strangled, snarling sob from Lionel.

Sakr-el-Bahr turned slowly. He eyed the fellow a moment in silence, then he laughed.

"Ha! My sometime brother. A pretty fellow, as God lives, is it not? Consider him, Rosamund. Behold how gallantly misfortune is borne by this pillar of manhood upon which you would have leaned, by this stalwart husband of your choice. Look at him! Look at this dear brother of mine."

Under the lash of that mocking tongue Lionel's mood was stung to anger where before it had held naught but fear.

"You are no brother of mine," he retorted fiercely. "Your mother was a wanton who betrayed my father."

Sakr-el-Bahr quivered a moment as if he had been struck. Yet he controlled himself.

"Let me hear my mother's name but once again on thy foul tongue, and I'll have it ripped out by the roots. Her memory, I thank God, is far above the insults of such a crawling thing as you. None the less, take care not to speak of the only woman whose name I reverence."

And then, turning at bay, as even the rat will do, Lionel sprang upon him, with clawing hands outstretched to reach his throat. But Sakr-el-Bahr caught him in a grip that bent him howling to his knees.

"You find me strong, eh?" he gibed. "Is it matter for wonder? Consider that for six endless months I toiled at the oar of a galley, and you'll understand what it was that turned my body into iron and robbed me of a soul."

He flung him off, and sent him crashing into the rosebush and the lattice over which it rambled.

"Do you realize the horror of the rower's bench? to sit day in day out, night in night out, chained naked to the oar, amid the reek and stench of your fellows in misfortune, unkempt, unwashed save by the rain, broiled and roasted by the sun, festering with sores, lashed and cut and scarred by the boatswain's whip as you faint under the ceaseless, endless, cruel toil?

"Do you realize it?" From a tone of suppressed fury his voice rose suddenly to a roar. "You shall. For that horror which was mine by your contriving shall now be yours until you die."

He paused; but Lionel made no attempt to avail himself of this. His courage all gone out of him again, as suddenly as it had flickered up, he cowered where he had been flung.

"Before you go there is something else," Sakr-el-Bahr resumed, "something for which I have had you brought hither to-night.

"Not content with having delivered me to all this, not content with having branded me a murderer, destroyed my good name, filched my possessions and driven me into the very path of hell, you must further set about usurping my place in the false heart of this woman I once loved.

"I hope," he went on reflectively, "that in your own poor way you love her, too, Lionel. Thus to the torment that awaits your body shall be added torment for your treacherous soul—such torture of mind as only the damned may know. To that end have I brought you hither. That you may realize something of what is in store for this woman at my hands; that you may take the thought of it with you to be to your mind worse than the boatswain's lash to your pampered body."

"You devil!" snarled Lionel. "O, you fiend out of hell!"

"If you will manufacture devils, little toad of a brother, do not upbraid them for being devils when next you meet them."

"Give him no heed, Lionel!" said Rosamund. "I shall prove him as much a boaster as he has proved himself a villain. Never think that he will be able to work his evil will."

"'T is you are the boaster there," said Sakr-el-Bahr. "And for the rest, I am what you and he, between you, have made me."

"Did we make you liar and coward?—for that is what you are indeed," she answered.

"Coward?" he echoed, in genuine surprise. "'T will be some lie that he has told you with the others. In what, pray, was I ever a coward?"

"In what? In this that you do now; in this taunting and torturing of two helpless beings in your power."

"I speak not of what I am," he replied, "for I have told you that I am what you have made me. I speak of what I was. I speak of the past."

She looked at him and she seemed to measure him with her unwavering glance.

"You speak of the past?" she echoed, her voice low. "You speak of the past and to me? You dare?"

"It is that we might speak of it together that I have fetched you all the way from England; that at last I may tell you things I was a fool to have kept from you five years ago; that we may resume a conversation which you interrupted when you dismissed me."

"I did you a monstrous injury, no doubt," she answered him, with bitter irony. "I was surely wanting in consideration. It would have become me better to have smiled and fawned upon my brother's murderer."

"I swore to you, then, that I was not his murderer," he reminded her in a voice that shook.

"And I answered you that you lied."

"Ay, and on that you dismissed me—the word of the man whom you professed to love, the word of the man to whom you had given your trust weighing for naught with you."

"When I gave you my trust," she retorted, "I did so in ignorance of your true self, in a headstrong wilful ignorance that would not be guided by what all the world said of you and your wild ways. For that blind wilfulness I have been punished, as perhaps I deserved to be."

"Lies—all lies!" he stormed. "Those ways of mine—and God knows they were none so wild, when all is said—I abandoned when I came to love you. No lover since the world began was ever so cleansed, so purified, so sanctified by love as was I."

"Spare me this at least!" she cried on a note of loathing.

"Spare you?" he echoed. "What shall I spare you?"

"The shame of it all; the shame that is ever mine in the reflection that for a season I believed I loved you."

He smiled. "If you can still feel shame, it shall overwhelm you ere I have done. For you shall hear me out. Here there are none to interrupt us, none to thwart my sovereign will. Reflect then, and remember. Remember what a pride you took in the change you had wrought in me. Your vanity welcomed that flattery, that tribute

to the power of your beauty. Yet, all in a moment, upon the paltriest
grounds, you believed me the murderer of your brother."

"The paltriest grounds?" she cried, protesting almost despite
herself.

"So paltry that the justices at Truro would not move against me."

"Because," she cut in, "they accounted that you had been sufficiently provoked. Because you had not sworn to them as you swore
to me that no provocation should ever drive you to raise your hand
against my brother. Because they did not realize how false and how
forsworn you were."

He considered her a moment. Then he took a turn on the terrace. Lionel crouching ever by the rose-tree was almost entirely
forgotten by him now.

"God give me patience with you!" he said at length. "I need it.
For I desire you to understand many things this night. I mean you
to see how just is my resentment; how just the punishment that is
to overtake you for what you have made of my life and perhaps of
my hereafter. Justice Baine and another who is dead, knew me for
innocent."

"They knew you for innocent?" There was scornful amazement
in her tone. "Were they not witnesses of the quarrel betwixt you
and Peter and of your oath that you would kill him?"

"That was an oath sworn in the heat of anger. Afterwards I
bethought me that he was your brother."

"Afterwards?" said she. "After you had murdered him?"

"I say again," Oliver replied calmly, "that I did not do this
thing."

"And I say again that you lie."

He considered her for a long moment; then he laughed. "Have
you ever," he asked, "known a man to lie without some purpose?
Men lie for the sake of profit, they lie out of cowardice or malice, or
else because they are vain and vulgar boasters. I know of no other
causes that will drive a man to falsehood, save that—ah yes!—"

(and he flashed a sidelong glance at Lionel)—"save that sometimes a man will lie to shield another, out of self-sacrifice. There you have all the spurs that urge a man to falsehood. Can any of these be urging me to-night? Reflect! Ask yourself what purpose I could serve by lying to you now. Consider further that I have come to loathe you for your unfaith; that I desire naught so much as to punish you for that and for all its bitter consequences to me; that I have brought you hither to exact payment from you to the uttermost farthing. What end then can I serve by falsehood?"

"All this being so, what end could you serve by truth?" she countered.

"To make you realize to the full the injustice that you did. To make you understand the wrongs for which you are called to pay. To prevent you from conceiving yourself a martyr; to make you perceive in all its deadly bitterness that what now comes to you is the inevitable fruit of your own faithlessness."

"Sir Oliver, do you think me a fool?" she asked him.

"Madam, I do—and worse," he answered.

"Ay, that is clear," she agreed scornfully, "since even now you waste breath in attempting to persuade me against my reason. But words will not blot out facts. And though you talk from now till the day of judgment no word of yours can efface those bloodstains in the snow that formed a trail from that poor murdered body to your own door; no word of yours can extinguish the memory of the hatred between him and you, and of your own threat to kill him; nor can it stifle the recollection of the public voice demanding your punishment. You dare to take such a tone as you are taking with me? You dare here under Heaven to stand and lie to me that you may give a false gloze to the villainy of your present deed—for that is the purpose of your falsehood, since you asked me what purpose there could be for it. What had you to set against all that, to convince me that your hands were clean, to induce me to keep the troth which—God forgive me!—I had plighted to you?"

"My word," he answered her in a ringing voice.

"Your lie," she amended.

"Do not suppose," said he, "that I could not support my word by proofs if called upon to do so."

"Proofs?" She stared at him, wide-eyed a moment. Then her lip curled. "And that no doubt was the reason of your flight when you heard that the Queen's pursuivants were coming in response to the public voice to call you to account."

He stood at gaze a moment, utterly dumbfounded. "My flight?" he said. "What fable's that?"

"You will tell me next that you did not flee. That that is another false charge against you?"

"So," he said slowly, "it was believed I fled!"

And then light burst upon him, to dazzle and stun him. It was so inevitably what must have been believed, and yet it had never crossed his mind. Oh the damnable simplicity of it! At another time his disappearance must have provoked comment and investigation, perhaps. But, happening when it did, the answer to it came promptly and convincingly, and no man troubled to question further. Thus was Lionel's task made doubly easy, thus was his own guilt made doubly sure in the eyes of all. His head sank upon his breast. What had he done? Could he still blame Rosamund for having been convinced by so overwhelming a piece of evidence? Could he still blame her if she had burnt unopened the letter which he had sent her by the hand of Pitt? What else indeed could any suppose, but that he had fled? And that being so, clearly such a flight must brand him irrefutably for the murderer he was alleged to be. How could he blame her if she had ultimately been convinced by the only reasonable assumption possible?

A sudden sense of the wrong he had done rose now like a tide about him.

"My God!" he groaned, like a man in pain. "My God!"

He looked at her, and then averted his glance again, unable now to endure the haggard, stained yet fearless gaze of those brave eyes of hers.

"What else, indeed, could you believe?" he muttered brokenly, thus giving some utterance to what was passing through his mind.

"Naught else but the whole vile truth," she answered fiercely, and thereby stung him anew, whipped him out of his sudden weakening back to his mood of resentment and vindictiveness.

She had shown herself, he thought in that moment of reviving anger, too ready to believe what told against him.

"The truth?" he echoed, and eyed her boldly now. "Do you know the truth when you see it? We shall discover. For by God's light you shall have the truth laid stark before you now, and you shall find it hideous beyond all your hideous imaginings."

There was something so compelling now in his tone and manner that it drove her to realize that some revelation was impending. She was conscious of a faint excitement, a reflection perhaps of the wild excitement that was astir in him.

"Your brother," he began, "met his death at the hands of a false weakling whom I loved, towards whom I had a sacred duty. Straight from the deed he fled to me for shelter. A wound he had taken in the struggle left that trail of blood to mark the way he had come." He paused, and his tone became gentler, it assumed the level note of one who reasons impassively. "Was it not an odd thing, now, that none should ever have paused to seek with certainty whence that blood proceeded, and to consider that I bore no wound in those days? Master Baine knew it, for I submitted my body to his examination, and a document was drawn up and duly attested which should have sent the Queen's pursuivants back to London with drooping tails had I been at Penarrow to receive them."

Faintly through her mind stirred the memory that Master Baine had urged the existence of some such document, that in fact he had gone so far as to have made oath of this very circumstance now urged by Sir Oliver; and she remembered that the matter had been brushed aside as an invention of the justice's to answer the charge of laxity in the performance of his duty, particularly as the only co-witness he could cite was Sir Andrew Flack, the parson, since deceased. Sir Oliver's voice drew her attention from that memory.

"But let that be," he was saying. "Let us come back to the story itself. I gave the craven weakling shelter. Thereby I drew down suspicion upon myself, and since I could not clear myself save by denouncing him, I kept silent. That suspicion drew to certainty when the woman to whom I was betrothed, recking nothing of my oaths, freely believing the very worst of me, made an end of our betrothal and thereby branded me a murderer and a liar in the eyes of all. Indignation swelled against me. The Queen's pursuivants were on their way to do what the justices of Truro refused to do.

"So far I have given you facts. Now I give you surmise—my own conclusions—but surmise that strikes, as you shall judge, the very bull's-eye of truth. That dastard to whom I had given sanctuary, to whom I had served as a cloak, measured my nature by his own and feared that I must prove unequal to the fresh burden to be cast upon me. He feared lest under the strain of it I should speak out, advance my proofs, and so destroy him. There was the matter of that wound, and there was something still more unanswerable he feared I might have urged. There was a certain woman—a wanton up at Malpas—who could have been made to speak, who could have revealed a rivalry concerning her betwixt the slayer and your brother. For the affair in which Peter Godolphin met his death was a pitifully, shamefully sordid one at bottom."

For the first time she interrupted him, fiercely. "Do you malign the dead?"

"Patience, mistress," he commanded. "I malign none. I speak the truth of a dead man that the truth may be known of two living ones. Hear me out, then! I have waited long and survived a deal that I might tell you this.

"That craven, then, conceived that I might become a danger to him; so he decided to remove me. He contrived to have me kidnapped one night and put aboard a vessel to be carried to Barbary and sold there as a slave. That is the truth of my disappearance. And the slayer, whom I had befriended and sheltered at my own bitter cost, profited yet further by my removal. God knows whether the prospect of such profit was a further temptation to him. In time he came to succeed me in my possessions, and at last to succeed me even in the affections of the faithless woman who once had been my affianced wife."

At last she started from the frozen patience in which she had listened hitherto. "Do you say that . . . that Lionel . . . ?" she was beginning in a voice choked by indignation.

And then Lionel spoke at last, straightening himself into a stiffly upright attitude.

"He lies!" he cried. "He lies, Rosamund! Do not heed him."

"I do not," she answered, turning away.

A wave of color suffused the swarthy face of Sakr-el-Bahr. A moment his eyes followed her as she moved away a step or two, then they turned their blazing light of anger upon Lionel. He strode silently across to him, his mien so menacing that Lionel shrank back in fresh terror.

Sakr-el-Bahr caught his brother's wrist in a grip that was as that of a steel manacle. "We'll have the truth this night if we have to tear it from you with red-hot pincers," he said between his teeth.

He dragged him forward to the middle of the terraces and held him there before Rosamund, forcing him down upon his knees into a cowering attitude by the violence of that grip upon his wrist.

"Do you know aught of the ingenuity of Moorish torture?" he asked him. "You may have heard of the rack and the wheel and the thumbscrew at home. They are instruments of voluptuous delight compared with the contrivances of Barbary to loosen stubborn tongues."

White and tense, her hands clenched, Rosamund seemed to stiffen before him.

"You coward! You cur! You craven renegade dog!" she branded him.

Oliver released his brother's wrist and beat his hands together. Without heeding Rosamund he looked down upon Lionel, who cowered shuddering at his feet.

"What do you say to a match between your fingers? Or do you think a pair of bracelets of living fire would answer better, to begin with?"

A squat, sandy-bearded, turbaned fellow, rolling slightly in his gait, came—as had been prearranged—to answer the corsair's summons.

With the toe of his slipper Sakr-el-Bahr stirred his brother.

"Look up, dog," he bade him. "Consider me that man, and see if you know him again. Look at him, I say!" And Lionel looked, yet since clearly he did so without recognition his brother explained: "His name among Christians was Jasper Leigh. He was the skipper you bribed to carry me into Barbary. He was taken in his own toils when his ship was sunk by Spaniards. Later he fell into my power, and because I forbore from hanging him he is to-day my faithful follower. I should bid him tell you what he knows," he continued, turning to Rosamund, "if I thought you would believe his tale. But since I am assured you would not, I will take other means." He swung round to Jasper again. "Bid Ali heat me a pair of steel manacles in a brazier and hold them in readiness against my need of them." And he waved his hand.

Jasper bowed and vanished.

"The bracelets shall coax confession from your own lips, my brother."

"I have naught to confess," protested Lionel. "You may force lies from me with your ruffianly tortures."

Oliver smiled. "Not a doubt but that lies will flow from you more readily than truth. But we shall have truth, too, in the end, never doubt it." He was mocking, and there was a subtle purpose underlying his mockery. "And you shall tell a full story," he continued, "in all its details, so that Mistress Rosamund's last doubt shall vanish. You shall tell her how you lay in wait for him that evening in Godolphin Park; how you took him unawares, and . . ."

"That is false!" cried Lionel in a passion of sincerity that brought him to his feet.

It was false, indeed, and Oliver knew it, and deliberately had recourse to falsehood, using it as a fulcrum upon which to lever out the truth. He was cunning as all the fiends, and never perhaps did he better manifest his cunning.

"False?" he cried with scorn. "Come, now, be reasonable. The truth, ere torture sucks it out of you. Reflect that I know all—exactly as you told it me. How was it, now? Lurking behind a bush you sprang upon him unawares and ran him through before he could so much as lay a hand to his sword, and so . . ."

"The lie of that is proven by the very facts themselves," was the furious interruption. A subtle judge of tones might have realized that here was truth indeed, angry indignant truth that compelled conviction. "His sword lay beside him when they found him."

But Oliver was loftily disdainful. "Do I not know? Yourself you drew it after you had slain him."

The taunt performed its deadly work. For just one instant Lionel was carried off his feet by the luxury of his genuine indignation, and in that one instant he was lost.

"As God's my witness, that is false!" he cried wildly. "And you know it. I fought him fair . . ." He checked on a long, shuddering, indrawn breath that was horrible to hear.

Then silence followed, all three remaining motionless as statues: Rosamund white and tense, Oliver grim and sardonic, Lionel limp, and overwhelmed by the consciousness of how he had been lured into self-betrayal.

At last it was Rosamund who spoke, and her voice shook and shifted from key to key despite her strained attempt to keep it level.

"What . . . what did you say, Lionel?" she asked.

Oliver laughed softly. "He was about to add proof of his statement, I think," he jeered. "He was about to mention the wound he took in that fight, which left those tracks in the snow, thus to prove that I lied—as indeed I did—when I said that he took Peter unawares."

"Lionel!" she cried. She advanced a step and made as if to hold out her arms to him, then let them fall again beside her. He stood stricken, answering nothing "Lionel!" she cried again, her voice growing suddenly shrill. "Is this true?"

"Did you not hear him say it?" quoth Oliver.

She stood swaying a moment, looking at Lionel, her white face distorted into a mask of unutterable pain. Oliver stepped towards her, ready to support her, fearing that she was about to fall. But with an imperious hand she checked his advance, and by a supreme effort controlled her weakness. Yet her knees shook under her, refusing their office. She sank down upon the divan and covered her face with her hands.

"God pity me!" she moaned, and sat huddled there, shaken with sobs.

Lionel started at that heart-broken cry. Cowering, he approached her, and Oliver, grim and sardonic, stood back, a spectator of the scene he had precipitated. He knew that given rope Lionel would enmesh himself still further. There must be explanations that would damn him utterly. Oliver was well content to look on.

"Rosamund!" came Lionel's piteous cry. "Rose! Have mercy! Listen ere you judge me. Listen lest you misjudge me!"

"Ay, listen to him," Oliver flung in, with his soft hateful laugh. "Listen to him. I doubt he'll be vastly entertaining."

That sneer was a spur to the wretched Lionel. "Rosamund, all that he has told you of it is false. I . . . I . . . It was done in self-defense. It is a lie that I took him unawares." His words came wildly now. "We had quarreled about . . . about . . . a certain matter, and as the devil would have it we met that evening in Godolphin

Park, he and I. He taunted me; he struck me, and finally he drew upon me and forced me to draw that I might defend my life. That is the truth. I swear to you here on my knees in the sight of Heaven! And . . ."

"Enough, sir! Enough!" she broke in, controlling herself to check these protests that but heightened her disgust.

"Nay, hear me yet, I implore you; that knowing all you may be merciful in your judgment."

"Merciful?" she cried, and almost seemed to laugh.

"It was an accident that I slew him," Lionel raved on. "I never meant it. I never meant to do more than ward and preserve my life. But when swords are crossed more may happen than a man intends. I take God to witness that his death was an accident resulting from his own fury."

She had checked her sobs, and she considered him now with eyes that were hard and terrible.

"Was it also an accident that you left me and all the world in the belief that the deed was your brother's?" she asked him.

He covered his face, as if unable to endure her glance. "Did you but know how I loved you—even in those days, in secret—you would perhaps pity me a little," he whimpered.

"Pity?" She leaned forward and seemed to spit the word at him. "'Sdeath, man! Do you sue for pity—you?"

"Yet you must pity me did you know the greatness of the temptation to which I succumbed."

"I know the greatness of your infamy, of your falseness, of your cowardice, of your baseness. Oh!"

He stretched out suppliant hands to her; there were tears now in his eyes. "Of your charity, Rosamund . . ." he was beginning, when at last Oliver intervened.

"I think you are wearying the lady," he said, and stirred him with his foot. "Relate to us instead some more of your astounding accidents. They are more diverting. Elucidate the accident by which you had me kidnapped to be sold into slavery. Tell us of the accident by which you succeeded to my property. Expound to the full the accidental circumstances of which throughout you have been the unfortunate victim. Come, man, ply your wits. 'T will make a pretty tale."

And then came Jasper to announce that Ali waited with the brazier and the heated manacles.

"They are no longer needed," said Oliver. "Take this slave hence with you. Bid Ali to take charge of him, and at dawn to see him chained to one of the oars of my galeasse. Away with him."

Lionel rose to his feet, his face ashen. "Wait! Ah, wait! Rosamund!" he cried.

Oliver caught him by the nape of his neck, spun him round, and flung him into the arms of Jasper. "Take him away!" he growled, and Jasper took the wretch by the shoulders and urged him out, leaving Rosamund and Oliver alone with the truth under the stars of Barbary.

CHAPTER XII

THE SUBTLETY
OF FENZILEH

OLIVER CONSIDERED the woman for a long moment as
she sat half-crouching on the divan, her hands locked, her
face set and stony, her eyes lowered. He sighed gently
and turned away. He paced to the parapet and looked out upon the
city bathed in the white glare of the full risen moon. There arose
thence a hum of sound, dominated, however, by the throbbing song
of a nightingale somewhere in his garden and the croaking of the
frogs by the pool in the valley.

Now that truth had been dragged from its well, and tossed, as it
were, into Rosamund's lap, he felt none of the fierce exultation
which he had conceived that such an hour as this must bring him.
Rather, indeed, was he saddened and oppressed. To poison the
unholy cup of joy which he had imagined himself draining with
such thirsty zest there was that discovery of a measure of justifica-
tion for her attitude towards him in her conviction that his disappearance was explained by flight.

He was weighed down by a sense that he had put himself
entirely in the wrong; that in his vengeance he had overreached

himself; and he found the fruits of it, which had seemed so desirably luscious, turning to ashes in his mouth.

Long he stood there, the silence between them entirely unbroken. Then at length he stirred, turned from the parapet, and paced slowly back until he came to stand beside the divan, looking down upon her from his great height.

"At last you have heard the truth," he said. And as she made no answer he continued: "I am thankful it was surprised out of him before the torture was applied, else you might have concluded that pain was wringing a false confession from him." He paused, but still she did not speak; indeed, she made no sign that she had heard him. "That," he concluded, "was the man whom you preferred to me. Faith, you did not flatter me, as perhaps you may have learnt."

At last she was moved from her silence, and her voice came dull and hard. "I have learnt how little there is to choose between you," she said. "It was to have been expected. I might have known that two brothers could not have been so dissimilar in nature. Oh, I am learning a deal, and swiftly!"

It was a speech that angered him, that cast out entirely the softer mood that had been growing in him.

"You are learning?" he echoed. "What are you learning?"

"Knowledge of the ways of men."

His teeth gleamed in his wry smile. "I hope the knowledge will bring you as much bitterness as the knowledge of women—of one woman—has brought me. To have believed me what you believed me—me whom you conceived yourself to love!" He felt perhaps the need to repeat it that he might keep the grounds of his grievance well before his mind.

"If I have a mercy to beg of you it is that you will not shame me with the reminder."

"Of your faithlessness?" he asked. "Of your disloyal readiness to believe the worst evil of me?"

"Of my ever having believed that I loved you. That is the

thought that shames me, as nothing else in life could shame me, as not even the slave-market and all the insult to which you have submitted me could shame me. You taunt me with my readiness to believe evil of you . . ."

"I do more than taunt you with it," he broke in, his anger mounting under the pitiless lash of her scorn. "I lay to your charge the wasted years of my life, all the evil that has followed out of it, all that I have suffered, all that I have lost, all that I am become."

She looked up at him coldly, astonishingly mistress of herself. "You lay all this to my charge?" she asked him.

"I do." He was very vehement. "Had you not used me as you did, had you not lent a ready ear to lies, that whelp my brother would never have gone to such lengths, nor should I ever have afforded him the opportunity."

She shifted on the cushions of the divan and turned her shoulder to him.

"All this is very idle," she said coldly. Yet perhaps because she felt that she had need to justify herself she continued: "If, after all, I was so ready to believe evil of you, it is that my instincts must have warned me of the evil that was ever in you. You have proved to me to-night that it was not you who murdered Peter; but to attain that proof you have done a deed that is even fouler and more shameful, a deed that reveals to the full the blackness of your heart. Have you not proved yourself a monster of vengeance and impiety?" She rose and faced him again in her sudden passion. "Are you not—you that were born a Cornish Christian gentleman—become a heathen and a robber, a renegade and a pirate? Have you not sacrificed your very God to your vengeful lust?"

He met her glance fully, never quailing before her denunciation, and when she had ended on that note of question he counter-questioned her.

"And your instincts had forewarned you of all this? God's life, woman! can you invent no better tale than that?" He turned aside as two slaves entered bearing an earthenware vessel. "Here comes your supper. I hope your appetite is keener than your logic."

They set the vessel, from which a savory smell proceeded, upon the little Moorish table by the divan. On the ground beside it they placed a broad dish of baked earth in which there were a couple of loaves and a red, short-necked amphora of water with a drinking-cup placed over the mouth of it to act as a stopper.

They salaamed profoundly and padded softly out again.

"Sup," he bade her shortly.

"I want no supper," she replied, her manner sullen.

His cold eye played over her. "Henceforth, girl, you will consider not what you want, but what I bid you do. I bid you eat; about it, therefore."

"I will not."

"Will not?" he echoed slowly. "Is that a speech from slave to master? Eat, I say."

"I cannot! I cannot!" she protested.

"A slave may not live who cannot do her master's bidding."

"Then kill me," she answered fiercely, leaping up to confront and dare him. "Kill me. You are used to killing, and for that at least I should be grateful."

"I will kill you if I please," he said in level icy tones. "But not to please you. You don't yet understand. You are my slave, my thing, my property, and I will not suffer you to be damaged save at my own good pleasure. Therefore, eat, or my Nubians shall whip you to quicken appetite."

For a moment she stood defiant before him, white and resolute. Then quite suddenly, as if her will was being bent and crumpled under the insistent pressure of his own, she drooped and sank down again to the divan. Slowly, reluctantly she drew the dish nearer. Watching her, he laughed quite silently.

She paused, appearing to seek for something. Failing to find it she looked up at him again, between scorn and intercession.

"Am I to tear the meat with my fingers?" she demanded.

His eyes gleamed with understanding, or at least with suspicion. But he answered her quite calmly—

"It is against the prophet's law to defile meat or bread by the contact of a knife. You must use the hands that God has given you."

"Do you mock me with the Prophet and his laws? What are the Prophet's laws to me? If eat I must, at least I will not eat like a heathen dog, but in Christian fashion."

To indulge her, as it seemed, he slowly drew the richly hilted dagger from his girdle. "Let that serve you, then," he said; and carelessly he tossed it down beside her.

With a quick indrawn breath she pounced upon it. "At last," she said, "you give me something for which I can be grateful to you." And on the words she laid the point of it against her breast.

Like lightning he had dropped to one knee, and his hand had closed about her wrist with such a grip that all her arm felt limp and powerless. He was smiling into her eyes, his swarthy face close to her own.

"Did you indeed suppose I trusted you? Did you really think me deceived by your sudden pretence of yielding? When will you learn that I am not a fool? I did it but to test your spirit."

"Then now you know its temper," she replied. "You know my intention."

"Forewarned, forearmed," said he.

She looked at him, with something that would have been mockery but for the contempt that colored it too deeply. "Is it so difficult a thing," she asked, "to snap the thread of life? Are there no ways of dying save by the knife? You boast yourself my master; that I am your slave; that, having bought me in the marketplace, I belong to you body and soul. How idle is that boast. My body you may bind and confine; but my soul . . . Be very sure that you shall be cheated of your bargain. You boast yourself lord of life and death. A lie! Death is all that you can command."

Quick steps came pattering up the stairs, and before he could answer her, before he had thought of words in which to do so, Ali confronted him with the astounding announcement that there was a woman below asking urgently to speak with him.

"A woman?" he questioned, frowning. "A Nasrani woman, do you mean?"

"No, my lord. A Muslim," was the still more surprising information.

"A Muslim woman, here? Impossible!"

But even as he spoke a dark figure glided like a shadow across the threshold onto the terrace. She was in black from head to foot, including the veil that shrouded her, a veil of the proportions of a mantle, serving to dissemble her very shape.

Ali swung upon her in a rage. "Did I not bid thee wait below, thou daughter of shame?" he stormed. "She has followed me up, my lord, to thrust herself in here upon you. Shall I drive her forth?"

"Let her be," said Sakr-el-Bahr. And he waved Ali away. "Leave us!"

Something about that black immovable figure arrested his attention and fired his suspicions. Unaccountably almost it brought to his mind the thought of Ayoub-el-Samin and the bidding there had been for Rosamund in the sôk.

He stood waiting for his visitor to speak and disclose herself. She on her side continued immovable until Ali's footsteps had faded in the distance. Then, with a boldness entirely characteristic, with the recklessness that betrayed her European origin, intolerant of the Muslim restraint imposed upon her sex, she did what no True-believing woman would have done. She tossed back that long black veil and disclosed the pale countenance and languorous eyes of Fenzileh.

For all that it was no more than he had expected, yet upon beholding her—her countenance thus bared to his regard—he recoiled a step.

"Fenzileh!" he cried. "What madness is this?"

Having announced herself in that dramatic fashion she composedly readjusted her veil so that her countenance should once more be decently concealed.

"To come here, to my house, and thus!" he protested. "Should this reach the ears of thy lord, how will it fare with thee and with me? Away, woman, and at once!" he bade her.

"No need to fear his knowing of this unless, thyself, thou tell him," she answered. "To thee I need no excuse if thou'lt but remember that like thyself I was not born a Muslim."

"But Algiers is not thy native Sicily, and whatever thou wast born it were well to remember what thou art become."

He went on at length to tell her of the precise degree of her folly, but she cut in, stemming his protestation in full flow.

"These are idle words that but delay me."

"To thy purpose then, in Allah's name, that thus thou mayest depart the sooner."

She came to it straight enough on that uncompromising summons. She pointed to Rosamund. "It concerns that slave," said she. "I sent my wazeer to the sôk to-day with orders to purchase her for me."

"So I had supposed," he said.

"But it seems that she caught thy fancy, and the fool suffered himself to be outbidden."

"Well?"

"Thou'lt relinquish her to me at the price she cost thee?" A faint note of anxiety trembled in her voice.

"I am anguished to deny thee, O Fenzileh. She is not for sale."

"Ah, wait," she cried. "The price paid was high—many times higher than I have ever heard tell was given for a slave, however lovely. Yet I covet her. 'T is a whim of mine, and I cannot suffer to be thwarted in my whims. To gratify this one I will pay three thousand philips."

He looked at her and wondered what devilries might be stirring in her mind, what evil purpose she desired to serve.

"Thou't pay three thousand philips?" he said slowly. Then bluntly asked her: "Why?"

"To gratify a whim, to please a fancy."

"What is the nature of this costly whim?" he insisted.

"The desire to possess her for my own," she answered evasively.

"And this desire to possess her, whence is it sprung?" he returned, as patient as he was relentless.

"You ask too many questions," she exclaimed with a flash of anger.

He shrugged and smiled. "You answer too few."

She set her arms akimbo and faced him squarely. Faintly through her veil he caught the gleam of her eyes, and he cursed the advantage she had in that her face was covered from his reading.

"In a word, Oliver-Reis," said she, "wilt sell her for three thousand philips?"

"In a word—no," he answered her.

"Thou't not? Not for three thousand philips?" Her voice was charged with surprise, and he wondered was it real or assumed.

"Not for thirty thousand," answered he. "She is mine, and I'll not relinquish her. So since I have proclaimed my mind, and since to tarry here is fraught with peril for us both, I beg thee to depart."

There fell a little pause, and neither of them noticed the alert interest stamped upon the white face of Rosamund. Neither of them suspected her knowledge of French which enabled her to follow most of what was said in the lingua franca they employed.

Fenzileh drew close to him. "Thou't not relinquish her, eh?" she asked, and he was sure she sneered. "Be not so confident. Thou't be forced to it, my friend—if not to me, why then, to Asad. He is coming for her, himself, in person."

"Asad?" he cried, startled now.

"Asad-ed-Din," she answered, and upon that resumed her

pleading. "Come, then! It were surely better to make a good bargain with me than a bad one with the Basha."

He shook his head and planted his feet squarely. "I intend to make no bargain with either of you. This slave is not for sale."

"Shalt thou dare resist Asad? I tell thee he will take her whether she be for sale or not."

"I see," he said, his eyes narrowing. "And the fear of this, then, is the source of thy whim to acquire her for thyself. Thou art not subtle, O Fenzileh. The consciousness that thine own charms are fading sets thee trembling lest so much loveliness should entirely cast thee from thy lord's regard, eh?"

If he could not see her face, and study there the effect of that thrust of his, at least he observed the quiver that ran through her muffled figure, he caught the note of anger that throbbed in her reply—"And if that were so, what is 't to thee?"

"It may be much or little," he replied thoughtfully.

"Indeed, it should be much," she answered quickly, breathlessly. "Have I not ever been thy friend? Have I not ever urged thy valor on my lord's notice and wrought like a true friend for thine advancement, Sakr-el-Bahr?"

He laughed outright. "Hast thou so?" quoth he.

"Laugh as thou wilt, but it is true," she insisted. "Lose me and thy most valuable ally is lost—one who has the ear and favor of her lord. For look, Sakr-el-Bahr, it is what would befall if another came to fill my place, another who might poison Asad's mind with lies against thee—for surely she cannot love thee, this Frankish girl whom thou hast torn from her home!"

"Be not concerned for that," he answered lightly, his wits striving in vain to plumb the depths and discover the nature of her purpose. "This slave of mine shall never usurp thy place beside Asad."

"O fool, Asad will take her whether she be for sale or not."

He looked down upon her, head on one side and arms akimbo. "If he can take her from me, the more easily can he take her from thee. No doubt thou hast considered that, and in some dark Sicilian way considered too how to provide against it. But the cost—hast thou counted that? What will Asad say to thee when he learns how thou hast thwarted him?"

"What do I care for that?" she cried in sudden fury, her gestures becoming a little wild. "She will be at the bottom of the harbor by then with a stone about her neck. He may have me whipped. No doubt he will. But 't will end there. He will require me to console him for his loss, and so all will be well again."

At last he had drawn her, pumped her dry as he imagined. Indeed, indeed, he thought, he had been right to say she was not subtle. He had been a fool to have permitted himself to be intrigued by so shallow, so obvious a purpose. He shrugged and turned away from her.

"Depart in peace, O Fenzileh," he said. "I yield her to none—be his name Asad or Shaitan."

His tone was final, and her answer seemed to accept at last his determination. Yet she was very quick with that answer; so quick that he might have suspected it to be preconceived.

"Then it is surely thine intent to wed her." No voice could have been more innocent and guileless than was hers now. "If so," she went on, "it were best done quickly, for marriage is the only barrier Asad will not overthrow. He is devout, and out of his deep reverence for the Prophet's law he would be sure to respect such a bond as that. But be very sure that he will respect nothing short of it."

Yet notwithstanding her innocence and assumed simplicity— because of it, perhaps—he read her as if she had been an open book; it no longer mattered that her face was veiled.

"And thy purpose would be equally well-served, eh?" he questioned her, sly in his turn.

"Equally," she admitted.

"Say 'better,' Fenzileh," he rejoined. "I said thou art not subtle. By the Koran, I lied. Thou art subtle as the serpent. Yet I see whither thou art gliding. Were I to be guided by thine advice a twofold purpose would be served. First, I should place her beyond Asad's reach, and second, I should be embroiled with him for having done so. What could more completely satisfy thy wishes?"

"Thou dost me wrong," she protested. "I have ever been thy friend. I would that . . ." She broke off suddenly to listen. The stillness of the night was broken by cries from the direction of the Bab-el-Oueb. She ran swiftly to the parapet whence the gate was to be seen and leaned far out.

"Look, look!" she cried, and there was a tremor of fear in her voice. "It is he—Asad-ed-Din."

Sakr-el-Bahr crossed to her side and in a glare of torches saw a body of men coming forth from the black archway of the gate.

"It almost seems as if, departing from thy usual custom, thou hast spoken truth, O Fenzileh."

She faced him, and he suspected the venomous glance darted at him through her veil. Yet her voice when she spoke was cold. "In a moment thou'lt have no single doubt of it. But what of me?" The question was added in a quickening tone. "He must not find me here. He would kill me, I think."

"I am sure he would," Sakr-el-Bahr agreed. "Yet muffled thus, who should recognize thee? Away, then, ere he comes. Take cover in the courtyard until he shall have passed. Didst thou come alone?"

"Should I trust anyone with the knowledge that I had visited thee?" she asked, and he admired the strong Sicilian spirit in her that not all these years in the Basha's hareem had sufficed to extinguish.

She moved quickly to the door, to pause again on the threshold.

"Thou'lt not relinquish her? Thou'lt not . . .?"

"Be at ease," he answered her, on so resolved a note that she departed satisfied.

CHAPTER XIII

IN THE SIGHT OF ALLAH

SAKR-EL-BAHR stood lost in thought after she had gone. Again he weighed her every word and considered precisely how he should meet Asad, and how refuse him, if the Basha's were indeed such an errand as Fenzileh had heralded.

Thus in silence he remained waiting for Ali or another to summon him to the presence of the Basha. Instead, however, when Ali entered it was actually to announce Asad-ed-Din, who followed immediately upon his heels, having insisted in his impatience upon being conducted straight to the presence of Sakr-el-Bahr.

"The peace of the Prophet upon thee, my son," was the Basha's greeting.

"And upon thee, my lord." Sakr-el-Bahr salaamed. "My house is honored." With a gesture he dismissed Ali.

"I come to thee a suppliant," said Asad, advancing.

"A suppliant, thou? No need, my lord. I have no will that is not the echo of thine own."

The Basha's questing eyes went beyond him and glowed as they rested upon Rosamund.

"I come in haste," he said, "like any callow lover, guided by my every instinct to the presence of her I seek—this Frankish pearl, this peri-faced captive of thy latest raid. I was away from the Kasbah when that pig Tsamanni returned thither from the sôk; but when at last I learnt that he had failed to purchase her as I commanded, I could have wept for very grief. I feared at first that some merchant from the Sus might have bought her and departed; but when I heard—blessed be Allah!—that thou wert the buyer, I was comforted again. For thou'lt yield her up to me, my son."

He spoke with such confidence that Oliver had a difficulty in choosing the words that were to disillusion him. Therefore he stood in hesitancy a moment.

"I will make good thy loss," Asad ran on. "Thou shalt have the sixteen hundred philips paid and another five hundred to console thee. Say that will content thee; for I boil with impatience."

Sakr-el-Bahr smiled grimly. "It is an impatience well known to me, my lord, where she is concerned," he answered slowly. "I boiled with it myself for five interminable years. To make an end of it I went a distant perilous voyage to England in a captured Frankish vessel. Thou didst not know, O Asad, else thou wouldst . . ."

"Bah!" broke in the Basha. "Thou'rt a huckster born. There is none like thee, Sakr-el-Bahr, in any game of wits. Well, well, name thine own price, strike thine own profit out of my impatience and let us have done."

"My lord," he said quietly, "it is not the profit that is in question. She is not for sale."

Asad blinked at him, speechless, and slowly a faint color crept into his sallow cheeks.

"Not . . . not for sale?" he echoed, faltering in his amazement.

"Not if thou offered me thy Bashalik as the price of her," was the solemn answer. Then more warmly, in a voice that held a note of intercession—"Ask anything else that is mine," he continued, "and gladly will I lay it at thy feet in earnest of my loyalty and love for thee."

"But I want nothing else." Asad's tone was impatient, petulant almost. "I want this slave."

"Then," replied Oliver, "I cast myself upon thy mercy and beseech thee to turn thine eyes elsewhere."

Asad scowled upon him. "Dost thou deny me?" he demanded, throwing back his head.

"Alas!" said Sakr-el-Bahr.

There fell a pause. Darker and darker grew the countenance of Asad, fiercer glowed the eyes he bent upon his lieutenant. "I see," he said at last, with a calm so oddly at variance with his looks as to be sinister. "I see. It seems that there is more truth in Fenzileh than I suspected. So!" He considered the corsair a moment with his sunken smouldering eyes.

Then he addressed him in a tone that vibrated with his suppressed anger. "Bethink thee, Sakr-el-Bahr, of what thou art, of what I have made thee. Bethink thee of all the bounty these hands have lavished on thee. Thou art my own lieutenant, and mayest one day be more. In Algiers there is none above thee save myself. Art, then, so thankless as to deny me the first thing I ask of thee? Truly is it written 'Ungrateful is Man.'"

"Didst thou know," began Sakr-el-Bahr, "all that is involved for me in this . . ."

"I neither know nor care," Asad cut in. "Whatever it may be, it should be as naught when set against my will." Then he discarded anger for cajolery. He set a hand upon Sakr-el-Bahr's stalwart shoulder. "Come, my son. I will deal generously with thee out of my love, and I will put thy refusal from my mind."

"Be generous, my lord, to the point of forgetting that ever thou didst ask me for her."

"Dost still refuse?" The voice, honeyed an instant ago, rang harsh again. "Take care how far thou strain my patience. Even as I have raised thee from the dirt, so at a word can I cast thee down again. Even as I broke the shackles that chained thee to the rower's bench, so can I rivet them on thee anew."

"All this canst thou do," Sakr-el-Bahr agreed. "And since, knowing it, I still hold to what is doubly mine—by right of capture and of purchase—thou mayest conceive how mighty are my reasons. Be merciful, then, Asad . . ."

"Must I take her by force in spite of thee?" roared the Basha.

Sakr-el-Bahr stiffened. He threw back his head and looked the Basha squarely in the eyes.

"Whilst I live, not even that mayest thou do," he answered.

"Disloyal, mutinous dog! Wilt thou resist me—*me?*"

"It is my prayer that thou'lt not be so ungenerous and unjust as to compel thy servant to a course so hateful."

Asad sneered. "Is that thy last word?" he demanded.

"Save only that in all things else I am thy slave, O Asad."

A moment the Basha stood regarding him, his glance baleful. Then deliberately, as one who has taken his resolve, he strode to the door. On the threshold he paused and turned again. "Wait!" he said, and on that threatening word departed.

Sakr-el-Bahr remained a moment where he had stood during the interview, then with a shrug he turned. He met Rosamund's eyes fixed intently upon him, and invested with a look he could not read. He found himself unable to meet it, and he turned away. It was inevitable that in such a moment the earlier stab of remorse should be repeated. He had overreached himself indeed. Despair settled down upon him, a full consciousness of the horrible thing he had done, which seemed now so irrevocable. In his silent anguish he almost conceived that he had mistaken his feelings for Rosamund; that far from hating her as he had supposed, his love for her had not yet been slain, else surely he should not be tortured now by the thought of her becoming Asad's prey. If he hated her, indeed, as he had supposed, he would have surrendered her and gloated.

He wondered was his present frame of mind purely the result of his discovery that the appearances against him had been stronger far than he imagined, so strong as to justify her conviction that he was her brother's slayer.

And then her voice, crisp and steady, cut into his torture of consideration.

"Why did you deny him?"

He swung round again to face her, amazed, horror-stricken.

"You understood?" he gasped.

"I understood enough," said she. "This lingua franca is none so different from French." And again she asked—"Why did you deny him?"

He paced across to her side and stood looking down at her.

"Do you ask why?"

"Indeed," she said bitterly, "there is scarce the need perhaps. And yet can it be that your lust of vengeance is so insatiable that sooner than willingly forgo an ounce of it you will lose your head?"

His face became grim again. "Of course," he sneered, "it would be so that you'ld interpret me."

"Nay. If I have asked it is because I doubt."

"Do you realize what it can mean to become the prey of Asad-ed-Din?"

She shuddered, and her glance fell from his, yet her voice was composed when she answered him—

"Is it so very much worse than becoming the prey of Oliver-Reis or Sakr-el-Bahr, or whatever they may call you?"

"If you say that it is all one to you there's an end to my opposing him," he answered coldly. "You may go to him. If I resisted him—like a fool, perhaps—it was for no sake of vengeance upon you. It was because the thought of it fills me with horror."

"Then it should fill you with horror of yourself no less," said she.

His answer startled her.

"Perhaps it does," he said, scarcely above a murmur. "Perhaps it does."

She flashed him an upward glance and looked as if she would have spoken. But he went on, suddenly passionate, without giving her time to interrupt him. "O God! It needed this to show me the vileness of the thing I have done. Asad has no such motives as had I. I wanted you that I might punish you. But he . . . O God!" he groaned, and for a moment put his face to his hands.

She rose slowly, a strange agitation stirring in her, her bosom galloping. But in his overwrought condition he failed to observe it. And then like a ray of hope to illumine his despair came the counsel that Fenzileh had given him, the barrier which she had said that Asad, being a devout Muslim, would never dare to violate.

"There is a way," he cried. "There is the way suggested by Fenzileh at the promptings of her malice." An instant he hesitated, his eyes averted. Then he made his plunge. "You must marry me."

It was almost as if he had struck her. She recoiled. Instantly suspicion awoke in her; swiftly it drew to a conviction that he had but sought to trick her by a pretended penitence.

"Marry you!" she echoed.

"Ay," he insisted. And he set himself to explain to her how if she were his wife she must be sacred and inviolable to all good Muslimeen, that none could set a finger upon her without doing outrage to the Prophet's holy law, and that, whoever might be so disposed, Asad was not of those, since Asad was perfervidly devout. "Thus only," he ended, "can I place you beyond his reach."

But she was still scornfully reluctant.

"It is too desperate a remedy even for so desperate an ill," said she, and thus drove him into a frenzy of impatience with her.

"You must, I say," he insisted, almost angrily. "You must—or else consent to be borne this very night to Asad's hareem—and not even as his wife, but as his slave. Oh, you must trust me for your own sake! You must!"

"Trust you!" she cried, and almost laughed in the intensity of her scorn. "Trust you! How can I trust one who is a renegade and worse?"

He controlled himself that he might reason with her, that by cold logic he might conquer her consent.

"You are very unmerciful," he said. "In judging me you leave out of all account the suffering through which I have gone and what yourself contributed to it. Knowing now how falsely I was accused and what other bitter wrongs I suffered, consider that I was one to whom the man and the woman I most loved in all this world had proven false. I had lost faith in man and in God, and if I became a Muslim, a renegade, and a corsair, it was because there was no other gate by which I could escape the unutterable toil of the oar to which I had been chained." He looked at her sadly. "Can you find no excuse for me in all that?"

It moved her a little, for if she maintained a hostile attitude, at least she put aside her scorn.

"No wrongs," she told him, almost with sorrow in her voice, "could justify you in outraging chivalry, in dishonoring your manhood, in abusing your strength to persecute a woman. Whatever the causes that may have led to it, you have fallen too low, sir, to make it possible that I should trust you."

He bowed his head under the rebuke which already he had uttered in his own heart. It was just and most deserved, and since he recognized its justice he found it impossible to resent it.

"I know," he said. "But I am not asking you to trust me to my profit, but to your own. It is for your sake alone that I implore you to do this." Upon a sudden inspiration he drew the heavy dagger from his girdle and proffered it, hilt foremost. "If you need an earnest of my good faith," he said, "take this knife with which to-night you attempted to stab yourself. At the first sign that I am false to my trust, use it as you will—upon me or upon yourself."

She pondered him in some surprise. Then slowly she put out her hand to take the weapon, as he bade her.

"Are you not afraid," she asked him, "that I shall use it now, and so make an end?"

"I am trusting you," he said, "that in return you may trust me. Further, I am arming you against the worst. For if it comes to choice between death and Asad, I shall approve your choice of death. But let me add that it were foolish to choose death whilst yet there is a chance of life."

"What chance?" she asked, with a faint return of her old scorn. "The chance of life with you?"

"No," he answered firmly. "If you will trust me, I swear that I will seek to undo the evil I have done. Listen. At dawn my galeasse sets out upon a raid. I will convey you secretly aboard and find a way to land you in some Christian country—Italy or France— whence you may make your way home again."

"But meanwhile," she reminded him, "I shall have become your wife."

He smiled wistfully. "Do you still fear a trap? Can naught convince you of my sincerity? A Muslim marriage is not binding upon a Christian, and I shall account it no marriage. It will be no more than a pretence to shelter you until we are away."

"How can I trust your word in that?"

"How?" He paused, baffled; but only for a moment. "You have the dagger," he answered pregnantly.

She stood considering, her eyes upon the weapon's lividly gleaming blade. "And this marriage?" she asked. "How is it to take place?"

He explained to her then that by the Muslim law all that was required was a declaration made before a kadi, or his superior, and in the presence of witnesses. He was still at his explanation when from below there came a sound of voices, the tramp of feet, and the flash of torches.

"Here is Asad returning in force," he cried, and his voice trembled. "Do you consent?"

"But the kadi?" she inquired, and by the question he knew that she was won to his way of saving her.

"I said the kadi or his superior. Asad himself shall be our priest, his followers our witnesses."

"And if he refuses? He will refuse!" she cried, clasping her hands before her in her excitement.

"I shall not ask him. I shall take him by surprise."

"It . . . it must anger him. He may avenge himself for what he must deem a trick."

"Ay," he answered, wild-eyed. "I have thought of that, too. But it is a risk we must run. If we do not prevail, then—"

"I have the dagger," she cried fearlessly.

"And for me there will be the rope or the sword," he answered. "Be calm! They come!"

But the steps that pattered up the stairs were Ali's. He flung upon the terrace in alarm.

"My lord, my lord! Asad-ed-Din is here in force. He has an armed following with him!"

"There is naught to fear," said Sakr-el-Bahr, with every show of calm. "All will be well."

Asad swept up the stairs and out upon that terrace to confront his rebellious lieutenant. After him came a dozen black-robed janissaries with scimitars along which the light of the torches rippled in little runnels as of blood.

The Basha came to a halt before Sakr-el-Bahr, his arms majestically folded, his head thrown back, so that his long white beard jutted forward.

"I am returned," he said, "to employ force where gentleness will not avail. Yet I pray that Allah may have lighted thee to a wiser frame of mind."

"He has, indeed, my lord," replied Sakr-el-Bahr.

"The praise to Him!" exclaimed Asad in a voice that rang with joy. "The girl, then!" And he held out a hand.

Sakr-el-Bahr stepped back to her and took her hand in his as if to lead her forward. Then he spoke the fateful words.

"In Allah's Holy Name and in His All-seeing eyes, before thee, Asad-ed-Din, and in the presence of these witnesses, I take this woman to be my wife by the merciful law of the Prophet of Allah the All-wise, the All-pitying."

The words were out and the thing was done before Asad had realized the corsair's intent. A gasp of dismay escaped him; then his visage grew inflamed, his eyes blazed.

But Sakr-el-Bahr, cool and undaunted before that royal anger, took the scarf that lay about Rosamund's shoulders, and raising it, flung it over her head, so that her face was covered by it.

"May Allah rot off the hand of him who in contempt of our Lord Mahomet's holy law may dare to unveil that face, and may Allah bless this union and cast into the pit of Gehenna any who shall attempt to dissolve a bond that is tied in His All-seeing eyes."

It was formidable. Too formidable for Asad-ed-Din. Behind him his janissaries like hounds in leash stood eagerly awaiting his command. But none came. He stood there breathing heavily, swaying a little, and turning from red to pale in the battle that was being fought within him between rage and vexation on the one hand and his profound piety on the other. And as he yet hesitated perhaps Sakr-el-Bahr assisted his piety to gain the day.

"Now you will understand why I would not yield her, O mighty Asad," he said. "Thyself hast thou oft and rightly reproached me with my celibacy, reminding me that it is not pleasing in the sight of Allah, that it is unworthy a good Muslim. At last it hath pleased the Prophet to send me such a maid as I could take to wife."

Asad bowed his head. "What is written is written," he said in the voice of one who admonished himself. Then he raised his arms aloft. "Allah is All-knowing," he declared. "His will be done!"

"Ameen," said Sakr-el-Bahr very solemnly and with a great surge of thankful prayer to his own long-forgotten God.

The Basha stayed yet a moment, as if he would have spoken. Then abruptly he turned and waved a hand to his janissaries. "Away!" was all he said to them, and stalked out in their wake.

CHAPTER XIV

THE SIGN

FROM BEHIND her lattice, still breathless from the haste she had made, and with her whelp Marzak at her side, Fenzileh had witnessed that first angry return of the Basha from the house of Sakr-el-Bahr.

She had heard him bawling for Abdul Mohktar, the leader of his janissaries, and she had seen the hasty mustering of a score of these soldiers in the courtyard, where the ruddy light of torches mingled with the white light of the full moon. She had seen them go hurrying away with Asad himself at their head, and she had not known whether to weep or to laugh, whether to fear or to rejoice.

"It is done," Marzak had cried exultantly. "The dog hath withstood him and so destroyed himself. There will be an end to Sakr-el-Bahr this night." And he had added: "The praise to Allah!"

But from Fenzileh came no response to his prayer of thanksgiving. True, Sakr-el-Bahr must be destroyed, and by a sword that she herself had forged. Yet was it not inevitable that the stroke which laid him low must wound her on its repercussion? That was the question to which now she sought an answer. For all her eagerness to speed the corsair to his doom, she had paused sufficiently to weigh the consequences to herself; she had not overlooked the circumstance that an inevitable result of this must be Asad's appropriation of that Frankish slave-girl. But at the time it had seemed to her that even this price was worth paying to remove Sakr-el-Bahr definitely and finally from her son's path—which shows that, after all, Fenzileh the mother was capable of some self-sacrifice. She comforted herself now with the reflection that the influence, whose waning she feared might be occasioned by the introduction of a rival into Asad's hareem, would no longer be so vitally necessary to herself and Marzak once Sakr-el-Bahr were removed. The rest mattered none so much to her. Yet it mattered something, and the present state of things left her uneasy, her mind a cockpit of emotions. Her grasp could not encompass all her desires at once, it seemed; and whilst she could gloat over the gratification of one, she must bewail the frustration of another. Yet in the main she felt that she should account herself the gainer.

In this state of mind she had waited, scarce heeding the savagely joyous and entirely selfish babblings of her cub, who cared little what might betide his mother as the price of the removal of that hated rival from his path. For him, at least, there was nothing but profit in the business, no cause for anything but satisfaction; and that satisfaction he voiced with a fine contempt for his mother's feelings.

Anon they witnessed Asad's return. They saw the janissaries come swinging into the courtyard and range themselves there whilst the Basha made his appearance, walking slowly, with steps that dragged a little, his head sunk upon his breast, his hands behind him. They waited to see slaves following him, leading or carrying the girl he had gone to fetch. But they waited in vain, intrigued and uneasy.

They heard the harsh voice in which Asad dismissed his followers, and the clang of the closing gate; and they saw him pacing there alone in the moonlight, ever in that attitude of dejection.

What had happened? Had he killed them both? Had the girl resisted him to such an extent that he had lost all patience and in one of those rages begotten of such resistance made an end of her?

Thus did Fenzileh question herself, and since she could not doubt but that Sakr-el-Bahr was slain, she concluded that the rest must be as she conjectured. Yet, the suspense torturing her, she summoned Ayoub and sent him to glean from Abdul Mohktar the tale of what had passed. In his own hatred of Sakr-el-Bahr, Ayoub went willingly enough and hoping for the worst. He returned disappointed, with a tale that sowed dismay in Fenzileh and Marzak.

Fenzileh, however, made a swift recovery. After all, it was the best that could have happened. It should not be difficult to transmute that obvious dejection of Asad's into resentment, and to fan this into a rage that must end by consuming Sakr-el-Bahr. And so the thing could be accomplished without jeopardy to her own place at Asad's side. For it was inconceivable that he should now take Rosamund to his hareem. Already the fact that she had been paraded with naked face among the Faithful must in itself have been a difficult obstacle to his pride. But it was utterly impossible that he could so subject his self-respect to his desire as to take to himself a woman who had been the wife of his servant.

Fenzileh saw her way very clearly. It was through Asad's devoutness—as she herself had advised, though scarcely expecting such rich results as these—that he had been thwarted by Sakr-el-Bahr. That same devoutness must further be played upon now to do the rest.

Taking up a flimsy silken veil, she went out to him where he now sat on the divan under the awning, alone there in the tepid-scented summer night. She crept to his side with the soft, graceful, questing movements of a cat, and sat there a moment unheeded almost—such was his abstraction—her head resting lightly against his shoulder.

"Lord of my soul," she murmued presently, "thou art sorrowing." Her voice was in itself a soft and soothing caress.

He started, and she caught the gleam of his eyes turned suddenly upon her.

"Who told thee so?" he asked suspiciously.

"My heart," she answered, her voice melodious as a viol. "Can sorrow burden thine and mine go light?" she wooed him. "Is happiness possible to me when thou art downcast? In there I felt thy melancholy, and thy need of me, and I am come to share thy burden, or to bear it all for thee." Her arms were raised, and her fingers interlocked themselves upon his shoulder.

He looked down at her, and his expression softened. He needed comfort, and never was she more welcome to him.

Gradually and with infinite skill she drew from him the story of what had happened. When she had gathered it, she loosed her indignation.

"The dog!" she cried. "The faithless, ungrateful hound! Yet have I warned thee against him, O light of my poor eyes, and thou hast scorned me for the warnings uttered by my love. Now at last thou knowest him, and he shall trouble thee no longer. Thou'lt cast him off, reduce him again to the dust from which thy bounty raised him."

But Asad did not respond. He sat there in a gloomy abstraction, staring straight before him. At last he sighed wearily. He was just, and he had a conscience, as odd a thing as it was awkward in a corsair Basha.

"In what hath befallen," he answered moodily, "there is naught to justify me in casting aside the stoutest soldier of Islam. My duty to Allah will not suffer it."

"Yet his duty to thee suffered him to thwart thee, O my lord," she reminded him very softly.

"In my desires—ay!" he answered, and for a moment his voice quivered with passion. Then he repressed it, and continued more calmly—"Shall my self-seeking overwhelm my duty to the Faith? Shall the matter of a slave-girl urge me to sacrifice the bravest sol-

dier of Islam, the stoutest champion of the Prophet's law? Shall I
bring down upon my head the vengeance of the One by destroying
a man who is a scourge of scorpions unto the infidel—and all this
that I may gratify my personal anger against him, that I may avenge
the thwarting of a petty desire?"

"Dost thou still say, O my life, that Sakr-el-Bahr is the stoutest
champion of the Prophet's law?" she asked him softly, yet on a note
of amazement.

"It is not I that say it, but his deeds," he answered sullenly.

"I know of one deed no True-Believer could have wrought. If
proof were needed of his infidelity he hath now afforded it in taking
to himself a Nasrani wife. Is it not written in the Book to be Read:
'Marry not idolatresses'? Is not that the Prophet's law, and hath he
not broken it, offending at once against Allah and against thee, O
fountain of my soul?"

Asad frowned. Here was truth indeed, something that he had
entirely overlooked. Yet justice compelled him still to defend
Sakr-el-Bahr, or else perhaps he but reasoned to prove to himself
that the case against the corsair was indeed complete.

"He may have sinned in thoughtlessness," he suggested.

At that she cried out in admiration of him. "What a fount of
mercy and forbearance art thou, O father of Marzak! Thou'rt right
as in all things. It was no doubt in thoughtlessness that he offended,
but would such thoughtlessness be possible in a True-Believer—in
one worthy to be dubbed by thee the champion of the Prophet's
Holy Law?"

It was a shrewd thrust, that pierced the armor of conscience in
which he sought to empanoply himself. He sat very thoughtful,
scowling darkly at the inky shadow of the wall which the moon was
casting. Suddenly he rose.

"By Allah, thou art right!" he cried. "So that he thwarted me
and kept that Frankish woman for himself, he cared not how he
sinned against the law."

She glided to her knees and coiled her arms about his waist, looking up at him. "Still art thou ever merciful, ever sparing in adverse judgment. Is that all his fault, O Asad?"

"All?" he questioned, looking down at her. "What more is there?"

"I would there were no more. Yet more there is, to which thy angelic mercy blinds thee. He did worse. Not merely was he reckless of how he sinned against the law, he turned the law to his own base uses and so defiled it."

"How?" he asked quickly, eagerly almost.

"He employed it as a bulwark behind which to shelter himself and her. Knowing that thou who art the Lion and defender of the Faith wouldst bend obediently to what is written in the Book, he married her to place her beyond thy reach."

"The praise to Him who is All-wise and lent me strength to do naught unworthy!" he cried in a great voice, glorifying himself. "I might have slain him to dissolve the impious bond, yet I obeyed what is written."

"Thy forbearance hath given joy to the angels," she answered him, "and yet a man was found so base as to trade upon it and upon thy piety, O Asad!"

He shook off her clasp, and strode away from her a prey to agitation. He paced to and fro in the moonlight there, and she, well-content, reclined upon the cushions of the divan, a thing of infinite grace, her gleaming eyes discreetly veiled from him—waiting until her poison should have done its work.

She saw him halt, and fling up his arms, as if apostrophizing Heaven, as if asking a question of the stars that twinkled in the wide-flung nimbus of the moon.

Then at last he paced slowly back to her. He was still undecided. There was truth in what she had said; yet he knew and weighed her hatred of Sakr-el-Bahr, knew how it must urge her to put the worst construction upon any act of his, knew her jealousy for Marzak, and so he mistrusted her arguments and mistrusted himself. Also there was his own love of Sakr-el-Bahr that would insist upon a place in the balance of his judgment. His mind was in turmoil.

"Enough," he said almost roughly. "I pray that Allah may send me counsel in the night." And upon that he stalked past her, up the steps, and so into the house.

She followed him. All night she lay at his feet to be ready at the first peep of dawn to buttress a purpose that she feared was still weak, and whilst he slept fitfully, she slept not at all, but lay wide-eyed and watchful.

At the first note of the mueddin's voice, he leapt from his couch obedient to its summons, and scarce had the last note of it died upon the winds of dawn than he was afoot, beating his hands together to summon slaves and issuing his orders, from which she gathered that he was for the harbor there and then.

"May Allah have inspired thee, O my lord!" she cried. And asked him: "What is thy resolve?"

"I go to seek a sign," he answered her, and upon that departed, leaving her in a frame of mind that was far from easy.

She summoned Marzak, and bade him accompany his father, breathed swift instructions of what he should do and how do it.

"Thy fate has been placed in thine own hands," she admonished him. "See that thou grip it firmly now."

In the courtyard Marzak found his father in the act of mounting a white mule that had been brought him. He was attended by his wazeer Tsamanni, Biskaine, and some other of his captains. Marzak begged leave to go with him. It was carelessly granted, and they set out, Marzak walking by his father's stirrup, a little in advance of the others. For awhile there was silence between father and son, then the latter spoke.

"It is my prayer, O my father, that thou art resolved to depose the faithless Sakr-el-Bahr from the command of this expedition."

Asad considered his son with a somber eye. "Even now the galeasse should be setting out if the argosy is to be intercepted," he said. "If Sakr-el-Bahr does not command, who shall, in Heaven's name?"

"Try me, O my father," cried Marzak.

Asad smiled with grim wistfulness. "Art weary of life, O my son, that thou wouldst go to thy death and take the galeasse to destruction?"

"Thou art less than just, O my father," Marzak protested.

"Yet more than kind, O my son," replied Asad, and they went on in silence thereafter, until they came to the mole.

The splendid galeasse was moored alongside, and all about her there was great bustle of preparation for departure. Porters moved up and down the gangway that connected her with the shore, carrying bales of provisions, barrels of water, kegs of gunpowder, and other necessaries for the voyage, and even as Asad and his followers reached the head of that gangway, four negroes were staggering down it under the load of a huge palmetto bale that was slung from staves yoked to their shoulders.

On the poop stood Sakr-el-Bahr with Othmani, Ali, Jasper-Reis, and some other officers. Up and down the gangway paced Larocque and Vigitello, two renegade boatswains, one French and the other Italian, who had sailed with him on every voyage for the past two years. Larocque was superintending the loading of the vessel, bawling his orders for the bestowal of provisions here, of water yonder, and of powder about the mainmast. Vigitello was making a final inspection of the slaves at the oars.

As the palmetto pannier was brought aboard, Larocque shouted to the negroes to set it down by the mainmast. But here Sakr-el-Bahr interfered, bidding them, instead, to bring it up to the stern and place it in the poop-house.

Asad had dismounted, and stood with Marzak at his side at the head of the gangway when the youth finally begged his father himself to take command of this expedition, allowing him to come as his lieutenant and so learn the ways of the sea.

Asad looked at him curiously, but answered nothing. He went aboard, Marzak and the others following him. It was at this moment that Sakr-el-Bahr first became aware of the Basha's presence, and he came instantly forward to do the honors of his galley. If there was a sudden uneasiness in his heart his face was calm and his glance as arrogant and steady as ever.

"May the peace of Allah overshadow thee and thy house, O mighty Asad," was his greeting. "We are on the point of casting off, and I shall sail the more securely for thy blessing."

Asad considered him with eyes of wonder. So much effrontery, so much ease after their last scene together seemed to the Basha a thing incredible, unless, indeed, it were accompanied by a conscience entirely at peace.

"It has been proposed to me that I shall do more than bless this expedition—that I shall command it," he answered, watching Sakr-el-Bahr closely. He observed the sudden flicker of the corsair's eyes, the only outward sign of his inward dismay.

"Command it?" echoed Sakr-el-Bahr. "'T was proposed to thee?" And he laughed lightly as if to dismiss that suggestion.

That laugh was a tactical error. It spurred Asad. He advanced slowly along the vessel's waist-deck to the mainmast—for she was rigged with main and foremasts. There he halted again to look into the face of Sakr-el-Bahr who stepped along beside him.

"Why didst thou laugh?" he questioned shortly.

"Why? At the folly of such a proposal," said Sakr-el-Bahr in haste, too much in haste to seek a diplomatic answer.

Darker grew the Basha's frown. "Folly?" quoth he. "Wherein lies the folly?"

Sakr-el-Bahr made haste to cover his mistake. "In the suggestion that such poor quarry as waits us should be worthy thine endeavor, should warrant the Lion of the Faith to unsheathe his mighty claws. Thou," he continued with ringing scorn, "thou the inspirer of a hundred glorious fights in which whole fleets have

been engaged, to take the seas upon so trivial an errand—one galeasse to swoop upon a single galley of Spain! It were unworthy thy
great name, beneath the dignity of thy valor!" and by a gesture he
contemptuously dismissed the subject.

But Asad continued to ponder him with cold eyes, his face
inscrutable. "Why, here's a change since yesterday!" he said.

"A change, my lord?"

"But yesterday in the marketplace thyself didst urge me to join
this expedition and to command it," Asad reminded him, speaking
with deliberate emphasis. "Thyself invoked the memory of the days
that are gone, when, scimitar in hand, we charged side by side
aboard the infidel, and thou didst beseech me to engage again
beside thee. And now . . ." He spread his hands, anger gathered in
his eyes. "Whence this change?" he demanded sternly.

Sakr-el-Bahr hesitated, caught in his own toils. He looked away
from Asad a moment; he had a glimpse of the handsome flushed
face of Marzak at his father's elbow, of Biskaine, Tsamanni, and the
others all staring at him in amazement, and even of some grimy
sunburned faces from the rowers' bench on his left that were looking on with dull curiosity.

He smiled, seeming outwardly to remain entirely unruffled.
"Why . . . it is that I have come to perceive thy reasons for refusing.
For the rest, it is as I say, the quarry is not worthy of the hunter."

Marzak uttered a soft sneering laugh, as if the true reason of the
corsair's attitude were quite clear to him. He fancied too, and he
was right in this, that Sakr-el-Bahr's odd attitude had accomplished
what persuasions addressed to Asad-ed-Din might to the end have
failed to accomplish—had afforded him the sign he was come to
seek. For it was in that moment that Asad determined to take command himself.

"It almost seems," he said slowly, smiling, "as if thou didst not
want me. If so, it is unfortunate; for I have long neglected my duty
to my son, and I am resolved at last to repair that error. We accom-

pany thee upon this expedition, Sakr-el-Bahr. Myself I will command it, and Marzak shall be my apprentice in the ways of the sea."

Sakr-el-Bahr said not another word in protest against that proclaimed resolve. He salaamed, and when he spoke there was almost a note of gladness in his voice.

"The praise to Allah, then, since thou'rt determined. It is not for me to urge further the unworthiness of the quarry since I am the gainer by thy resolve."

CHAPTER XV

THE VOYAGE

HIS RESOLVE being taken, Asad drew Tsamanni aside and spent some moments in talk with him, giving him certain instructions for the conduct of affairs ashore during his absence. That done, and the wazeer dismissed, the Basha himself gave the order to cast off, an order which there was no reason to delay, since all was now in readiness.

The gangway was drawn ashore, the boatswain's whistle sounded, and the steersmen leapt to their niches in the stern, grasping the shafts of the great steering-oars. A second blast rang out, and down the gangway-deck came Vigitello and two of his mates, all three armed with long whips of bullock-hide, shouting to the slaves to make ready. And then, on the note of a third blast of Larocque's whistle, the fifty-four poised oars dipped to the water, two hundred and fifty bodies bent as one, and when they heaved themselves upright again the great galeasse shot forward and so set out upon her adventurous voyage. From her mainmast the red flag with its green crescent was unfurled to the breeze, and from the crowded mole, and the beach where a long line of spectators had gathered, there burst a great cry of valediction.

That breeze blowing stiffly from the desert was Lionel's friend that day. Without it his career at the oar might have been short indeed. He was chained, like the rest, stark naked, save for a loin-cloth, in the place nearest the gangway on the first starboard bench abaft the narrow waist-deck, and ere the galeasse had made the short distance between the mole and the island at the end of it, the boatswain's whip had coiled itself about his white shoulders to urge him to better exertion than he was putting forth. He had screamed under the cruel cut, but none had heeded him. Lest the punishment should be repeated, he had thrown all his weight into the next strokes of the oar, until by the time the Peñon was reached the sweat was running down his body and his heart was thudding against his ribs. It was not possible that it could have lasted, and his main agony lay in that he realized it, and saw himself face to face with horrors inconceivable that must await the exhaustion of his strength. He was not naturally robust, and he had led a soft and pampered life that was very far from equipping him for such a test as this.

But as they reached the Peñon and felt the full vigor of that warm breeze, Sakr-el-Bahr, who by Asad's command remained in charge of the navigation, ordered the unfurling of the enormous lateen sails on main and foremasts. They ballooned out, swelling to the wind, and the galeasse surged forward at a speed that was more than doubled. The order to cease rowing followed, and the slaves were left to return thanks to Heaven for their respite, and to rest in their chains until such time as their sinews should be required again.

The vessel's vast prow, which ended in a steel ram and was armed with a culverin on either quarter, was crowded with loung-ing corsairs, who took their ease there until the time to engage should be upon them. They leaned on the high bulwarks or squat-ted in groups, talking, laughing, some of them tailoring and repair-ing garments, others burnishing their weapons or their armor, and one swarthy youth there was who thrummed a gimri and sang a melancholy Shilha love-song to the delight of a score or so of blood-thirsty ruffians squatting about him in a ring of variegated color.

The gorgeous poop was fitted with a spacious cabin, to which admission was gained by two archways curtained with stout silken tapestries upon whose deep red ground the crescent was wrought in brilliant green. Above the cabin stood the three cressets or stern-lamps, great structures of gilded iron surmounted each by the orb and crescent. As if to continue the cabin forward and increase its size, a green awning was erected from it to shade almost half the poop-deck. Here cushions were thrown, and upon these squatted now Asad-ed-Bin with Marzak, whilst Biskaine and some three or four other officers who had escorted him aboard and whom he had retained beside him for that voyage, were lounging upon the gilded balustrade at the poop's forward end, immediately above the rowers' benches.

Sakr-el-Bahr alone, a solitary figure, resplendent in caftan and turban that were of cloth of silver, leaned upon the bulwarks of the larboard quarter of the poop-deck, and looked moodily back upon the receding city of Algiers which by now was no more than an agglomeration of white cubes piled up the hillside in the morning sunshine.

Asad watched him silently awhile from under his beetling brows, then summoned him. He came at once, and stood respect-fully before his prince.

Asad considered him a moment solemnly, whilst a furtive mali-cious smile played over the beautiful countenance of his son.

"Think not, Sakr-el-Bahr," he said at length, "that I bear thee resentment for what befell last night or that that happening is the sole cause of my present determination. I had a duty—a long-neglected duty—to Marzak, which at last I have undertaken to perform." He seemed to excuse himself almost, and Marzak mis-liked both words and tone. Why, he wondered, must this fierce old man, who had made his name a terror throughout Christendom, be

ever so soft and yielding where that stalwart and arrogant infidel
was concerned?

Sakr-el-Bahr bowed solemnly. "My lord," he said, "it is not for
me to question thy resolves or the thoughts that may have led to
them. It suffices me to know thy wishes; they are my law."

"Are they so?" said Asad tartly. "Thy deeds will scarce bear out
thy protestations." He sighed. "Sorely was I wounded yesternight
when thy marriage thwarted me and placed that Frankish maid
beyond my reach. Yet I respect this marriage of thine, as all Muslims must—for all that in itself it was unlawful. But there!" he
ended with a shrug. "We sail together once again to crush the
Spaniard. Let no ill-will on either side o'er-cloud the splendor of
our task."

"Ameen to that, my lord," said Sakr-el-Bahr devoutly. "I almost
feared . . ."

"No more!" the Basha interrupted him. "Thou wert never a
man to fear anything, which is why I have loved thee as a son."

But it suited Marzak not at all that the matter should be thus
dismissed, that it should conclude upon a note of weakening from
his father, upon what indeed amounted to a speech of reconcilia-
tion. Before Sakr-el-Bahr could make answer he had cut in to set
him a question laden with wicked intent.

"How will thy bride beguile the season of thine absence, O
Sakr-el-Bahr?"

"I have lived too little with women to be able to give thee an
answer," said the corsair.

Marzak winced before a reply that seemed to reflect upon himself. But he returned to the attack.

"I compassionate thee that art the slave of duty, driven so soon
to abandon the delight of her soft arms. Where hast thou bestowed
her, O captain?"

"Where should a Muslim bestow his wife but according to the
biddings of the Prophet—in the house?"

Marzak sneered. "Verily, I marvel at thy fortitude in quitting her so soon!"

But Asad caught the sneer, and stared at his son. "What cause is there to marvel in that a true Muslim should sacrifice his inclinations to the service of the Faith?" His tone was a rebuke; but it left Marzak undismayed. The youth sprawled gracefully upon his cushions, one leg tucked under him.

"Place no excess of faith in appearances, O my father!" he said.

"No more!" growled the Basha. "Peace to thy tongue, Marzak, and may Allah the All-knowing smile upon our expedition, lending strength to our arms to smite the infidel to whom the fragrance of the garden is forbidden."

To this again Sakr-el-Bahr replied "Ameen," but an uneasiness abode in his heart summoned thither by the questions Marzak had set him. Were they idle words calculated to do no more than plague him, and to keep fresh in Asad's mind the memory of Rosamund, or were they based upon some actual knowledge?

His fears were to be quickened soon on that same score. He was leaning that afternoon upon the rail, idly observing the doling out of the rations to the slaves, when Marzak came to join him.

For some moments he stood silently beside Sakr-el-Bahr watching Vigitello and his men as they passed from bench to bench serving out biscuits and dried dates to the rowers—but sparingly, for oars move sluggishly when stomachs are too well nourished—and giving each to drink a cup of vinegar and water in which floated a few drops of added oil.

Then he pointed to a large palmetto bale that stood on the waist-deck near the mainmast about which the powder barrels were stacked.

"That pannier," he said, "seems to me oddly in the way yonder. Were it not better to bestow it in the hold, where it will cease to be an encumbrance in case of action?"

Sakr-el-Bahr experienced a slight tightening at the heart. He knew that Marzak had heard him command that bale to be borne into the poop-cabin, and that anon he had ordered it to be fetched thence when Asad had announced his intention of sailing with him. He realized that this in itself might be a suspicious circumstance; or, rather, knowing what the bale contained, he was too ready to fear suspicion. Nevertheless he turned to Marzak with a smile of some disdain.

"I understood, Marzak, that thou art sailing with us as apprentice."

"What then?" quoth Marzak.

"Why merely that it might become thee better to be content to observe and learn. Thou'lt soon be telling me how grapnels should be slung, and how an action should be fought." Then he pointed ahead to what seemed to be no more than a low cloud-bank towards which they were rapidly skimming before that friendly wind. "Yonder," he said, "are the Balearics. We are making good speed."

Although he said it without any object other than that of turning the conversation, yet the fact itself was sufficiently remarkable to be worth a comment. Whether rowed by her two hundred and fifty slaves, or sailed under her enormous spread of canvas, there was no swifter vessel upon the Mediterranean than the galeasse of Sakr-el-Bahr. Onward she leapt now with bellying lateens, her well-greased keel slipping through the wind-whipped water at a rate which perhaps could not have been bettered by any ship that sailed.

"If this wind holds we shall be under the Point of Aguila before sunset, which will be something to boast of hereafter," he promised.

Marzak, however, seemed but indifferently interested; his eyes continued awhile to stray towards that palmetto bale by the mainmast. At length, without another word to Sakr-el-Bahr, he made his way abaft, and flung himself down under the awning, beside his father. Asad sat there in a moody abstraction, already regretting that he should have lent an ear to Fenzileh to the extent of coming upon this voyage, and assured by now that at least there was no cause to mistrust Sakr-el-Bahr. Marzak came to revive that droop-ing mistrust. But the moment was ill-chosen, and at the first words he uttered on the subject, he was growled into silence by his sire.

"Thou dost but voice thine own malice," Asad rebuked him. "And I am proven a fool in that I have permitted the malice of oth-ers to urge me in this matter. No more, I say."

Thereupon Marzak fell silent and sulking, his eyes ever follow-ing Sakr-el-Bahr, who had descended the three steps from the poop to the gangway and was pacing slowly down between the rowers' benches.

The corsair was supremely ill at ease, as a man must be who has something to conceal, and who begins to fear that he may have been betrayed. Yet who was there could have betrayed him? But three men aboard that vessel knew his secret—Ali, his lieutenant, Jasper, and the Italian Vigitello. And Sakr-el-Bahr would have staked all his possessions that neither Ali nor Vigitello would have betrayed him, whilst he was fairly confident that in his own inter-ests Jasper also must have kept faith. Yet Marzak's allusion to that palmetto bale had filled him with an uneasiness that sent him now in quest of his Italian boatswain whom he trusted above all others.

"Vigitello," said he, "is it possible that I have been betrayed to the Basha?"

Vigitello looked up sharply at the question, then smiled with confidence. They were standing alone by the bulwarks on the waist-deck.

"Touching what we carry yonder?" quoth he, his glance shifting to the bale. "Impossible. If Asad had knowledge he would have betrayed it before we left Algiers, or else he would never have sailed without a stouter bodyguard of his own."

"What need of bodyguard for him?" returned Sakr-el-Bahr. "If it should come to grips between us—as well it may if what I suspect be true—there is no doubt as to the side upon which the corsairs would range themselves."

"Is there not?" quoth Vigitello, a smile upon his swarthy face. "Be not so sure. These men have most of them followed thee into a score of fights. To them thou art the Basha, their natural leader."

"Maybe. But their allegiance belongs to Asad-ed-Din, the exalted of Allah. Did it come to a choice between us, their faith would urge them to stand beside him in spite of any past bonds that may have existed between them and me."

"Yet there were some who murmured when thou wert superseded in the command of this expedition," Vigitello informed him. "I doubt not that many would be influenced by their faith, but many would stand by thee against the Grand Sultan himself. And do not forget," he added, instinctively lowering his voice, "that many of us are renegadoes like myself and thee, who would never know a moment's doubt if it came to a choice of sides. But I hope," he ended in another tone, "there is no such danger here."

"And so do I, in all faith," replied Sakr-el-Bahr, with fervor. "Yet I am uneasy, and I must know where I stand if the worst takes place. Go thou amongst the men, Vigitello, and probe their real feelings, gauge their humor and endeavor to ascertain upon what numbers I may count if I have to declare war upon Asad or if he declares it upon me. Be cautious."

Vigitello closed one of his black eyes portentously. "Depend upon it," he said, "I'll bring you word anon."

On that they parted, Vigitello to make his way to the prow and there engage in his investigations, Sakr-el-Bahr slowly to retrace his steps to the poop. But at the first bench abaft the gangway he paused, and looked down at the dejected, white-fleshed slave who sat shackled there. He smiled cruelly, his own anxieties forgotten in the savor of vengeance.

"So you have tasted the whip already," he said in English. "But that is nothing to what is yet to come. You are in luck that there is a wind to-day. It will not always be so. Soon shall you learn what it was that I endured by your contriving."

Lionel looked up at him with haggard, blood-injected eyes. He wanted to curse his brother, yet was he too overwhelmed by the sense of the fitness of this punishment.

"For myself I care nothing," he replied.

"But you will, sweet brother," was the answer. "You will care for yourself most damnably and pity yourself most poignantly. I speak from experience. 'T is odds you will not live, and that is my chief regret. I would you had my thews to keep you alive in this floating hell."

"I tell you I care nothing for myself," Lionel insisted. "What have you done with Rosamund?"

"Will it surprise you to learn that I have played the gentleman and married her?" Oliver mocked him.

"Married her?" his brother gasped, blenching at the very thought. "You hound!"

"Why abuse me? Could I have done more?" And with a laugh he sauntered on, leaving Lionel to writhe there with the torment of his half-knowledge.

An hour later, when the cloudy outline of the Balearic Isles had acquired density and color, Sakr-el-Bahr and Vigitello met again on the waist-deck, and they exchanged some few words in passing.

"It is difficult to say exactly," the boatswain murmured, "but from what I gather I think the odds would be very evenly balanced, and it were rash in thee to precipitate a quarrel."

"I am not like to do so," replied Sakr-el-Bahr. "I should not be like to do so in any case. I but desired to know how I stand in case a quarrel should be forced upon me." And he passed on.

Yet his uneasiness was no whit allayed; his difficulties were very far from solved. He had undertaken to carry Rosamund to France or Italy; he had pledged her his word to land her upon one or the other shore, and should he fail, she might even come to conclude that such had never been his real intention. Yet how was he to succeed, now, since Asad was aboard the galeasse? Must he be constrained to carry her back to Algiers as secretly as he had brought her thence, and to keep her there until another opportunity of setting her ashore upon a Christian country should present itself? That was clearly impracticable and fraught with too much risk of detection. Indeed, the risk of detection was very imminent now. At any moment her presence in that pannier might be betrayed. He could think of no way in which to redeem his pledged word. He could but wait and hope, trusting to his luck and to some opportunity which it was impossible to foresee.

And so for a long hour and more he paced there moodily to and fro, his hands clasped behind him, his turbaned head bowed in thought, his heart very heavy within him. He was taken in the toils of the evil web which he had spun; and it seemed very clear to him now that nothing short of his life itself would be demanded as the price of it. That, however, was the least part of his concern. All things had miscarried with him and his life was wrecked. If at the price of it he could ensure safety to Rosamund, that price he would gladly pay. But his dismay and uneasiness all sprang from his inability to discover a way of achieving that most desired of objects even at such a sacrifice. And so he paced on alone and very lonely, waiting and praying for a miracle.

CHAPTER XVI

THE PANNIER

H E WAS still pacing there when an hour or so before sunset—some fifteen hours after setting out—they stood before the entrance of a long bottle-necked cove under the shadow of the cliffs of Aquila Point on the southern coast of the Island of Formentera. He was rendered aware of this and roused from his abstraction by the voice of Asad calling to him from the poop and commanding him to make the cove.

Already the wind was failing them, and it became necessary to take to the oars, as must in any case have happened once they were through the cove's narrow neck in the becalmed lagoon beyond. So Sakr-el-Bahr, in his turn, lifted up his voice, and in answer to his shout came Vigitello and Larocque.

A blast of Vigetello's whistle brought his own men to heel, and they passed rapidly along the benches ordering the rowers to make ready, whilst Jasper and a half-dozen Muslim sailors set about furling the sails that already were beginning to flap in the shifting and intermittent gusts of the expiring wind. Sakr-el-Bahr gave the word to row, and Vigitello blew a second and longer blast. The oars dipped, the slaves strained and the galeasse ploughed forward, time being kept by a boatswain's mate who squatted on the waist-deck and beat a tom-tom rhythmically. Sakr-el-Bahr, standing on the poop-deck, shouted his order to the steersmen in their niches on either side of the stern, and skillfully the vessel was maneuvered through the narrow passage into the calm lagoon whose depths were crystal clear. Here before coming to rest, Sakr-el-Bahr followed the invariable corsair practice of going about, so as to be ready to leave his moorings and make for the open again at a moment's notice.

She came at last alongside the rocky buttresses of a gentle slope that was utterly deserted by all save a few wild goats browsing near the summit. There were clumps of broom, thick with golden flower, about the base of the hill. Higher, a few gnarled and aged olive trees reared their gray heads from which the rays of the westering sun struck a glint as of silver.

Larocque and a couple of sailors went over the bulwarks on the larboard quarter, dropped lightly to the horizontal shafts of the oars, which were rigidly poised, and walking out upon them gained the rocks and proceeded to make fast the vessel by ropes fore and aft.

Sakr-el-Bahr's next task was to set a watch, and he appointed Larocque, sending him to take his station on the summit of the head whence a wide range of view was to be commanded.

Pacing the poop with Marzak the Basha grew reminiscent of former days when roving the seas as a simple corsair he had used this cove both for purposes of ambush and concealment. There were, he said, few harbors in all the Mediterranean so admirably suited to the corsairs' purpose as this; it was a haven of refuge in case of peril, and an unrivaled lurking-place in which to lie wait for the prey. He remembered once having lain there with the formidable Dragut-Reis, a fleet of six galleys, their presence entirely unsuspected by the Genoese admiral, Doria, who had passed majestically along with three caravels and seven galleys.

Marzak, pacing beside his father, listened but half-heartedly to these reminiscences. His mind was all upon Sakr-el-Bahr, and his suspicions of that palmetto bale were quickened by the manner in which for the last two hours he had seen the corsair hovering thoughtfully in its neighborhood.

He broke in suddenly upon his father's memories with an expression of what was in his mind.

"The thanks to Allah," he said, "that it is thou who command this expedition, else might this cove's advantages have been neglected."

"Not so," said Asad. "Sakr-el-Bahr knows them as well as I do. He has used this vantage point aforetime. It was himself who suggested that this would be the very place in which to await this Spanish craft."

"Yet had he sailed alone I doubt if the Spanish argosy had concerned him greatly. There are other matters on his mind, O my father. Observe him yonder, all lost in thought. How many hours of this voyage has he spent thus. He is as a man trapped and desperate. There is some fear rankling in him. Observe him, I say."

"Allah pardon thee," said his father, shaking his old head and sighing over so much impetuosity of judgment. "Must thy imagination be for ever feeding on thy malice? Yet I blame not thee, but thy Sicilian mother, who has fostered this hostility in thee. Did she not hoodwink me into making this unnecessary voyage?"

"I see thou hast forgot last night and the Frankish slave-girl," said his son.

"Nay, then thou seest wrong. I have not forgot it. But neither have I forgot that since Allah hath exalted me to be Basha of Algiers, He looks to me to deal in justice. Come, Marzak, set an end to all this. Perhaps to-morrow thou shalt see him in battle, and after such a sight as that never again wilt thou dare say evil of him. Come, make thy peace with him, and let me see better relations betwixt you hereafter."

And raising his voice he called Sakr-el-Bahr, who immediately turned and came up the gangway. Marzak stood by in a sulky mood, with no notion of doing his father's will by holding out an olive branch to the man who was like to cheat him of his birthright ere all was done. Yet was it he who greeted Sakr-el-Bahr when the corsair set foot upon the poop.

"Does the thought of the coming fight perturb thee, dog of war?" he asked.

"Am I perturbed, pup of peace?" was the crisp answer.

"It seems so. Thine aloofness, thine abstractions . . ."

"Are signs of perturbation, dost suppose?"

"Of what else?"

Sakr-el-Bahr laughed. "Thou'lt tell me next that I am afraid. Yet I should counsel thee to wait until thou hast smelt blood and powder, and learnt precisely what fear is."

The slight altercation drew the attention of Asad's officers who were idling there. Biskaine and some three others lounged forward to stand behind the Basha, looking on in some amusement, which was shared by him.

"Indeed, indeed," said Asad, laying a hand upon Marzak's shoulder, "his counsel is sound enough. Wait, boy, until thou hast gone beside him aboard the infidel, ere thou judge him easily perturbed."

Petulantly Marzak shook off that gnarled old hand.

"Dost thou, O my father, join with him in taunting me upon my lack of knowledge. My youth is sufficient answer. But at least," he added, prompted by a wicked notion suddenly conceived, "at least you cannot taunt me with lack of address with weapons."

"Give him room," said Sakr-el-Bahr, with ironical good-humor, "and he will show us prodigies."

Marzak looked at him with narrowing gleaming eyes.

"Give me a cross-bow," he retorted, "and I'll show thee how to shoot," was his amazing boast.

"Thou'lt show him?" roared Asad. "Thou'lt show him!" And his laugh rang loud and hearty. "Go smear the sun's face with clay, boy."

"Reserve thy judgment, O my father," begged Marzak, with frosty dignity.

"Boy, thou'rt mad! Why Sakr-el-Bahr's quarrel will check a swallow in its fight."

"That is his beast, belike," replied Marzak.

"And what may thine be?" quoth Sakr-el-Bahr, "To hit the Island of Formentera at this distance?"

"Does dare to sneer at me?" cried Marzak, ruffling.

"What daring would that ask?" wondered Sakr-el-Bahr.

"By Allah, thou shalt learn."

"In all humility I await the lesson."

"And thou shalt have it," was the answer viciously delivered. Marzak strode to the rail. "Ho there! Vigitello! A cross-bow for me, and another for Sakr-el-Bahr."

Vigitello sprang to obey him, whilst Asad shook his head and laughed again.

"An it were not against the Prophet's law to make a wager . . ." he was beginning, when Marzak interrupted him.

"Already should I have proposed one."

"So that," said Sakr-el-Bahr, "thy purse would come to match thine head for emptiness."

Marzak looked at him and sneered. Then he snatched from Vigitello's hands one of the cross-bows that he bore and set a shaft to it. And then at last Sakr-el-Bahr was to learn the malice that was at the root of all this odd pretence.

"Look now," said the youth, "there is on that palmetto bale a speck of pitch scarce larger than the pupil of my eye, Thou'lt need to strain thy sight to see it. Observe how my shaft will find it. Canst thou better such a shot?"

His eyes, upon Sakr-el-Bahr's face, watching it closely, observed the pallor by which it was suddenly overspread. But the corsair's recovery was almost as swift. He laughed, seeming so entirely care-less that Marzak began to doubt whether he had paled indeed or whether his own imagination had led him to suppose it.

"Ay, thou'lt choose invisible marks, and wherever the arrow enters thou'lt say 't was there! An old trick, O Marzak. Go cozen women with it."

"Then," said Marzak, "we will take instead the slender cord that binds the bale," And he leveled his bow. But Sakr-el-Bahr's hand closed upon his arm in an easy yet paralyzing grip.

"What," he said, "Thou'lt choose another mark for several rea-sons. For one, I'll not have thy shaft blundering through my oars-men and haply killing one of them. Most of them are slaves specially chosen for their brawn, and I cannot spare any. Another reason is that the mark is a foolish one. The distance is not more than ten paces. A childish test, which, maybe, is the reason why thou hast chosen it."

Marzak lowered his bow and Sakr-el-Bahr released his arm. They looked at each other, the corsair supremely master of himself and smiling easily, no faintest trace of the terror that was in his soul show-ing upon his swarthy bearded countenance or in his hard pale eyes.

He pointed up the hillside to the nearest olive tree, a hundred paces distant. "Yonder," he said, "is a man's mark. Put me a shaft through the long branch of that first olive."

Asad and his officers voiced approval.

"A man's mark, indeed," said the Basha, "so that he be a marks-man."

But Marzak shrugged his shoulders with make-believe con-tempt. "I knew he would refuse the mark I set," said he. "As for the olive-branch, it is so large a butt that a child could not miss it at this distance."

"If a child could not, then thou shouldst not," said Sakr-el-Bahr, who had so placed himself that his body was now between Marzak and the palmetto bale. "Let us see thee hit it, O Marzak." And as he spoke he raised his cross-bow, and scarcely seeming to take aim, he loosed his shaft. It flashed away to be checked, quivering, in the branch he had indicated.

A chorus of applause and admiration greeted the shot, and drew the attention of all the crew to what was toward.

Marzak tightened his lips, realizing how completely he had been outwitted. Willy-nilly he must now shoot at that mark. The choice had been taken out of his hands by Sakr-el-Bahr. He never doubted that he must cover himself with ridicule in the performance, and that there he would be constrained to abandon this pretended match.

"By the Koran," said Biskaine, "thou'lt need all thy skill to equal such a shot, Marzak."

"'T was not the mark I chose," replied Marzak sullenly.

"Thou wert the challenger, O Marzak," his father reminded him. "Therefore the choice of mark was his. He chose a man's mark, and by the beard of Mohammed, he showed us a man's shot."

Marzak would have flung the bow from him in that moment, abandoning the method he had chosen to investigate the contents of the suspicious palmetto bale; but he realized that such a course must now cover him with scorn. Slowly he leveled his bow at that distant mark.

"Have a care of the sentinel on the hill-top," Sakr-el-Bahr admonished him, provoking a titter.

Angrily the youth drew the bow. The cord hummed, and the shaft sped to bury itself in the hill's flank a dozen yards from the mark.

Since he was the son of the Basha none dared to laugh outright save his father and Sakr-el-Bahr. But there was no suppressing a titter to express the mockery to which the proven braggart must ever be exposed.

Asad looked at him, smiling almost sadly. "See now," he said, "what comes of boasting thyself against Sakr-el-Bahr."

"My will was crossed in the matter of a mark," was the bitter answer. "You angered me and made my aim untrue."

Sakr-el-Bahr strode away to the starboard bulwarks, deeming the matter at an end. Marzak observed him.

"Yet at that small mark," he said, "I challenge him again." As he spoke he fitted a second shaft to his bow.

"Behold!" he cried, and took aim.

But swift as thought, Sakr-el-Bahr—heedless now of all consequences—leveled at Marzak the bow which he still held.

"Hold!" he roared. "Loose thy shaft at the bale, and I loose this at thy throat. I never miss!" he added grimly.

There was a startled movement in the ranks of those who stood behind Marzak. In speechless amazement they stared at Sakr-el-Bahr, as he stood there, white-faced, his eyes aflash, his bow drawn taut and ready to launch that death-laden quarrel as he threatened.

Slowly then, smiling with unutterable malice, Marzak lowered his bow. He was satisfied. His true aim was reached. He had drawn his enemy into self-betrayal.

Asad's was the voice that shattered that hush of consternation.

"Kellamullah!" he bellowed. "What is this? Art thou mad, too, O Sakr-el-Bahr?"

"Ay, mad indeed," said Marzak, "mad with fear." And he stepped quickly aside so that the body of Biskaine should shield him from any sudden consequences of his next words.

"Ask him what he keeps in that pannier. O my father."

"Ay, what, in Allah's name?" demanded the Basha, advancing towards his captain.

Sakr-el-Bahr lowered his bow, master of himself again. His composure was beyond all belief.

"I carry in it goods of price, which I'll not see riddled to please a pert boy," he said.

"Goods of price?" echoed Asad, with a snort. "They'll need to be of price indeed that are valued above the life of my son. Let us see these goods of price." And to the men upon the waist-deck he shouted. "Open me that pannier."

Sakr-el-Bahr sprang forward, and laid a hand upon the Basha's arm.

"Stay, my lord!" he entreated almost fiercely. "Consider that this pannier is my own. That its contents are my property: that none has a right to . . ."

"Wouldst babble of right to me, who am thy lord?" blazed the Basha, now in a towering passion. "Open me that pannier, I say."

They were quick to his bidding. The ropes were slashed away, and the front of the pannier fell open on its palmetto hinges. There was a half-repressed chorus of amazement from the men. Sakr-el-Bahr stood frozen in horror of what must follow.

"What is it? What have you found?" demanded Asad.

In silence the men swung the bale about, and disclosed to the eyes of those upon the poop-deck the face and form of Rosamund Godolphin. Then Sakr-el-Bahr, rousing himself from his trance of horror, reckless of all but her, flung down the gangway to assist her from the pannier, and thrusting aside those who stood about her, took his stand at her side.

CHAPTER XVII

THE DUPE

For a little while Asad stood at gaze, speechless in his incredulity. Then to revive the anger that for a moment had been whelmed in astonishment came the reflection that he had been duped by Sakr-el-Bahr, duped by the man he trusted most. He had snarled at Fenzileh and scorned Marzak when they had jointly warned him against his lieutenant; if at times he had been in danger of heeding them, yet sooner or later he had concluded that they but spoke to vent their malice. And yet it was proven now that they had been right in their estimate of this traitor, whilst he himself had been a poor, blind dupe, needing Marzak's wit to tear the bandage from his eyes.

Slowly he went down the gangway, followed by Marzak, Biskaine, and the others. At the point where it joined the waist-deck he paused, and his dark old eyes smoldered under his beetling brows.

"So," he snarled. "These are thy goods of price. Thou lying dog, what was thine aim in this?"

Defiantly Sakr-el-Bahr answered him: "She is my wife. It is my right to take her with me where I go." He turned to her, and bade her veil her face, and she immediately obeyed him with fingers that shook a little in her agitation.

"None questions thy right to that," said Asad. "But being resolved to take her with thee, why not take her openly? Why was she not housed in the poop-house, as becomes the wife of Sakr-el-Bahr? Why smuggle her aboard in a pannier, and keep her there in secret?"

"And why," added Marzak, "didst thou lie to me when I questioned thee upon her whereabouts?—telling me she was left behind in thy house in Algiers?"

"All this I did," replied Sakr-el-Bahr, with a lofty—almost a disdainful—dignity, "because I feared lest I should be prevented from bearing her away with me," and his bold glance, beating full upon Asad, drew a wave of color into the gaunt old cheeks.

"What could have caused that fear?" he asked. "Shall I tell thee? Because no man sailing upon such a voyage as this would have desired the company of his new-wedded wife. Because no man would take a wife with him upon a raid in which there is peril of life and peril of capture."

"Allah has watched over me his servant in the past," said Sakr-el-Bahr, "and I put my trust in Him."

It was a specious answer. Such words—laying stress upon the victories Allah sent him—had aforetime served to disarm his enemies. But they served not now. Instead, they did but fan the flames of Asad's wrath.

"Blaspheme not," he croaked, and his tall form quivered with rage, his sallow old face grew vulturine. "She was brought thus aboard in secret out of fear that were her presence known thy true purpose too must stand revealed."

"And whatever that true purpose may have been," put in Marzak, "it was not the task entrusted thee of raiding the Spanish treasure-galley."

"'T is what I mean, my son," Asad agreed. Then with a commanding gesture: "Wilt thou tell me without further lies what thy purpose was?" he asked.

"How?" said Sakr-el-Bahr, and he smiled never so faintly. "Hast thou not said that this purpose was revealed by what I did? Rather, then, I think is it for me to ask thee for some such information. I do assure thee, my lord, that it was no part of my intention to neglect the task entrusted me. But just because I feared lest knowledge of her presence might lead my enemies to suppose what thou art now supposing, and perhaps persuade thee to forget all that I have done for the glory of Islam, I determined to bring her secretly aboard.

"My real aim, since you must know it, was to land her somewhere on the coast of France, whence she might return to her own land, and her own people. That done, I should have set about intercepting the Spanish galley, and never fear but that by Allah's favor I should have succeeded."

"By the horns of Shaitan," swore Marzak, thrusting himself forward, "he is the very father and mother of lies. Wilt thou explain this desire to be rid of a wife thou hadst but wed?" he demanded.

"Ay," growled Asad. "Canst answer that?"

"Thou shalt hear the truth," said Sakr-el-Bahr.

"The praise to Allah!" mocked Marzak.

"But I warn you," the corsair continued, "that to you it will seem less easy to believe by much than any falsehood I could invent. Years ago in England where I was born I loved this woman and should have taken her to wife. But there were men and circumstances that defamed me to her so that she would not wed me, and I went forth with hatred of her in my heart. Last night the love of her which I believed to be dead and turned to loathing, proved to be still a living force. Loving her, I came to see that I had used her unworthily, and I was urged by a desire above all others to undo the evil I had done."

On that he paused, and after an instant's silence, Asad laughed angrily and contemptuously. "Since when has man expressed his love for a woman by putting her from him?" he asked in a voice of scorn that showed the precise value he set upon such a statement.

"I warned thee it would seem incredible," said Sakr-el-Bahr.

"Is it not plain, O my father, that this marriage of his was no more than a pretence?" cried Marzak.

"As plain as the light of day," replied Asad. "Thy marriage with that woman made an impious mock of the True Faith. It was no marriage. It was a blasphemous pretence, thine only aim to thwart me, abusing my regard for the Prophet's Holy Law, and to set her beyond my reach." He turned to Vigitello, who stood a little behind Sakr-el-Bahr. "Bid thy men put me this traitor into irons," he said.

"Heaven hath guided thee to a wise decision, O my father!" cried Marzak, his voice jubilant. But his was the only jubilant note that sounded, his the only voice that was raised.

"The decision is more like to guide you both to Heaven," replied Sakr-el-Bahr, undaunted. On the instant he had resolved upon his course. "Stay!" he said, raising his hand to Vigitello, who, indeed, had shown no sign of stirring. He stepped close up to Asad, and what he said did not go beyond those who stood immediately about the Basha and Rosamund, who strained her ears that she might lose no word of it.

"Do not think, Asad," he said, "that I will submit me like a camel to its burden. Consider thy position well. If I but raise my voice to call my sea-hawks to me, only Allah can tell how many will be left to obey thee. Darest thou put this matter to the test?" he asked, his countenance grave and solemn, but entirely fearless, as of a man in whom there is no doubt of the issue as it concerns himself.

Asad's eyes glittered dully, his color faded to a deathly ashen hue. "Thou infamous traitor . . ." he began in a thick voice, his body quivering with anger.

"Ah no," Sakr-el-Bahr interrupted him. "Were I a traitor it is what I should have done already, knowing as I do that in any division of our forces, numbers will be heavily on my side. Let then my silence prove my unswerving loyalty, Asad. Let it weigh with thee in considering my conduct, nor permit thyself to be swayed by Marzak there, who recks nothing so that he vents his petty hatred of me."

"Do not heed him, O my father!" cried Marzak. "It cannot be that . . ."

"Peace!" growled Asad, somewhat stricken on a sudden.

And there was peace whilst the Basha stood moodily combing his white beard, his glittering eyes sweeping from Oliver to Rosamund and back again. He was weighing what Sakr-el-Bahr had said. He more than feared that it might be no more than true, and he realized that if he were to provoke a mutiny here he would be putting all to the test, setting all upon a throw in which the dice might well be cogged against him.

If Sakr-el-Bahr prevailed, he would prevail not merely aboard this galley, but throughout Algiers, and Asad would be cast down never to rise again. On the other hand, if he bared his scimitar and called upon the faithful to support him, it might chance that recognizing in him the exalted of Allah to whom their loyalty was due, they would rally to him. He even thought it might be probable. Yet the stake he put upon the board was too vast. The game appalled him, whom nothing yet had appalled, and it scarce needed a muttered caution from Biskaine to determine him to hold his hand.

He looked at Sakr-el-Bahr again, his glance now sullen. "I will consider thy words," he announced in a voice that was unsteady. "I would not be unjust, nor steer my course by appearances alone. Allah forbid!"

CHAPTER XVIII

SHEIK MAT

U NDER THE inquisitive gaping stare of all about them stood Rosamund and Sakr-el-Bahr regarding each other in silence for a little spell after the Basha's departure. The very galley-slaves, stirred from their habitual lethargy by happenings so curious and unusual, craned their sinewy necks to peer at them with a flicker of interest in their dull, weary eyes.

Sakr-el-Bahr's feelings as he considered Rosamund's white face in the fading light were most oddly conflicting. Dismay at what had befallen and some anxious dread of what must follow were leavened by a certain measure of relief.

He realized that in no case could her concealment have continued long. Eleven mortal hours had she spent in the cramped and almost suffocating space of that pannier, in which he had intended to do no more than carry her aboard. The uneasiness which had been occasioned him by the impossibility to deliver her from that close confinement when Asad had announced his resolve to accompany them upon that voyage, had steadily been increasing as hour succeeded hour, and still he found no way to release her from a situation in which sooner or later, when the limits of her endurance were reached, her presence must be betrayed. This release which he could not have contrived had been contrived for him by the suspicions and malice of Marzak. That was the one grain of consolation in the present peril—to himself who mattered nothing and to her who mattered all. Adversity had taught him to prize benefits however slight and to confront perils however over-whelming. So he hugged the present slender benefit, and res-olutely braced himself to deal with the situation as he found it, taking the fullest advantage of the hesitancy which his words had sown in the heart of the Basha. He hugged, too, the thought that as things had fallen out, from being oppressor and oppressed, Rosamund and he were become fellows in misfortune, sharing now a common peril. He found it a sweet thought to dwell on. Therefore was it that he faintly smiled as he looked into Rosamund's white, strained face.

That smile evoked from her the question that had been burden-ing her mind.

"What now? What now?" she asked huskily, and held out appealing hands to him.

"Now," said he coolly, "let us be thankful that you are delivered from quarters destructive both to comfort and to dignity. Let me lead you to those I had prepared for you, which you would have occupied long since but for the ill-timed coming of Asad. Come." And he waved an inviting hand towards the gangway leading to the poop.

She shrank back at that, for there on the poop sat Asad under his awning with Marzak, Biskaine, and his other officers in attendance.

"Come," he repeated, "there is naught to fear so that you keep a bold countenance. For the moment it is Sheik Mat—check to the king."

"Naught to fear?" she echoed, staring.

"For the moment, naught," he answered firmly. "Against what

the future may hold, we must determine. Be sure that fear will not assist our judgment."

She stiffened as if he had charged her unjustly.

"I do not fear," she assured him, and if her face continued white, her eyes grew steady, her voice was resolute.

"Then come," he repeated, and she obeyed him instantly now as if to prove the absence of all fear.

Side by side they passed up the gangway and mounted the steps of the companion to the poop, their approach watched by the group that was in possession of it with glances at once of astonishment and resentment.

Asad's dark, smoldering eyes were all for the girl. They followed her every movement as she approached, and never for a moment left her to turn upon her companion.

Outwardly she bore herself with a proud dignity and an unfaltering composure under that greedy scrutiny; but inwardly she shrank and writhed in a shame and humiliation that she could hardly define. In some measure Oliver shared her feelings, but blent with anger; and urged by them he so placed himself at last that he stood between her and the Basha's regard to screen her from it as he would have screened her from a lethal weapon. Upon the poop he paused, and salaamed to Asad.

"Permit, exalted lord," said he, "that my wife may occupy the quarters I had prepared for her before I knew that thou wouldst honor this enterprise with thy presence."

Curtly, contemptuously, Asad waved a consenting hand without vouchsafing to reply in words. Sakr-el-Bahr bowed again, stepped forward, and put aside the heavy red curtain upon which the crescent was wrought in green. From within the cabin the golden light of a lamp came out to merge into the blue-gray twilight, and to set a shimmering radiance about the white-robed figure of Rosamund.

Thus for a moment Asad's fierce, devouring eyes observed her, then she passed within. Sakr-el-Bahr followed, and the screening curtain swung back into its place.

The small interior was furnished by a divan spread with silken carpets, a low Moorish table in colored wood mosaics bearing the newly lighted lamp, and a tiny brazier in which aromatic gums were burning and spreading a sweetly pungent perfume for the fumigation of all True-Believers.

Out of the shadows in the farther corners rose silently Sakr-el-Bahr's two Nubian slaves, Abiad and Zal-Zer, to salaam low before him. But for their turbans and loincloths in spotless white their dusky bodies must have remained invisible, shadowy among the shadows.

The captain issued an order briefly, and from a hanging cupboard the slaves took meat and drink and set it upon the low table—a bowl of chicken cooked in rice and olives and prunes, a dish of bread, a melon, and a clay amphora of water. Then at another word from him, each took a naked scimitar and they passed out to place themselves on guard beyond the curtain. This was not an act in which there was menace or defiance, nor could Asad so interpret it. The acknowledged presence of Sakr-el-Bahr's wife in that poop-house, rendered the place the equivalent of his hareem, and a man defends his hareem as he defends his honor; it is a spot sacred to himself which none may violate, and it is fitting that he take proper precautions against any impious attempt to do so.

Rosamund sank down upon the divan, and sat there with bowed head, her hands folded in her lap. Sakr-el-Bahr stood by in silence for a long moment contemplating her.

"Eat," he bade her at last. "You will need strength and courage, and neither is possible to a fasting body."

She shook her head. Despite her long fast, food was repellent. Anxiety was thrusting her heart up into her throat to choke her.

"I cannot eat," she answered him. "To what end? Strength and courage cannot avail me now."

"Never believe that," he said. "I have undertaken to deliver you alive from the perils into which I have brought you, and I shall keep my word."

So resolute was his tone that she looked up at him, and found his bearing equally resolute and confident.

"Surely," she cried, "all chance of escape is lost to me."

"Never count it lost whilst I am living," he replied.

She considered him a moment, and there was the faintest smile on her lips.

"Do you think that you will live long now?" she asked him.

"Just as long as God pleases," he replied quite coolly. "What is written is written. So that I live long enough to deliver you, then . . . why, then, faith I shall have lived long enough."

Her head sank. She clasped and unclasped the hands in her lap. She shivered slightly.

"I think we are both doomed," she said in a dull voice. "For if you die, I have your dagger still, remember. I shall not survive you."

He took a sudden step forward, his eyes gleaming, a faint flush glowing through the tan of his cheeks. Then he checked. Fool! How could he so have misread her meaning even for a moment? Were not its exact limits abundantly plain, even without the words which she added a moment later?

"God will forgive me if I am driven to it—if I choose the easier way of honor; for honor, sir," she added, clearly for his benefit, "is ever the easier way, believe me."

"I know," he replied contritely. "I would to God I had followed it."

He paused there, as if hoping that his expression of penitence might evoke some answer from her, might spur her to vouchsafe him some word of forgiveness. Seeing that she continued, mute and absorbed, he sighed heavily, and turned to other matters.

"Here you will find all that you can require," he said. "Should you lack aught you have but to beat your hands together, one or the other of my slaves will come to you. If you address them in French they will understand you. I would I could have brought a woman to minister to you, but that was impossible, as you'll perceive." He stepped to the entrance.

"You are leaving me?" she questioned him in sudden alarm.

"Naturally. But be sure that I shall be very near at hand. And meanwhile be no less sure that you have no cause for immediate fear. At least, matters are no worse than when you were in the pannier. Indeed, much better, for some measure of ease and comfort is now possible to you. So be of good heart; eat and rest. God guard you! I shall return soon after sunrise."

Outside on the poop-deck he found Asad alone now with Marzak under the awning. Night had fallen, the great crescent lanterns on the stern rail were alight and cast a lurid glow along the vessel's length, picking out the shadowy forms and gleaming faintly on the naked backs of the slaves in their serried ranks along the benches, many of them bowed already in attitudes of uneasy slumber. Another lantern swung from the mainmast, and yet another from the poop-rail for the Basha's convenience. Overhead the clustering stars glittered in a cloudless sky of deepest purple. The wind had fallen entirely, and the world was wrapped in stillness broken only by the faint rustling break of waves upon the beach at the cove's end.

Sakr-el-Bahr crossed to Asad's side, and begged for a word alone with him.

"I am alone," said the Basha curtly.

"Marzak is nothing, then," said Sakr-el-Bahr. "I have long suspected it."

Marzak showed his teeth and growled inarticulately, whilst the Basha, taken aback by the ease reflected in the captain's careless, mocking words, could but quote a line of the Koran with which Fenzileh of late had often nauseated him.

"A man's son is the partner of his soul. I have no secrets from Marzak. Speak, then, before him, or else be silent and depart."

"He may be the partner of thy soul, Asad," replied the corsair with his bold mockery, "but I give thanks to Allah he is not the partner of mine. And what I have to say in some sense concerns my soul."

"I thank thee," cut in Marzak, "for the justice of thy words. To be the partner of thy soul were to be an infidel unbelieving dog."

"Thy tongue, O Marzak, is like thine archery," said Sakr-el-Bahr.

"Ay—in that it pierces treachery," was the swift retort.

"Nay—in that it aims at what it cannot hit. Now, Allah, pardon me! Shall I grow angry at such words as thine? Hath not the One proven full oft that he who calls me infidel dog is a liar predestined to the Pit? Are such victories as mine over the fleets of the unbelievers vouchsafed by Allah to an infidel? Foolish blasphemer, teach thy tongue better ways lest the All-wise strike thee dumb."

"Peace!" growled Asad. "Thine arrogance is out of season."

"Haply so," said Sakr-el-Bahr, with a laugh. "And my good sense, too, it seems. Since thou wilt retain beside thee this partner of thy soul, I must speak before him. Have I thy leave to sit?"

Lest such leave should be denied him he dropped forthwith to the vacant place beside Asad and tucked his legs under him.

"Lord," he said, "there is a rift dividing us who should be united for the glory of Islam."

"It is of thy making, Sakr-el-Bahr," was the sullen answer, "and it is for thee to mend it."

"To that end do I desire thine ear. The cause of this rift is yonder." And he jerked his thumb backward over his shoulder towards the poop-house. "If we remove that cause, of a surety the rift itself will vanish, and all will be well again between us."

He knew that never could all be well again between him and Asad. He knew that by virtue of his act of defiance he was irrevocably doomed, that Asad having feared him once, having dreaded his power to stand successfully against his face and overbear his will, would see to it that he never dreaded it again. He knew that if he returned to Algiers there would be a speedy end to him. His only chance of safety lay, indeed, in stirring up mutiny upon the spot and striking swiftly, venturing all upon that desperate throw. And he knew that this was precisely what Asad had cause to fear. Out of this assurance had he conceived his present plan, deeming that if he offered to heal the breach, Asad might pretend to consent so as to weather his present danger, making doubly sure of his vengeance by waiting until they should be home again.

Asad's gleaming eyes considered him in silence for a moment.

"How remove that cause?" he asked. "Wilt thou atone for the mockery of thy marriage, pronounce her divorced and relinquish her?"

"That were not to remove her," replied Sakr-el-Bahr. "Consider well, Asad, what is thy duty to the Faith. Consider that upon our unity depends the glory of Islam. Were it not sinful, then, to suffer the intrusion of aught that may mar such unity? Nay, nay, what I propose is that I should be permitted—assisted even—to bear out the project I had formed, as already I have frankly made confession. Let us put to sea again at dawn—or this very night if thou wilt—make for the coast of France, and there set her ashore that she may go back to her own people and we be rid of her disturbing presence. Then we will return— there is time and to spare—and here or elsewhere lurk in wait for this Spanish argosy, seize the booty and sail home in amity to Algiers, this incident, this little cloud in the splendor of our comradeship, behind us and forgotten as though it had never been. Wilt thou, Asad—for the glory of the Prophet's Law?"

The bait was cunningly presented, so cunningly that not for a moment did Asad or even the malicious Marzak suspect it to be just a bait and no more. It was his own life, become a menace to Asad, that Sakr-el-Bahr was offering him in exchange for the life and liberty of that Frankish slave-girl, but offering it as if unconscious that he did so.

Asad considered, temptation gripping him. Prudence urged him to accept, so that affecting to heal the dangerous breach that now existed he might carry Sakr-el-Bahr back to Algiers, there, beyond the aid of any friendly mutineers, to have him strangled. It was the course to adopt in such a situation, the wise and sober course by which to ensure the overthrow of one who from an obedient and submissive lieutenant had suddenly shown that it was possible for him to become a serious and dangerous rival.

Sakr-el-Bahr watched the Basha's averted, gleaming eyes under their furrowed, thoughtful brows, he saw Marzak's face white, tense and eager in his anxiety that his father should consent. And since his father continued silent, Marzak, unable longer to contain himself, broke into speech.

"He is wise, O my father!" was his crafty appeal. "The glory of Islam above all else! Let him have his way in this, and let the infidel woman go. Thus shall all be well between us and Sakr-el-Bahr!" He laid such a stress upon these words that it was obvious he desired them to convey a second meaning.

Asad heard and understood that Marzak, too, perceived what was here to do; tighter upon him became temptation's grip; but tighter, too, became the grip of a temptation of another sort. Before his fierce eyes there arose a vision of a tall stately maiden with softly rounded bosom, a vision so white and lovely that it enslaved him. And so he found himself torn two ways at once. On the one hand, if he relinquished the woman, he could make sure of his vengeance upon Sakr-el-Bahr, could make sure of removing that rebel from his path. On the other hand, if he determined to hold fast to his desires and to be ruled by them, he must be prepared to risk a mutiny aboard the galeasse, prepared for battle and perhaps for defeat. It was a stake such as no sane Basha would have consented to set upon the board. But since his eyes had again rested upon Rosamund, Asad was no longer sane. His thwarted desires of yesterday were the despots of his wits.

He leaned forward now, looking deep into the eyes of Sakr-el-Bahr.

"Since for thyself thou dost not want her, why dost thou thwart me?" he asked, and his voice trembled with suppressed passion. "So long as I deemed thee honest in taking her to wife I respected that bond as became a good Muslim; but since 't is manifest that it was no more than a pretence, a mockery to serve some purpose hostile to myself, a desecration of the Prophet's Holy Law, I, before whom this blasphemous marriage was performed, do pronounce it to be no marriage. There is no need for thee to divorce her. She is no longer thine. She is for any Muslim who can take her."

Sakr-el-Bahr laughed unpleasantly. "Such a Muslim," he announced, "will be nearer my sword than the Paradise of Mahomet." And on the words he stood up, as if in token of his readiness.

Asad rose with him in a bound of a vigor such as might scarce have been looked for in a man of his years.

"Dost threaten?" he cried, his eyes aflash.

"Threaten?" sneered Sakr-el-Bahr. "I prophesy."

And on that he turned, and stalked away down the gangway to the vessel's waist. There was no purpose in his going other than his perceiving that here argument were worse than useless, and that the wiser course were to withdraw at once, avoiding it and allowing his veiled threat to work upon the Basha's mind.

Quivering with rage Asad watched his departure. On the point of commanding him to return, he checked, fearing lest in his present mood Sakr-el-Bahr should flout his authority and under the eyes of all refuse him the obedience due. He knew that it is not good to command where we are not sure of being obeyed or of being able to enforce obedience, that an authority once successfully flouted is in itself half-shattered.

Whilst still he hesitated, Marzak, who had also risen, caught him by the arm and poured into his ear hot, urgent arguments enjoining him to yield to Sakr-el-Bahr's demand.

"It is the sure way," he cried insistently. "Shall all be jeopardized for the sake of that whey-faced daughter of perdition? In the name of Shaitan, let us be rid of her; set her ashore as he demands, as the price of peace between us and him, and in the security of that peace let him be strangled when we come again to our moorings in Algiers. It is the sure way—the sure way!"

Asad turned at last to look into that handsome eager face. For a moment he was at a loss; then he had recourse to sophistry. "Am I a coward that I should refuse all ways but sure ones?" he demanded in a withering tone. "Or art thou a coward who can counsel none other?"

"My anxiety is all for thee, O my father," Marzak defended himself indignantly. "I doubt if it be safe to sleep, lest he should stir up mutiny in the night."

"Have no fear," replied Asad. "Myself I have set the watch, and the officers are all trustworthy. Biskaine is even now in the forecastle taking the feeling of the men. Soon we shall know precisely where we stand."

"In thy place I would make sure. I would set a term to this danger of mutiny. I would accede to his demands concerning the woman, and settle afterwards with himself."

"Abandon that Frankish pearl?" quoth Asad. Slowly he shook his head. "Nay, nay! She is a garden that shall yield me roses. Together we shall yet taste the sweet sherbet of Kansar, and she shall thank me for having led her into Paradise. Abandon that rosy-limbed loveliness!" He laughed softly on a note of exaltation, whilst in the gloom Marzak frowned, thinking of Fenzileh.

"She is an infidel," his son sternly reminded him, "so forbidden thee by the Prophet. Wilt thou be as blind to that as to thine own peril?" Then his voice gathering vehemence and scorn as he proceeded: "She has gone naked of face through the streets of Algiers; she has been gaped at by the rabble in the sôk; this loveliness of hers has been deflowered by the greedy gaze of Jew and Moor and Turk; galley-slaves and negroes have feasted their eyes upon her unveiled beauty; one of thy captains hath owned her his wife." He laughed. "By Allah, I do not know thee, O my father! Is this the woman thou wouldst take for thine own? This the woman for whose possession thou wouldst jeopardize thy life and perhaps the very Bashalik itself!"

Asad clenched his hands until the nails bit into his flesh. Every word his son had uttered had been as a lash to his soul. The truth of it was not be to contested. He was humiliated and shamed. Yet was he not conquered of his madness, nor diverted from his course. Before he could make answer, the tall martial figure of Biskaine came up the companion.

"Well?" the Basha greeted him eagerly, thankful for this chance to turn the subject.

Biskaine was downcast. His news was to be read in his countenance. "The task appointed me was difficult," said he. "I have done my best. Yet I could scarce go about it in such a fashion as to draw definite conclusions. But this I know, my lord, that he will be reckless indeed if he dares to take up arms against thee and challange thine authority. So much at least I am permitted to conclude."

"No more than that?" asked Asad. "And if I were to take up arms against him, and to seek to settle this matter out of hand?"

Biskaine paused a moment ere replying. "I cannot think but that Allah would vouchsafe thee victory," he said. But his words did not delude the Basha. He recognized them to be no more than those which respect for him dictated to his officer. "Yet," continued Biskaine, "I should judge thee reckless too, my lord, as reckless as I should judge him in the like circumstances."

"I see," said Asad. "The matter stands so balanced that neither of us dare put it to the test."

"Thou hast said it."

"Then is thy course plain to thee!" cried Marzak, eager to renew his arguments. "Accept his terms, and . . ."

But Asad broke in impatiently. "Every thing in its own hour and each hour is written. I will consider what to do."

Below on the waist-deck Sakr-el-Bahr was pacing with Vigitello, and Vigitello's words to him were of a tenor identical almost with those of Biskaine to the Basha.

"I scarce can judge," said the Italian renegade. "But I do think that it were not wise for either thou or Asad to take the first step against the other."

"Are matters, then, so equal between us?"

"Numbers, I fear," replied Vigitello, "would be in favor of Asad. No truly devout Muslim will stand against the Basha, the representative of the Sublime Portal, to whom loyalty is a question of religion. Yet they are accustomed to obey thee, to leap at thy command, and so Asad himself were rash to put it to the test."

"Ay—a sound argument," said Sakr-el-Bahr. "It is as I had thought."

Upon that he quitted Vigitello, and slowly, thoughtfully, returned to the poop-deck. It was his hope—his only hope now—that Asad might accept the proposal he had made him. As the price of it he was fully prepared for the sacrifice of his own life, which it must entail. But it was not for him to approach Asad again; to do so would be to argue doubt and anxiety and so to court refusal. He must possess his soul in what patience he could. If Asad persisted in his refusal undeterred by any fear of mutiny, then Sakr-el-Bahr knew not what course remained him to accomplish Rosamund's deliverance. Proceed to stir up mutiny he dared not. It was too desperate a throw. In his own view it offered him no slightest chance of success, and did it fail, then indeed all would be lost, himself destroyed, and Rosamund at the mercy of Asad. He was as one walking along a sword-edge. His only chance of present immunity for himself and Rosamund lay in the confidence that Asad would dare no more than himself to take the initiative in aggression. But that was only for the present, and at any moment Asad might give the word to put about and steer for Barbary again; in no case could that be delayed beyond the plundering of the Spanish argosy. He nourished the faint hope that in that coming fight—if indeed the Spaniards did show fight—some chance might perhaps present itself, some unexpected way out of the present situation.

He spent the night under the stars, stretched across the threshold of the curtained entrance to the poop-house, making thus a barrier of his body whilst he slept, and himself watched over in his turn by his faithful Nubians who remained on guard. He awakened when the first violet tints of dawn were in the east, and quietly dismissing the weary slaves to their rest, he kept watch alone thereafter. Under the awning on the starboard quarter slept the Basha and his son, and near them Biskaine was snoring.

CHAPTER XIX

THE MUTINEERS

L ATER THAT morning, some time after the galeasse had
awakened to life and such languid movement as might be
looked for in a waiting crew, Sakr-el-Bahr went to visit
Rosamund.

He found her brightened and refreshed by sleep, and he
brought her reassuring messages that all was well, encouraging her
with hopes which himself he was very far from entertaining. If her
reception of him was not expressedly friendly, neither was it
unfriendly. She listened to the hopes he expressed of yet effecting
her safe deliverance, and whilst she had no thanks to offer him for
the efforts he was to exert on her behalf—accepting them as her
absolute due, as the inadequate liquidation of the debt that lay
between them—yet there was now none of that aloofness amounting almost to scorn which hitherto had marked her bearing
towards him.

He came again some hours later, in the afternoon, by when his
Nubians were once more at their post. He had no news to bring her
beyond the fact that their sentinel on the heights reported a sail to

westward, beating up towards the island before the very gentle breeze that was blowing. But the argosy they awaited was not yet in sight, and he confessed that certain proposals which he had made to Asad for landing her in France had been rejected. Still she need have no fear, he added promptly, seeing the sudden alarm that quickened in her eyes. A way would present itself. He was watching, and would miss no chance.

"And if no chance should offer?" she asked him.

"Why then I will make one," he answered, lightly almost, "I have been making them all my life, and it would be odd if I should have lost the trick of it on my life's most important occasion."

This mention of his life led to a question from her.

"How did you contrive the chance that has made you what you are? I mean," she added quickly, as if fearing that the purport of that question might be misunderstood, "that has enabled you to become a corsair captain."

"'T is a long story that," he said. "I should weary you in the telling of it."

"No," she replied, and shook her head, her clear eyes solemnly meeting his clouded glance. "You would not weary me. Chances may be few in which to learn it."

"And you would learn it?" quoth he, and added, "That you may judge me?"

"Perhaps," she said, and her eyes fell.

With bowed head he paced the length of the small chamber, and back again. His desire was to do her will in this, which is natural enough—for if it is true that who knows all must perforce forgive all, never could it have been truer than in the case of Sir Oliver Tressilian.

So he told his tale. Pacing there he related it at length, from the days when he had toiled at an oar on one of the galleys of Spain down to that hour in which aboard the Spanish vessel taken under Cape Spartel he had determined upon that voyage to England to present his reckoning to his brother. He told his story simply and without too great a wealth of detail, yet he omitted nothing of all that had gone to place him where he stood. And she, listening, was so profoundly moved that at one moment her eyes glistened with tears which she sought vainly to repress. Yet he, pacing there, absorbed, with head bowed and eyes that never once strayed in her direction, saw none of this.

"And so," he said, when at last that odd narrative had reached its end, "you know what the forces were that drove me. Another stronger than myself might have resisted and preferred to suffer death. But I was not strong enough. Or perhaps it is that stronger than myself was my desire to punish, to vent the bitter hatred into which my erstwhile love for Lionel was turned."

"And for me, too—as you have told me," she added.

"Not so," he corrected her. "I hated you for your unfaith, and most of all for your having burnt unread the letters that I sent you by the hand of Pitt. In doing that you contributed to the wrongs I was enduring, you destroyed my one chance of establishing my innocence and seeking rehabilitation, you doomed me for life to the ways which I was treading. But I did not then know what ample cause you had to believe me what I seemed. I did not know that it was believed I had fled. Therefore I forgive you freely a deed for which at one time I confess that I hated you, and which spurred me to bear you off when I found you under my hand that night at Arwenack when I went for Lionel."

"You mean that it was no part of your intent to have done so?" she asked him.

"To carry you off together with him?" he asked. "I swear to God I had not premeditated that. Indeed, it was done because not pre-meditated, for had I considered it, I do think I should have been proof against any such temptation. It assailed me suddenly when I beheld you there with Lionel, and I succumbed to it. Knowing what I now know I am punished enough, I think."

"I think I can understand," she murmured gently, as if to comfort him, for quick pain had trembled in his voice.

He tossed back his turbaned head. "To understand is something," said he. "It is halfway at least to forgiveness. But ere forgiveness can be accepted the evil done must be atoned for to the full."

"If possible," said she.

"It must be made possible," he answered her with heat, and on that he checked abruptly, arrested by a sound of shouting from without.

He recognized the voice of Larocque, who at dawn had returned to his sentinel's post on the summit of the headland, relieving the man who had replaced him there during the night.

"My lord! My lord!" was the cry, in a voice shaken by excitement, and succeeded by a shouting chorus from the crew.

Sakr-el-Bahr turned swiftly to the entrance, whisked aside the curtain, and stepped out upon the poop. Larocque was in the very act of clambering over the bulwarks amidships, towards the waist-deck where Asad awaited him in company with Marzak and the trusty Biskaine. The prow, on which the corsairs had lounged at ease since yesterday, was now a seething mob of inquisitive babbling men, crowding to the rail and even down the gangway in their eagerness to learn what news it was that brought the sentinel aboard in such excited haste.

From where he stood Sakr-el-Bahr heard Larocque's loud announcement.

"The ship I sighted at dawn, my lord!"

"Well?" barked Asad.

"She is here—in the bay beneath that headland. She has just dropped anchor."

"No need for alarm in that," replied the Basha at once. "Since she has anchored there it is plain that she has no suspicion of our presence. What manner of ship is she?"

"A tall galleon of twenty guns, flying the flag of England."

"Of England!" cried Asad in surprise. "She'll need be a stout vessel to hazard herself in Spanish waters."

Sakr-el-Bahr advanced to the rail.

"Does she display no further device?" he asked.

Larocque turned at the question. "Ay," he answered, "a narrow blue pennant on her mizzen is charged with a white bird—a stork, I think."

"A stork?" echoed Sakr-el-Bahr thoughtfully. He could call to mind no such English blazon, nor did it seem to him that it could possibly be English. He caught the sound of a quickly indrawn breath behind him. He turned to find Rosamund standing in the entrance, not more than half concealed by the curtain. Her face showed white and eager, her eyes were wide.

"What is 't?" he asked her shortly.

"A stork, he thinks," she said, as though that were answer enough.

"I' faith an unlikely bird," he commented. "The fellow is mistook."

"Yet not by much, Sir Oliver."

"How? Not by much?" Intrigued by something in her tone and glance, he stepped quickly up to her, whilst below the chatter of voices increased.

"That which he takes to be a stork is a heron—a white heron, and white is argent in heraldry, is 't not?"

"It is. What then?"

"D' ye not see? That ship will be the *Silver Heron*."

He looked at her. "'S life!" said he, "I reck little whether it be the silver heron or the golden grasshopper. What odds?"

"It is Sir John's ship—Sir John Killigrew's," she explained. "She was all but ready to sail when . . . when you came to Arwenack. He was for the Indies. Instead—don't you see?—out of love for me he will have come after me upon a forlorn hope of overtaking you ere you could make Barbary."

"God's light!" said Sakr-el-Bahr, and fell to musing. Then he raised his head and laughed. "Faith, he's some days late for that!"

But the jest evoked no response from her. She continued to stare at him with those eager yet timid eyes.

"And yet," he continued, "he comes opportunely enough. If the breeze that has fetched him is faint, yet surely it blows from Heaven."

"Were it . . .?" she paused, faltering a moment. Then, "Were it possible to communicate with him?" she asked, yet with hesitation.

"Possible—ay," he answered. "Though we must needs devise the means, and that will prove none so easy."

"And you would do it?" she inquired, an undercurrent of wonder in her question, some recollection of it in her face.

"Why readily," he answered, "since no other way presents itself. No doubt 't will cost some lives," he added, "but then . . ." And he shrugged to complete the sentence.

"Ah, no, no! Not at that price!" she protested. And how was he to know that all the price she was thinking of was his own life, which she conceived would be forfeited if the assistance of the *Silver Heron* were invoked?

Before he could return her any answer his attention was diverted. A sullen threatening note had crept into the babble of the crew, and suddenly one or two voices were raised to demand insistently that Asad should put to sea at once and remove his vessel from a neighborhood become so dangerous. Now, the fault of this was Marzak's. His was the voice that first had uttered that timid suggestion, and the infection of his panic had spread instantly through the corsair ranks.

Asad, drawn to the full of his gaunt height, turned upon them the eyes that had quelled greater clamors, and raised the voice which in its day had hurled a hundred men straight into the jaws of death without a protest.

"Silence!" he commanded. "I am your lord and need no counselors save Allah. When I consider the time come, I will give the word to row, but not before. Back to your quarters, then, and peace!"

He disdained to argue with them, to show them what sound reasons there were for remaining in this secret cove and against putting forth into the open. Enough for them that such should be his will. Not for them to question his wisdom and his decisions.

But Asad-ed-Din had lain overlong in Algiers whilst his fleets under Sakr-el-Bahr and Biskaine had scoured the inland sea. The men were no longer accustomed to the goad of his voice, their confidence in his judgment was not built upon the sound basis of past experience. Never yet had he led into battle the men of this crew and brought them forth again in triumph and enriched by spoil.

So now they set their own judgment against his. To them it seemed a recklessness—as, indeed, Marzak had suggested—to linger here, and his mere announcement of his purpose was far from sufficient to dispel their doubts.

The murmurs swelled, not to be overborne by his fierce presence and scowling brow, and suddenly one of the renegades —secretly prompted by the wily Vigitello—raised a shout for the captain whom they knew and trusted.

"Sakr-el-Bahr! Sakr-el-Bahr! Thou'lt not leave us penned in this cove to perish like rats!"

It was as a spark to a train of powder. A score of voices instantly took up the cry; hands were flung out towards Sakr-el-Bahr, where he stood above them and in full view of all, leaning impassive and stern upon the poop-rail, whilst his agile mind weighed the opportunity thus thrust upon him, and considered what profit was to be extracted from it.

Asad fell back a pace in his profound mortification. His face was livid, his eyes glared furiously, his hand flew to the jeweled hilt of his scimitar, yet forbore from drawing the blade. Instead he let loose upon Marzak the venom kindled in his soul by this evidence of how shrunken was his authority.

"Thou fool!" he snarled. "Look on thy craven's work. See what a devil thou hast raised with thy woman's counsels. Thou to command a galley! Thou to become a fighter upon the seas! I would that Allah had stricken me dead ere I begat me such a son as thou!"

Marzak recoiled before the fury of words that he feared might be followed by yet worse. He dared make no answer, offer no excuse: in that moment he scarcely dared breathe.

Meanwhile Rosamund in her eagerness had advanced until she stood at Sakr-el-Bahr's elbow.

"God is helping us!" she said in a voice of fervent gratitude. "This is your opportunity. The men will obey you."

He looked at her, and smiled faintly upon her eagerness. "Ay, mistress, they will obey me," he said. But in the few moments that were sped he had taken his resolve. Whilst undoubtedly Asad was right, and the wise course was to lie close in this sheltering cove where the odds of their going unperceived were very heavily in their favor, yet the men's judgment was not altogether at fault. If they were to put to sea, they might by steering an easterly course pass similarly unperceived, and even should the splash of their oars reach the galleon beyond the headland, yet by the time she had weighed anchor and started in pursuit they would be well away straining every ounce of muscle at the oars, whilst the breeze—a heavy factor in his considerations—was become so feeble that they could laugh at pursuit by a vessel that depended upon wind alone. The only danger, then, was the danger of the galleon's cannon, and that danger was none so great as from experience Sakr-el-Bahr well knew.

Thus was he reluctantly forced to the conclusion that in the main the wiser policy was to support Asad, and since he was full confident of the obedience of the men he consoled himself with the reflection that a moral victory might be in store for him out of which some surer profit might presently be made.

In answer, then, to those who still called upon him, he leapt down the companion and strode along the gangway to the waist-deck to take his stand at the Basha's side. Asad watched his approach with angry misgivings; it was with him a foregone conclusion that things being as they were Sakr-el-Bahr would be ranged against him to obtain complete control of these mutineers and to cull the fullest advantage from the situation. Softly and slowly he unsheathed his scimitar, and Sakr-el-Bahr seeing this out of the corner of his eye, yet affected not to see, but stood forward to address the men.

"How now?" he thundered wrathfully. "What shall this mean? Are ye all deaf that ye have not heard the commands of your Basha, the exalted of Allah, that ye dare raise your mutinous voices and say what is your will?"

Sudden and utter silence followed that exhortation. Asad listened in relieved amazement; Rosamund caught her breath in sheer dismay.

What could he mean, then? Had he but fooled and duped her? Were his intentions towards her the very opposite to his protestations? She leant upon the poop-rail straining to catch every syllable of that speech of his in the lingua franca, hoping almost that her indifferent knowledge of it had led her into error on the score of what he had said.

She saw him turn with a gesture of angry command upon Larocque, who stood there by the bulwarks, waiting.

"Back to thy post up yonder, and keep watch upon that vessel's movements, reporting them to us. We stir not hence until such be our lord Asad's good pleasure. Away with thee!"

Larocque without a murmur threw a leg over the bulwarks and dropped to the oars, whence he clambered ashore as he had been bidden. And not a single voice was raised in protest.

Sakr-el-Bahr's dark glance swept the ranks of the corsairs crowding the forecastle.

"Because this pet of the hareem," he said, immensely daring, indicating Marzak by a contemptuous gesture, "bleats of danger into the ears of men, are ye all to grow timid and foolish as a herd of sheep? By Allah! What are ye? Are ye the fearless sea-hawks that have flown with me, and struck where the talons of my grappling-hooks were flung, or are ye but scavenging crows?"

He was answered by an old rover whom fear had rendered greatly daring.

"We are trapped here as Dragut was trapped at Jerba."

"Thou liest," he answered. "Dragut was not trapped, for Dragut found a way out. And against Dragut there was the whole navy of Genoa, whilst against us there is but one single galleon. By the Koran if she shows fight, have we no teeth? Will it be the first galleon whose decks we have overrun? But if ye prefer a coward's counsel, ye sons of shame, consider that once we take the open sea our discovery will be assured, and Larocque hath told you that she carries twenty guns. I tell you that if we are to be attacked by her, best be attacked at close quarters, and I tell you that if we lie close and snug in here it is long odds that we shall never be attacked at all. That she has no inkling of our presence is proven, since she has cast anchor round the headland. And consider that if we fly from a danger that doth not exist, and in our flight are so fortunate as not to render real that danger and to court it, we abandon a rich argosy that shall bring profit to us all.

"But I waste my breath in argument," he ended abruptly. "You have heard the commands of your lord, Asad-ed-Din, and that should be argument enough. No more of this, then."

Without so much as waiting to see them disperse from the rail and return to their lounging attitudes about the forecastle, he turned to Asad.

"It might have been well to hang the dog who spoke of Dragut and Jerba," he said. "But it was never in my nature to be harsh with those who follow me." And that was all.

Asad from amazement had passed quickly to admiration and a

sort of contrition, into which presently there crept a poisonous tinge of jealousy to see Sakr-el-Bahr prevail where he himself alone must utterly have failed. This jealousy spread all-pervadingly, like an oil stain. If he had come to bear ill-will to Sakr-el-Bahr before, that ill-will was turned of a sudden into positive hatred for one in whom he now beheld a usurper of the power and control that should reside in the Basha alone. Assuredly there was no room for both of them in the Bashalik of Algiers.

Therefore the words of commendation which had been rising to his lips froze there now that Sakr-el-Bahr and he stood face to face. In silence he considered his lieutenant through narrowing evil eyes, whose message none but a fool could have misunderstood.

Sakr-el-Bahr was not a fool, and he did not misunderstand it for a moment. He felt a tightening at the heart, and ill-will sprang to life within him responding to the call of that ill-will. Almost he repented him that he had not availed himself of that moment of weakness and mutiny on the part of the crew to attempt the entire superseding of the Basha.

The conciliatory words he had in mind to speak he now suppressed. To that venomous glance he opposed his ever-ready mockery. He turned to Biskaine.

"Withdraw," he curtly bade him, "and take that stout sea-warrior with thee." And he indicated Marzak.

Biskaine turned to the Basha. "Is it thy wish, my lord?" he asked.

Asad nodded in silence, and motioned him away together with the cowed Marzak.

"My lord," said Sakr-el-Bahr, when they were alone, "yesterday I made thee a proposal for the healing of this breach between us, and it was refused. But now had I been the traitor and mutineer thou hast dubbed me I could have taken full advantage of the humor of my corsairs. Had I done that it need no longer have been mine to propose or to sue. Instead it would have been mine to dictate. Since I have given thee such crowning proof of my loyalty, it is my hope and trust that I may be restored to the place I had lost in thy confidence, and that this being so thou wilt accede now to that proposal of mine concerning the Frankish woman yonder."

It was unfortunate perhaps that she should have been standing there unveiled upon the poop within the range of Asad's glance; for the sight of her it may have been that overcame his momentary hesitation and stifled the caution which prompted him to accede. He considered her a moment, and a faint color kindled in his cheeks which anger had made livid.

"It is not for thee, Sakr-el-Bahr," he answered at length, "to make me proposals. To dare it, proves thee far removed indeed from the loyalty thy lips profess. Thou knowest my will concerning her. Once hast thou thwarted and defied me, misusing to that end the Prophet's Holy Law. Continue a barrier in my path and it shall be at thy peril." His voice was raised and it shook with anger.

"Not so loud," said Sakr-el-Bahr, his eyes gleaming with a response of anger. "For should my men overhear these threats of thine I will not answer for what may follow. I oppose thee at my peril sayest thou. Be it so, then." He smiled grimly. "It is war between us, Asad, since thou hast chosen it. Remember hereafter when the consequences come to overwhelm thee that the choice was thine."

"Thou mutinous, treacherous son of a dog!" blazed Asad.

Sakr-el-Bahr turned on his heel. "Pursue the path of an old man's folly," he said over his shoulder, "and see whither it will lead thee."

Upon that he strode away up the gangway to the poop, leaving the Basha alone with his anger and some slight fear evoked by that last bold menace. But notwithstanding that he menaced boldly the heart of Sakr-el-Bahr was surcharged with anxiety. He had conceived a plan; but between the conception and its execution he realized that much ill might lie.

"Mistress," he addressed Rosamund as he stepped upon the poop. "You are not wise to show yourself so openly."

To his amazement she met him with a hostile glance.

"Not wise?" said she, her countenance scornful. "You mean that I may see more than was intended for me. What game do you play here, sir, that you tell me one thing and show me by your actions that you desire another?"

He did not need to ask her what she meant. At once he perceived how she had misread the scene she had witnessed.

"I'll but remind you," he said very gravely, "that once before you did me a wrong by over-hasty judgment, as has been proven to you."

It overthrew some of her confidence. "But then . . ." she began.

"I do but ask you to save your judgment for the end. If I live I shall deliver you. Meanwhile I beg that you will keep your cabin. It does not help me that you be seen."

She looked at him, a prayer for explanation trembling on her lips. But before the calm command of his tone and glance she slowly lowered her head and withdrew beyond the curtain.

CHAPTER XX

THE MESSENGER

For the rest of the day she kept the cabin, chafing with anxiety to know what was toward and the more racked by it because Sakr-el-Bahr refrained through all those hours from coming to her. At last towards evening, unable longer to contain herself, she went forth again, and as it chanced she did so at an untimely moment.

The sun had set, and the evening prayer was being recited aboard the galeasse, her crew all prostrate. Perceiving this, she drew back again instinctively, and remained screened by the curtain until the prayer was ended. Then putting it aside, but without stepping past the Nubians who were on guard, she saw that on her left Asad-ed-Din, with Marzak, Biskaine, and one or two other officers, was again occupying the divan under the awning. Her eyes sought Sakr-el-Bahr, and presently they beheld him coming up the gangway with his long, swinging stride, in the wake of the boatswain's mates who were doling out the meager evening meal to the slaves.

Suddenly he halted by Lionel, who occupied a seat at the head of his oar immediately next to the gangway. He addressed him harshly in the lingua franca, which Lionel did not understand, and his words rang clearly and were heard—as he intended that they should be—by all upon the poop.

"Well, dog? How does galley-slave fare suit thy tender stomach?"

Lionel looked up at him.

"What are you saying?" he asked in English.

Sakr-el-Bahr bent over him, and his face as all could see was evil and mocking. No doubt he spoke to him in English also, but no more than a murmur reached the straining ears of Rosamund, though from his countenance she had no doubt of the purport of his words. And yet she was far indeed from a correct surmise. The mockery in his countenance was but a mask.

"Take no heed of my looks," he was saying. "I desire them up yonder to think that I abuse you. Look as a man would who were being abused. Cringe or snarl, but listen. Do you remember once when as lads we swam together from Penarrow to Trefusis Point?"

"What do you mean?" quoth Lionel, and the natural sullenness of his mien was all that Sakr-el-Bahr could have desired.

"I am wondering whether you could still swim as far. If so you might find a more appetizing supper awaiting you at the end—aboard Sir John Killigrew's ship. You had not heard? The *Silver Heron* is at anchor in the bay beyond that headland. If I afford you the means, could you swim to her do you think?"

Lionel stared at him in profoundest amazement. "Do you mock me?" he asked at length.

"Why should I mock you on such a matter?"

"Is it not to mock me to suggest a way for my deliverance?"

Sakr-el-Bahr laughed, and he mocked now in earnest. He set his left foot upon the rowers' stretcher, and leaned forward and down his elbow upon his raised knee so that his face was close to Lionel's.

"For your deliverance?" said he. "God's life! Lionel, your mind was ever one that could take in naught but your own self. 'T is that has made a villain of you. Your deliverance! God's wounds! Is there none but yourself whose deliverance I might desire? Look you now, I want you to swim to Sir John's ship and bear him word of the presence here of this galeasse and that Rosamund is aboard it. 'T is for her that I am concerned, and so little for you that should you chance to be drowned in the attempt my only regret will be that the message was not delivered. Will you undertake that swim? It is your one sole chance short of death itself of escaping from the rower's bench. Will you go?"

"But how?" demanded Lionel, still mistrusting him.

"Will you go?" his brother insisted.

"Afford me the means and I will," was the answer.

"Very well." Sakr-el-Bahr leaned nearer still. "Naturally it will be supposed by all who are watching us that I am goading you to desperation. Act, then, your part. Up, and attempt to strike me. Then when I return the blow—and I shall strike heavily that no make-believe may be suspected—collapse on your oar pretending to swoon. Leave the rest to me. Now," he added sharply, and on the word rose with a final laugh of derision as if to take his departure.

But Lionel was quick to follow the instructions. He leapt up in his bonds, and reaching out as far as they would permit him, he struck Sakr-el-Bahr heavily upon the face. On his side, too, there was to be no make-believe apparent. That done he sank down with a clank of shackles to the bench again, whilst every one of his fellow-slaves that faced his way looked on with fearful eyes.

Sakr-el-Bahr was seen to reel under the blow, and instantly there was a commotion on board. Biskaine leapt to his feet with a half-cry of astonishment; even Asad's eyes kindled with interest at so unusual a sight as that of a galley-slave attacking a corsair. Then with a snarl of anger, the snarl of an enraged beast almost, Sakr-el-Bahr's great arm was swung aloft and his fist descended like a hammer upon Lionel's head.

Lionel sank forward under the blow, his senses swimming. Sakr-el-Bahr's arm swung up a second time.

"Thou dog!" he roared, and then checked, perceiving that Lionel appeared to have swooned.

He turned and bellowed for Vigitello and his mates in a voice that was hoarse with passion. Vigitello came at a run, a couple of his men at his heels.

"Unshackle me this carrion, and heave it overboard," was the harsh order. "Let that serve as an example to the others. Let them learn thus the price of mutiny in their lousy ranks. To it, I say."

Away sped a man for hammer and chisel. He returned with them at once. Four sharp metallic blows rang out, and Lionel was dragged forth from his place to the gang-way-deck. Here he revived, and screamed for mercy as though he were to be drowned in earnest.

Biskaine chuckled under the awning, Asad looked on approvingly, Rosamund drew back, shuddering, choking, and near to fainting from sheer horror.

She saw Lionel borne struggling in the arms of the boatswain's men to the starboard quarter, and flung over the side with no more compunction or care than had he been so much rubbish. She heard the final scream of terror with which he vanished, the splash of his fall, and then in the ensuing silence the laugh of Sakr-el-Bahr.

For a spell she stood there with horror and loathing of that renegade corsair in her soul. Her mind was bewildered and confused. She sought to restore order in it, that she might consider this fresh deed of his, this act of wanton brutality and fratricide. And all that she could gather was the firm conviction that hitherto he had cheated her; he had lied when he swore that his aim was to effect her deliverance. It was not in such a nature to know a gentle mood of penitence for a wrong done. What might be his purpose she could not yet perceive, but that it was an evil one she never doubted, for no purpose of his could be aught but evil. So overwrought was she now that she forgot all Lionel's sins, and found her heart filled with compassion for him hurled in that brutal fashion to his death.

And then, quite suddenly a shout rang out from the forecastle. "He is swimming!"

Sakr-el-Bahr had been prepared for the chance of this.

"Where? Where?" he cried, and sprang to the bulwarks.

"Yonder!" A man was pointing. Others had joined him and were peering through the gathering gloom at the moving object that was Lionel's head and the faintly visible swirl of water about it which indicated that he swam.

"Out to sea!" cried Sakr-el-Bahr, "He'll not swim far in any case. But we will shorten his road for him." He snatched a cross-bow from the rack about the mainmast, fitted a shaft to it and took aim.

On the point of loosing the bolt he paused.

"Marzak!" he called. "Here, thou prince of marksmen, is a butt for thee!"

From the poop-deck whence with his father he too was watching the swimmer's head, which at every moment became more faint in the failing light, Marzak looked with cold disdain upon his challenger, making no reply. A titter ran through the crew.

"Come now," cried Sakr-el-Bahr. "Take up thy bow!"

"If thou delay much longer," put in Asad, "he will be beyond thine aim. Already he is scarcely visible."

"The more difficult a butt, then," answered Sakr-el-Bahr, who was but delaying to gain time. "The keener test. A hundred philips, Marzak, that thou'lt not hit me that head in three shots, and that I'll sink him at the first! Wilt take the wager?"

"The unbeliever is for ever peeping forth from thee," was Marzak's dignified reply. "Games of chance are forbidden by the Prophet."

"Make haste, man!" cried Asad. "Already I can scarce discern him. Loose thy quarrel."

"Pooh," was the disdainful answer. "A fair mark still for such an eye as mine. I never miss—not even in the dark."

"Vain boaster," said Marzak.

"Am I so?" Sakr-el-Bahr loosed his shaft at last into the gloom, and peered after it following its flight, which was wide of the direction of the swimmer's head. "A hit!" he cried brazenly. "He's gone!"

"I think I see him still," said one.

"Thine eyes deceive thee in this light. No man was ever known to swim with an arrow through his brain."

"Ay," put in Jasper, who stood behind Sakr-el-Bahr. "He has vanished."

"'T is too dark to see," said Vigitello.

And then Asad turned from the vessel's side. "Well, well—shot or drowned, he's gone," he said, and there the matter ended.

Sakr-el-Bahr replaced the cross-bow in the rack, and came slowly up to the poop.

In the gloom he found himself confronted by Rosamund's white face between the two dusky countenances of his Nubians. She drew back before him as he approached, and he, intent upon imparting his news to her, followed her within the poop-house, and bade Abiad bring lights.

When these had been kindled they faced each other, and he perceived her profound agitation and guessed the cause of it. Suddenly she broke into speech.

"You beast! You devil!" she panted. "God will punish you! I shall spend my every breath in praying Him to punish you as you deserve. You murderer! You hound! And I like a poor simpleton was heeding your false words. I was believing you sincere in your repentance of the wrong you have done me. But now you have shown me . . ."

"How have I hurt you in what I have done to Lionel?" he cut in, a little amazed by so much vehemence.

"Hurt me!" she cried, and on the words grew cold and calm again with very scorn. "I thank God it is beyond your power to hurt me. And I thank you for correcting my foolish misconception of you, my belief in your pitiful pretence that it was your aim to save me. I would not accept salvation at your murderer's hands. Though, indeed, I shall not be put to it. Rather," she pursued, a little wildly now in her deep mortification, "are you like to sacrifice me to your own vile ends, whatever they may be. But I shall thwart you, Heaven helping me. Be sure I shall not want courage for that." And with a shuddering moan she covered her face, and stood swaying there before him.

He looked on with a faint, bitter smile, understanding her mood just as he understood her dark threat of thwarting him.

"I came," he said quietly, "to bring you the assurance that he has got safely away, and to tell you upon what manner of errand I have sent him."

Something compelling in his voice, the easy assurance with which he spoke, drew her to stare at him again.

"I mean Lionel, of course," he said, in answer to her questioning glance. "That scene between us—the blow and the swoon and the rest of it—was all make-believe. So afterwards the shooting. My challenge to Marzak was a ruse to gain time—to avoid shooting until Lionel's head should have become so dimly visible in the dusk that none could say whether it was still there or not. My shaft went wide of him, as I intended. He is swimming round the head with my message to Sir John Killigrew. He was a strong swimmer in the old days, and should easily reach his goal. That is what I came to tell you."

For a long spell she continued to stare at him in silence.

"You are speaking the truth?" she asked at last, in a small voice.

He shrugged. "You will have a difficulty in perceiving the object I might serve by falsehood."

She sat down suddenly upon the divan; it was almost as if she collapsed bereft of strength; and as suddenly she fell to weeping softly.

"And . . . and I believed that you . . . that you . . ."

"Just so," he grimly interrupted. "You always did believe the best of me."

And on that he turned and went out abruptly.

CHAPTER XXI

MORITURUS

H E DEPARTED from her presence with bitterness in his heart, leaving a profound contrition in her own. The sense of this her last injustice to him so overwhelmed her that it became the gauge by which she measured that other earlier wrong he had suffered at her hands. Perhaps her overwrought mind falsified the perspective, exaggerating it until it seemed to her that all the suffering and evil with which this chronicle has been concerned were the direct fruits of her own sin of unfaith.

Since all sincere contrition must of necessity bring forth an ardent desire to atone, so was it now with her. Had he but refrained from departing so abruptly he might have had her on her knees to him suing for pardon for all the wrongs which her thoughts had done him, proclaiming her own utter unworthiness and baseness. But since his righteous resentment had driven him from her presence she could but sit and brood upon it all, considering the words in which to frame her plea for forgiveness when next he should return.

But the hours sped, and there was no sign of him. And then, almost with a shock of dread came the thought that ere long perhaps Sir John Killigrew's ship would be upon them. In her distraught state of mind she had scarcely pondered that contingency. Now that it occurred to her all her concern was for the result of it to Sir Oliver. Would there be fighting, and would he perhaps perish in that conflict at the hands either of the English or of the corsairs whom for her sake he had betrayed, perhaps without ever hearing her confession of penitence, without speaking those words of forgiveness of which her soul stood in such thirsty need?

It would be towards midnight when unable longer to bear the suspense of it, she rose and softly made her way to the entrance. Very quietly she lifted the curtain, and in the act of stepping forth almost stumbled over a body that lay across the threshold. She drew back with a startled gasp; then stooped to look, and by the faint rays of the lanterns on mainmast and poop-rail she recognized Sir Oliver, and saw that he slept. She never heeded the two Nubians immovable as statues who kept guard. She continued to bend over him, and then gradually and very softly sank down on her knees beside him. There were tears in her eyes—tears wrung from her by a tender emotion of wonder and gratitude at so much fidelity. She did not know that he had slept thus last night. But it was enough for her to find him here now. It moved her oddly, profoundly, that this man whom she had ever mistrusted and misjudged should even when he slept make of his body a barrier for her greater security and protection.

A sob escaped her, and at the sound, so lightly and vigilantly did he take his rest, he came instantly if silently to a sitting attitude; and so they looked into each other's eyes, his swarthy, bearded hawk face on a level with her white gleaming countenance.

"What is it?" he whispered.

She drew back instantly, taken with sudden panic at that question. Then recovering, and seeking woman-like to evade and dissemble the thing she was come to do, now that the chance of doing it was afforded her—

"Do you think," she faltered, "that Lionel will have reached Sir John's ship?"

He flashed a glance in the direction of the divan under the awning where the Basha slept. There all was still. Besides, the question had been asked in English. He rose and held out a hand to help her to her feet. Then he signed to her to re-enter the poop-house, and followed her within.

"Anxiety keeps you wakeful?" he said, half-question, half-assertion.

"Indeed," she replied.

"There is scarce the need," he assured her. "Sir John will not be like to stir until dead of night, that he may make sure of taking us unawares. I have little doubt that Lionel would reach him. It is none so long a swim. Indeed, once outside the cove he could take to the land until he was abreast of the ship. Never doubt he will have done his errand."

She sat down, her glance avoiding his; but the light falling on her face showed him the traces there of recent tears.

"There will be fighting when Sir John arrives?" she asked him presently.

"Like enough. But what can it avail? We shall be caught—as was said to-day—in just such a trap as that in which Andrea Doria caught Dragut at Jerba, saving that whilst the wily Dragut found a way out for his galleys, here none is possible. Courage, then, for the hour of your deliverance is surely at hand." He paused, and then in a softer voice, humbly almost, "It is my prayer," he added, "that hereafter in a happy future these last few weeks shall come to seem no more than an evil dream to you."

To that prayer she offered no response. She sat bemused, her brow wrinkled.

"I would it might be done without fighting," she said presently, and sighed wearily.

"You need have no fear," he assured her. "I shall take all precautions for you. You shall remain here until all is over and the entrance will be guarded by a few whom I can trust."

"You mistake me," she replied, and looked up at him suddenly. "Do you suppose my fears are for myself?" She paused again, and then abruptly asked him, "What will befall you?"

"I thank you for the thought," he replied gravely. "No doubt I shall meet with my deserts. Let it but come swiftly when it comes."

"Ah, no, no!" she cried. "Not that!" And rose in her sudden agitation.

"What else remains?" he asked, and smiled. "What better fate could anyone desire me?"

"You shall live to return to England," she surprised him by exclaiming. "The truth must prevail, and justice be done you."

He looked at her with so fierce and searching a gaze that she averted her eyes. Then he laughed shortly.

"There's but one form of justice I can look for in England," said he. "It is a justice administered in hemp. Believe me, mistress, I am grown too notorious for mercy. Best end it here to-night. Besides," he added, and his mockery fell from him, his tone became gloomy, "bethink you of my present act of treachery to these men of mine, who, whatever they may be, have followed me into a score of perils and but to-day have shown their love and loyalty to me to be greater than their devotion to the Basha himself. I shall have delivered them to the sword. Could I survive with honor? They may be but poor heathens to you and yours, but to me they are my sea-hawks, my warriors, my faithful gallant followers, and I were a dog indeed did I survive the death to which I have doomed them."

As she listened and gathered from his words the apprehension of a thing that had hitherto escaped her, her eyes grew wide in sudden horror.

"Is that to be the cost of my deliverance?" she asked him fearfully.

"I trust not," he replied. "I have something in mind that will perhaps avoid it."

"And save your own life as well?" she asked him quickly.

"Why waste a thought upon so poor a thing? My life was forfeit already. If I go back to Algiers they will assuredly hang me. Asad will see to it, and not all my sea-hawks could save me from my fate."

She sank down again upon the divan, and sat there rocking her arms in a gesture of hopeless distress.

"I see," she said. "I see. I am bringing this fate upon you. When you sent Lionel upon that errand you voluntarily offered up your life to restore me to my own people. You had no right to do this without first consulting me. You had no right to suppose I would be a party to such a thing. I will not accept the sacrifice. I will not, Sir Oliver."

"Indeed, you have no choice, thank God!" he answered her. "But you are astray in your conclusions. It is I alone who have brought this fate upon myself. It is the very proper fruit of my insensate deed. It recoils upon me as all evil must upon him that does it." He shrugged his shoulders as if to dismiss the matter. Then in a changed voice, a voice singularly timid, soft, and gentle, "It were perhaps too much to ask," said he, "that you should forgive me all the suffering I have brought you?"

"I think," she answered him, "that it is for me to beg forgiveness of you."

"Of me?"

"For my unfaith, which has been the source of all. For my readiness to believe evil of you five years ago, for having burnt unread your letter and the proof of your innocence that accompanied it."

He smiled upon her very kindly. "I think you said your instinct guided you. Even though I had not done the thing imputed to me, your instinct knew me for evil; and your instinct was right, for evil I am—I must be. These are your own words. But do not think that I mock you with them. I have come to recognize their truth."

She stretched out her hands to him. "If . . . if I were to say that I have come to realize the falsehood of all that?"

"I should understand it to be the charity which your pitiful heart extends to one in my extremity. Your instinct was not at fault."

"It was! It was!"

But he was not to be driven out of his conviction. He shook his head, his countenance gloomy. "No man who was not evil could have done by you what I have done, however deep the provocation. I perceive it clearly now—as men in their last hour perceive hidden things."

"Oh, why are you so set on death?" she cried upon a despairing note.

"I am not," he answered with a swift resumption of his more habitual manner. "'T is death that is so set on me. But at least I meet it without fear or regret. I face it as we must all face the inevitable—the gifts from the hands of destiny. And I am heartened—gladdened almost—by your sweet forgiveness."

She rose suddenly, and came to him. She caught his arm, and standing very close to him, looked up now into his face.

"We have need to forgive each other, you and I, Oliver," she said. "And since forgiveness effaces all, let . . . let all that has stood between us these last five years be now effaced."

He caught his breath as he looked down into her white, straining face.

"Is it impossible for us to go back five years? Is it impossible for us to go back to where we stood in those old days at Godolphin Court?"

The light that had suddenly been kindled in his face faded slowly, leaving it gray and drawn. His eyes grew clouded with sorrow and despair.

"Who has erred must abide by his error—and so must the generations that come after him. There is no going back ever. The gates of the past are tight-barred against us."

"Then let us leave them so. Let us turn our backs upon that past, you and I, and let us set out afresh together, and so make amends to each other for what our folly has lost to us in those years."

He set his hands upon her shoulders, and held her so at arm's length from him considering her with very tender eyes.

"Sweet lady!" he murmured, and sighed heavily. "God! How happy might we not have been but for that evil chance . . ." He checked abruptly. His hands fell from her shoulders to his sides, he half-turned away, brusque now in tone and manner. "I grow maudlin. Your sweet pity has so softened me that I had almost spoke of love; and what have I to do with that? Love belongs to life; love is life; whilst I . . . Moriturus te salutat!"

"Ah, no, no!" She was clinging to him again with shaking hands, her eyes wild.

"It is too late," he answered her. "There is no bridge can span the pit I have dug myself. I must go down into it as cheerfully as God will let me."

"Then," she cried in sudden exaltation, "I will go down with you. At the last, at least, we shall be together."

"Now here is midsummer frenzy!" he protested, yet there was a tenderness in the very impatience of his accents. He stroked the golden head that lay against his shoulder. "How shall that help me?" he asked her. "Would you embitter my last hour—rob death of all its glory? Nay, Rosamund, you can serve me better far by living. Return to England, and publish there the truth of what you have learnt. Be yours the task of clearing my honor of this stain upon it, proclaiming the truth of what drove me to the infamy of becoming a renegade and a corsair." He started from her. "Hark! What's that?"

From without had come a sudden cry, "Afoot! To arms! To arms! Holâ! Balâk! Balâk!"

"It is the hour," he said, and turning from her suddenly sprang to the entrance and plucked aside the curtain.

CHAPTER XXII

THE SURRENDER

UP THE GANGWAY between the lines of slumbering slaves came a quick patter of feet. Ali, who since sunset had been replacing Larocque on the heights, sprang suddenly upon the poop still shouting,

"Captain! Captain! My lord! Afoot! Up! or we are taken!"

Throughout the vessel's length came the rustle and stir of waking men. A voice clamored somewhere on the forecastle. Then the flap of the awning was suddenly whisked aside and Asad himself appeared with Marzak at his elbow.

From the starboard side as suddenly came Biskaine and Othmani, and from the waist Vigitello, Jasper—that latest renegade—and a group of alarmed corsairs.

"What now?" quoth the Basha.

Ali delivered his message breathlessly. "The galleon has weighed anchor. She is moving out of the bay."

Asad clutched his beard, and scowled. "Now what may that portend? Can knowledge of our presence have reached them?"

"Why else should she move from her anchorage thus in the dead of night?" said Biskaine.

"Why else, indeed?" returned Asad, and then he swung upon Oliver standing there in the entrance of the poop-house. "What sayest thou, Sakr-el-Bahr?" he appealed to him.

Sakr-el-Bahr stepped forward, shrugging. "What is there to say? What is there to do?" he asked. "We can but wait. If our presence is known to them we are finely trapped, and there's an end to all of us this night."

His voice was cool as ice, contemptuous almost, and whilst it struck anxiety into more than one it awoke terror in Marzak.

"May thy bones rot, thou ill-omened prophet!" he screamed, and would have added more but that Sakr-el-Bahr silenced him.

"What is written is written!" said he in a voice of thunder and reproof.

"Indeed, indeed," Asad agreed, grasping at the fatalist's consolation. "If we are ripe for the gardener's hand, the gardener will pluck us."

Less fatalistic and more practical was the counsel of Biskaine. "It were well to act upon the assumption that we are indeed discovered, and make for the open sea while yet there may be time."

"But that were to make certain what is still doubtful," broke in Marzak, fearful ever. "It were to run to meet the danger."

"Not so!" cried Asad in a loud confident voice. "The praise to Allah who sent us this calm night. There is scarce a breath of wind. We can row ten leagues while they are sailing one."

A murmur of quick approval sped through the ranks of officers and men.

"Let us but win safely from this cove and they will never overtake us," announced Biskaine.

"But their guns may," Sakr-el-Bahr quietly reminded them to damp their confidence. His own alert mind had already foreseen this one chance of escaping from the trap, but he had hoped that it would not be quite so obvious to the others.

"That risk we must take," replied Asad. "We must trust to the night. To linger here is to await certain destruction." He swung briskly about to issue his orders. "Ali, summon the steersmen. Hasten! Vigitello, set your whips about the slaves, and rouse them." Then as the shrill whistle of the boatswain rang out and the whips of his mates went hissing and cracking about the shoulders of the already half-awakened slaves, to mingle with all the rest of the stir and bustle aboard the galeasse, the Basha turned once more to Biskaine. "Up thou to the prow," he commanded, "and marshal the men. Bid them stand to their arms lest it should come to boarding. Go!" Biskaine salaamed and sprang down the companion. Above the rumbling din and scurrying toll of preparation rang Asad's voice. "Crossbowmen, aloft! Gunners to the carronades! Kindle your linstocks! Put out all lights!"

An instant later the cressets on the poop-rail were extinguished, as was the lantern swinging from the rail, and even the lamp in the poop-house which was invaded by one of the Basha's officers for that purpose. The lantern hanging from the mast alone was spared against emergencies; but it was taken down, placed upon the deck, and muffled.

Thus was the galeasse plunged into a darkness that for some moments was black and impenetrable as velvet. Then slowly, as the eyes became accustomed to it, this gloom was gradually relieved. Once more men and objects began to take shape in the faint, steely radiance of the summer night.

After the excitement of that first stir the corsairs went about their tasks with amazing calm and silence. None thought now of reproaching the Basha or Sakr-el-Bahr with having delayed until the moment of peril to take the course which all of them had demanded should be taken when first they had heard of the neighborhood of that hostile ship. In lines three deep they stood ranged along the ample fighting platform of the prow; in the foremost line were the archers, behind them stood the swordsmen, their weapons gleaming lividly in the darkness. They crowded to the bulwarks of the waist-deck and swarmed upon the ratlines of the mainmast. On the poop three gunners stood to each of the two small cannon, their faces showing faintly ruddy in the glow of the ignited match.

Asad stood at the head of the companion, issuing his sharp brief commands, and Sakr-el-Bahr, behind him, leaning against the timbers of the poop-house with Rosamund at his side, observed that the Basha had studiously avoided entrusting any of this work of preparation to himself.

The steersmen climbed to their niches, and the huge steering oars creaked as they were swung out. Came a short word of command from Asad and a stir ran through the ranks of the slaves, as they threw forward their weight to bring the oars to the level. Thus a moment, then a second word, the premonitory crack of a whip in the darkness of the gangway, and the tom-tom began to beat the time. The slaves heaved, and with a creak and splash of oars the great galeasse skimmed forward towards the mouth of the cove.

Up and down the gangway ran the boatswain's mates, cutting fiercely with their whips to urge the slaves to the very utmost effort. The vessel gathered speed. The looming headland slipped by. The mouth of the cove appeared to widen as they approached it. Beyond spread the dark steely mirror of the dead-calm sea.

Rosamund could scarcely breathe in the intensity of her suspense. She set a hand upon the arm of Sakr-el-Bahr.

"Shall we elude them, after all?" she asked in a trembling whisper.

"I pray that we may not," he answered, muttering. "But this is the handiwork I feared. Look!" he added sharply, and pointed.

They had shot clear to the headland. They were out of the cove, and suddenly they had a view of the dark bulk of the galleon, studded with a score of points of light, riding a cable's length away on their larboard quarter.

"Faster!" cried the voice of Asad. "Row for your lives, you infidel swine! Lay me your whips upon these hides of theirs! Bend me these dogs to their oars, and they'll never overtake us now."

Whips sang and thudded below them in the waist, to be

answered by more than one groan from the tormented panting slaves, who already were spending every ounce of strength in this cruel effort to elude their own chance of salvation and release. Faster beat the tom-tom marking the desperate time, and faster in response to it came the creak and dip of oars and the panting, stertorous breathing of the rowers.

"Lay on! Lay on!" cried Asad, inexorable. Let them burst their lungs—they were but infidel lungs!—so that for an hour they but maintained the present pace.

"We are drawing away!" cried Marzak in jubilation. "The praise to Allah!"

And so indeed they were. Visibly the lights of the galleon were receding. With every inch of canvas spread yet she appeared to be standing still, so faint was the breeze that stirred. And whilst she crawled, the galeasse raced as never yet she had raced since Sakr-el-Bahr had commanded her, for Sakr-el-Bahr had never yet turned tail upon the foe in whatever strength he found him.

Suddenly over the water from the galleon came a loud hail. Asad laughed, and in the darkness shook his fist at them, cursing them in the name of Allah and his Prophet. And then, in answer to that curse of his, the galleon's side belched fire; the calm of the night was broken by a roar of thunder, and something smote the water ahead of the Muslim vessel with a resounding thudding splash.

In fear Rosamund drew closer to Sakr-el-Bahr. But Asad laughed again.

"No need to fear their marksmanship," he cried. "They cannot see us. Their own lights dazzle them. On! On!"

"He is right," said Sakr-el-Bahr. "But the truth is that they will not fire to sink us because they know you to be aboard."

She looked out to sea again, and beheld those friendly lights falling farther and farther astern.

"We are drawing steadily away," she groaned. "They will never overtake us now."

So feared Sakr-el-Bahr. He more than feared it. He knew that save for some miraculous rising of the wind it must be as she said. And then out of his despair leapt inspiration—a desperate inspiration, true child of that despair of which it was begotten.

"There is a chance," he said to her. "But it is as a throw of the dice with life and death for stakes."

"Then seize it," she bade him instantly. "For though it should go against us we shall not be losers."

"You are prepared for anything?" he asked her.

"Have I not said that I will go down with you this night? Ah, don't waste time in words!"

"Be it so, then," he replied gravely, and moved away a step, then checked. "You had best come with me," he said.

Obediently she complied and followed him, and some there were who stared as these two passed down the gangway, yet none attempted to hinder her movements. Enough and to spare was there already to engage the thoughts of all aboard that vessel.

He thrust a way for her, past the boatswain's mates who stood over the slaves ferociously plying tongues and whips, and so brought her to the waist. Here he took up the lantern which had been muffled, and as its light once more streamed forth, Asad shouted an order for its extinction. But Sakr-el-Bahr took no least heed of that command. He stepped to the mainmast, about which the powder kegs had been stacked. One of these had been broached against its being needed by the gunners on the poop. The unfastened lid rested loosely atop of it. That lid Sakr-el-Bahr knocked over; then he pulled one of the horn sides out of the lantern, and held the now half-naked flame immediately above the powder.

A cry of alarm went up from some who had watched him. But above that cry rang his sharp command:

"Cease rowing!"

The tom-tom fell instantly silent, but the slaves took yet another stroke.

"Cease rowing!" he commanded again. "Asad!" he called. "Bid them pause, or I'll blow you all straight into the arms of Shaitan." And he lowered the lantern until it rested on the very rim of the powder keg.

At once the rowing ceased. Slaves, corsairs, officers, and Asad himself stood paralyzed, all at gaze upon that grim figure illumined by the lantern, threatening them with doom. It may have crossed the minds of some to throw themselves forthwith upon him; but to arrest them was the dread lest any movement towards him should precipitate the explosion that must blow them all into the next world.

At last Asad addressed him, his voice half-choked with rage.

"May Allah strike thee dead! Art thou djinn-possessed?"

Marzak, standing at his father's side, set a quarrel to the bow which he had snatched up. "Why do you all stand and stare?" he cried. "Cut him down, one of you!" And even as he spoke he raised his bow. But his father checked him, perceiving what must be the inevitable result.

"If any man takes a step towards me, the lantern goes straight into the gunpowder," said Sakr-el-Bahr serenely. "And if you shoot me as you intend, Marzak, or if any other shoots, the same will happen of itself. Be warned unless you thirst for the Paradise of the Prophet."

"Sakr-el-Bahr!" cried Asad, and from its erstwhile anger his voice had now changed to a note of intercession. He stretched out his arms appealingly to the captain whose doom he had already pronounced in his heart and mind. "Sakr-el-Bahr, I conjure thee by the bread and salt we have eaten together, return to thy senses, my son."

"I am in my sense," was the answer, "and being so I have no mind for the fate reserved me in Algiers—by the memory of that same bread and salt. I have no mind to go back with thee to be hanged or sent to toil at an oar again."

"And if I swear to thee that naught of this shall come to pass?"

"Thou'lt be forsworn. I would not trust thee now, Asad. For thou art proven a fool, and in all my life I never found good in a fool and never trusted one—save once, and he betrayed me. Yesterday I pleaded with thee, showing thee the wise course, and affording thee thine opportunity. At a slight sacrifice thou mightest have had me and hanged me at thy leisure. 'T was my own life I offered thee, and for all that thou knewest it, yet thou knewest not that I knew." He laughed. "See now what manner of fool art thou? Thy greed hath wrought thy ruin. Thy hands were opened to grasp more than they could hold. See now the consequence. It comes yonder in that slowly but surely approaching galleon."

Every word of it sank into the brain of Asad thus tardily to enlighten him. He wrung his hands in his blended fury and despair. The crew stood in appalled silence, daring to make no movement that might precipitate their end.

"Name thine own price," cried the Basha at length, "and I swear to thee by the beard of the Prophet it shall be paid thee."

"I named it yesterday, but it was refused. I offered thee my liberty and my life if that were needed to gain the liberty of another."

Had he looked behind him he might have seen the sudden lighting of Rosamund's eyes, the sudden clutch at her bosom, which would have announced to him that his utterances were none so cryptic but that she had understood them.

"I will make thee rich and honored, Sakr-el-Bahr," Asad continued urgently. "Thou shalt be as mine own son. The Bashalik itself shall be thine when I lay it down, and all men shall do thee honor in the meanwhile as to myself."

"I am not to be bought, O mighty Asad. I never was. Already wert thou set upon my death. Thou canst command it now, but only upon the condition that thou share the cup with me. What is written is written. We have sunk some tall ships together in our day, Asad. We'll sink together in our turn to-night if that be thy desire."

"May thou burn for evermore in hell, thou black-hearted traitor!" Asad cursed him, his anger bursting all the bonds he had imposed upon it.

And then, of a sudden, upon that admission of defeat from their Basha, there arose a great clamor from the crew. Sakr-el-Bahr's sea-hawks called upon him, reminding him of their fidelity and love, and asking could he repay it now by dooming them all thus to destruction.

"Have faith in me!" he answered them. "I have never led you into aught but victory. Be sure that I shall not lead you now into defeat—on this the last occasion that we stand together."

"But the galleon is upon us!" cried Vigitello.

And so, indeed, it was, creeping up slowly under that faint breeze, her tall bulk loomed now above them, her prow ploughing slowly forward at an acute angle to the prow of the galeasse. Another moment and she was alongside, and with a swing and clank and a yell of victory from the English seamen lining her bulwarks her grappling irons swung down to seize the corsair ship at prow and stern and waist. Scarce had they fastened, than a torrent of men in breastplates and morions poured over her side, to alight upon the prow of the galeasse, and not even the fear of the lantern held above the powder barrel could now restrain the corsairs from giving these hardy boarders the reception they reserved for all infidels. In an instant the fighting platform on the prow was become a raging, seething hell of battle luridly illumined by the ruddy glow from the lights aboard the *Silver Heron*. Foremost among those who had leapt down had been Lionel and Sir John Killigrew. Foremost among those to receive them had been Jasper Leigh, who had passed his sword through Lionel's body even as Lionel's feet came to rest upon the deck, and before the battle was joined.

A dozen others went down on either side before Sakr-el-Bahr's ringing voice could quell the fighting, before his command to them to hear him was obeyed.

"Hold there!" he had bellowed to his sea-hawks, using the lingua

franca. "Back, and leave this to me. I will rid you of these foes."
Then in English he had summoned his countrymen also to desist.
"Sir John Killigrew!" he called in a loud voice. "Hold your hand until
you have heard me! Call your men back and let none others come
aboard! Hold until you have heard me, I say, then wreak your will."

Sir John, perceiving him by the mainmast with Rosamund at his
side, and leaping at the most inevitable conclusion that he meant to
threaten her life, perhaps to destroy her if they continued their
advance, flung himself before his men, to check them.

Thus almost as suddenly as it had been joined the combat
paused.

"What have you to say, you renegade dog?" Sir John demanded.

"This, Sir John, that unless you order your men back aboard
your ship, and make oath to desist from this encounter, I'll take you
straight down to hell with us at once. I'll heave this lantern into the
powder here, and we sink and you come down with us held by your
own grappling hooks. Obey me and you shall have all that you have
come to seek aboard this vessel. Mistress Rosamund shall be delivered up to you."

Sir John glowered upon him a moment from the poop, considering. Then—

"Though not prepared to make terms with you," he announced,
"yet I will accept the conditions you impose, but only provided that
I have all indeed that I am come to seek. There is aboard this galley
an infamous renegade hound whom I am bound by my knightly
oath to take and hang. He, too, must be delivered up to me. His
name was Oliver Tressilian."

Instantly, unhesitatingly, came the answer—

"Him, too, will I surrender to you upon your sworn oath that
you will then depart and do here no further hurt."

Rosamund caught her breath, and clutched Sakr-el-Bahr's arm,
the arm that held the lantern.

"Have a care, mistress," he bade her sharply, "or you will
destroy us all."

"Better that!" she answered him.

And then Sir John pledged him his word that upon his own surrender and that of Rosamund he would withdraw nor offer hurt to any there.

Sakr-el-Bahr turned to his waiting corsairs, and briefly told them what the terms he had made.

He called upon Asad to pledge his word that these terms would be respected, and no blood shed on his behalf, and Asad answered him, voicing the anger of all against him for his betrayal.

"Since he wants thee that he may hang thee, he may have thee and so spare us the trouble, for 't is no less than thy treachery deserves from us."

"Thus, then, I surrender," he announced to Sir John, and flung the lantern overboard.

One voice only was raised in his defence, and that voice was Rosamund's. But even that voice failed, conquered by weary nature. This last blow following upon all that lately she had endured bereft her of all strength. Half swooning she collapsed against Sakr-el-Bahr even as Sir John and a handful of his followers leapt down to deliver her and make fast their prisoner.

The corsairs stood looking on in silence; the loyalty to their great captain, which would have made them spend their last drop of blood in his defence, was quenched by his own act of treachery which had brought the English ship upon them. Yet when they saw him pinioned and hoisted to the deck of the *Silver Heron*, there was a sudden momentary reaction in their ranks. Scimitars were waved aloft, and cries of menace burst forth. If he had betrayed them, yet he had so contrived that they should not suffer by that betrayal. And that was worthy of the Sakr-el-Bahr they knew and loved; so worthy that their love and loyalty leapt full-armed again upon the instant.

But the voice of Asad called upon them to bear in mind what in their name he had promised, and since the voice of Asad alone might not have sufficed to quell that sudden spark of revolt, there came down to them the voice of Sakr-el-Bahr himself issuing his last command.

"Remember and respect the terms I have made for you! Mektub! May Allah guard and prosper you!"

A wail was his reply, and with that wail ringing in his ears to assure him that he did not pass unloved, he was hurried below to prepare him for his end.

The ropes of the grapnels were cut, and slowly the galleon passed away into the night, leaving the galley to replace what slaves had been maimed in the encounter and to head back for Algiers, abandoning the expedition against the argosy of Spain.

Under the awning upon the poop Asad now sat like a man who has awakened from an evil dream. He covered his head and wept for one who had been as a son to him, and whom through his madness he had lost. He cursed all women, and he cursed destiny; but the bitterest curse of all was for himself.

In the pale dawn they flung the dead overboard and washed the decks, nor did they notice that a man was missing in token that the English captain, or else his followers, had not kept strictly to the letter of the bond.

They returned in mourning to Algiers—mourning not for the Spanish argosy which had been allowed to go her ways unmolested, but for the stoutest captain that ever bared his scimitar in the service of Islam. The story of how he came to be delivered up was never clearly told; none dared clearly tell it, for none who had participated in the deed but took shame in it thereafter, however clear it might be that Sakr-el-Bahr had brought it all upon himself. But, at least, it was understood that he had not fallen in battle, and hence it was assumed that he was still alive. Upon that presumption there was built up a sort of legend that he would one day come back; and redeemed captives returning a half-century later related how in Algiers to that day the coming of Sakr-el-Bahr was still confidently expected and looked for by all true Muslimeen.

CHAPTER XXIII

THE HEATHEN CREED

SAKR-EL-BAHR was shut up in a black hole in the forecastle of the *Silver Heron* to await the dawn and to spend the time in making his soul. No words had passed between him and Sir John since his surrender. With wrists pinioned behind him, he had been hoisted aboard the English ship, and in the waist of her he had stood for a moment face to face with an old acquaintance—our chronicler, Lord Henry Goade. I imagine the florid countenance of the Queen's Lieutenant wearing a preternaturally grave expression, his eyes forbidding as they rested upon the renegade. I know—from Lord Henry's own pen—that no word had passed between them during those brief moments before Sakr-el-Bahr was hurried away by his guards to be flung into those dark, cramped quarters reeking of tar and bilge.

For a long hour he lay where he had fallen, believing himself alone; and time and place would no doubt conduce to philosophical reflection upon his condition. I like to think that he found that when all was considered, he had little with which to reproach himself. If he had done evil he had made ample amends. It can scarcely

be pretended that he had betrayed those loyal Muslimeen followers of his, or, if it is, at least it must be added that he himself had
paid the price of that betrayal. Rosamund was safe, Lionel would
meet the justice due to him, and as for himself, being as good as
dead already, he was worth little thought. He must have derived
some measure of content from the reflection that he was spending
his life to the very best advantage. Ruined it had been long since.
True, but for his ill-starred expedition of vengeance he might long
have continued to wage war as a corsair, might even have risen to
the proud Muslim eminence of the Bashalik of Algiers and become
a feudatory prince of the Grand Turk. But for one who was born a
Christian gentleman that would have been an unworthy way to
have ended his days. The present was the better course.

A faint rustle in the impenetrable blackness of his prison turned
the current of his thoughts. A rat, he thought, and drew himself to
a sitting attitude, and beat his slippered heels upon the ground to
drive away the loathly creature. Instead, a voice challenged him out
of the gloom.

"Who's there?"

It startled him for a moment, in his complete assurance that he
had been alone.

"Who's there?" the voice repeated, querulously to add: "What
black hell be this? Where am I?"

And now he recognized the voice for Jasper Leigh's, and marveled how that latest of his recruits to the ranks of Mohammed
should be sharing this prison with him.

"Faith," said he, "you're in the forecastle of the *Silver Heron*;
though how you come here is more than I can answer."

"Who are ye?" the voice asked.

"I have been known in Barbary as Sakr-el-Bahr."

"Sir Oliver!"

"I suppose that is what they will call me now. It is as well perhaps that I am to be buried at sea, else it might plague these Chris-

tian gentlemen what legend to inscribe upon my headstone. But you—how come you hither? My bargain with Sir John was that none should be molested, and I cannot think Sir John would be forsworn."

"As to that I know nothing, since I did not even know where I was bestowed until ye informed me. I was knocked senseless in the fight, after I had put my bilbo through your comely brother. That is the sum of my knowledge."

Sir Oliver caught his breath. "What do you say? You killed Lionel?"

"I believe so," was the cool answer. "At least I sent a couple of feet of steel through him—'t was in the press of the fight when first the English dropped aboard the galley; Master Lionel was in the van—the last place in which I should have looked to see him."

There fell a long silence. At length Sir Oliver spoke in a small voice.

"Not a doubt but you gave him no more than he was seeking. You are right, Master Leigh; the van was the last place in which to look for him, unless he came deliberately to seek steel that he might escape a rope. Best so, no doubt. Best so! God rest him!"

"Do you believe in God?" asked the sinful skipper on an anxious note.

"No doubt they took you because of that," Sir Oliver pursued, as if communing with himself. "Being in ignorance perhaps of his deserts, deeming him a saint and martyr, they resolved to avenge him upon you, and dragged you hither for that purpose." He sighed. "Well, well, Master Leigh, I make no doubt that knowing yourself for a rascal you have all your life been preparing your neck for a noose; so this will come as no surprise to you."

The skipper stirred uneasily, and groaned. "Lord, how my head aches!" he complained.

"They've a sure remedy for that," Sir Oliver comforted him. "And you'll swing in better company than you deserve, for I am to be hanged in the morning too. You've earned it as fully as have I,

Master Leigh. Yet I am sorry for you—sorry you should suffer where I had not so intended."

Master Leigh sucked in a shuddering breath, and was silent for awhile.

Then he repeated an earlier question.

"Do you believe in God, Sir Oliver?"

"There is no God but God, and Mohammed is his Prophet," was the answer, and from his tone Master Leigh could not be sure that he did not mock.

"That's a heathen creed," said he in fear and loathing.

"Nay, now; it's a creed by which men live. They perform as they preach, which is more than can be said of any Christians I have ever met."

"How can you talk so upon the eve of death?" cried Leigh in protest.

"Faith," said Sir Oliver, "it's considered the season of truth above all others."

"Then ye don't believe in God?"

"On the contrary, I do."

"But not in the real God?" the skipper insisted.

"There can be no God but the real God—it matters little what men call Him."

"Then if ye believe, are ye not afraid?"

"Of what?"

"Of hell, damnation, and eternal fire," roared the skipper, voicing his own belated terrors.

"I have but fulfilled the destiny which in His Omniscience He marked out for me," replied Sir Oliver. "My life hath been as He designed it, since naught may exist or happen save by His Will. Shall I then fear damnation for having been as God fashioned me?"

"'T is the heathen Muslim creed!" Master Leigh protested.

"'T is a comforting one," said Sir Oliver, "and it should comfort such a sinner as thou."

But Master Leigh refused to be comforted. "Oh!" he groaned miserably. "I would that I did not believe in God!"

"Your disbelief could no more abolish Him than can your fear create Him," replied Sir Oliver. "But your mood being what it is, were it not best you prayed?"

"Will not you pray with me?" quoth that rascal in his sudden fear of the hereafter.

"I shall do better," said Sir Oliver at last. "I shall pray for you—to Sir John Killigrew, that your life be spared."

"Sure he'll never heed you!" said Master Leigh with a catch in his breath.

"He shall. His honor is concerned in it. The terms of my surrender were that none else aboard the galley should suffer any hurt."

"But I killed Master Lionel."

"True—but that was in the scrimmage that preceded my making terms. Sir John pledged me his word, and Sir John will keep to it when I have made it clear to him that honor demands it."

A great burden was lifted from the skipper's mind—that great shadow of the fear of death that had overhung him. With it, it is greatly to be feared that his desperate penitence also departed. At least he talked no more of damnation, nor took any further thought for Sir Oliver's opinions and beliefs concerning the hereafter. He may rightly have supposed that Sir Oliver's creed was Sir Oliver's affair, and that should it happen to be wrong he was scarcely himself a qualified person to correct it. As for himself, the making of his soul could wait until another day, when the necessity for it should be more imminent.

Upon that he lay down and attempted to compose himself to sleep, though the pain in his head proved a difficulty. Finding slumber impossible after a while he would have talked again: but by that time his companion's regular breathing warned him that Sir Oliver had fallen asleep during the silence.

Now this surprised and shocked the skipper. He was utterly at a loss to understand how one who had lived Sir Oliver's life, been a renegade and a heathen, should be able to sleep tranquilly in the knowledge that at dawn he was to hang. His belated Christian zeal prompted him to rouse the sleeper and to urge him to spend the little time that yet remained him in making his peace with God. Humane compassion on the other hand suggested to him that he had best leave him in the peace of that oblivion. Considering matters he was profoundly touched to reflect that in such a season Sir Oliver could have found room in his mind to think of him and his fate and to undertake to contrive that he should be saved from the rope. He was the more touched when he bethought him of the extent to which he had himself been responsible for all that happened to Sir Oliver. Out of the consideration of heroism, a certain heroism came to be begotten in him, and he fell to pondering how in his turn he might perhaps serve Sir Oliver by a frank confession of all that he knew of the influences that had gone to make Sir Oliver what he was. This resolve uplifted him, and oddly enough it uplifted him all the more when he reflected that perhaps he would be jeopardizing his own neck by the confession upon which he had determined.

So through that endless night he sat, nursing his aching head, and enheartened by the first purpose he had ever conceived of a truly good and altruistic deed. Yet fate it seemed was bent upon frustrating that purpose of his. For when at dawn they came to hale Sir Oliver to his doom, they paid no heed to Jasper Leigh's demands that he, too, should be taken before Sir John.

"Thee bean't included in our orders," said a seaman shortly.

"Maybe not," retorted Master Leigh, "because Sir John little knows what it is in my power to tell him. Take me before him, I say, that he may hear from me the truth of certain matters ere it be too late."

"Be still," the seaman bade him, and struck him heavily across the face, so that he reeled and collapsed into a corner. "Thee turn will come soon. Just now our business be with this other heathen."

"Naught that you can say would avail," Sir Oliver assured him quietly. "But I thank you for the thought that marks you for my friend. My hands are bound, Jasper. Were it otherwise I would beg leave to clasp your own. Fare you well!"

Sir Oliver was led out into the golden sunlight which almost blinded him after his long confinement in that dark hole. They were, he gathered, to conduct him to the cabin where a short mockery of a trial was to be held. But in the waist their progress was arrested by an officer, who bade them wait.

Sir Oliver sat down upon a coil of rope, his guard about him, an object of curious inspection to the rude seamen. They thronged the forecastle and the hatchways to stare at this formidable corsair who once had been a Cornish gentleman and who had become a renegade Muslim and a terror to Christianity.

Truth to tell, the sometime Cornish gentleman was difficult to discern in him as he sat there still wearing the caftan of cloth of silver over his white tunic and a turban of the same material swathed about his steel headpiece that ended in a spike. Idly he swung his brown sinewy legs, naked from knee to ankle, with the inscrutable calm of the fatalist upon his swarthy hawk face with its light agate eyes and black forked beard; and those callous seamen who had assembled there to jeer and mock him were stricken silent by the intrepidity and stoicism of his bearing in the face of death.

If the delay chafed him, he gave no outward sign of it. If his hard, light eyes glanced hither and thither it was upon no idle quest. He was seeking Rosamund, hoping for a last sight of her before they launched him upon his last dread voyage.

But Rosamund was not to be seen. She was in the cabin at the time. She had been there for this hour past, and it was to her that the present delay was due.

CHAPTER XXIV

THE JUDGES

I N THE ABSENCE of any woman into whose care they might
entrust her, Lord Henry, Sir John, and Master Tobias, the ship's
surgeon, had amongst them tended Rosamund as best they
could when numbed and half-dazed she was brought aboard the
Silver Heron.

Master Tobias had applied such rude restoratives as he commanded, and having made her as comfortable as possible upon a
couch in the spacious cabin astern, he had suggested that she
should be allowed the rest of which she appeared so sorely to stand
in need. He had ushered out the commander and the Queen's Lieutenant, and himself had gone below to a still more urgent case that
was demanding his attention—that of Lionel Tressilian, who had
been brought limp and unconscious from the galeasse together with
some four other wounded members of the *Silver Heron's* crew.

At dawn Sir John had come below, seeking news of his wounded
friend. He found the surgeon kneeling over Lionel. As he entered,
Master Tobias turned aside, rinsed his hands in a metal basin
placed upon the floor, and rose wiping them on a napkin.

"I can do no more, Sir John," he muttered in a despondent voice. "He is sped."

"Dead, d' ye mean?" cried Sir John, a catch in his voice.

The surgeon tossed aside the napkin, and slowly drew down the upturned sleeves of his black doublet. "All but dead," he answered. "The wonder is that any spark of life should still linger in a body with that hole in it. He is bleeding inwardly, and his pulse is steadily weakening. It must continue so until imperceptibly he passes away. You may count him dead already, Sir John." He paused. "A merciful, painless end," he added, and sighed perfunctorily, his pale shaven face decently grave, for all that such scenes as these were commonplaces in his life. "Of the other four," he continued, "Blair is dead; the other three should all recover."

But Sir John gave little heed to the matter of those others. His grief and dismay at this quenching of all hope for his friend precluded any other consideration at the moment.

"And he will not even recover consciousness?" he asked insisting, although already he had been answered.

"As I have said, you may count him dead already, Sir John. My skill can do nothing for him."

Sir John's head drooped, his countenance drawn and grave. "Nor can my justice," he added gloomily. "Though it avenge him, it cannot give me back my friend." He looked at the surgeon. "Vengeance, sir, is the hollowest of all the mockeries that go to make up life."

"Your task, Sir John," replied the surgeon, "is one of justice, not vengeance."

"A quibble, when all is said." He stepped to Lionel's side, and looked down at the pale, handsome face over which the dark shadows of death were already creeping. "If he would but speak in the interests of this justice that is to do! If we might but have the evidence of his own words, lest I should ever be asked to justify the hanging of Oliver Tressilian."

"Surely, sir," the surgeon ventured, "there can be no such question ever. Mistress Rosamund's word alone should suffice, if indeed so much as that even were required."

"Ay! His offences against God and man are too notorious to leave grounds upon which any should ever question my right to deal with him out of hand."

There was a tap at the door and Sir John's own body servant entered with the announcement that Mistress Rosamund was asking urgently to see him.

"She will be impatient for news of him," Sir John concluded, and he groaned. "My God! How am I to tell her? To crush her in the very hour of her deliverance with such news as this! Was ever irony so cruel?" He turned, and stepped heavily to the door. There he paused. "You will remain by him to the end?" he bade the surgeon interrogatively.

Master Tobias bowed. "Of course, Sir John." And he added. "'T will not be long."

Sir John looked across at Lionel again—a glance of valediction. "God rest him!" he said hoarsely, and passed out.

In the waist he paused a moment, turned to a knot of lounging seamen, and bade them throw a halter over the yard-arm, and hale the renegade Oliver Tressilian from his prison. Then with slow heavy step and heavier heart he went up the companion to the vessel's castellated poop.

The sun, new risen in a faint golden haze, shone over a sea faintly rippled by the fresh clean winds of dawn to which their every stitch of canvas was now spread. Away on the larboard quarter, a faint cloudy outline, was the coast of Spain.

Sir John's long sallow face was preternaturally grave when he entered the cabin, where Rosamund awaited him. He bowed to her with a grave courtesy, doffing his hat and casting it upon a chair. The last five years had brought some strands of white into his thick black hair, and at the temples in particular it showed very gray, giving him an appearance of age to which the deep lines in his brow contributed.

He advanced towards her, as she rose to receive him.

"Rosamund, my dear!" he said gently, and took both her hands. He looked with eyes of sorrow and concern into her white, agitated face. "Are you sufficiently rested, child?"

"Rested?" she echoed on a note of wonder that he should suppose it.

"Poor lamb, poor lamb!" he murmured, as a mother might have done, and drew her towards him, stroking that gleaming auburn head. "We'll speed us back to England with every stitch of canvas spread. Take heart then, and . . ."

But she broke in impetuously, drawing away from him as she spoke, and his heart sank with foreboding of the thing she was about to inquire.

"I overheard a sailor just now saying to another that it is your intent to hang Sir Oliver Tressilian out of hand—this morning."

He misunderstood her utterly. "Be comforted," he said. "My justice shall be swift; my vengeance sure. The yard-arm is charged already with the rope on which he shall leap to his eternal punishment."

She caught her breath, and set a hand upon her bosom as if to repress its sudden tumult.

"And upon what grounds," she asked him with an air of challenge, squarely facing him, "do you intend to do this thing?"

"Upon what grounds?" he faltered. He stared and frowned, bewildered by her question and its tone. "Upon what grounds?" he repeated, foolishly almost in the intensity of his amazement. Then he considered her more closely, and the wildness of her eyes bore to him slowly an explanation of words that at first had seemed beyond explaining.

"I see!" he said in a voice of infinite pity; for the conviction to which he had leapt was that her poor wits were all astray after the horrors through which she had lately traveled. "You must rest," he said gently, "and give no thought to such matters as these. Leave them to me, and be very sure that I shall avenge you as is due."

"Sir John, you mistake me, I think. I do not desire that you avenge me. I have asked you upon what grounds you intend to do this thing, and you have not answered me."

In increasing amazement he continued to stare. He had been wrong, then. She was quite sane and mistress of her wits. And yet instead of the fond inquiries concerning Lionel which he had been dreading came this amazing questioning of his grounds to hang his prisoner.

"Need I state to you—of all living folk—the offences which that dastard has committed?" he asked, expressing thus the very question that he was setting himself.

"You need to tell me," she answered, "by what right you constitute yourself his judge and executioner; by what right you send him to his death in this peremptory fashion, without trial." Her manner was as stern as if she were invested with all the authority of a judge.

"But you," he faltered in his ever-growing bewilderment, "you, Rosamund, against whom he has offended so grievously, surely you should be the last to ask me such a question! Why, it is my intention to proceed with him as is the manner of the sea with all knaves taken as Oliver Tressilian was taken. If your mood be merciful towards him—which as God lives, I can scarce conceive—consider that this is the greatest mercy he can look for."

"You speak of mercy and vengeance in a breath, Sir John." She was growing calm, her agitation was quieting and a grim sternness was replacing it.

He made a gesture of impatience. "What good purpose could it serve to take him to England?" he demanded. "There he must stand his trial, and the issue is foregone. It were unnecessarily to torture him."

"The issue may be none so foregone as you suppose," she replied. "And that trial is his right."

Sir John took a turn in the cabin, his wits all confused. It was preposterous that he should stand and argue upon such a matter with Rosamund of all people, and yet she was compelling him to it against his every inclination, against common sense itself.

"If he so urges it, we'll not deny him," he said at last, deeming it best to humor her. "We'll take him back to England if he demands it, and let him stand his trial there. But Oliver Tressilian must realize too well what is in store for him to make any such demand." He passed before her, and held out his hands in entreaty. "Come, Rosamund, my dear! You are distraught, you . . ."

"I am indeed distraught, Sir John," she answered, and took the hands that he extended. "Oh, have pity!" she cried with a sudden change to utter intercession. "I implore you to have pity!"

"What pity can I show you child? You have but to name . . ."

"'T is not pity for me, but pity for him that I am beseeching of you."

"For him?" he cried, frowning again.

"For Oliver Tressilian."

He dropped her hands and stood away. "God's light!" he swore. "You sue for pity for Oliver Tressilian, for that renegade, that incarnate devil? Oh, you are mad!" he stormed. "Mad!" and he flung away from her, whirling his arms.

"I love him," she said simply.

That answer smote him instantly still. Under the shock of it he just stood and stared at her again, his jaw fallen.

"You love him!" he said at last below his breath. "You love him! You love a man who is a pirate, a renegade, the abductor of yourself and of Lionel, the man who murdered your brother!"

"He did not." She was fierce in her denial of it. "I have learnt the truth of that matter."

"From his lips, I suppose?" said Sir John, and he was unable to repress a sneer. "And you believed him?"

"Had I not believed him I should not have married him."

"Married him?" Sudden horror came now to temper his bewilderment. Was there to be no end to these astounding revelations? Had they reached the climax yet, he wondered, or was there still more to come? "You married that infamous villain?" he asked, and his voice was expressionless.

"I did—in Algiers on the night we landed there."

He stood gaping at her whilst a man might count to a dozen, and then abruptly he exploded. "It is enough!" he roared, shaking a clenched fist at the low ceiling of the cabin. "It is enough, as God's my Witness. If there were no other reason to hang him, that would be reason and to spare. You may look to me to make an end of this infamous marriage within the hour."

"Ah, if you will but listen to me!" she pleaded.

"Listen to you?" He paused by the door to which he had stepped in his fury, intent upon giving the word that there and then should make an end, and summoning Oliver Tressilian before him, announce his fate to him and see it executed on the spot. "Listen to you?" he repeated, scorn and anger blending in his voice. "I have heard more than enough already!"

It was the Killigrew way, Lord Henry Goade assures us, pausing here at long length for one of those digressions into the history of families whose members chance to impinge upon his chronicle. "They were," he says, "ever an impetuous, short-reasoning folk, honest and upright enough so far as their judgment carried them, but hampered by a lack of penetration in that judgment."

Sir John, as much in his earlier commerce with the Tressilians as in this pregnant hour, certainly appears to justify his lordship of that criticism. There were a score of questions a man of perspicuity would now have asked, not one of which appears to have occurred to the knight of Arwenack. If anything arrested him upon the cabin's threshold, delayed him in the execution of the thing he had resolved upon, no doubt it was sheer curiosity as to what further extravagances Rosamund might yet have it in her mind to utter.

"This man has suffered," she told him, and was not put off by the hard laugh with which he mocked that statement. "God alone knows what he has suffered in body and in soul for sins which he never committed. Much of that suffering came to him through me. I know to-day that he did not murder Peter. I know that but for a disloyal act of mine he would be in a position incontestably to prove it without the aid of any man. I know that he was carried off, kidnapped before ever he could clear himself of the accusation, and that as a consequence no life remained him but the life of a renegade which he chose. Mine was the chief fault. And I must make amends. Spare him to me! If you love me . . ."

But he had heard enough. His sallow face was flushed to a flaming purple.

"Not another word!" he blazed at her. "It is because I do love you—love and pity you from my heart—that I will not listen. It seems I must save you not only from that knave, but from yourself. I were false to my duty by you, false to your dead father and murdered brother else. Anon, you shall thank me, Rosamund." And again he turned to depart.

"Thank you?" she cried in a ringing voice. "I shall curse you. All my life I shall loathe and hate you, holding you in horror for a murderer if you do this thing. You fool! Can you not see? You fool!"

He recoiled. Being a man of position and importance, quick, fearless, and vindictive of temperament—and also, it would seem, extremely fortunate—it had never happened to him in all his life to be so uncompromisingly and frankly judged. She was by no means the first to account him a fool, but she was certainly the first to call him one to his face; and whilst to the general it might have proved her extreme sanity, to him it was no more than the culminating proof of her mental distemper.

"Pish!" he said, between anger and pity, "you are mad, stark mad! Your mind's unhinged, your vision's all distorted. This fiend incarnate is become a poor victim of the evil of others; and I am become a murderer in your sight—a murderer and a fool. God's

Life! Bah! Anon when you are rested, when you are restored, I pray that things may once again assume their proper aspect."

He turned, all aquiver still with indignation, and was barely in time to avoid being struck by the door which opened suddenly from without.

Lord Henry Goade, dressed—as he tells us—entirely in black, and with his gold chain of office—an ominous sign could they have read it—upon his broad chest, stood in the doorway, silhouetted sharply against the flood of morning sunlight at his back. His benign face would, no doubt, be extremely grave to match the suit he had put on, but its expression will have lightened somewhat when his glance fell upon Rosamund standing there by the table's edge.

"I was overjoyed," he writes, "to find her so far recovered, and seeming so much herself again, and I expressed my satisfaction."

"She were better abed," snapped Sir John, two hectic spots burning still in his sallow cheeks. "She is distempered, quite."

"Sir John is mistaken, my lord," was her calm assurance, "I am very far from suffering as he conceives."

"I rejoice therein, my dear," said his lordship, and I imagine his questing eyes speeding from one to the other of them, and marking the evidences of Sir John's temper, wondering what could have passed. "It happens," he added somberly, "that we may require your testimony in this grave matter that is toward." He turned to Sir John. "I have bidden them bring up the prisoner for sentence. Is the ordeal too much for you, Rosamund?"

"Indeed, no, my lord," she replied readily. "I welcome it." And threw back her head as one who braces herself for a trial of endurance.

"No, no," cut in Sir John, protesting fiercely. "Do not heed her, Harry. She . . ."

"Considering," she interrupted, "that the chief count against the prisoner must concern his . . . his dealings with myself, surely the matter is one upon which I should be heard."

"Surely, indeed," Lord Henry agreed, a little bewildered, he confesses, "always provided you are certain it will not overtax your endurance and distress you overmuch. We could perhaps dispense with your testimony."

"In that, my lord, I assure you that you are mistaken," she answered. "You cannot dispense with it."

"Be it so, then," said Sir John grimly, and he strode back to the table, prepared to take his place there.

Lord Henry's twinkling blue eyes were still considering Rosamund somewhat searchingly, his fingers tugging thoughtfully at his short tuft of ashen-colored beard. Then he turned to the door. "Come in, gentlemen," he said, "and bid them bring up the prisoner."

Steps clanked upon the deck, and three of Sir John's officers made their appearance to complete the court that was to sit in judgment upon the renegade corsair, a judgment whose issue was foregone.

CHAPTER XXV

THE ADVOCATE

C HAIRS WERE set at the long brown table of massive oak,
and the officers sat down, facing the open door and the
blaze of sunshine on the poop-deck, their backs to the other
door and the horn windows which opened upon the stern-gallery.
The middle place was assumed by Lord Henry Goade by virtue of
his office of Queen's Lieutenant, and the reason for his chain of
office became now apparent. He was to preside over this summary
court. On his right sat Sir John Killigrew, and beyond him an officer
named Youldon. The other two, whose names have not survived,
occupied his lordship's left.

A chair had been set for Rosamund at the table's extreme right
and across the head of it, so as to detach her from the judicial
bench. She sat there now, her elbows on the polished board, her
face resting in her half-clenched hands, her eyes scrutinizing the
five gentlemen who formed this court.

Steps rang on the companion, and a shadow fell athwart the
sunlight beyond the open door. From the vessel's waist came a
murmur of voices and a laugh. Then Sir Oliver appeared in the

doorway guarded by two fighting seamen in corselet and morion with drawn swords.

He paused an instant in the doorway, and his eyelids flickered as if he had received a shock when his glance alighted upon Rosamund. Then under the suasion of his guards he entered, and stood forward, his wrists still pinioned behind him, slightly in advance of the two soldiers.

He nodded perfunctorily to the court, his face entirely calm.

"A fine morning, sirs," said he.

The five considered him in silence, but Lord Henry's glance, as it rested upon the corsair's Muslim garb, was eloquent of the scorn which he tells us filled his heart.

"You are no doubt aware, sir," said Sir John after a long pause, "of the purpose for which you have been brought hither."

"Scarcely," said the prisoner. "But I have no doubt whatever of the purpose for which I shall presently be taken hence. However," he continued, cool and critical, "I can guess from your judicial attitudes the superfluous mockery that you intend. If it will afford you entertainment, faith I do not grudge indulging you. I would observe only that it might be considerate in you to spare Mistress Rosamund the pain and weariness of the business that is before you."

"Mistress Rosamund herself desired to be present," said Sir John, scowling.

"Perhaps," said Sir Oliver, "she does not realize . . ."

"I have made it abundantly plain to her," Sir John interrupted, almost vindictively.

The prisoner looked at her as if in surprise, his brows knit. Then with a shrug he turned to his judges again.

"In that case," said he, "there's no more to be said. But before you proceed, there is another matter upon which I desire an understanding.

"The terms of my surrender were that all others should be permitted to go free. You will remember, Sir John, that you pledged me your knightly word for that. Yet I find aboard here one who was lately with me upon my galeasse—a sometime English seaman, named Jasper Leigh, whom you hold a prisoner."

"He killed Master Lionel Tressilian," said Sir John coldly.

"That may be, Sir John. But the blow was delivered before I made my terms with you, and you cannot violate these terms without hurt to your honor."

"D' ye talk of honor, sir?" said Lord Henry.

"Of Sir John's honor, my lord," said the prisoner, with mock humility.

"You are here, sir, to take your trial," Sir John reminded him.

"So I had supposed. It is a privilege for which you agreed to pay a certain price, and now it seems you have been guilty of filching something back. It seems so, I say. For I cannot think but that the arrest was inadvertently effected, and that it will suffice that I draw your attention to the matter of Master Leigh's detention."

Sir John considered the table. It was beyond question that he was in honor bound to enlarge Master Leigh, whatever the fellow might have done; and, indeed, his arrest had been made without Sir John's knowledge until after the event.

"What am I to do with him?" he growled sullenly.

"That is for yourself to decide, Sir John. But I can tell you what you may not do with him. You may not keep him a prisoner, or carry him to England, or injure him in any way. Since his arrest was a pure error, as I gather, you must repair that error as best you can. I am satisfied that you will do so, and need say no more. Your servant, sirs," he added to intimate that he was now entirely at their disposal, and he stood waiting.

There was a slight pause, and then Lord Henry, his face inscrutable, his glance hostile and cold, addressed the prisoner.

"We have had you brought hither to afford you an opportunity of urging any reasons why we should not hang you out of hand, as is our right."

Sir Oliver looked at him in almost amused surprise. "Faith!" he said at length. "It was never my habit to waste breath."

"I doubt you do not rightly apprehend me, sir," returned his lordship, and his voice was soft and silken as became his judicial position. "Should you demand a formal trial, we will convey you to England that you may have it."

"But lest you should build unduly upon that," cut in Sir John fiercely, "let me warn you that as the offences for which you are to suffer were chiefly committed within Lord Henry Goade's own jurisdiction, your trial will take place in Cornwall, where Lord Henry has the honor to be Her Majesty's Lieutenant and dispenser of justice."

"Her Majesty is to be congratulated," said Sir Oliver elaborately.

"It is for you to choose, sir," Sir John ran on, "whether you will be hanged on sea or land."

"My only possible objection would be to being hanged in the air. But you're not likely to heed that," was the flippant answer.

Lord Henry leaned forward again. "Let me beg you, sir, in your own interests to be serious," he admonished the prisoner.

"I confess the occasion, my lord. For if you are to sit in judgment upon my piracy, I could not desire a more experienced judge of the matter on sea or land than Sir John Killigrew."

"I am glad to deserve your approval," Sir John replied tartly. "Piracy," he added, "is but the least of the counts against you."

Sir Oliver's brows went up, and he stared at the row of solemn faces.

"As God's my life, then, your other counts must needs be sound—or else, if there be any justice in your methods, you are like to be disappointed of your hopes of seeing me swing. Proceed, sirs, to the other counts. I vow you become more interesting than I could have hoped."

"Can you deny the piracy?" quoth Lord Henry.

"Deny it? No. But I deny your jurisdiction in the matter, or that of any English court, since I have committed no piracy in English waters."

Lord Henry admits that the answer silenced and bewildered him, being utterly unexpected. Yet what the prisoner urged was a truth so obvious that it was difficult to apprehend how his lordship had come to overlook it. I rather fear that despite his judicial office, jurisprudence was not a strong point with his lordship. But Sir John, less perspicuous or less scrupulous in the matter, had his retort ready.

"Did you not come to Arwenack and forcibly carry off thence . . ."

"Nay, now, nay now," the corsair interrupted, good-humoredly. "Go back to school, Sir John, to learn that abduction is not piracy."

"Call it abduction, if you will," Sir John admitted.

"Not if I will, Sir John. We'll call it what it is, if you please."

"You are trifling, sir. But we shall mend that presently," and Sir John banged the table with his fist, his face flushing slightly in anger. (Lord Henry very properly deplores this show of heat at such a time.) "You cannot pretend to be ignorant," Sir John continued, "that abduction is punishable by death under the law of England." He turned to his fellow-judges. "We will then, sirs, with your concurrence, say no more of the piracy."

"Faith," said Lord Henry in his gentle tones, "in justice we cannot." And he shrugged the matter aside. "The prisoner is right in what he claims. We have no jurisdiction in that matter, seeing that he committed no piracy in English waters, nor—so far as our knowledge goes—against any vessel sailing under the English flag."

Rosamund stirred. Slowly she took her elbows from the table, and folded her arms resting them upon the edge of it. Thus leaning forward she listened now with an odd brightness in her eye, a slight flush in her cheeks reflecting some odd excitement called into life by Lord Henry's admission—an admission which sensibly whittled down the charges against the prisoner.

Sir Oliver, watching her almost furtively, noted this and marveled, even as he marveled at her general composure. It was in vain that he sought to guess what might be her attitude of mind towards himself now that she was safe again among friends and protectors.

But Sir John, intent only upon the business ahead, plunged angrily on.

"Be it so," he admitted impatiently. "We will deal with him upon the counts of abduction and murder. Have you anything to say?"

"Nothing that would be like to weigh with you," replied Sir Oliver. And then with a sudden change from his slightly derisive manner to one that was charged with passion: "Let us make an end of this comedy," he cried, "of this pretence of judicial proceedings. Hang me, and have done, or set me to walk the plank. Play the pirate, for that is a trade you understand. But a' God's name don't disgrace the Queen's commission by playing the judge."

Sir John leapt to his feet, his face aflame. "Now, by Heaven, you insolent knave . . ."

But Lord Henry checked him, placing a restraining hand upon his sleeve, and forcing him gently back into his seat. Himself he now addressed the prisoner.

"Sir, your words are unworthy one who, whatever his crimes, has earned the repute of being a sturdy valiant fighter. Your deeds are so notorious—particularly that which caused you to flee from England and take to roving, and that of your reappearance at Arwenack and the abduction of which you were then guilty—that your sentence in an English court is a matter foregone beyond all possible doubt. Nevertheless, it shall be yours, as I have said, for the asking. Yet," he added, and his voice was lowered and very earnest, "were I your friend, Sir Oliver, I would advise you that you rather choose to be dealt with in the summary fashion of the sea."

"Sirs," replied Sir Oliver, "your right to hang me I have not disputed, nor do I. I have no more to say."

"But I have."

Thus Rosamund at last, startling the court with her crisp, sharp utterance. All turned to look at her as she rose, and stood tall and compelling at the table's end.

"Rosamund!" cried Sir John, and rose in his turn. "Let me implore you . . ."

She waved him peremptorily, almost contemptuously, into silence.

"Since in this matter of the abduction with which Sir Oliver is charged," she said, "I am the person said to have been abducted, it were perhaps well that before going further in this matter you should hear what I may hereafter have to say in an English court."

Sir John shrugged, and sat down again. She would have her way, he realized; just as he knew that its only result could be to waste their time and protract the agony of the doomed man.

Lord Henry turned to her, his manner full of deference. "Since the prisoner has not denied the charge, and since wisely he refrains from demanding to be taken to trial, we need not harass you, Mistress Rosamund. Nor will you be called upon to say anything in an English court."

"There you are at fault, my lord," she answered, her voice very level. "I shall be called upon to say something when I impeach you all for murder upon the high seas, as impeach you I shall if you persist in your intent."

"Rosamund!" cried Oliver in his sudden amazement—and it was a cry of joy and exultation.

She looked at him, and smiled—a smile full of courage and friendliness and something more, a smile for which he considered that his impending hanging was but a little price to pay. Then she turned again to that court, into which her words had flung a sudden consternation.

"Since he disdains to deny the accusation, I must deny it for him," she informed them. "He did not abduct me, sirs, as is alleged. I love Oliver Tressilian. I am of full age and mistress of my

actions, and I went willingly with him to Algiers where I became
his wife."

Had she flung a bomb amongst them she could hardly have
made a greater disorder of their wits. They sat back, and stared at
her with blank faces, muttering incoherencies.

"His . . . his wife?" babbled Lord Henry. "You became his . . ."

And then Sir John cut in fiercely. "A lie! A lie to save that foul
villain's neck!"

Rosamund leaned towards him, and her smile was almost a
sneer. "Your wits were ever sluggish, Sir John," she said. "Else you
would not need reminding that I could have no object in lying to
save him if he had done me the wrong that is imputed to him."
Then she looked at the others. "I think, sirs, that in this matter my
word will outweigh Sir John's or any man's in any court of justice."

"Faith, that's true enough!" ejaculated the bewildered Lord
Henry. "A moment, Killigrew!" And again he stilled the impetuous
Sir John. He looked at Sir Oliver, who in truth was very far from
being the least bewildered in that company. "What do you say to
that, sir?" he asked.

"To that?" echoed the almost speechless corsair. "What is there
left to say?" he evaded.

"'T is all false," cried Sir John again. "We were witnesses of the
event—you and I, Harry—and we saw , , ,"

"You saw," Rosamund interrupted. "But you did not know what
had been concerted."

For a moment that silenced them again. They were as men who
stand upon crumbling ground, whose every effort to win to a safer
footing but occasioned a fresh slide of soil. Then Sir John sneered,
and made his riposte.

"No doubt she will be prepared to swear that her betrothed,
Master Lionel Tressilian, accompanied her willingly upon that
elopement."

"No," she answered. "As for Lionel Tressilian he was carried off that he might expiate his sins—sins which he had fathered upon his brother there, sins which are the subject of your other count against him."

"Now what can you mean by that?" asked his lordship.

"That the story that Sir Oliver killed my brother is a calumny; that the murderer was Lionel Tressilian, who, to avoid detection and to complete his work, caused Sir Oliver to be kidnapped that he might be sold into slavery."

"This is too much!" roared Sir John. "She is trifling with us, she makes white black and black white. She has been bewitched by that crafty rogue, by Moorish arts that . . ."

"Wait!" said Lord Henry, raising his hand. "Give me leave." He confronted her very seriously. "This . . . this is a grave statement, mistress. Have you any proof—anything that you conceive to be a proof—of what you are saying?"

But Sir John was not to be repressed. "'T is but the lying tale this villain told her. He has bewitched her, I say. 'T is plain as the sunlight yonder."

Sir Oliver laughed outright at that. His mood was growing exultant, buoyant, and joyous, and this was the first expression of it. "Bewitched her? You're determined never to lack for a charge. First 't was piracy, then abduction and murder, and now 't is witchcraft!"

"Oh, a moment, pray!" cried Lord Henry, and he confesses to some heat at this point. "Do you seriously tell us, Mistress Rosamund, that it was Lionel Tressilian who murdered Peter Godolphin?"

"Seriously?" she echoed, and her lips were twisted in a little smile of scorn. "I not merely tell it you, I swear it here in the sight of God. It was Lionel who murdered my brother and it was Lionel who put it about that the deed was Sir Oliver's. It was said that Sir Oliver had run away from the consequences of something discovered against him, and I to my shame believed the public voice. But I have since discovered the truth . . ."

"The truth, do you say, mistress?" cried the impetuous Sir John in a voice of passionate contempt. "The truth . . ."

Again his Lordship was forced to intervene.

"Have patience, man," he admonished the knight. "The truth will prevail in the end, never fear, Killigrew."

"Meanwhile we are wasting time," grumbled Sir John, and on that fell moodily silent.

"Are we further to understand you to say, mistress," Lord Henry resumed, "that the prisoner's disappearance from Penarrow was due not to flight, as was supposed, but to his having been trepanned by order of his brother?"

"That is the truth as I stand here in the sight of Heaven," she replied in a voice that rang with sincerity and carried conviction to more than one of the officers seated at that table. "By that act the murderer sought not only to save himself from exposure, but to complete his work by succeeding to the Tressilian estates. Sir Oliver was to have been sold into slavery to the Moors of Barbary. Instead the vessel upon which he sailed was captured by Spaniards, and he was sent to the galleys by the Inquisition. When his galley was captured by Muslim corsairs he took the only way of escape that offered. He became a corsair and a leader of corsairs, and then . . ."

"What else he did we know," Lord Henry interrupted. "And I assure you it would all weigh very lightly with us or with any court if what else you say is true."

"It is true. I swear it, my lord," she repeated.

"Ay," he answered, nodding gravely. "But can you prove it?"

"What better proof can I offer you than that I love him, and have married him?"

"Bah!" said Sir John.

"That, mistress," said Lord Henry, his manner extremely gentle, "is proof that yourself you believe this amazing story. But it is not proof that the story itself is true. You had it, I suppose," he continued smoothly, "from Oliver Tressilian himself?"

"That is so; but in Lionel's own presence, and Lionel himself confirmed it—admitting its truth."

"You dare say that?" cried Sir John, and stared at her in incredulous anger. "My God! You dare say that?"

"I dare and do," she answered him, giving him back look for look.

Lord Henry sat back in his chair, and tugged gently at his ashen tuft of beard, his florid face overcast and thoughtful. There was something here he did not understand at all. "Mistress Rosamund," he said quietly, "let me exhort you to consider the gravity of your words. You are virtually accusing one who is no longer able to defend himself; if your story is established, infamy will rest for ever upon the memory of Lionel Tressilian. Let me ask you again, and let me entreat you to answer scrupulously. Did Lionel Tressilian admit the truth of this thing with which you say that the prisoner charged him?"

"Once more I solemnly swear that what I have spoken is true; that Lionel Tressilian did in my presence, when charged by Sir Oliver with the murder of my brother and the kidnapping of himself, admit those charges. Can I make it any plainer, sirs?"

Lord Henry spread his hands. "After that, Killigrew, I do not think we can go further in this matter. Sir Oliver must go with us to England, and there take his trial."

But there was one present—that officer named Youldon—whose wits, it seems, were of keener temper.

"By your leave, my lord," he now interposed, and he turned to question the witness. "What was the occasion on which Sir Oliver forced this admission from his brother?"

Truthfully she answered. "At his house in Algiers on the night he . . ." She checked suddenly, perceiving then the trap that had been set for her. And the others perceived it also. Sir John leapt into the breach which Youldon had so shrewdly made in her defences.

"Continue, pray," he bade her. "On the night he . . ."

"On the night we arrived there," she answered desperately, the color now receding slowly from her face.

"And that, of course," said Sir John slowly, mockingly almost, "was the first occasion on which you heard this explanation of Sir Oliver's conduct?"

"It was," she faltered—perforce.

"So that," insisted Sir John, determined to leave her no loophole whatsoever, "so that until that night you had naturally continued to believe Sir Oliver to be the murderer of your brother?"

She hung her head in silence, realizing that the truth could not prevail here since she had hampered it with a falsehood, which was now being dragged into the light.

"Answer me!" Sir John commanded.

"There is no need to answer," said Lord Henry slowly, in a voice of pain, his eyes lowered to the table. "There can, of course, be but one answer. Mistress Rosamund has told us that he did not abduct her forcibly; that she went with him of her own free will and married him; and she has urged that circumstance as a proof of her conviction of his innocence. Yet now it becomes plain that at the time she left England with him she still believed him to be her brother's slayer. Yet she asks us to believe that he did not abduct her." He spread his hands again and pursed his lips in a sort of grieved contempt.

"Let us make an end, a' God's name?" said Sir John, rising.

"Ah, wait!" she cried. "I swear that all that I have told you is true—all but the matter of the abduction. I admit that, but I condoned it in view of what I have since learnt."

"She admits it!" mocked Sir John.

But she went on without heeding him. "Knowing what he has suffered through the evil of others, I gladly own him my husband, hoping to make some amends to him for the part I had in his wrongs. You must believe me, sirs. But if you will not, I ask you is his action of yesterday to count for naught? Are you not to remember that but for him you would have had no knowledge of my whereabouts?"

They stared at her in fresh surprise.

"To what do you refer now, mistress? What action of his is responsible for this?"

"Do you need to ask? Are you so set on murdering him that you affect ignorance? Surely you know that it was he dispatched Lionel to inform you of my whereabouts?"

Lord Henry tells us that at this he smote the table with his open palm, displaying an anger he could no longer curb. "This is too much!" he cried. "Hitherto I have believed you sincere but misguided and mistaken. But so deliberate a falsehood transcends all bounds. What has come to you, girl? Why, Lionel himself told us the circumstances of his escape from the galeasse. Himself he told us how that villain had him flogged and then flung him into the sea for dead."

"Ah!" said Sir Oliver between his teeth. "I recognize Lionel there! He would be false to the end, of course. I should have thought of that."

Rosamund at bay, in a burst of regal anger leaned forward to face Lord Henry and the others. "He lied, the base, treacherous dog!" she cried.

"Madam," Sir John rebuked her, "you are speaking of one who is all but dead."

"And more than damned," added Sir Oliver. "Sirs," he cried, "you prove naught but your own stupidity when you accuse this gentle lady of falsehood."

"We have heard enough, sir," Lord Henry interrupted.

"Have you so, by God!" he roared, stung suddenly to anger. "You shall hear yet a little more. The truth will prevail, you have said yourself; and prevail the truth shall since this sweet lady so desires it."

He was flushed, and his light eyes played over them like points of steel, and like points of steel they carried a certain measure of compulsion. He had stood before them half-mocking and indifferent, resigned to hang and desiring the thing might be over and ended as speedily as possible. But all that was before he suspected that life could still have anything to offer him, whilst he conceived that Rosamund was definitely lost to him. True he had the memory of a certain tenderness she had shown him yesternight aboard the galley, but he had deemed that tenderness to be no more than such as the situation itself begot. Almost he had deemed the same to be here the case until he had witnessed her fierceness and despair in fighting for his life, until he had heard and gauged the sincerity of her avowal that she loved him and desired to make some amends to him for all that he had suffered in the past. That had spurred him, and had a further spur been needed, it was afforded him when they branded her words with falsehood, mocked her to her face with what they supposed to be her lies. Anger had taken him at that to stiffen his resolve to make a stand against them and use the one weapon that remained him—that a merciful chance, a just God had placed within his power almost despite himself.

"I little knew, sirs," he said, "that Sir John was guided by the hand of destiny itself when last night, in violation of the terms of my surrender, he took a prisoner from my galeasse. That man is, as I have said, a sometime English seaman, named Jasper Leigh. He fell into my hands some months ago, and took the same road to escape from thraldom that I took myself under the like circumstances. I was merciful in that I permitted him to do so, for he is the very skipper who was suborned by Lionel to kidnap me and carry me into Barbary. With me he fell into the hands of the Spaniards. Have him brought hither, and question him."

In silence they all looked at him, but on more than one face he saw the reflection of amazement at his impudence, as they conceived it.

It was Lord Henry who spoke at last. "Surely, sir, this is most oddly, most suspiciously apt," he said, and there could be no doubt that he was faintly sneering. "The very man to be here aboard, and taken prisoner thus, almost by chance . . ."

"Not quite by chance, though very nearly. He conceives that he has a grudge against Lionel, for it was through Lionel that misfortune overtook him. Last night when Lionel so rashly leapt aboard the galley, Jasper Leigh saw his opportunity to settle an old score and took it. It was as a consequence of that that he was arrested."

"Even so, the chance is still miraculous."

"Miracles, my lord, must happen sometimes if the truth is to prevail," Sir Oliver replied with a tinge of his earlier mockery. "Fetch him hither, and question him. He knows naught of what has passed here. It were a madness to suppose him primed for a situation which none could have foreseen. Fetch him hither, then."

Steps sounded outside but went unheeded at the moment.

"Surely," said Sir John, "we have been trifled with by liars long enough!"

The door was flung open, and the lean black figure of the surgeon made its appearance.

"Sir John!" he called urgently, breaking without ceremony into the proceedings, and never heeding Lord Henry's scowl. "Master Tressilian has recovered consciousness. He is asking for you and for his brother. Quick, sirs! He is sinking fast."

CHAPTER XXVI

THE JUDGMENT

To that cabin below the whole company repaired in all speed in the surgeon's wake, Sir Oliver coming last between his guards. They assembled about the couch where Lionel lay, leaden-hued of face, his breathing labored, his eyes dull and glazing.

Sir John ran to him, went down upon one knee to put loving arms about that chilling clay, and very gently raised him in them, and held him so resting against his breast.

"Lionel!" he cried in stricken accents. And then as if thoughts of vengeance were to soothe and comfort his sinking friend's last moments, he added: "We have the villain fast."

Very slowly and with obvious effort Lionel turned his head to the right, and his dull eyes went beyond Sir John and made quest in the ranks of those that stood about him.

"Oliver?" he said in a hoarse whisper. "Where is Oliver?"

"There is not the need to distress you . . ." Sir John was beginning, when Lionel interrupted him.

"Wait!" he commanded in a louder tone. "Is Oliver safe?"

"I am here," said Sir Oliver's deep voice, and those who stood between him and his brother drew aside that they might cease from screening him.

Lionel looked at him for a long moment in silence, sitting up a little. Then he sank back again slowly against Sir John's breast.

"God has been merciful to me a sinner," he said, "since He accords me the means to make amends, tardily though it be." Then he struggled up again, and held out his arms to Sir Oliver, and his voice came in a great pleading cry. "Noll! My brother! Forgive!"

Oliver advanced, none hindering until, with his hands still pinioned behind him he stood towering there above his brother, so tall that his turban brushed the low ceiling of the cabin. His countenance was stern and grim.

"What is it that you ask me to forgive?" he asked.

Lionel struggled to answer, and sank back again into Sir John's arms, fighting for breath; there was a trace of blood-stained foam about his lips.

"Speak! Oh, speak, in God's name!" Rosamund exhorted him from the other side, and her voice was wrung with agony.

He looked at her, and smiled faintly. "Never fear," he whispered, "I shall speak. God has spared me to that end. Take your arms from me, Killigrew. I am the . . . the vilest of men. It . . . it was I who killed Peter Godolphin."

"My God!" groaned Sir John, whilst Lord Henry drew a sharp breath of dismay and realization.

"Ah, but that is not my sin," Lionel continued. "There was no sin in that. We fought, and in self-defence I slew him—fighting fair. My sin came afterwards. When suspicion fell on Oliver, I nourished it . . . Oliver knew the deed was mine, and kept silent that he might screen me. I feared the truth might become known for all that . . . and . . . and I was jealous of him, and . . . and I had him kidnapped to be sold . . ."

His fading voice trailed away into silence. A cough shook him, and the faint crimson foam on his lips was increased. But he rallied again, and lay there panting, his fingers plucking at the coverlet.

"Tell them," said Rosamund, who in her desperate fight for Sir Oliver's life kept her mind cool and steady and directed towards essentials, "tell them the name of the man you hired to kidnap him."

"Jasper Leigh, the skipper of the *Swallow*," he answered whereupon she flashed upon Lord Henry a look that contained a gleam of triumph for all that her face was ashen and her lips trembled.

Then she turned again to the dying man, relentlessly almost in her determination to extract all vital truth from him ere he fell silent.

"Tell them," she bade him, "under what circumstances Sir Oliver sent you last night to the *Silver Heron*."

"Nay, there is no need to harass him," Lord Henry interposed. "He has said enough already. May God forgive us our blindness, Killigrew!"

Sir John bowed his head in silence over Lionel.

"Is it you, Sir John?" whispered the dying man. "What? Still there? Ha!" he seemed to laugh faintly, then checked. "I am going . . ." he muttered, and again his voice grew stronger, obeying the last flicker of his shrinking will. "Noll! I am going! I . . . I have made reparation . . . all that I could. Give me . . . give me thy hand!" Gropingly he put forth his right.

"I should have given it you ere this but that my wrists are bound," cried Oliver in a sudden frenzy. And then exerting that colossal strength of his, he suddenly snapped the cords that pinioned him as if they had been thread. He caught his brother's extended hand, and dropped upon his knees beside him. "Lionel . . . Boy!" he cried. It was as if all that had befallen in the last five years had been wiped out of existence. His fierce relentless hatred of his half-brother, his burning sense of wrong, his parching thirst for vengeance, became on the instant all dead, buried, and forgotten.

More, it was as if they had never been. Lionel in that moment was again the weak, comely, beloved brother whom he had cherished and screened and guarded, and for whom when the hour arrived he had sacrificed his good name, and the woman he loved, and placed his life itself in jeopardy.

"Lionel, boy!" was all that for a moment he could say. Then: "Poor lad! Poor lad!" he added. "Temptation was too strong for thee." And reaching forth he took the other white hand that lay beyond the couch, and so held both tight-clasped within his own.

From one of the ports a ray of sunshine was creeping upwards towards the dying man's face. But the radiance that now overspread it was from an inward source. Feebly he returned the clasp of his brother's hands.

"Oliver, Oliver!" he whispered. "There is none like thee! I ever knew thee as noble as I was base. Have I said enough to make you safe? Say that he will be safe now," he appealed to the others, "that no . . ."

"He will be safe," said Lord Henry stoutly. "My word on 't."

"It is well. The past is past. The future is in your hands, Oliver. God's blessing on 't." He seemed to collapse, to rally yet again. He smiled pensively, his mind already wandering. "That was a long swim last night—the longest I ever swam. From Penarrow to Trefusis—a fine long swim. But you were with me, Noll. Had my strength given out . . . I could have depended on you. I am still chill from it, for it was cold . . . cold . . . ugh!" He shuddered, and lay still.

Gently Sir John lowered him to his couch. Beyond it Rosamund fell upon her knees and covered her face, whilst by Sir John's side Oliver continued to kneel, clasping in his own his brother's chilling hands.

There ensued a long spell of silence. Then with a heavy sigh Sir Oliver folded Lionel's hands across his breast, and slowly, heavily rose to his feet.

The others seemed to take this for a signal. It was as if they had but waited mute and still out of deference to Oliver. Lord Henry moved softly round to Rosamund and touched her lightly upon the shoulder. She rose and went out in the wake of the others, Lord Henry following her, and none remaining but the surgeon.

Outside in the sunshine they checked. Sir John stood with bent head and hunched shoulders, his eyes upon the white deck. Timidly almost—a thing never seen before in this bold man—he looked at Sir Oliver.

"He was my friend," he said sorrowfully, and as if to excuse and explain himself, "and . . . and I was misled through love of him."

"He was my brother," replied Sir Oliver solemnly. "God rest him!"

Sir John, resolved, drew himself up into an attitude preparatory to receiving with dignity a rebuff should it be administered him.

"Can you find it in your generosity, sir, to forgive me?" he asked, and his air was almost one of challenge.

Silently Sir Oliver held out his hand. Sir John fell upon it almost in eagerness.

"We are like to be neighbors again," he said, "and I give you my word I shall strive to be a more neighborly one than in the past."

"Then, sirs," said Sir Oliver, looking from Sir John to Lord Henry, "I am to understand that I am no longer a prisoner."

"You need not hesitate to return with us to England, Sir Oliver," replied his lordship. "The Queen shall hear your story, and we have Jasper Leigh to confirm it if need be, and I will go warranty for your complete reinstatement. Count me your friend, Sir Oliver, I beg." And he, too, held out his hand. Then turning to the others: "Come, sirs," he said, "we have duties elsewhere, I think."

They tramped away, leaving Oliver and Rosamund alone. The twain looked long each at the other. There was so much to say, so much to ask, so much to explain, that neither knew with what words to begin. Then Rosamund suddenly came up to him, holding out her hands.

"Oh, my dear!" she said, and that, after all, summed up a deal.

One or two over-inquisitive seamen, lounging on the forecastle and peeping through the shrouds, were disgusted to see the lady of Godolphin Court in the arms of a beturbaned bare-legged follower of Mahound.

THE END